DIRTY CILLIAN

THE HUDSON DUSTERS MOB COLLECTION: ONE

HARLEY DIAMOND

FIRST EDITION

Published by House of Books Press

www.harleydiamond.com

Edited by Karen Sanders Editing

https://www.karensandersediting.com/

PA Services by Arcane and Reverie

contact@arcaneandreverie.com

Proofreading Services by Proofreading by Mich

https://www.instagram.com/proofreadingbymichx/

PR Services by Peachy Keen Author Services

https://www.peachykeenauthorservices.com/

Cover Design by Vicious Desires Design

https://www.instagram.com/viciousdesires/

Cover Model is Eddy Grim via Wander Aguiar Photography

https://www.instagram.com/eddygrim/

http://wanderaguiar.com/

Created with Vellum

Blurb

MY SAVIOR. MY SIN.

With blood on my hands, I ran for seven years.

Now the prodigal sister has returned to the city that never sleeps.

New York.

For once, this biker chick needed saving. Turns out my black knight's a mobster.

Dirty. Deadly. Irish.

Cillian O'Connell's not offering me a happily ever after. All he's offering is sinful, no-strings sex.

Run from the big bad Duster wolf?

He doesn't realize this little Red is just as fucked up as he is.

He'll find out soon enough that we're a match made in outlaw hell.

In our world, that makes us perfect.

Lyrics

How long will I love you?
As long as stars are above you
And longer if I can

Ellie Goulding

Trigger Warning

This book contains mature content, violence, swearing, and other potentially triggering situations that some readers may find offensive.

Please do not read this story if you are uncomfortable with any of the above.

Thank you.

Author's Note

CILLIAN'S story starts from where ACE ends (EXCLUDING the epilogue).

Although CILLIAN is standalone within the Dirty Dusters Series and can be enjoyed in its own right, it is also the second story in a CROSSOVER UNIVERSE between the Angels, Scorpions, and Dusters.

CILLIAN is also BOOK 2 in an initial series of novels containing an ONGOING STORYLINE that concludes in BOOK 6 of the crossover universe, DIRTY PADRAIG.

For the BEST OVERALL EXPERIENCE, the books should be read in their CROSSOVER ORDER.

ACE, DIRTY CILLIAN, RAZR, DIRTY DYLAN, DIRTY EOIN, DIRTY PADRAIG

CHAPTER ONE

CILLIAN

The Hudson Dusters' HQ, Manhattan, New York

Happy Families.

We're a faction in a mobster game of Happy fucking Families.

Or maybe we O'Connells are the modern-day equivalent of the knights of the round table. It's circular, after all, and we have been known to venture out at night to kidnap unsuspecting, traitorous fuckers from their beds before sending them to meet their maker by sinking them into a watery grave.

I take in its leather-topped black surface, which reeks of expensive polish. Vanilla. The stench of it lingers in the air, so potent I can almost taste it. I fucking hate vanilla. The table stands on a marble floor surrounded by white walls filled with priceless works of art. Some purchased. Most stolen.

Well, it wasn't out and out theft, to be fair. Da likes to think of them as heirlooms inherited from those whose lives we have ended.

Keepsakes. The room is over the top ostentatious and depicts just how disgustingly wealthy we truly are. Never rich enough for Da, though, or powerful enough either.

The view? The Hudson. What the fuck else?

I scan the space and take in my brothers. They look bored rigid like me. We're all suited and booted, as per the old man's request.

There's our Padraig sitting across from me, who refuses to make eye contact with anyone. As usual, the finest selection of refreshments is on offer, but he's chosen to sample a whiskey, and it's only mid-day. Paddy's the baby of the family at twenty-eight. With poster-boy good looks, jet black hair, and piercing blue eyes, he's quite the catch. So tall, dark, and handsome, the majority of Manhattan's high society females are queuing up to bed the best-looking one of us. I'm sure his bank balance turns them on almost as much as his appearance.

Paddy's a bit of a smart alec and is our legal guru. Brains as well as looks. He's the complete package. He's also Ma's favorite. She'd never admit as much, but the rest of us are fully aware.

Personality-wise, he's also the one with the sunniest disposition. Paddy even smiles when he ends a life. He's a charming fecker. Extremely sociable and with—as Ma calls it—the gift of the Irish gab. He's the life and soul of every party with his winning personality.

Or at least, he was.

Now, he sits there like his life has ended, looking for answers at the bottom of a bottle where everyone with half a brain knows there's none to be found. Several bottles, in fact. Every day. It turns out, even though he could have his pick of the finest women in the city, the love of his life is some badass MC chick. A few months ago she chose a hairy biker over him. Go figure.

Still, none of that matters. Da's signed the poor fucker's life away in an arranged marriage to some silly teenage Sicilian mafia princess. In my mind, Paddy doesn't know how lucky he is. I dread to think who the rest of us will end up with if Da has his way.

My eyes then drift to our Eoin. Visually, he's an older version of Padraig, but a tad taller, broader, and with smarter hair. He looks a bit like one of those magazine models, all primped and preened to perfection. He must spend hours in the morning in front of a mirror getting himself ready. Worse than a woman I reckon. The eldest at thirty-six, Eoin's still never taken himself a wife. He's under pressure to do so now, but it's a tough role to fill. The poor girl will have to put up with his arrogant arse as well as be the big ma of The Hudson Dusters. It's a hands-on role. She'll need to roll her sleeves up like the rest of us. Our ma will also be looking over her shoulder at every opportunity. Critiquing her every fucking move to make sure she's doing things just right. Nope. Not for the faint-hearted, and she'll almost certainly have to be someone of high rank from *the life*—a woman who can handle a weapon and stand the sight of blood and all other bodily fluids.

It's the equivalent of looking for a rainbow-shitting unicorn.

Eoin's definitely got the skills to take over the reins from Da, though. As well as being a financial analyst and economics whiz kid, he's a murderous bastard and has probably taken as many souls as the rest of us brothers put together.

Finally, there's our Dylan, who's twenty-nine. He's the same coloring as the other two, but with a self-inflicted buzzcut. He looks way more pale and peaky but that's only because he's the opposite of Paddy. He's an anti-social little fecker with no friends and who never leaves his apartment, so he seldom sees the light of day. He spends all his time looking over the properties like it's a one-person game of Monopoly, making sure everything's secure at all times. He's probably some sort of peeping Tom with all the surveillance he's got going on. Dyl also does investigative work. If you want intel on anything or anyone, he's your man. He can do all that from the comfort of his own home. That's just how he likes it.

Actually, I take back the friend comment.

I think he's got at least one, as he's taken to messaging constantly and partaking in whispered phone conversations. Not sure who it is or even if they're male or female, but he spends a lot of time looking at his screen these days. The fucker even smiles from time to time, which is quite disconcerting. Maybe it's that surreptitious sniper, The Exterminator, who refuses to deal with any of the rest of us.

Dylan's taken less than a dozen lives, which is not a lot in this life. Just enough to convince Da that he's not a big girl's blouse.

I'm the odd one out. My hair is auburn, and my eyes are green like my ma's. At thirty-four, I'm the second born child. The one in every family that no one gives a fuck about. It's like we don't exist half the time. I'm also the biggest toy soldier. The one who does the real work. I walk the streets and take care of the day-to-day shite that no one else wants to do, getting my hands dirty and doing the wet work alongside our Paddy. I also handle the add-on services to the people who have purchased Duster properties and the like. Drugs, prostitutes, weapons. You name it. We don't do heroin, though. If you want that, you need to deal with the Sicilians.

"Cillian? Cillian? Are you fucking listening?" I zone back into the boring as fuck conversation and quickly duck as whatever paperweight he's flung disintegrates as it makes contact with the wall behind me.

"Aye, Da. I can hear you," I mutter.

"What was I saying then, smart arse?" he grumbles as he looks at me over the top of his reading glasses. He's trying to catch me out.

At sixty-five, Da's still a handsome fucker, even if his once jet-black hair is now pure white. He blames us for that. Then again, he blames us for everything, as he can do no wrong. The male equivalent of Mary Poppins. Practically perfect in every way. Everything he says has a large pinch of hindsight thrown in just for good measure.

"You were saying there's a rumor going around that the new pakhan’s been chosen, Da."

"Aye. That's it." No acknowledgment of the fact that I was actually listening. No apology that he almost sent me to an early grave by flinging a glass dome at my fucking head. "And they’re baying for The Exterminator's blood now he's murdered their two head honchos, Gorbachev and that other one."

"Lebedev and Sokolov," Paddy huffs.

We all turn to stare at him. Normally, he never shuts up; he loves the sound of his own voice. Recently, he's barely spoken. I'm sure there's stuff they're not telling me about what's gone down with him and that biker chick, Jaine Jones. They think because I'm not an academic like them that I'm thick as fuck and clueless so I don't need to know any of the finer details. Like I drag my knuckles along the ground like some sort of crazed neanderthal, bashing arseholes over the head with a club. Some fucker had to stay here and take care of business whilst they all gallivanted off to fancy colleges.

"I'm sure The Exterminator can take care of himself, Da," I reply. “It's not our problem. We paid for our hit, and receipt was acknowledged. If he's anyone's responsibility, he's the Scorpions’. They're the ones who launder the cash on his behalf."

"Well, he seems to have gone to ground since. Maybe waiting for the dust to settle. Sensible lad. Dylan, make sure you send him that list I prepared, will you, son?"

"Already done, Da," Dylan replies, his face still in his phone.

"Not sure why the sniper's insisting on dealing with your mardy arse, but each to their own," Da mumbles as he flicks through his pad, pretending he's prepared notes. Has he fuck.

"I've had a conversation with Paul Delaney aka Razr this morning. Apparently, Luciano Ruocco has been purchasing properties around ones currently owned by Delaney Enterprises. He's not happy. He's convinced there's something tactical going down, especially with the upcoming alliance between the Dusters and the Sicilian mafia." I throw that in there.

"Maybe that means I won't have to marry the fucking teenager, then," Paddy mumbles as he tosses back yet another whiskey.

Da shuffles in his chair, then wags his pointer finger at him. "There's no law against purchasing property. Hell's Kitchen and Hudson Yards are ours, mind you, so no fucker best tread on our toes or there'll be hell to pay. No pun intended."

"We don't want to be falling out with the MC. Paul Delaney won't take kindly to anyone devaluing his properties. They'll be rewarded with their throat on a plate," Eoin interjects.

He's right. Razr's a fucking madman. Anyone who crosses him needs their head examined. I'm game for a tussle with most, but fuck taking him on.

"Paddy. You need to be building relationships with Luc. He's going to be your brother-in-law, son. Find out what game he's playing and be quick about it."

Paddy rolls his eyes. He'd best watch his insolence. He's only lucky the paperweight's already been slung today, although I'm sure old Fergal can quickly lay his hands on something else to chuck.

"Cill, you speak to Razr. Assure him there are no underhand tactics going on that the Dusters are aware of or that we condone, but we are asking the appropriate questions discreetly. Eoin, my lad, you keep your finger on the pulse of the Bratva situation. The kiddie sex trafficking is still going on, so those dirty vermin must be working with someone else and bringing them in from another location. Let's hope it's not those car-bombing Mexicans. I wouldn't trust those yellow-bellied fuckers as far as I can throw them."

"Will do, Da," I reply, while Eoin just nods. He's got sense. Best to open your mouth as little as possible or that lunatic will deliberately misinterpret what you've said and use it as an excuse to launch something at you.

Still, it's all in a day's work when you're a Duster.

CHAPTER TWO

SARAH

Mexico City

"SORRY! I don't speak any Spanish." I'm lying. I'm fluent. I just don't want to make unnecessary small talk. The guy leaning against the bar staring at me is hot. Like, Joe Manganiello in his heyday hot. I'm sorely tempted to take what he's so blatantly offering as he undresses me with his chocolate orbs.

His dick.

I mean, I *am* itching to get laid. I'm not promiscuous or anything. You could count on two hands the number of guys I've slept with. I don't do one-night stands. I'm a modern girl. I have fuck buddies. No strings attached relationships that suit both parties. It's been a few months, though, and that itch is way more than any vibrator on the market can scratch.

Trust me. I've tried—several times.

He smiles at me, showing off white teeth as perfect as the rest of him as he motions to the bartender to bring us a round of drinks. The barman winks at him, and they share a knowing smile. Who would have thought I'd run into a hottie like this guy in a shitty little backstreet bar? I look around the dark, dingy establishment with its sticky floors and almost offensive-sounding guitar-playing live music. No wonder we're the only people in the place. It's a dive.

Any other time, I'd have been tempted to take him up on his unspoken offer, but I'm on my way home. To the city that never sleeps. Somewhere I haven't been in seven years. My guts fleetingly fill with dread at the thought. The prodigal daughter returns. Or should that be sister? Both my folks have passed, and the only kin I have left is my older brother.

"You speak English?"

"Colombian." He then lifts his shoulders exaggeratedly in response to indicate he doesn't understand.

Is he lying too? Most likely. The movement causes his crisp white shirt to cling to his rather impressive pecs and biceps. He reaches out and snakes his arm around my waist, pulling me against his rock-hard body. His musky cologne engulfs me as he drops his hands to cup my ass.

Fast mover.

I do love a man who knows what he wants and just goes for it. Draping my arms around his neck, I let his bourbon-flavored tongue fuck my mouth, then groan against his lips as he grabs my hips and yanks me firmly against his erection.

Yup. Just as I thought. He's a big boy. Such a fucking shame I'll have to pass up his tempting offer. My hands instinctively drop to his ass that's wrapped snugly in a pair of tight blue designer jeans.

With reluctance, I eventually pull our mouths apart. I need to get going. We're flying out in two hours from MEX to JFK. I spin around to look at my best friend. "You ready to go, Laila?"

She's perched on a barstool, looking at me in disgust over the top of her little round spectacles, her straight, mid-brown, mid-length locks tucked behind her ears. She's wearing a shift dress with zero shape. I'm sure she deliberately tries to look as unappealing to the opposite sex as she can. Not that there's anything wrong with that. It's her choice.

"Yes, I’m just waiting for you to put your friend down." She huffs, rolling her eyes exaggeratedly as she pulls her laptop strap over her shoulder.

"I only wish I had time to fuck him. From what I can tell, his cock's massive," I whisper, grinning as her cheeks redden.

She eyes me distastefully. Laila believes you shouldn't have sex before marriage. She's a born-again Christian or whatever. It's what they tried to instill in us at the convent school we both attended. Screw that. I grew up in the MC life, where your next breath could be your last. I'll likely never get married, and I refuse to die a virgin. Laila doesn't swear either. I think the first word I said as a baby was *fuck*.

I know. I'm a real disappointment.

We down the shots he's bought us in one. It's clear-colored, so it's a liquid pretending to be vodka or gin, but it tastes more like paint stripper. I grimace in distaste. Still, it's free. Not that I'm poor by any means, but why turn down a freebie drink?

The nameless smoking hot guy puts his arm around my shoulder. I look at him apologetically and shrug it off. Fun's over. Not that it ever really began. Laila and I pick up our backpacks containing our worldly possessions and make our way outside. I suddenly wish I’d worn more sensible footwear like her. I take in her brown flats, then glance down at my white four-inch heels. My feet will be killing me by the end of the night. I run my hands down my pale blue skinny jeans and tuck in my white tank top before slinging my bag over my shoulder.

Outside, it's muggy, and the smell of coffee fills the air from the little shop next door. Suddenly feeling woozy, I place my hand against the building to steady myself. Our Colombian buddy smiles at me, gripping my shoulder tightly when I almost fall over.

"Did you… did you fuck with our drinks, you son of a bitch?"

Posing that question is the last thing I remember.

My mouth feels as dry as Gandhi's sandals, and my breath probably smells no better. I try to spread my saliva, but it doesn't help. There isn't enough to go around. I'm parched, and my tongue's literally stuck to the roof of my mouth. The aftertaste of that rancid, definitely-tampered-with drink is making me gag.

Wherever I am, the floor's rocking, and the little air there is lacks oxygen and is hot as hell. It's also pungent with the smell of unclean bodies, feces, and urine. I wrinkle my nose in disgust. Forcing my eyes open, I try to rub them with my hands, but I can't. Someone's bound them tightly behind my back.

My face is pressed against the floor. It's metal. Its cool temperature is the only thing welcomed in these stifling conditions.

I lift my head and move my body so I'm in a sitting position. I feel drugged and disorientated. My head spins, and nausea grips me, but I bite it back. Adding the smell of vomit to the already repugnant aroma won't help matters.

"Laila," I mumble. Where the fuck is my friend? Then I spot her, still out cold, on the floor beside me. I frown as I take in my surroundings. Dozens of pairs of eyes stare back at me from the partially lit space. "What the fuck is going on? Where are we?" I whisper.

We're in some sort of long vehicle. Cages line the walls. Cages filled with young children of varying ages. Some are sobbing, but most are quiet. Accepting of their fate. What fate? Older children and teenagers sit like me, bound and with their backs to the wall of the vehicle. There must be around one hundred of us in these cramped conditions.

"They're taking us to America to sell us to the wealthy men." My gaze moves to the teenage girl facing me, who replied in broken English. Even in these shitty conditions, she's beautiful, with her long dark hair and large doe brown eyes.

"We're being trafficked?" I speak in Spanish.

"Yes."

I try to get my head around it. I've spent most of the past seven years living and working in Bolivia in a little village just outside La Paz. Every morning, a headcount would be taken to work out if any children or young people had been kidnapped overnight. I knew it went on. It's a lucrative business. Cheap labor. Sex workers. Porn stars. You name it. I just never expected to become part of it.

"What's your name?"

"Mia."

"You know how many people are transporting us, Mia?"

"I believe it's just the driver for now. I… I overheard them talking. Once we've crossed the border out of Mexico, he's going to make a stop. We'll then be split into smaller groups and distributed."

I stare at her. The poor girl looks at me like she's lost the will to live.

"What age are you?"

"I just turned fifteen last week," she replies sadly.

"Well, rest assured, I am going to get us out of this."

I've seen shit. I've done shit. I've killed. Only one and a long time ago. I guess it's like riding a bike, though, or it better be. There's no fucking way I'm going to be sold on to some rich fucker as a sex slave. There's no way anyone in this vehicle is. They've picked on the wrong girl this time. The driver is about to become my new best friend when I finally get the chance to meet him.

FUCK KNOWS HOW LONG WE'VE BEEN STUCK IN THIS VEHICLE. Could be hours. Could be days. I refuse to piss myself. I refuse to sit in my own filth, but I'm getting desperate now. The human bladder can only hold so much.

"I need to pee." Laila's been saying it over and over ever since she woke up. She's like a broken record. It's the equivalent of Chinese water torture.

"Yeah, well, we all need to pee." I reply with the same response I do every time.

Just when I'm about to give in and humiliate myself by urinating in my pants, the vehicle comes to an abrupt standstill.

"He'll let us older ones out to relieve ourselves. The young children don't get out," Mia mumbles, no doubt having encountered this situation several times on the journey.

So, the younger ones have to just piss and shit themselves. What sort of fucking sick, twisted assholes are we dealing with here?

"Will he unbind us?" I ask, wondering how the hell we can do anything with our hands tied.

"Usually just one or two of us, and we have to help the others."

Jesus Christ, how humiliating. So, someone has to pull your pants up and down. Wipe your ass if need be.

"Who does he normally choose?"

"Me and Paolo, usually." She motions her head towards a young boy whose dark hair falls into his eyes. He looks to be around twelve, and his cheeks are tear-stained. I guess they don't want boys to be any older as they won't be as appealing then. As young men, they'd also be powerful enough to fight back.

The doors on the rear of the vehicle finally open. I close my eyes as blinding, brilliant sunlight streams in. Fresh air embraces us, and I inhale it deeply into my lungs, vowing to never take it for granted again.

The driver climbs up into the trailer. He appears to be mid-thirties and is Hispanic-looking, clean-shaven, and sporting a buzzcut. I take in his short stature and slightly rotund stomach, trying to gauge if I can over-power him if the opportunity arises. Maybe. Maybe not. I lean forward and smile at him, flicking my hair as flirtatiously as I can over my shoulder. His impassive gaze drifts over me. Handsome, he's not.

"You." He points at me, speaking in English. "And you." He points at Paolo.

I get to my feet and walk to the door. I watch as he unbinds Paolo, who, when released, immediately sees to the needs of the other males.

I hold my wrists out. "Sarah," I say, introducing myself. "I don't speak Spanish." I add it loudly enough for everyone to hear. I don't want him to know I'm fluent.

"Mario." He smiles as he unbinds me, his eyes leering at my body. I rub my chaffed wrists and step down from the vehicle, then take in my surroundings. It's a woodland area, probably in the middle of nowhere, so there's no point trying to make a run for it. Not that I would. The others need me to save the day. Going behind a tree, I relieve myself, then escort the girls out one by one, all the while smiling coyly at my new best friend, Mario.

Walking across to him, I bite my lip. His eyes darken as he takes me in.

"You must get lonely up front all by yourself, Mario," I whisper as I deliberately rub my hand over his dick. He smells of cigarettes and sweat, which he’s tried and failed to disguise with cheap cologne. He curses quietly, and I feel his appendage grow hard underneath my hand.

"I can ride up front with you if you like." My breath is deliberately hot in his ear.

"Yes." He nods, motioning his head towards the cabin.

Unbinding Mia, he has her and Paolo hand out water and food rations to the others before retying them and closing the back of the trailer.

I climb in beside him.

Sarah 1. Pedo fuckers 0.

SPANISH MUSIC PLAYS IN THE BACKGROUND. I'M NOT SURE IF IT'S A radio channel or some shitty CD.

"Yes, yes. I will reach the stop-off point in around forty-eight hours." Mario is on the phone. It sounds like it's another member of his gang he's talking to. I'm riding shotgun and have been for three days now. I'm pretending to be asleep, but there's no need. He thinks I don't understand a word anyway, so he doesn't even try to be discrete.

Fucking fool.

It's difficult to tell if he's working for the Mexicans or the Colombians. I think it's the latter that instigated this fucking shitshow. They always were the scum of the outlaw world. Them and the fucking Russian vermin Then again, the Sicilians were only ever one step up. Not that I remember that much, given I abandoned *the life* when I was twenty-one. The lowlife pecking order could well have changed since then.

He disconnects the call, and I stretch and look at him. He smirks at me, then leans back in his seat while shuffling his hips forward before motioning his head towards his groin. As I've been doing these past three days, I smile sweetly, unzip him, and pull out his limp dick. He grunts in approval, his eyes remaining fixed on the road as I work his minuscule cock with steady strokes, focusing my attention on the little hula dancer attached to the dashboard. I’m sure she’s fucking smirking at me. She’ll get hers.

God wasn't kind to Mario. He's an ugly fucker, and his dick size is as unimpressive as his staying power. Thirty seconds later, he's roaring in appreciation as his hips thrust against my fist and his jizz covers my hand.

I grab an oily cloth from the back and wipe his muck off, grimacing inwardly as I do. It's a small price to pay to get to ride up front and hear what's going on.

"I want to fuck you," he grumbles as he folds his flaccid dick back in his jeans and zips himself up.

"When my period’s over, lover boy," I promise hotly into his ear.

I'm not on. Thank fuck. How unhygienic would that be with no access to wash facilities? Even though I can't abide his hands being on me, I let him rub me through my jeans, then I fake an orgasm. Mario now thinks he's a sex god, and it keeps him at bay. Once we get closer to the drop-off point, which I now know to be Washington DC, that's when I'll make my move.

Two fucking days more of this shit.

CHAPTER THREE

CILLIAN

Cillian's Apartment, Hudson Yards, New York

"HARDER, CILL!'

Her voice is shrill, and it’s grating on my last fucking nerve.

"Get on your hands and knees," I grunt. Maybe it'll be less off-putting if she's facing the other way.

She does as she's told, and I ram my cock back in to the hilt. Her snatch is hot and tight as it clamps around my length. Next time, I might just gag the bitch. If there is a next time, that is.

"Fuck, Cill. Give it to me, baby."

Or earplugs. Earplugs would be good.

I pound my dick into her over and over, sweat running down my face. Even if she is annoying and I just want this to be over and done with, I'm still going to make sure it's the best fuck of her life.

I drop my hand underneath and circle her clit, her legs shaking in response. When I know she's almost there, I press firmly against it, and her pussy walls squeeze around my cock as she comes, gripping me like a vice and causing my balls to swell painfully and then explode.

"Fuck." I grunt as she milks me dry.

I kiss her on the shoulder and pull out, walking to the bathroom to deal with the condom and wipe the sweat off my face.

"You need to go, Angie. I've work to do."

She huffs, but she doesn't argue. Angie is one of three women I fuck regularly. No, I take that back. I fuck Cara regularly. I alternate between Amber and Angie when she's busy. Angie's a *Sports Illustrated* model or something. All endless legs, false tits, and blonde hair. She's beautiful, I'll give her that, but spending any time with her aside from fucking is about as interesting as watching paint dry. She's arm candy, and that's about it.

"Can't I just stay over, Cill?"

"No, you cannot. You know the script. No one sleeps over. Not ever. Don't be getting all possessive now. You know that shite won't fly with me." I slap her arse. Hard. "Get up and get going, or it'll be the last time I invite you back here."

I watch as she stands up, her bottom lip jutting out sulkily. It has me wondering what age she is, and I estimate her to be around twenty-five. It takes her five seconds to put her clothes back on as all she's wearing is a black tube dress with fuck all underneath. She walks to the door, then turns back in the hope I'll have changed my mind. I haven't. She leaves without a word, and I head for the shower.

I've got a shipment of coke coming tonight, and I need to take delivery.

"Tam." I call my right-hand man. Well, one of them. The other's Johnny. We've all known each other since we were single figures. They live a good life being as high up as they are in the Duster ranks. Both of them are married with fuck knows how many children between them. Too many. I'm not seeing that on the cards for me any time soon. Not with the recently introduced golden rule that our brides need to be from the life. Women who won't raise an eyebrow if we come home covered in blood. Even better if they're happy to roll up their sleeves and take part like Ma does.

"Yeah, Cill?"

"Meet me downstairs in fifteen minutes."

"Will do."

PADRAIG

Padraig's Apartment, Hudson Yards, New York

We've been talking business. Now that's over with, I change the subject.

"How's she keeping?" I can't stop myself from asking the question. It pisses me off that I still care as much as I ever did. I glance around my apartment as I await his response, taking in the new cream and navy décor. I needed a change. The monochrome had to go after I spent days staring at it while throwing crystal glasses against the stone fireplace during the worst days of my fucking life.

"Who?" the mardy arse fecker finally replies. For a minute, I thought he'd hung up to avoid answering.

"You know fine well who, Dyl."

I've been biding my time for weeks. He speaks to her every day. It should be me she's talking to. It's been three months or so now since she told me she didn't love me. That she never fucking had. That all I'd been to her was a substitute for *him*. I've spent every day since wallowing in self-pity and disbelief, trying to get my head around it. Trying to drink my memories of her away and eradicate the last nine fucking years. Trying to forget how she looks, how she smells, how she tastes. I spent countless hours searching for answers at the bottom of a bottle, but there were no messages to be found.

I regret telling her she was dead to me. It was immature. I reacted badly, but who can blame me?

I miss her so fucking much. I never thought it was possible to miss someone this much. Love someone this much. I pick up my phone several times a day, and my finger hovers over her number. Call her? Message her? She told me not to. She made her choice, cut her ties. Would she answer if I called? If I messaged? The ball's in her court. Then again, it always has been. It never stopped me before, though.

It seems I have an addictive personality where Jaine Jones is concerned. It seems I'll forgive the love of my life anything. Yes, I have forgiven her for taking herself away. Now I want her back. Even if it's only her friendship. Beggars can't be choosers. I'll take anything I can get.

"She's fine, Paddy. Getting on with her life, and you should be doing the same." He then quietly adds, "She's nine weeks pregnant."

Those words hit me like a sucker punch. I feel like I've been gutted. I run my hands through my hair and try to remember how to breathe. It should have been my baby in her belly. No one else's. Ace has everything I've ever wanted—Jaine, pregnant with his offspring. Meanwhile, I have to court a spoiled brat of a Sicilian teenager who thinks she's God's gift, and that she's doing me a huge favor by accepting me. To keep my da off my back, I've agreed to meet with Sophia once a month for lunch, but that's it. It's about as much as I can stomach someone so vacuous. Someone who wiles away her days spending her family's fortune on designer clothes and beauty treatments. She'd have been way better suited to our Dyl, as she's definitely not a murderous bastard like me.

Like Jaine.

"I'm sorry. I had to tell you. It's best you know before it's announced and becomes common knowledge, Paddy. Please don't mention it to anyone else. It's not my news to broadcast."

There's a pause.

"She's happy, for what it's worth. But if it's any consolation, I'm certain she misses you too. She doesn't say anything. She doesn't have to. I can tell. You need to take a leaf out of her book, though, and just move on."

So, Dyl thinks Jaine misses me. For some reason, that gives me hope. False hope? Fuck knows. I'll cling on to anything. I might not get her back in my life today or tomorrow or any time soon, but there's no way what we shared was destined to end up dead and buried like the feckers we both kill.

No fucking way.

"Dylan, I hear what you're saying, but I need to ask you a gigantic favor. I know before I ask that you're not going to like it but think of it as my coping mechanism."

"I'm not sure I like the sound of that."

"Just hear me out."

CHAPTER FOUR

JAINE

Jaine's House, Rising, California

I PRESS my ass against his groin, and his grip around my waist tightens. I'm such a selfish bitch. He's been on the road for four days, and he's only just got back. He must be fucking exhausted.

"What you chasing, PJ?" His voice is hot and husky in my ear, and I'm pretty sure my arousal is running down my thighs.

"I need to fuck, Ace. I know you're tired, and I'm a needy asshole, but I've missed you."

"You missed me or my dick?"

"I've missed you both."

Chuckling softly, his hand drops lower, and he runs his calloused fingers up and down my folds, dipping them into my slickness before settling on my clit. My center coils in anticipation.

"So damn wet." He nuzzles behind my ear and kisses my tattoo. I can tell he's smirking as I can feel the upward curve of his lips against my skin. Arrogant fucker. He loves how much I want him. How much I always fucking want him.

Small, lazy circles. He knows my body so well. The release is imminent. He stops his movements, and I groan loudly in frustration.

"Quit complaining. I thought you said you wanted to fuck."

He rolls onto his back on the bed, and I immediately turn around and kneel to look down at him.

Facial hair covers his jaw, more so than usual. My eyes graze over his rugged features. Cheekbones to die for. His midnight-black hair lays in waves over the pillow, longer than it's ever been. He should be on the cover of a goddamn magazine. My eyes drift down his torso. He's got it all going on with that sinful, naked body of his caressed with tattoos and carved to perfection by Lucifer himself. I trace my fingers over his most recent ink.

PJ.

Over his heart.

"Quit staring and hop on, sweetheart." He eyes darken in response to my blatant admiration.

Our gazes connect. Blue on green. His are as blue as the bluest thing ever and shining with love and desire for me.

My eyes drift to his dick and my mouth waters. It's ramrod straight, its tip leaking. I wrap my hand around the thick, silk-wrapped steel. He closes his eyes and lifts his hips, growling in appreciation. My hand tightens, and I pump him a few times, causing his abs to clench in response. Jesus Christ, I could never tire of just looking at him.

"You sure, Ace?"

"You keep up with the questions and I might change my goddamn mind." He smirks at me as he lies there with his hands behind his head. Liar. He wants to fuck as much as I do. I drop my head and suck his glistening tip into my mouth. He immediately fists my hair and yanks my head back hard.

"No sucking, baby. I'm not clean."

Like I care if he's showered. I love it when he tells me what to do. Only in the bedroom, though. He knows not to pull that shit anywhere else.

Straddling him, I lean forward and press my nose to his neck. He smells of hard-working male. Sweat, leather, and raw masculinity. Such a heady combination. My nipples agree and tighten in response. I press my lips against his, and his large hand grips the back of my head, his tongue immediately taking ownership of my mouth as he pulls me closer and kisses me like a man who's been starved.

Positioning his blunt head at my entrance, I lower myself, gasping as his dick stretches and fills me completely.

"Take what you need, sweetheart." He grunts as the flat of his tongue licks the length of my throat.

Locking our fingers together, I rock back and forth so his dick rubs against my sweet spot, my clit against his groin.

The closer I get to the high I crave, the faster my movements become. He grips my hips painfully, holding me in place so he can thrust upwards and bang against all the pleasure points.

"Shit, Ace." I mewl as I finally reach the pinnacle, my nails digging into his taut stomach as the waves course through my body.

Flipping me onto my back, he presses my legs against my torso and drives into me.

"Touch yourself."

It's not a request. It's an order. I reach for my clit as he thrusts, his focus now on reaching his own end. He's sheened with sweat. He closes his eyes, his movements becoming more erratic as he claims his release, taking me with him a second time before filling me with his cum.

He collapses on top of me, careful not to squash my stomach.

My fingers reach for his hair, running through its silky length.

"I love you, Ace," I whisper.

"Love you too, PJ."

Rolling over onto his back, he pulls me with him, kisses my forehead, and within seconds, my beautiful boy is fast asleep.

Do I have any regrets? About Ace? About Rising?

It's been two months since I moved back home and, in a word… nope.

PADRAIG

Padraig's Apartment, Hudson Yards, New York

Was I right to ask such a favor of our Dyl? To drag him into the web of deceit I want to create to stop myself drowning in whiskey every day?

Probably not, but I selfishly waved an empty bottle in his face, played the martyr card, and did it anyway. I'm not proud of it. But this is all about survival. I'm not surviving without her.

My finger hovers over my phone as I think about what to say in a message that's from me but not.

I need to connect with her, and even if she doesn't know it's me… I'll take what I can get.

Lies, deceit, and pretense. No good will ever come of it. I tell myself that maybe, in time, I can wean myself away. That's another lie. I know I'll only stop when she finds out. And find out she will.

Padraig: *You there?*
Jaine: *Where else would I be, Dyl?*

It's not my name she's saying as I message her from my brother's number. But it's her. That's all that matters. My heart jolts at this small piece of contact.

Padraig: *Murdering someone in cold blood.*
Jaine: *Nope. Not today. I need to cut back, just so you know. At least for now.*
Padraig: *My da won't be happy to hear that.*
Jaine: *I'll take the urgent ones where I can, but my hormones are all over the place. The last person I shot, I cried over. His brains were splattered all over a family photo that had children in it. I was an emotional fucking wreck. Don't get me wrong, he deserved the engraved bullet. But my hormones are giving me a big fat conscience these days. I can't afford to feel guilty. I can't afford to hesitate and then miss.*
Padraig: *Understood. By all accounts, the Russians are baying for your blood, so it's maybe best you lie low for a while.*
Jaine: *Those fuckers can join the queue.*
Padraig: *How many weeks along are you now? Nine you said?*
Jaine: *Yes.*
Padraig: *You excited?*
Jaine: *I guess. I wasn't to start with as it wasn't planned, but now we're happy.*
Padraig: *Speaking of we, where's Ace*?
Jaine: *In bed. He's only just got back this morning after being on a four-day run. So, I'm all on my lonesome, wearing a string bikini and lounging by the pool.*
Padraig: *Are you going to send me one of those images? You know, the ones girls take of their legs, and then I have to decide if they're hot dogs or not.*

Jaine: *You want me to send you a pic of my legs? You got the hots for me or something? I mean, I can send you one if you like.*

Shite. It's so easy to slip back into our familiar flirty ways. I need to remember who I'm supposed to be.

Padraig: *Don't be daft. I thought it was meant to be a joke thing.*
Jaine: *Dylan and Jaine sitting in a tree. K.I.S.S.I.N.G.*
Padraig: *Shut up, you eejit.*
Jaine: *You want to check out my hot dog legs. Said so yourself. I reckon you want to be my boyfriend!!! I'm telling Ace.*
Padraig: *Don't you dare.*
Jaine: *Why? He won't mind. He's secure enough in himself. Plus, he knows I have a weird fetish for Irishmen.*
Padraig: *All Irishmen?*
Jaine: *Well, apart from Eoin. I'd need to draw the line at him. Cillian too. I have a type, it seems, and it's black hair and blue eyes, so as much as Cill's good-looking, auburn just doesn't do it for me.*
Padraig: *I'll be sure to let them both know. They'll be sorely disappointed.*
Jaine: *Oh, I'm sure Eoin will weep into his breakfast cereal at the news that I'm not interested in becoming Ma Duster.*
Jaine: *Sends pic.*
Jaine: *My legs.*
Padraig: *Those are definitely hot dogs.*
Jaine: *You're an idiot, Dylan O'Connell.*
Padraig: *You know what they say. It takes one to know one.*
Jaine: *Go away.*
Padraig: *Bye, Jaine*

JAINE

Jaine's House, Rising, California

Smiling to myself, I put my burner phone on the glass table beside me. Stretching out on the recliner, I lift my face to the Californian sun and inhale the familiar smell of wildflowers. Dyl is so easy to tease, and he does seem to enjoy the banter. It's not like him to flirt, though. My thoughts immediately drift to *my* Irish. My life is pretty much perfect right now. He's the only exception. I miss him.

So. Fucking. Much.

I rub my hand over my stomach. There's nothing to see yet. It's still flat. I guess that will all change soon enough. I know I can find out now who my baby daddy is. What's the point, though? It won't change anything.

I'm fifteen weeks. I lied. I don't like having to do that, but it's not like I have much choice. It wouldn't take a rocket scientist to work out that I fell pregnant around the time we were being held by the Russians. Questions would be asked.

"Morning, Cherry." I take the call from my other phone.

"Morning, babe. Ace back?"

"Yeah. He got back this morning."

"You fucked him yet?"

"None of your business."

"That means you did."

"Why are you so interested in my sex life?"

"You seen Jefferson lately?"

"Yeah. He came over yesterday with the paperwork for the two new titty bars they're opening in Depling."

"Did he ask about me?"

"No, he didn't, babe, but I could tell he wanted to. Listen, you need to just ask him outright if he's moving to Manhattan or not."

"I will."

She lets out the longest sigh. Now's as good a time as any to broach the other sensitive subject.

"Have you thought about what I asked, Cherry? I need to know because I have to plan accordingly."

"Will you come back and show me the ropes?"

"Of course."

"I can't believe you want me to run JAL."

"Just until after the baby's born and until I can work out how best to move things forward."

"I'm nervous about having to deal with Razr."

I laugh. "Delaney's a pussy cat. He won't give you any problems, and if he does, you just tell me, and I'll handle him."

"I'm also worried about having to deal with Prescott."

"Easy. Just flash Gabe your cleavage now and then and read him the riot act. That asshole likes to be dominated and told what to do. I'm pretty sure he's a kinky fucker and into all that BDSM shit. I reckon if you started playing with his handcuffs, he'd come in his pants. Again. I'm happy to fly in if it's something you need assistance with."

There's a pause.

"Do you know what? I'll do it."

I breathe a sigh of relief. "I've got a charity function I need to attend in Manhattan in around six weeks that I can't get out of, so let me kill two birds with one stone. In fact, you should go with me. There'll be a lot of JAL clients there, so I can introduce you around. I'll hand over the reins then."

"Sounds good. And let me know if Jefferson asks about me."

I roll my eyes. "Quit beating around the bush and just ask him outright. Anyway, speak soon. Love you."

"Love you too."

I disconnect the call and go into the house. It's all white walls and gray floors these days, but I've added back a lot of the old furniture and all the photo frames. Sitting on the ancient cream sofa, I grimace as the cold surface touches my bare skin. I run my hands across it comfortingly. There are over twenty years of memories engrained in its leather, which only smells of polish these days.

I'm not looking forward to returning to Manhattan. It's way too soon. Not enough time has passed since I had to let *him* go, so it holds too many unpleasant recent memories. I need to tie up loose ends and attend this damn event, though. When I first asked Cherry if she'd run the business in my absence, she point-blank refused. After weeks of persistence, it seems I've finally worn her down and got her to believe in herself enough to agree.

Thank fuck. It's not like I can hand over the reins to just any old lawyer. I have several accounts that need careful handling over and above the Scorpions' one.

I say a silent prayer that I don't run into any of the O'Connells when I'm in town. In fact, I may have to speak with Eoin in advance just to make sure. There's no point in tempting fate. The last thing I need to happen is for me to bump into Irish. Not that I ever have in the past at any function, but it would just be my luck.

CHAPTER FIVE

SARAH

In transport

"So, what's the plan?" Laila's voice is hushed as we stand behind a tree in a secluded, wooded area. It's dark and still, but dawn now beckons. The only sound is a lone owl hooting in the distance. It's break time, and I've just assisted the girls with their bodily functions.

"It's best you don't know."

"You will be careful, won't you, Sarah?"

I look down at my little friend. Not that I'm overly tall at five-eight, but she must be five-two at most. Plus, I'm wearing four-inch heels. Her expression is full of concern for me. Really, she should be worrying more about the predicament we'll all be in if I can't pull this off.

"Of course I will. But we've only got one shot at this, so you concentrate on praying to God and leave the rest to me." I smile, hoping it reassures her. Being a good Catholic girl, I know she will pray, and I'm going to need all the help I can get. False idols included. Right now, I'm not choosy.

I stare up at the full moon. It's been raining, and the musty smell from the wet undergrowth fills the air. I inhale it deeply into my lungs.

Once everyone is back in the vehicle, I get in the front beside Mario. He smiles at me, his teeth brilliant white against his tanned skin. We haven't spoken much on the journey, mainly because of the fake language barrier I've created, but we've sort of gotten used to being around each other. I feel bad about what I'm going to have to do, but it was his choice to hook up with a bunch of fuckers who thought it okay to traffick children.

Once we're on the move, I jerk him off, hopefully for the last time, then wipe my hand on the oily cloth. Resting my head against the seat. I pretend to sleep, but I don't. I can't. There's too much at stake.

We stop off once more, and in between, I pretend to doze. I welcome the signs for Richmond several hours later. The sun is setting, and the sky is glorious in shades of blues and pinks. In another half hour, it'll be dark. I groan loudly, pretending to wake, then stretch exaggeratedly, making sure my tits are pressed against my top as I do. Looking out the corner of my eye, I watch as Mario's gaze drops to my nipples. I turn and smile coyly, running my hands down my tits at the same time, making the tips pebble further. His eyes darken in response as he licks his lips before dropping his hand to his crotch to adjust his hardening junk.

I lean over and run my fingers up his short, stocky thigh, stopping just before I reach his puny dick.

"Want to fuck?" I bite my lip as I part my legs invitingly. Then, dropping my hand between my thighs, I rub my clit through my jeans.

He nods. "Next truck stop."

Ten minutes later, we're pulling into an empty parking lot. He chooses a spot that's as far back from the gas station as possible. The lights are on, but from what I can see, there are no customers inside or out. It's just an older man sitting behind the counter, reading a newspaper.

Once parked, Mario leans over and reaches for me, his hands automatically groping my tits, his wet mouth connecting with my neck.

Pulling back, I motion my head towards the door. "Let's go outside, Mario."

He looks like he's weighing up the options, and I panic. Please, God, don't let him refuse, or it's game fucking over.

Thankfully, when I smile and reach for the handle, he does the same.

I shiver as my feet connect with the tarmac. Is it because I'm cold or because of what I'm about to do? Can I do it? I have no choice. There's a trailer filled with children depending on me. There's also my best friend.

Mario approaches my side of the truck, which is shrouded in darkness and can't be seen by the elderly sales assistant.

His hands immediately lunge for my tits. I let him have his fun. It's the last grope he'll ever have of any female. As I'm way taller, he tries to pull my head down to kiss me, but I avoid him, so he makes do with my neck. I shiver in revulsion as his slimy tongue leaves a trail of saliva across my exposed skin, the wetness quickly cooling in the night air.

"Let me take off my shoes and pants," I whisper hotly in his ear. He steps back and rubs his hard-on through his jeans as he watches me remove my shoes. Using the oldest trick in the fucking book, I look over his shoulder, and he instinctively turns to see what I'm staring at. As he does, I swing my stiletto with such force it connects with the side of his head, just behind his eye, the steel tip penetrating his flesh. He pulls it out, then collapses to the ground, groaning in pain before passing out.

I roll him flat onto his back, knowing the blow won't have killed him. I have no choice but to complete the process, and quickly, as he won't be out for long.

Putting my shoes back on my feet. I raise my eyes to the sky and whisper a prayer, asking for forgiveness. The silvery moon glares back at me, silently condemning my outlaw soul as it bears witness to what I'm about to do. I know Mario's scum, but it doesn't make his murder any easier to commit.

Crossing myself beforehand, I lift my foot and slam the stiletto heel of my shoe right into where I know his jugular vein to be. Blood sprays everywhere. I wait until the spurting stops, then check for a pulse to make sure he's dead. Nothing. Leaning my arm against the vehicle, I heave up the bile from my empty stomach.

I'm way out of practice with this killing shit.

Rubbing the back of my hand across my mouth, I drag Mario's body to the side of the cabin. Then, grabbing the keys from his front pocket, I open up the trailer. I'm instantly accosted by the smell of piss and excrement. Poor fuckers. Pigs are better treated.

I had felt guilty for a moment. For having to kill him. We shared something fleetingly. Even if it was fucked up. Now I remember why the asshole deserved to die.

"Laila?"

I can hear her shuffle forward, along with several others.

"The rest of you stay inside," I order them. Not sure I would have listened to me if I could smell freedom, but they do as they're told and move back.

I help Laila down, then lock the trailer.

"What's going on, Sarah? What have you done?" she whispers up at me, her green eyes huge on her face.

"I killed the fucker, and I need your help getting him behind the passenger seat."

"WHAT DO WE DO NOW?" LAILA ALMOST PASSED OUT AT THE SIGHT of so much blood. She's riding shotgun, her arms wrapped around her knees, which are clutched to her chest. She's gagging. Most likely because Mario's corpse is squashed behind her seat, and what's left of his lifeblood is pooling in the footwell, the metallic stench almost overwhelming.

"Now I have to phone a friend."

Using Mario's phone, I dial the only number apart from my brother's and Laila's that I know off the top of my head. Why do I remember it? It ends in 666. It's unforgettable. Hopefully, so am I, as it's been a long time. Will she be able to help me? Who knows, but it's a chance I'll have to take.

"Cherry Avery speaking. Who is this?"

"Hi, Cherry. Blast from the past. It's Sarah Sanders."

There's a pause. She's no doubt trying to remember who the fuck I am.

"Sarah… from school, Sarah?"

"Yes, Sarah from school, Sarah."

I don't wait for a response.

"Listen, I'll explain everything later, but I need help, and yours is the only number I know off by heart. Can I trust you? You always said if I needed you for anything, you'd be there. We pinkie promised, and we swapped blood and all that other shit, remember?

Sorry to put you on the spot, but please tell me I can." The words tumble from my lips.

There's another pause while she catches up with what I'm saying. "Yes, of course. What do you need?"

"Are you still living in Manhattan?"

"Yes."

"And did you ever do that law thing your folks expected of you?"

"Yes. Why? What's going on, Sarah?"

"So, this conversation is confidential, right?"

"Of course."

"Okay." I take a deep breath to compose myself before I go on. "I'm currently driving a lorry filled with kids that were earmarked for trafficking. I need to speak to someone urgently about what to do next. I've killed the driver and am about to hit the road. I'm in Richmond and heading for New York. Do you know anyone who could help? I know contacting you is a long shot, but…"

There's no hesitation as she interjects.

"I know exactly who you need to speak to, Sarah. Her name is Jaine Jones. I'll get her to call you on this number right away."

"SARAH?"

"Yes," I answer as I try to navigate the vehicle out of the lorry park, knocking over a sign on the way whilst trying to yank the fucking annoying hula dancer off the dashboard. I swear silently before checking my mirrors, exiting the truck stop, and throwing the fucking thing out the window. Die, bitch.

"Sarah, it's Jaine. Cherry's filled me in. Tell me exactly what you need and where and when you need it."

"Jaine, I have dozens of children in the back of this vehicle. I have no idea what condition some of them are in as many have been caged for days, maybe even weeks. My friend and I were abducted in Mexico, so some of them may be from farther afield. They were scheduled to be handed over to Christ knows who in Washington DC in around one hour from now. I'm currently heading for New York. I need to know where to take them and who I can safely hand them over to. I may end up being tailed when the vehicle doesn't show up at its destination. I've also got a body in the back. The driver. Sorry. I don't even know you, and I'm dragging you into my shitty mess."

"Just keep calm, Sarah. You're doing great. You're my fucking hero. Listen, the main thing is don't crash and just keep heading for Manhattan. I'm not local to you at present, but I have some contacts who are…."

"Where are you?"

"I'm in California."

"Shit."

"Don't panic. So, since you know Cherry, I guess it's safe to assume you're a New Yorker?"

"Yes. Returning home after a sabbatical of sorts."

"Any names of people I should avoid?"

"It's not likely that you'll know him, but you can't contact Paul Delaney."

There's a pause. Shit. Does she know him?

"Any reason why?"

"Yes. I have a reason."

"Would you mind sharing that with me?"

I pause, wondering if it's safe to tell her. Then I realize I don't have any choice.

"He's my brother."

"Jesus Christ. You're the missing Sarah?" She sounds surprised, shocked even.

"You know Paul?"

"Yes, I know him."

"He can't find out. Not yet. I need to tell him I'm back in my own time."

There's a pause.

"Okay… no worries, Sarah. Does anyone there know your real name?"

"Just my friend Laila."

"You're strawberry blonde like Paul. I've seen photos. You got the temper to go with it?"

"You could say that."

She chuckles. "So, a short fuse like your brother. Okay, well, from now on, your name's Red."

"Thanks, Jaine."

"No worries. I'll always try to respect your wishes. Let me try my other contact. In the meantime, just keep driving."

CHAPTER SIX

JAINE

Jaine's House, Rising, California

"JAINE, WHAT'S UP?"

"Sorry to call, Dylan, but I've got an emergency on its way from Richmond to New York. I need the Dusters' help."

"We'll assist if we can. What's the problem?"

"A trailer filled with children is on its way to New York in a vehicle potentially being tailed. Some of them may be illegals; all of them were earmarked for trafficking. There's also a dead body. The girl driving, Red, needs to know what to do and where to take them. She's just set off from Richmond."

"Whoa, let me stop you there. What can the Dusters do?"

"Well, you need to do something as I can't because I'm in California."

"Shite." There's a pause. "You need to speak to our Eoin."

"Fuck that."

"There's no other choice, Jaine! It's not a decision I can make, and if they're expected to arrive in six hours or so, we need to start making the necessary arrangements."

"Give me his fucking number."

"Might be best if I give him yours."

"Oh, sure. I'm not worthy. Okay, but make sure you give him the other number. Not this one."

"Will do."

Great, now I need to speak to my arch fucking nemesis.

"Jaine, how are you?"

I immediately feel my blood pressure rise when I hear the deep, dangerous voice of the asshole I hate with a passion. The fucker who interfered with my life and who will pay for his divine intervention in due course, preferably with my engraved bullet between his aquamarine eyes.

"I'm fine, Eoin. Not that you're really interested, so don't pretend you are. Now, can we get straight to the matter at hand?"

"As you wish."

"I've got an emergency situation on its way from Richmond to New York. I need the Dusters' assistance."

"Dylan's filled me in. What do you want us to do?"

"Some of the children may be illegals—some not. While we figure shit out, we don't need any of them getting tied up in red tape. Not when we can get them straight home. They could spend months in the care system while things are addressed and processed, as you know. Some may wind up never being returned and stuck there indefinitely."

"So, you're convinced they were earmarked for trafficking?"

"The girl driving the vehicle seems to think so. She and her friend were abducted in Mexico, so we can only assume that's what the other captives have told them."

"So, what do you want us to do with them?"

"I don't know. Put them up in your apartment?"

"Be serious, Jaine. You're the one asking for the favor."

"Put them up in one of your hotels, then. That way, they can be gone through and dealt with individually."

"It's a big ask."

"Maybe so, but if it were your child, wouldn't you hope someone would do the decent thing by them if the situation arose and if they could?"

"Why can't you ask the Scorpions for help?"

"Because I can't."

"Why not?"

"I can't tell you."

"I'm intrigued. I need to know now."

"Fuck you."

"Your smart, vulgar mouth's not helping the situation when time's ticking, Miss Jones."

"I wish it was ticking under your ass in the shape of a fucking bomb," I mumble.

"I heard that."

"Sorry." Not sorry. "Look, are you going to help me or not?"

"I need to know why you can't ask the Scorpions."

"Nosy fucker, aren't you?"

"I prefer curious or inquisitive."

"Well, we both know what that did to the cat, don't we?"

"I'll take my chances."

"You're the kind that would have the nine guaranteed lives. You've probably already bought God and have his Almighty-self stuffed in your back pocket. Anyway, I can't tell you. I swore I wouldn't."

"You want the Dusters' help, then I need to know."

"Why do you need to know? Why are you asking this? You're deliberately being fucking obtuse just to piss me off."

"Not at all. I just don't want to trample on anyone's toes. If you're saying the girl involved is adamant she doesn't want to deal with the Scorpions, then that means she knows Razr. I'm not sure it's good business for the Dusters to make an enemy of him."

"I gave my word, Eoin."

"If you don't tell me, then you'll need to find someone else to assist."

The asshole's got me over a barrel for the second time in my life. It just makes me hate his guts all the more.

"Fine, but it goes no further. Not even to the other Dusters. Do I have your word?"

"Depending on the answer, then yes, of course."

"It's Delaney's long-lost sister."

"Sarah?" He sounds as shocked as I was.

"Yes. Sarah. That's strictly between us. For now, and to everyone else, she's called Red."

"Of course."

"So, you'll help?"

"Yes."

"Tell me where to send her and the details of who she's going to meet."

"I'll message you the intel. It will be our Cillian who will handle it. In situations like this, he goes by the name Ian. As you'll appreciate, we don't want to tarnish the Dusters' reputation if things don't go as planned."

"That's laughable. What goddamn reputation is there to uphold and protect?"

"You're pushing the boundaries, Miss Jones," he hisses.

It seems like I've touched a raw nerve. Shame. Now I want to just keep poking that big old Duster bear.

"What happens if I keep pushing, Eoin? Hm? Are you going to threaten to have me exterminated again? Or are you going to put me over your knee and spank me for being a naughty girl?"

There's no response, but I can almost feel his annoyance vibrating down the line.

"Oh, and there's one other thing."

"What now?"

"Don't be so fucking condescending." I smirk, relishing in just how much I've pissed him off.

"I'm waiting."

"I have to attend a charity function in New York six weeks this Saturday. I can't avoid it. One of my largest clients is hosting it. JAL is also a significant benefactor to the cause being represented. My client and I have a lot of mutual contacts, many of whom will also be in attendance. It's unlikely he would go as, in nine years, I've never bumped into him at a function, but I need you to make sure Padraig doesn't show up. As said, I can't get out of it. It's too important a client for me."

"Which client?"

"That's none of your business. Just make sure Padraig stays home that night. Cinderella cannot go to the goddamn ball."

I hear him sigh in frustration, which makes my smile widen. The arrogant fucker deserves to be wound up, tied up, and tossed into the Hudson.

"I'm waiting on a name, Miss Jones."

I don't reply immediately just to annoy him further. Immature, I know, but who gives a fuck?

"Leoluca Di Matteo," I answer eventually.

There's a pause. "He's your client?"

"Yes. What? Did you think my only client was Paul Delaney and the Iron Scorpions?"

"Leoluca has links with the Sicilian mafia."

"I'm well aware of that. As a result, Luciano will also be there, and maybe even his baby sister, Sophia." How fucking cozy will that be? I can hardly wait. "Between you and me, Leo should overthrow that waste of space Luc and take control. Turn that faction into one that people want to be associated with. Leo's a good man. Well, as far as the Cosa Nostra go."

"Leo. I'm told only his closest friends call him that."

"Yes? And?"

There's a pause. Maybe now he realizes the true extent of his underestimation of me.

"As you know, Paddy is engaged to Sophia Ruocco."

"Yes, I'm well aware of that. You paid me a visit to deliver the news personally, if you recall. To warn me never to contact him again. I'm sure you can't have forgotten, Eoin. It wasn't that long ago. I assure you I never will. I await my wedding invitation with bated breath."

Then I decide I'm on a roll.

"You know, maybe the Dusters should have considered marrying Irish off to a family that was going to be around for the long-term instead of the Ruoccos. They're already deemed untrustworthy by their peers after showing their true colors when they tried to short-change the Mexicans. Leoluca has a younger sister, Ava, and she's a credit to his famiglia. She would have made a much better match."

There's a pause. The fucker must know I have a point.

"Anyway, I'm just letting you know. Leo is expecting me. I can't let him down."

"I'll bear it in mind."

"You do that. I'll speak with Red now and let her know to

expect contact from Cillian, aka Ian. I won't mention the Dusters. Oh, and if you want to know who else is on my client list and who else I rub shoulders with, you can just fucking ask me. Then again, I know the minute I hang up, you'll have Dyl go through my business closet with a fine-tooth comb. Am I right?"

He doesn't reply. He knows I am. I exhale slowly and grit my teeth before I say something I'll regret. Not that I'd ever regret saying anything derogatory to this piece of shit.

"Anyway, thank you, Eoin." I play nice.

"You're welcome, Jaine."

Fucking pompous asshole.

"SARAH, IT'S ME. EVERYTHING OKAY?"

"Yeah. I've taken out one sign already, so I'm just concentrating on driving carefully and focusing my attention on the road and nothing else."

"Good idea. You're doing fantastic. Not much farther. Listen, can you put me on to your friend?"

"Yes. Will do. And Jaine?"

"Yeah?"

"Will I be able to meet you when this is over? You know, to thank you properly?"

Tears prick my eyes. Fucking hormones. "Sure, Sarah. I'd love to meet up. Let's make plans once everyone's safe."

"Thank you… for everything." I can hear the emotion in her voice.

"I'm only glad I could help."

"Hi, it's Laila." Her voice is barely audible. She sounds about ten years old.

"Hi, Laila. It's Jaine. Listen, I don't want to stress Sarah out any more than she already is. I'm going to message the details of where you need to go. My contact is called Ian, and he's aware of everything. He'll be in touch. Sarah's name is now Red. Don't refer to her as anything else."

"Noted."

CHAPTER SEVEN

CILLIAN

Cillian's Apartment, Hudson Yards, New York

"EOIN?" I'm draped across the brown leather sectional at home playing *Call of Duty* remotely against Paddy and Dyl. He's a competitive fucker, our Paddy. Dyl and I have found that keeping him entertained in the evenings stops him from reaching for the bottle, although he does seem to be a bit chirpier these days for some reason. Of course, it'll be something else that no fucker tells me anything about.

I mute them.

"Sorry, Cill. We've got an emergency. I've just had Jaine Jones on the phone."

"What? Paddy's Jaine?"

He pauses, obviously irritated at that moniker for her.

"Yes… Paddy's Jaine."

"What did she want?"

"There a vehicle with children heading for New York. They were earmarked for trafficking. I need you to intercept them at the docks and have the young ones transported to the new hotel that's scheduled to open soon. We can take care of everything else from there. There's also a body. Strip him, keep hold of his personal possessions, and have him tossed in the Hudson. Tip the vehicle in there too, provided it's not been followed."

"On it. Anyone I need to deal with?"

"Yes. Deal with the girl called Red."

I disconnect the call and stretch out. Fucking hell. First time it's been quiet in ages, and now it's going to be chaos.

I unmute my brothers.

"Dyl. Paddy. I need to head off. Work beckons. I'll speak to you pair tomorrow."

"You know what they say, Cill. No rest for the wicked."

"Well, in that case, Paddy, you should be coming with me."

He laughs. "Away you go. I'm a saint compared to you."

"Aye, only because you're a lazy swine, and as for Dyl, that eejit couldn't even kill a spider without bursting into guilty tears, so no one could ever refer to him as being wicked."

"I am still here, you know," Dyl mumbles in the background

"You know it's true, brother."

I disconnect them.

"Tam."

"Cill?"

"Meet me downstairs in fifteen minutes."

"Yes, boss."

DYLAN

Dylan's Apartment, Hudson Yards, New York

"Eoin." No sooner has he hung up on Cill, he's calling me.

"Jaine Jones."

"What about her?"

"I want everything you can find on her."

"We went through it before. Aside from the MC life, she's clean."

"I want to know who her business contacts are. Did you know Leoluca Di Matteo is her client?"

"No, I didn't know that."

"We need to know these things, Dyl!" he hisses.

"Why? She backed off from Paddy, so she's no threat to us now."

There's a pause. I can tell he's pissed off at my response. Maybe if he explained what he was getting at, the rest of us wouldn't have to second guess. He's far too much like Da.

"That's my point. Maybe she would have been the best match for Paddy after all if her social and business circle means she rubs shoulders with the people we want to be associated with."

"Bit late for that now. She's living with Ace in California."

I can hear him throw something across the room. Probably a paperweight. Like father like eldest son. "I still need to know. I need it by tomorrow."

"I'll start work on it in the morning."

"How is Paddy?"

I sigh. "Well, he's stopped looking for answers at the bottom of a whiskey bottle, and he seems brighter in himself. He'll never let Jaine go, though, and I doubt she'll ever let him go either."

"I can understand the attraction now I've spoken to her a few times. She's an intriguing woman, and very pretty, if I recall. Then again, she's also extremely irritating and with a mouth that would shame most sailors."

"Yes. Jaine says it how it is. There's no airs or graces with that girl." I chuckle.

He pauses again. Is he going to say something else about her?

"Anyway, get me that information, Dyl. Urgently."

"On it."

Disconnecting the call, I think about what Eoin's just said.

Has Jaine got my big brother's dick twitching?

CHAPTER EIGHT

SARAH

Seven Years Earlier (Age Twenty-One)
The Delaney Home, Brightling, New York

"YOU NEED to practice more on your aim, baby girl."

I roll my eyes at him and let out a huff as I place the heavy air pistol on the garden table.

"I'll never be any good at shooting, Daddy. We both know that."

I watch as the long-haired biker swaggers to the end of our perfectly mowed lawn and removes the paper target from the board it's affixed to. Lifting it to the cloudless blue sky, he looks at where my pellets have penetrated the card, frowning at how bad a shot I am.

He shakes his head in disappointment, then looks at me, smiles, and shakes it again. I know exactly what he's thinking. The daughter of the president of a one percent club, and I can't shoot for shit. I smirk in response as I take in the forty-eight-year-old. The most handsome man in the world. Both my older brother and I have inherited his strawberry blonde hair. Paul has Dad's green eyes and pale complexion, whereas I have my mother's hazel eyes and olive skin.

Despite approaching fifty, my dad's still got it all going on and has a queue of women lining up, all desperate to be his old lady. I know he gets his dick wet. He's old, not dead.

A couple of times, I've even walked in on him mid-fuck. He's had a couple of short-term relationships over the years, but none of them have ever amounted to anything serious. He's just never gotten over loving then losing my mom.

He walks back towards me with the evidence of how crap a shot I am in his hands.

"It's in the genes, baby girl. Your momma was a shit shot too," he says with a chuckle.

I walk towards him, and he envelopes me in his large arms. I close my eyes and inhale the familiar smell of his leather cut and cigarettes.

"Yeah, well, we can't be good at everything, Daddy." I laugh. Like my mom and my brother, my weapon of choice is a blade. Now, with that piece of metal, I'm incredibly talented.

He kisses the top of my head and gives me one final squeeze before picking up and placing the air gun down the front of his jeans.

"You run along and make your old man something to eat now, Sarah, before I have to head back to the clubhouse. That's a skill I'm grateful you did inherit from your momma. Damn, my Ella knew how to cook."

My thoughts immediately drift to my mom. She had a hemorrhage birthing me. The doctors couldn't pump blood into her tiny body as fast as she was losing it, and she went into cardiac arrest. They couldn't save her. She was only twenty-six years old. I think part of my daddy died that day too. They'd been childhood sweethearts. They thought they had their whole lives ahead of them, but I well and truly fucked that up by being born. I know my daddy doesn't resent me for what happened, but my brother does. We've never really been close, Paul and me. That's the reason.

He hates me.

Placing a kiss on my daddy's cheek, I turn to walk towards the house. My childhood home. I've lived here my whole life. It's a Tudor-style property with six bedrooms and in an extremely affluent area. I'm not stupid. I realize our money isn't earned legally, as do our neighbors. We never bring any trouble to our door, though, so I guess that's why they've always tolerated our biker asses.

The kitchen radio is playing soft rock music, and I hum along as I investigate the fridge's contents, contemplating what to make. It's then I hear the sirens.

My daddy is beside me in an instant. "Stay inside, Sarah." His tone is authoritative. He's King now. His road name. And he's in presidential mode. I know better than to disobey him. I continue making lunch, trying to distract myself, but a feeling of doom punches me in the gut, causing me to almost double over.

He's immediately on the phone to Wolf, the Scorpions' VP. I can't make out what they're saying, but there's a lot of hushed talking and swearing.

I hear the front door open and close. A few seconds later, I hear a gunshot. My blood runs cold.

"Daddy!" I sob.

Running to the door, I throw it wide open.

"Get down on the ground and don't move." I'm aware of the flashing lights only briefly as I drop to my knees in front of my daddy. He's panting and clutching his chest. He's been shot, his lifeblood quickly pooling on the driveway around him.

"Daddy." I pull his upper body into my arms, cradling him to me. I try to see where he's bleeding out from, but I can't. There's blood everywhere, pumping out of his body with every beat of his beautiful heart. It's all over me. Tainting me forever. I know it will never wash off. His blood will always be on my hands.

"Daddy, you're bleeding! What do I do? I don't know what to do." I'm screaming and crying. I want to stay calm for his sake, reassure him everything's going to be okay, but I can't. I'm panicking, failing him when he needs me most.

"Phone an ambulance," I scream at the half dozen police cars that now surround our home, my tears blinding me.

I touch his handsome face, and his skin feels cold and clammy.

I know what that means. Please, God, no.

"You hang on in there, Daddy. The ambulance will be here soon." I rock him in my arms, holding him close, trying to keep him warm while watching as the river of blood widens and flows.

Time ticks. Seconds. Minutes. Hours. Too long. Way too long.

Reality hits me like a truck. It hits him too. Then he voices what I fear hearing more than anything in this godforsaken world.

"Sarah… I'm not going to make it, baby girl… It's time for me to go be with your momma."

My chest constricts. My heart physically hurts.

Please, God, don't take my daddy. I beg you, please don't take him.

"Don't say that. You're going to be okay, Daddy." It doesn't sound like me. The words are panicked, pained, distraught.

Please, God. I'll do anything. Please take me instead. Please.

I'm begging, but I know my words will fall on deaf ears. See, God doesn't give a shit about the likes of us. Biker trash. If he did, he wouldn't have taken my momma.

And now he's going to take my daddy from me too.

"Sarah… tell your brother I love him and that he has to make me and your mom proud. Tell him… no matter what, that he's to take care of his baby sister." His voice is a whisper as he speaks in broken words.

"You can tell him yourself." I'm trying to be firm, not wanting to face the reality that the man who gave me life is about to die in my fucking arms. What did I ever do to deserve this shitty karma?

"I love you, baby girl. Don't you ever forget that," he whispers.

"I love you too, Daddy. So much." They were the last words he ever heard, and I'm so fucking glad I got the chance to say them.

He closes his eyes and frowns with the pain. His breathing is labored, and his skin is so cold.

"Where's the fucking ambulance?" I scream at the pigs, who are all still behind their open car doors with their weapons aimed at me. It's like they're waiting for him to die before they do anything.

"Just hang on, Daddy. Please hang on." I rock him back and forth, but he can't hear me anymore. Pushing his hair back from his face, I rub my hand over his to try to warm him back up.

I don't know how much time passes. Or maybe it just stopped. I'll never know how long it took from when my daddy got shot until he took his final breath in and then out.

Then his chest is still. Then there's just silence. Deathly silence.

I cry at the unfairness of it all as I clutch him to my chest, rocking him backward and forward.

The stillness of the day my daddy died will live with me forever. The silence so loud I can still hear it.

It's finally disturbed by the unwelcome sound of the ambulance, which is no longer needed, and the welcome sounds of hogs.

They have to prise my daddy from my grasp in the end as I refuse to let him go.

I don't remember anything after that.

Not until a few days later.

I was never told why the pigs turned up that day. It's not something womenfolk should know. We're only useful for cooking, cleaning, and fucking, after all.

What I was told is that it was a rookie police officer who shot my daddy. Apparently, he saw the gun tucked in the front of his jeans and panicked, thinking it was loaded, so he discharged his weapon.

Their excuse.

How was the young officer to know it was just an air pistol?

En-Route from Richmond to New York

"Why don't you want Paul to know you're back?"

My painful memories of the past are interrupted. I think about the question Laila's just asked. It's a good one.

I ran out on my brother when I was twenty-one years old, two months after my daddy passed in my arms. I spouted some bullshit about wanting to see the world. I lied. I watched my daddy die. I was responsible for the death of my mom.

Their blood was on my hands. Or at least that's what I thought for a long time.

I blamed myself. Paul did too. I know he did. At least for our momma. He made it pretty obvious by reminding me I killed her every opportunity he got.

My older brother would have been glad to see the back of me. He would have assumed I was taking off to go whoring and touring around the globe without a care in the world, especially with money being no object. I wasn't. I was coming to terms with it all. Or at least trying to. Learning how to live with it. Find peace. I've spent seven years in Bolivia, working in a little village hospital, being trained in how to help people. How to stop them from bleeding to death. I never want to witness that shit again.

Tears threaten, and I blink them back. If I'd known then what I know now, I could have saved my daddy.

Not my mom. She gave her life to give me mine. Hers was the ultimate sacrifice.

And now? Now I'm going to make a difference.

I'm going home to train to be a doctor. To help those who need it. I never want to feel helpless again in that situation. To feel useless as a person dies from a preventable death. Especially one who doesn't deserve it, and my daddy sure as hell didn't deserve it.

I left my brother to take over the reins of the MC and cope with the fallout on his own. I was a fucking coward. I should have been there. Been the sister I was born and raised to be in this fucked up outlaw world. But it was just too much. I was too young. I couldn't deal with it then. Couldn't deal with him. Shit, I don't know if I can deal with either now.

"I need to explain to Paul the reasons I left, and the reasons I've come back, Laila, but I have to get that shit straight in my head first. It's been seven years. Now is not that time. Not with all this going on. When I speak to my brother, I need our conversation to be the priority. Right now, it's not. You know?"

"Yeah. I know, Sarah… I mean… Red."

I laugh out loud as I run my fingers through my filthy hair. Strawberry blonde. A flattering description for those of us who are on the paler side of ginger. Same as Paul's. He's all the kin I have left. I love my big brother with all my heart. I've always loved him. I owed him a proper explanation then. I definitely owe him one now. Not that he was blameless. He was a cruel, heartless bastard to me then and likely still will be now. So, no. Given our past, I can't just contact my brother out of the blue then rock up to the Scorpions' clubhouse with all these kids in tow.

Thank God for Cherry. Thank God for Jaine. I've no idea who

she is or how she knows Paul, but I'll find out in due course, I'm sure. One thing I do know is that we owe her our lives.

"I've put the details into my phone. It's suggesting our ETA is one hour fifty."

Laila interrupts my thoughts a second time.

My stomach flips. I'm starting to see familiar sights now.

Welcome back, Sarah.

CHAPTER NINE

PADRAIG

Padraig's Apartment, Hudson Yards, New York

Padraig: *You there?*
Jaine: *Where the fuck else would I be, Dyl?*
Padraig: *Everything sorted?*
Jaine: *Yes, although it was like pulling teeth.*
Padraig: *Shall I tell you a joke to cheer you up?*
Jaine: *Sweet Baby Jesus.*
Padraig: *Okay, I won't bother, then.*
Jaine: *What the fuck? You sulking now? Since when did you grow a funny bone? Are you making me feel guilty for not wanting to hear your joke? Not trying to be nasty, but I think Irish is the comedian in the Duster household. Go on, then, before I change my mind.*
Padraig: *What do you call an Irishman whose bullet misses and bounces off the wall?*

Jaine: *Jesus Christ?*
Padraig: *No, darlin'. You're not even trying. It's not The Almighty. It's Rick O'Shea.*

THERE'S A PAUSE, and I know why. I've just dropped the ball.

Jaine: *You just called me darlin'.*
Padraig: *Am I not allowed to call you that?*
Jaine: *It's what Irish used to call me.*
Padraig: *You miss him?*
Jaine: *We're not meant to go there. We agreed we wouldn't go there with those sorts of prying questions.*
Padraig: *Sorry. My bad.*
Jaine: *You're a fucking idiot.*
Padraig: *I'll be whatever you want me to be, darlin'.*
Jaine: *I'm not sure I can cope with you calling me that.*
Padraig: *Why?*
Jaine: *Because it brings back too many memories. Please don't call me darlin'.*
Padraig: *I was just trying to be nice. I like talking to you, and I think you like talking to me too. In fact, I know you do.*
Jaine: *Vain much? Weirdo.*
Padraig: *Takes one to know one.*
Jaine: *Okay... you can call me darlin'.*
Padraig: *Thank you... darlin'.*

I smile at my phone screen. It feels like old times. Just me and her. Then my smile fades. Because it's not. It's her and Dylan. I'm hit by a melancholy moment of reflection. It's brief. Because I remind myself that this is way better than nothing.

JAINE

Jaine's House, Rising, California

I put my phone on the bed and immediately bite back tears.

Fucking hormones.

Tightening my bathrobe, I sit on the bed and brush my wet hair down my back. My and Ace's bedroom is in tones of greys and creams. It's Pop's old room—a grown-up space. I didn't have the heart to take apart my pink childhood bedroom with all its sparkly, feathery, and glittery things going on. I don't think Ace could bear to touch it either. It holds way too many special memories for us both. We figured if we're ever blessed with a daughter, then it will be perfect for her, just like it was for little Plain Jaine Jones.

Ace is at the clubhouse in a council meeting. I abstained from going despite Sasha's complaint that she hasn't seen me in days. Morning sickness is an all-day event. The pregnancy gurus lied through their teeth. There's nothing to goddamn glow about.

I lie back on the bed with my phone beside me. It'll be a long night, I'm sure, dealing with the Dusters, and Delaney's baby sister.

"Shit," I mutter as my tears ignore my futile attempts to hold them at bay.

My exchange with Dylan made me think of Padraig. I guess it's only to be expected, given they're brothers. There are bound to be similarities.

I laugh. I say that, but there are zero similarities between Irish and Eoin. Aside from looks, those two couldn't be more different if they tried.

I've been lying staring at the ceiling and feeling all melancholy for God knows how long when I feel the bed dip. Turning my head, I see Ace lying on his back, looking across at me as he takes in my broken expression. I never even realized he was home.

Wiping the last of the tears from my face, I shoot him a watery smile. He reaches for my hand, locking our fingers together and squeezing mine gently.

"You miss him, don't you?"

"Yeah," I whisper with a nod. There's no need to ask who he's referring to. No point in me lying either. I don't lie. Well, at least not if I can help it. And if I can't be honest with Ace, who can I be honest with?

There's a pause.

"You know you can talk to me about what happened if you want to, PJ? About why you and Padraig don't speak anymore. The only reason I haven't asked is that it's none of my business. Not because I don't care. You know that, right?"

I squeeze his hand. "I know."

"I love you. I'm so fucking glad to have you back in my life, but if what you need is to have us both, me and him, then I want you to know I'd be fine with that too."

More tears flow as I lift myself on my elbow to look down at him.

He's so damn selfless. So fucking forgiving.

"I don't deserve you, Jason Steele. I really don't."

Our gazes connect. He reaches up and tucks my hair gently behind my ear, and I lean into his palm.

"It's not about who deserves what. You know me. I live day by day. There are no guarantees in this life. You're all that matters to me. You're the only thing that's ever mattered." He sits up and turns to look at me before running his hand through his hair. "I just wish I could offer you more. Rising isn't like Manhattan. But you already know that. I guess I'm worried the novelty of being back here might wear off pretty damn quick. That this town and me are never going to be enough. Not now you've had a taste of success and the city."

I can tell the thought has been playing on his mind a whole heck of a lot.

Sitting up, I turn to face him. "I left everything I ever knew for ten years because of how much I loved you, Ace. I don't think you ever have to worry about how strong my feelings are."

He smirks smugly at me, and I lose myself in the bluest of eyes as I do every time.

"I know you love me, PJ. I don't doubt that for a second. But is life here going to be enough for you long term? I don't think it will be. Deep down, I think you know that too. You're not cut out just to be a mom and an old lady. Maybe when the baby's born, we need to look at you spending time in Manhattan. You've invested a lot in your business, and I don't want you to have to give that up. Not completely. Not for me."

"It's not a commutable journey, though, Ace." I sigh as I bite my lip, taking in what he's saying.

"Then you go for a few days at a time. Or even a week at a time. We can make things work. I don't want you to resent me or have any regrets about what we're doing here." He pauses. "And if it turns out the baby's Padraig's, we're going to have to work something out anyway. At some point, you'd have to tell him. It wouldn't be fair on him or the baby otherwise. So, we may as well get our heads around that and get used to the idea. Either way, I don't want you giving up something you've spent years creating. I'm so fucking proud of you. Of who you are. Of what you've achieved."

I lay my hands over my flat stomach, and he pulls me back against his chest and covers them with his own. "This baby in here is part of you, so whether it's mine or not, I'll love it all the same, sweetheart."

I lift my head and smile up at him. "I know that."

"And if it's not mine, then we'll just have to make ourselves another."

I chuckle up at him. "Oh, you think so, Prez?"

"I know so, sweetheart, and I think maybe we should start practicing right about now."

His breath is hot in my ear. I watch as he unties my robe, the coolness of his rough hands as they connect with my exposed skin causing me to shiver.

I stand and let it drop to the floor so I'm naked. Lifting his Henley over his head, I push him back onto the bed so he's resting on his elbows.

Straddling his slim hips, I run my hands through his hair as his mouth drops to my nipples, licking and sucking them into his mouth. I groan as he feasts on my over-sensitive tips, causing my core to pool with warmth.

He lifts his head, and I drop my lips to meet his, his tongue immediately filling my mouth possessively. His fingers dip into my slickness, causing me to groan in response.

Pressing my nose to his neck, I inhale his familiar scent before my lips move to trace his tattoos. My mouth covers his nipple, and I bite down hard. He flinches and curses before fisting my hair and yanking my head back.

"Careful with those goddamn teeth, PJ." He growls at me, his eyes dark and dangerous. He's like a wild animal. I love tormenting the beast in him and bringing that fucker to the surface.

I smirk, then drop lower, licking the sensitive skin at the top of his jeans with the flat of my tongue, causing his rock-hard abs to clench in response.

"You want to suck my dick, sweetheart?" I look up, and he drags his thumb across my lower lip before pushing its saltiness into my mouth. I tongue it before sucking hard, and his eyes darken further. His lips part and his breathing becomes uneven as he watches me kneel on the floor before unbuttoning his impressive length to freedom.

Rubbing the pre-cum around the crown with my thumb, I suck his slickness from the tip before taking his dick deep into my mouth. Fisting my hair, he closes his eyes, swearing as he thrusts past my lips.

"Take it deep. All the fucking way." He growls as he fucks me hard and fast in the mouth, causing a mixture of saliva and pre-cum to drip down my chin.

"Squeeze my balls, sweetheart."

I use one hand to grip them, keeping the other tight around the base of his shaft. With a sharp intake of breath, he curses loudly as his hot cum spurts against the back of my throat, and I swallow him down greedily.

I watch a slow smile cross his beautiful face as he lies there panting.

"Sit on my face, PJ."

Who am I to refuse? I crawl up his body and do just that.

CHAPTER TEN

SARAH

En-Route from Richmond to New York

"Could he be starting to decompose? I'm sure there's a smell like something's gone off."

I turn to glance at my little mousy friend, who's wrinkling up her nose in disgust, before quickly turning my attention back to the road.

"How long's it been?" I ask, frowning. I have no idea how much time has passed since I stabbed the fucker in the neck with my four-inch stiletto.

"About six hours, I reckon."

I shrug. "It's not likely that his corpse would be starting to smell already, although maybe he's pissed and shit himself again since. It does happen, you know. All the muscles in the body relax when you die, and…"

“Too much information, Sarah,” she interrupts. I hear her dry heave, and I chuckle inwardly.

“Then again, the blood in the footwell will be starting to congeal, so that may be causing the odor.”

“Okay, enough already!”

I struggle not to laugh out loud. Welcome to *the life,* little Laila.

I change the subject. “What’s our ETA?”

She’s been in charge of the phone ever since Jaine called. It’s safer that way. I need to keep focused on the road with no distractions. I don’t need to be drawing any unwanted attention to the vehicle by taking out any more signs.

“Around an hour.”

Shit. Do we need to make contact now we’re getting closer? I look out the driver side window. It’s two a.m., and it’s pitch black around the barely lit highway. I check the mirrors, but we don’t seem to be getting tailed. Should I phone Jaine? What time is it in California? Why didn’t I think to ask the most obvious of fucking questions?

“There’s an unknown number calling. What should I do?”

Laila’s holding the phone up like it’s about to explode in her hands. I bite my lip and try to think. We have no fucking choice.

“Answer it and put it on speaker. Whatever you do, don’t say anything. Let the caller speak first.”

She presses to accept. There’s silence initially.

“I need to talk to Red.” I sit up straight in my seat, my ears immediately tuned in to the deep voice with the Irish lilt. Fuck me. I can already feel myself getting wet. Is it possible to get turned on by just one short sentence?

I really have gone without for way too long.

“Red speaking. Who is this?” I sound breathless. Fucking great.

“Ian. How’s your time looking?”

"We'll reach the destination in around forty-five minutes," Laila answers.

"Who is this?" He sounds pissed as fuck.

"I'm Red's friend, Laila."

"I deal with Red only. No one fucking else."

"Sorry," she replies with a half sob, her shaky hands passing me the phone.

My blood boils in my veins. I'm tempted to say something bitchy to him for upsetting my friend, but I don't. This is the world we live in. The world I lived in. A world where there's no time or place for emotions. Those fuckers will only get you killed. The priority is the kids riding in the back, covered in their own piss and shit and missing their folks.

"Gotcha, Ian. I'll keep the phone in front of me and make sure it's on speaker at all times."

Asshole.

"If anyone calls, make sure you let them speak first."

"I'm not totally fucking stupid," I bite back, then curse myself inwardly for being so damn reactive. I need this Ian guy to think I'm just a trafficking victim.

"Temper, temper, Red." He laughs softly.

"Sorry." Not fucking sorry.

"When you get close, I'll send a car. I'll message the plate details. Follow him in."

The Docks, Hudson Yards

I pull the vehicle to a standstill, and it wheezes loudly. I know just how it feels.

Opening the driver's door, I jump down onto the dockside. I feel myself about to heave with the stress of the situation, but I hold it back. It's neither the time nor place. Leaning forward, I rest my hands on my thighs and inhale the air of my hometown, capturing it in my lungs and trapping it welcomingly in my veins.

New fucking York.

Standing up straight, I look around. We're hidden behind sky-high walls of stacked containers of every size and color. Some new with fresh advertisements on. Some ancient, their paint peeling thanks to the salt content in the brackish water of the Hudson.

I ignore the people now milling around like soldier ants. They're here to help, and that's what I'm going to let them do. I've played my part. I stare out across the river.

Seven fucking years. A blink of an eye or a lifetime? Both.

"Here." Shivers run down my spine when I hear *his* voice. The Irish lilt isn't uncommon in New York. Hell's Kitchen is full of people claiming to be from the Emerald Isle, but most accents are fake. His isn't.

I turn to look at him and accept the bottle of water he's offering.

"Thank you. Ian, I take it?" My gaze drifts over the man who's saved the day. Saved me. Saved all of us.

He's lean and tall. Around six-three, I'd say, since he's taller than me, even though I'm still wearing my murder weapons on my feet. He's wearing black jeans and a black Henley.

Like a fucking ninja.

He nods.

"I didn't realize it was Halloween." I motion my head at the balaclava he's wearing.

He snorts. "I'm not allowed to reveal my true identity, unfortunately."

"Like Batman," I mumble.

He snickers.

I drink down the small bottle of water in one, and he passes me his partially drunk one, which I gratefully accept. For some reason,

I like the fact that his lips have been on it. It's like some sort of unintentional kiss.

"How did you know I was Red?" I look at him. I'm itching to pull the balaclava off his head. I want to see him. Fuck the consequences. I want to see the man behind the lilting voice that's making my panties wet.

He reaches out, his fingers brushing my hair. "Red."

I feel myself blush at the intimate gesture. Thankfully, it's dark enough for it not to be noticeable. At least, I hope so. "Strawberry blonde."

"Still red." He chuckles.

I smile. He's right, of course. There's no fucking dressing up ginger by trying to pretend to be blonde.

We stand in silence for several minutes. Strangely, it's a comfortable silence. We've known each other for five seconds, but it feels like we've known each other forever.

"This is the driver's phone. His name was Mario. He's behind the passenger seat. Not sure if that was his real name or not." I pass him the phone, and our fingers touch briefly. I shiver at the connection.

I stare at him, and he stares back.

"Red, I got our bags from the back. Uh… it stinks in there." Laila interrupts our ongoing silent assessment of each other.

We turn simultaneously and take in my tiny friend, who's dragging our bags across the dock, the one containing her laptop clutched tightly in her hands. She stops when she sees who she suspects to be Ian. Then, hesitating, she points back towards the vehicle.

"I… I can come back… when it's convenient. Or wait over there?" She looks between us like she's disturbing something. Is the connection that obvious?

"I'll come and find you in ten, Laila," I reply.

I turn back around and gaze out across the river once more.

"Do you need anything else from me, or can I leave this situation in your capable hands, Ian? Jaine may have told you already, but I'm a New Yorker. We were picked up by the traffickers in Mexico on our way back."

"Yes, she mentioned. I may need to speak to you if I have any questions. Do you have a phone? A contact number?"

I shake my head. "No. The guy who drugged us must have kept it." It's a lie. I do have a phone in my bag, but it's my actual number. The number I use when I'm Sarah Sanders Delaney. I can't give that to this Irish stranger. He walks off. Since he never said goodbye, I guess I have to stay where I am like a good fucking girl. My temper flares again.

"Here." He passes me a handset. "It's a burner phone. The only number in it is mine."

"Thank you."

I shiver.

"Cold, Red?"

I don't reply. I've got a feeling he knows the reason I shivered, and it has nothing to do with the temperature. I pause before I speak again.

"What if I don't answer?"

He spins me around to face him, his fingers digging into my arms and bruising my skin. His fingertips feel like they're burning my flesh, branding the memory of him on my skin so I'll never forget him. Wetness pools between my legs. I like his rough handling.

He looks down at me and I inhale his woodsy cologne. It's addictive—almost overpowering in its subtlety. I want to bottle it up, spray it on my pillow, then get myself off to it over and over again. He's so close his breath is warm on my face. He exhales. I breathe in. Cigarettes. Peppermint. I lick my lips, desperately wanting the taste on my tongue. Not from the candy or piece of gum. I want it straight from his mouth. I look at his lips, then I'm conscious I'm staring. I curse inwardly. He'll think I want him to kiss me. Which I fucking do.

"I think we both know you'll answer." He laughs quietly. Smugly.

I fight the urge to slap him. Instead, I glare at the conceited fucker, spin around, and storm off, heading towards Laila.

"Do you need a lift, Red?" he shouts across, and I can hear the mocking tone in his voice.

Asshole.

"No." I'm annoyed with myself for letting him know that he's pissed me off. I left New York to get away from the life, and the arrogant, chauvinistic assholes who surrounded me, and here I am, on my return, colliding with yet another. Well, fuck him. Then I curse myself again as I know that's most likely what I'll end up doing. And doesn't he just know it?

"Tam, drop them where they need to go," Ian instructs him. I don't say anything. I do need a ride.

I turn around to look at Tam. He's probably about seven feet tall by half that wide. A powerhouse so large he should have his own zip code, and all finished off with a face only a mother could love. His hair is ginger. It's the only positive thing he's got going for him. I smile and he ignores me. Then I find myself wondering if he can actually speak. A neanderthal, maybe? Nope. Most probably another chauvinist.

He leads us to a black SUV, and we clamber into the back. The radio's on, playing classical music, and the vehicle smells of vanilla. I hate vanilla. I give him the directions to an apartment block in Brooklyn. We don't live there, but I'm hoping Paul still owns the property and the one next door. They were the first two buildings he bought. The entry code is Mom's birthday. I don't want this goon to know anything about Laila or me. He's also likely being tailed just to make doubly sure Ian knows precisely where I live. I'm not stupid, even though Tam and his Irish boss would love to think I am.

"Thank you," I mumble as we reach our destination. We walk towards the four-story recently-painted building that gleams white, contrasting against the night sky. I pray to God the code is unchanged.

March 13th. 0313.

The door clicks open.

Thank. Fuck.

We wave our thanks at Mr. Zero Personality and go inside before descending into the basement area. Both buildings are interconnected. We cross to the basement of the adjoining property.

The code? 0308. Mine and Paul's days of birth. Laila and I quickly exit the building at street level. Thankfully, a yellow cab is passing, which we flag down.

"Brightling, please."

I lean my head back against the seat with a smirk. Unfortunately, my good mood lasts for a nanosecond when I realize I'm about to return to the house where my dad was murdered in cold blood. In front of me.

Home sweet fucking home.

CHAPTER ELEVEN

CILLIAN

The Docks, Hudson Yards

I WATCH as she storms off across the dock. I've just pissed her off. I'm sure I saw her clench her fists before she took flight. Maybe she was going to slap me. Not sure what her problem is. The admiration's mutual. Why the fuck try to deny it? See, that's what's wrong with most women. They can't just admit it when they find someone attractive. Her red hair's whipping out behind her like Medusa due to the speed she's walking, trying to put as much distance as possible between her and me because she now thinks I'm an arrogant swine. My eyes drop to her arse: slim hips and long legs. She's a bit too skinny for my taste, but she has a fine set of tits on her. A perfect handful, with just a bit extra spilling over the top. And she's fucking stunning with her dark eyes and lips that look like they were made for sucking cock.

My cock.

She's a fiery little thing. It'll be that red hair. Reactive as fuck, just like me. Bring it fucking on.

She'll be back. With what just fired up between us, there's no way she won't be. That's why I gave her the phone. It's a burner phone linked to my burner phone. I've no idea who she is, what her background is, or where she lives, but I'm going to make it my business to find out.

I doubt very much that Red is her real name.

I watch as she and her pocket-sized friend get in the back of the black SUV.

I call Tam's earpiece after he's texted me the zip code.

"Drop them off, give it fifteen, then go inside the building and knock on all the doors. I want to know which apartment she lives in."

I call Jonny.

"Follow Tam. I don't want any slip-ups. If they try to leave the building, I want you to follow them."

"Got it, Cill."

I walk back to the vehicle used for trafficking. Aidan and Jack —brothers and two of my other trusted men—deal with the dead driver. He's Colombian. Or at least it looks that way. They pass me his personal items, which I'll give to Dyl when I get back. With him on the case, in a day or two, we'll know everything worth knowing about the dead pedo.

"How was he killed?" I ask Jack as I look at the short little fuck who's been bent over double like a flick knife.

"Stabbed in the jugular."

"Weapon?"

"Nothing found."

I nod. Did Red kill him, I wonder, or one of the others in the back?

"Tam?" I answer my phone as I stand having a smoke while waiting for the last of the kids to be shipped out. "Did you find out which apartment?"

There's a pause.

"We lost them, Cill."

I can feel my blood boiling in my veins, and I punch the side of the vehicle so hard I dent the fucking thing.

"What the fuck do you mean you lost them?" I rasp.

"They went into the building. We followed as you said, fifteen minutes later, then went around all the apartments, but they'd vanished. No one was hiding them. We checked every property. Jonny and I searched the basement and found a door leading to the adjoining building. We can only assume they knew the code and exited through there."

"Fuck sake, Tam!" I growl.

I hang up. I want to kill some fucker now. I take deep breaths in and out to calm myself down.

I take out the burner phone and call her. She answers straight away.

"You want to tell me where you actually fucking live?" I hiss.

"Nope." She sounds smug as fuck.

"Don't play games with me, Red."

"It's none of your business where I live."

"I've made it my business."

"Then un-make it."

"I'll find you. You can't hide from me."

"I'm a victim of trafficking. Why do you need to know where I live?"

"Did you kill the driver?"

"Might have."

"What the fuck do you mean you might have?"

"Maybe he tripped and fell."

"And landed on something that penetrated his jugular?"

"The laws of probability would deem that it's not impossible."

"What? Are you a mathematician now? Did you kill him?"

"Yes."

"With?"

"My shoe."

"Innovative."

"Why, thank you. I'll take that as a compliment."

"It is. When can I see you?"

"Cocky much?"

"Not at all. I just live in the moment, sweetheart." It's partially true, but she's also right. I am a cocky fecker. Always have been. Always will be. I've got a feeling admitting to that right now will just cause her temper to flare further, though. That red hair of hers must get her into so much trouble.

"Listen, Ian, if that's your real name, which I very much doubt. I'm throwing this cell in the trash so you can't track me. I'll have the SIM destroyed, don't worry. I'll call you before midnight if I decide I want to see you again. If you don't hear from me, take that as thanks for the very tempting offer, but no thanks."

Then she hangs up. I call back, but it goes straight to voicemail.

I punch the vehicle in frustration again. If she doesn't call me back, I'm going to make it my life's fucking mission to track her down. That little minx thinks she can give an O'Connell the slip. She doesn't know who the fuck she's dealing with.

I need to find out who owns that building. She must know them if she had the basement code. That wouldn't be given out to just anyone.

"Dyl?"

"Cill?"

"I've some details on the driver. I'll have Tam bring them to you. I also need you to find out the owner of a property." I give him the address, then hang up.

"You can run, little Red, but you'll never escape the clutches of the Big Bad Duster Wolf."

Cillian's Apartment, Hudson Yards, New York

"I fold," Eoin announces. You'd think being the head honcho after Da, he would be ruthless and competitive at poker. He's not.

It's our weekly get-together—the only time we're guaranteed to spend time with each other as brothers and not as mobsters.

I look at Dyl. He's the strategic one. Analytical. The fucker probably spends all his free time playing sudoku and coloring in those mindfulness books or whatever the fuck they're called. We're all casually dressed in jeans. He looks like a college professor as he sits in a cream button-down and navy slacks, with his reading glasses perched on the end of his nose.

Meanwhile, Paddy is face studying. It's like he can see what's whirring away inside your head. They must teach that shite at law school.

"I fold too," Dyl announces.

Paddy's burner phone lights up, and he places his cards on the tabletop face down, a grin taking over his face that would make the Cheshire Cat envious. What the fuck's going on with him? Last week, he was borderline suicidal, and now he's happy as Larry.

"I fold too, Cill. You win," he says without looking at me, his face now lost in his screen. I reckon even if he were holding a royal flush, he'd still have folded.

Dyl frowns at him. Those two have always had a close connection, being so similar in age. They're almost telepathic. Ma was pretty much pregnant with Padraig the minute she dropped Dylan, the gap so short they almost shared a womb. They're hiding something. Still, at least whatever it is has cheered Paddy up and stopped him from drinking.

I look at my phone. It's almost midnight, and still nothing from Red since I spoke to her. Maybe she's going to turn me down. I've never been fucking turned down before. Guess there's a first time for everything.

"All sorted with the trafficked kids now, Eoin?" I look at my big brother, who's standing at the fireplace, swirling whiskey in a glass. He's never got a hair out of place. Mr. Fucking Immaculate. He's also staring at his phone screen. Probably lining up a woman for later. I wonder if his hair gets messed up when he fucks or if he tells her to keep her hands off.

Not that I want to think about my big brother dicking anyone.

"Pretty much. One of the older girls was able to help, so there's only a handful whose parents haven't been found yet."

I nod. "Has Red been in contact with you?" I try to appear disinterested.

"Why do you ask?" His attention switches from his phone to my face.

Nosy fucker.

"Tam dropped her off, but it was a bogus address. She gave him and Jonny the slip in the end."

He smirks at me.

"Her name's not really Red, is it?"

He shrugs. "I'm not sure. Jaine's been dealing with her direct." He's a lying fucker. He does know.

I glance at Paddy, who immediately looks up at hearing the name of the love of his life.

"You spoke to Jaine?" He frowns at Eoin, no doubt jealous as fuck.

"Yes. She needed our help with something."

"How's she keeping?"

"She's fine. Abusive and swearing like a trooper, if you must know. Very ladylike."

"She's from the life, Eoin. No one ever said Jaine was a lady." He smiles almost proudly, then turns his attention back to his phone. I'm surprised he's not being more inquisitive. Maybe he really has moved on.

My phone vibrates. It's 11.59 p.m..

Sarah: *Where and when?*
Cillian: *Like leaving things to the last minute, Red?*
Sarah: *I'm a fly by the seat of my pants kind of girl, what can I say? Were you getting worried I'd turn you down?*
Cillian: *Not at all.*
Sarah: *You were. Don't lie.*

I smirk. She's fucking right.

Cillian: *Tomorrow. I'll get someone to pick you up.*
Sarah: *Not a chance, lover boy. I want a location where I can just show up.*
Cillian: *Are you always this suspicious?*
Sarah: *Yes. My thinking is you are too, so don't judge. Are you going to be wearing that balaclava?*

I frown at that. Fuck. She can't know who I am. I still have no idea who she is or if she can be trusted, so it's safer for everyone concerned for her not to know.

Cillian: *Not sure the balaclava will work. Can I blindfold you instead?*

Sarah: *Are you into that BDSM shit? Is this just an excuse so you can tie me up?*
Cillian: *I never mentioned bondage, but I'm game if you are.*
Sarah: *I'll pass. I don't trust you enough, plus, I like to use my hands.*
Cillian: *Really? What do you like to do with your hands, exactly?*
Sarah: *Listen, if you want sex chat, pay a premium rate like everyone else.*

I snicker as I adjust my cock, which is now rock fucking hard. Finally, I send her a postcode.

Cillian: *I'll have you picked up from there tomorrow at seven p.m. Oh, and Red?*
Sarah: *Yeah?*
Cillian: *Don't wear any panties.*

CHAPTER TWELVE

JAINE

Jaine's House, Rising, California

Jaine: *Can I have an update on the kids, Dyl?*
Padraig: *As far as I know, the last little one's parents were found this morning, darlin'.*
Jaine: *Thank God.*
Padraig: *Thank the Dusters, you mean?*
Jaine: *Yeah, I guess you guys helped.*
Padraig: *Really? That's all the credit we're getting.*
Jaine: *Okay, I'll admit you helped a lot. Thank you, Dyl. You've been a Godsend to me recently.*
Padraig: *Remind me again of just how wonderful I am.*
Jaine: *Are you angling for compliments? Jesus Christ. What's gotten into you these last few days? With all the Irish stuff.*
Padraig: *Irish?*

Jaine: *Padraig.*
Padraig: *Oh, that Irish.*
Jaine: *How is he?*
Padraig: *Not sure what he's been up to. No good, obviously, as he's been smiling. A lot. He's been more like his old self.*
Jaine: *No doubt he'll be charming Sophia.*
Padraig: *You jealous, Jaine?*
Jaine: *We're not going there. Off limits, remember.*
Padraig: *Sorry. I forgot.*
Jaine: *Anyway, I'm in Manhattan soon if you want to meet for a catch-up.*

THERE'S A PAUSE.

Jaine: *Dyl? What's with the tumbleweed moment? If you don't want to meet up just say so. I won't be offended.*
Padraig: *Send me the dates and let me check my calendar.*
Jaine: *You have a calendar?*
Padraig: *Even Batman needs to have a calendar.*
Jaine: *Fuck me. I thought I just needed to shine a light in the night sky, and hey presto.*

SMILING, I FLOP DOWN ON THE SOFA, THEN GRIMACE AS THE COLD leather touches my exposed skin. I dial the new number Sarah messaged to my phone. There's no time like the present to let her know I was her brother's girlfriend for four years. I mean, it's bound to come up sooner rather than later.

She answers straight away.

"Sarah, hi. It's Jaine."

"Jaine. It's good to hear from you. Any update on the trafficked kids?"

"Yeah. I just spoke to my contact. The last child's parents were found this morning."

She sighs with relief, followed by a sob. God bless her. It must have been quite the traumatic ordeal.

"You did good, Sarah. Fuck knows where they'd be now if you hadn't stepped up to the plate."

"I had to kill the driver." Her voice is quiet. Hesitant. Like she doesn't want to admit it.

"I know you did, babe. You had no choice. In this life, we seldom do, so we do what needs to be done."

"Have you killed anyone before, Jaine?"

What a question to ask The Exterminator.

"Two or three. And it wasn't easy. It's never easy taking a life." I grimace as I lie through my teeth. Two or three hundred more like, and most I'd willingly do again, even without payment. Still, she doesn't need to know that I'm a mass murderer.

"He was my second. My brother has killed a lot of people. Did you know that?"

"I know he has."

I've witnessed several first-hand.

"So, how do you know Paul?"

I pause only briefly. "Delaney's my ex-boyfriend."

"No way!"

"Yes way. It's true what they say. It really is a small goddamn world."

"So, you know all about the Scorpions?"

"Yes. I'm their legal representation. Now, I'm trusting you with all of this. This conversation stays strictly between you and me." I say it quietly but firmly.

"Yes, of course. You can trust me completely."

"Good to know."

"So, you say ex. When did you and Paul split up? Were you together for long?"

"We split up fairly recently. We were together for four years."

"Shit. So, you really do know him well."

"Probably better than anyone."

"Why did you split up?"

"Honestly? Delaney wanted more from me than I could give him. Our lives can be short in this life, as you know. I wanted him to find someone who could give him the world. Marriage. Kids. That's what he wants, and he deserves that and so much more. He's a bit volatile and hot-headed, but he's a good man."

She huffs.

"I know you and he had your moments, but it was seven years ago. It's in the past, so my advice is to leave it where it belongs. A lot's changed. He's missed you so much. You're all the family he has left."

"So, how do you know Cherry?"

I chuckle at her blatant change of subject.

"We went to Yale together. You?"

"We went to convent school together."

"The daughter of the prez of the Iron Scorpions went to a convent school? Jesus. I've heard it all now."

"I know, right? The only way my folks could get me in was using my mom's maiden name."

"Part of the reason I was surprised when you said you were Delaney's missing sister."

She laughs. "My daddy was insistent I go. He was prepared to do anything including hide the fact that I was the daughter of the prez of an MC. I was sworn to secrecy. I think he wanted me to do penance in advance. Build up some good karma. I also think he wanted to keep me away from those dirty biker boys."

"Makes sense."

"Yeah. Didn't work, though. My first proper boyfriend was Blaze. Anyway, listen, Jaine. I'd love to meet up and talk more. You mentioned you're not in New York, though?"

"Nope. I'm currently in my hometown in California with my biker boyfriend. I'm heading your way in a few weeks, though, so I'm happy to get together then. I can drop by the Scorpions' clubhouse and kill two birds with one stone. I'll need to catch up with Delaney while I'm in town, anyway."

"Sure thing. Let me know the dates."

"I will. And Sarah?"

"Yeah?"

"Our conversations. No further. Remember."

"Understood, Jaine."

"And please let Delaney know you're back before he finds out from someone else."

"You'd tell him?"

"No. Not me. I try never to betray a confidence. But if you're back in Brightling, there's a chance you'll be seen. If you haven't already, that is. Especially if you're back at the old house."

"Noted. Oh, and one last thing. Who is Ian? I'm guessing that's not his real name."

"Why do you ask?"

"No reason in particular."

I sigh. These fucking Irish men with their charming personalities, winning their way into ladies' panties.

"If he won't reveal his identity to you, I can't either. I have to respect his wishes the same as I have to respect yours."

"I appreciate that."

"Are you going to fuck him?"

"Maybe."

I sigh. "Listen, he's a murderous bastard, but he's a good guy. Completely trustworthy. He won't harm you in any way."

"Thanks, Jaine. That was all I needed to know."

Jaine: *Eoin, my flight details are attached.*

Eoin: *And? Why do I need them?*

One word. Asshole. In fact. Second word. Dick. I call his number.

"Just so you know when I'll be in town. So you can keep Irish occupied."

"Ah, yes, of course."

"The charity function is on Saturday night. Note the date. Leoluca has confirmed that both Luc and Sophia will be attending. If Sophia asks Irish to go with her, you need to make sure he declines. I can't be held responsible if our paths cross, Eoin."

"It's unlikely she will, but if she does, I'll ensure something Duster-related comes up."

"Thank you."

"You seem to be saying that a lot, and I get the impression every time it's through gritted teeth. I'm not a bad person, you know."

"You're a mobster. Of course you're a bad person. There's no such thing as a good mobster. That would be an oxymoron."

He chuckles. "What else are you doing when you're in town?"

"Always the nosy fucker."

He doesn't reply. I get the distinct impression he doesn't like women swearing. It just makes me want to cuss even more. Fuck him.

"I'm meeting with a colleague and then with several clients. Not that it's any of your goddamn business. Then again, if I tell you, it saves you from having me tailed. I wouldn't suggest you do that shit when I visit Delaney, though, unless you want to lose your throat."

"Ah, yes. I forgot you were his old lady at one point."

"I was never his old lady. We talked, and we fucked for four years and wound up as friends."

"Friends."

"That was all I could offer him in the end."

"Because you were in love with my brother."

"Yes. Amongst other things. Not that that's any of your business either."

"I like to make things my business."

"No? I hadn't noticed."

"Sarcasm is the lowest form of wit."

I roll my eyes. "So they say. And for the record, I'm not trying to be amusing."

"Provided we're straight with each other and you have nothing to hide, then we'll get along just fine."

"Goodbye, Eoin."

I disconnect the call then stare at my phone. My blood is boiling in my veins. Where the fuck does he get off? Who the fuck does he think he is? Then I smirk. One day I will be straight with him. One day he'll know exactly who I am, and he'd best hope it's not when I have my finger over the trigger and there's an X on his forehead marking the goddamn spot.

EOIN

Eoin's Apartment, Hudson Yards, New York

"Dylan. What did you find out?"

"About?"

"Jaine Jones. Her business contacts."

"Okay. Yes. So, Leoluca Di Matteo is definitely a client and has been for some time."

I wait for him to continue and I'm annoyed when he doesn't.

"And? Who else?" I snap.

"Well, JAL has a lot of clients. They've just taken on another six full-time lawyers, taking the team total to almost twenty."

"Who, Dyl?"

"Rodolfo Flores."

"So, she has links with La eMe, the Mexican mafia?"

"Seems like it. I'm not sure to what extent. As you know, they tend to stick to the west coast. Proximity would surely have been an issue previously, but now Jaine's back living in Rising, who knows? Then again, maybe it's not mafia-related and it's just personal for Rodolfo. He's a very successful businessman."

I exhale. Dylan can be so naïve.

"Anyone else of note?"

"Senator Bidewell."

"Lawrence Bidewell? Rumor has it he's earmarked for a presidential election in the future."

Dylan doesn't reply.

"What makes these high-caliber clients flock to her, I wonder?" I'm thinking out loud more than anything, but Dylan answers regardless.

"Jaine's trustworthy. Her word means everything to her. Like the Dusters' word does. She prides herself on it. It also makes sense that if she can get MCs and mobsters off the hook, then she's exactly who her clients want on their side. They're not choosing her because she's squeaky clean. They're choosing her because she isn't. They know she'll always have their back, and she'll play every dirty trick in the book to get them off. Legally, of course. Rumor has it she also has some of the NYPD pigs eating out of the palm of her hand, so I wouldn't be surprised if the same applies to her employees. You know, recruiting ones with contacts already in their pockets. They're being recruited from all over the U.S., and they're flocking to Manhattan. She pays top dollar and also offers an enviable benefits package. She'll be hiring dirty just as much as she plays it. She's good, Eoin. She's very, very good. Maybe you've underestimated…"

"Thanks for the intel, Dyl."

I cut him off, then hang up. He's right, of course. I have underestimated her. My curiosity is definitely piqued.

I run an internet search. The first image is a recent one of her shaking hands with Detective Gabriel Prescott of NYPD. Is he one of the officers eating out of the palm of her hand, I wonder? It's something else he wants to be eating, given the way he's ogling her tits. Still, who can blame him?

I curse myself for not looking at her in detail. I wrongly assumed she was just a biker's old lady. I didn't realize how successful she was. How many connections she has. When I met her, she was dressed down in combats. Maybe she likes to give a false impression.

Not maybe. Definitely.

I look at the image of her in her ten-thousand-dollar suit. I know the cut. I know the tailor. I use the same one. Her business is doing well. But well enough to afford that level of luxury? I open the folder Dyl raised on her from before. She has several bank accounts. Hundreds of millions of personal dollars at her fingertips. Countless large deposits from Paul Delaney. I mean, Razr can give her money if he wants to. It's his to do with as he pleases. Something doesn't sit right with me, though. He's too generous. Why so much and why so often?

"Dyl. Get me Jaine Jones's most recent bank statements. The same accounts as before."

"Will do."

DYLAN

Dylan's Apartment, Hudson Yards, New York

"Jaine, I'm telling you this as a friend."

"Go on."

"Eoin is asking for your bank statements up to date. I'm thinking he's noticed the monies going in from Razr."

"So? Delaney can give me money if he wants to. There's no law against that. Maybe I'm just a really good fuck."

"You make yourself sound like a high-end call girl. You're also not together anymore. I'm just letting you know. He's also aware that Bidewell and Flores are two of your clients."

"I have many influential clients throughout the U.S. I'm merely their legal representation. Your big brother needs to butt out of my business, Dylan. Why the fuck is he sticking his nose in, anyway? I'm not sticking my nose into Duster affairs, and we both know I could if I wanted to, but I have better things to do with my time. For one, I have a life. Maybe Eoin needs to get himself one of those."

"You know this is difficult for me, Jaine. I promised to honor The Exterminator's confidence, and I will, but when it comes to anything else, I'm a Duster."

"I understand that. I've never asked anything of you apart from keeping that one piece of information to yourself. You have my word that I will never expect you to betray your family. What's Eoin's fascination with me all of a sudden, though? I stepped away from Irish, didn't I? I've left him alone so he can fulfill his Duster obligations. Eoin needs to back off before I start getting annoyed. My business is my business. He needs to concentrate on his own affairs and watch where he sticks that nose of his if he doesn't want to end up having the thing shot off."

"Now, now, Jaine. Let's not be making empty threats. I just wanted to give you the heads-up."

"I appreciate that, Dyl."

I disconnect the call.

Why the fuck is our Eoin so interested in Jaine all of a sudden? I ask myself the question, but I already know the answer.

I reckon he wants her for himself. She's intriguing him. She's already check marking all his mobster boxes, and that's without the revelation that she's The Exterminator. In his mind, she'd already make the perfect ma Duster. That would just be the cherry on top.

He forgets Jaine's in love with our baby brother and that she hates his guts.

Then again, I'm not sure that will deter him if he decides to pursue her. See, for Eoin, this isn't about love. It's about outlaw chess.

CHAPTER THIRTEEN

SARAH

Upper East Side, New York

I'VE DECIDED to ride my Night Train into Manhattan and park in the basement of Delaney Enterprises' office block. Paul will have CCTV for sure. Will he recognize the hog and know it's me? Is it live-streamed or not? Knowing him, it probably is. He'll have a group of overpaid people carrying out twenty-four-hour surveillance on all his properties. It's not like he can't afford it. He's a billionaire, after all. Manhattan's most eligible bachelor, so I'm told, along with the O'Connell brothers. They're referred to as The Hudson Dusters, if I recall. Mobsters. Irish ones.

I've decided I might call Paul tomorrow. Let him know I'm back. That the prodigal younger sister has finally returned home to a house where everything has remained exactly as it was when I left seven years ago.

Like time stood still.

Or maybe not.

My hog hasn't been used since I left, but Daddy taught me how to service my bike, so I've topped up all the levels and checked the brakes. I know I shouldn't be riding without it having had a good going over, but I figured it was better to chance breaking down than risk Ian or one of his goons following me if I caught a cab.

I'm dressed all in black leather with a full black helmet and visor. I'd generally wear a half-helmet, but I want to be invisible. Cloaked in the darkness of the night. My boots are long and high. They're my height of choice. Four-inch and stiletto. Handy, as they proved when I killed Mario.

Who needs to carry a weapon when you can wear them on your feet?

I straddle my hog on the same driveway my daddy died on. A lump forms in my throat, but I swallow it down. Guilt then floods me.

I could have saved him.

I've slept since I got home and haven't done much else apart from going into the garage to prepare my ride. I'll worry about everything else tomorrow.

I switch on my hog's engine and rev it up. I can already see the curtain twitchers in the neighboring properties. Looking at me, watching me. They probably thought I was dead. They'll have been praying for Paul to sell the house so they wouldn't have to put up with biker trash living on their doorstep. Tarnishing their perfect lives with pigs, sirens, blue flashing lights, and the stink of death.

I glance at the house on the opposite side, four down. Laila's. I messaged her earlier. Like me, she's done nothing but sleep. She's traumatized—poor thing. We grew up together, but she seldom frequented the clubhouse or witnessed the darker side of the MC life. My daddy didn't think it was appropriate. Her parents didn't think it was either.

I haven't told her about Ian. About my secret rendezvous with him. I'm hoping fucking him will bring the closure I need to forget about all of this. That I can then put it behind me. Sort shit out with my brother. Go to medical school. Move on with my life. Save lives rather than take them.

I head for the freeway, taking in all the familiar sights, relishing in the feel of the hog's engine thrumming between my thighs. Best feeling in the world. Once a biker, always a biker.

Everything's changed, but then again, nothing's changed. Timing is everything, I guess. I couldn't cope then. I can now. Hopefully. I'm older. Wiser. I've forgiven myself.

Well, as much as I ever can.

I welcome the sights and sounds of the city that never sleeps. The beeping of the yellow cabs and the cussing of their drivers as they wave frustrated fists out their windows or flick each other the bird. It's a camaraderie of sorts—part of what makes them belong together.

The air is pungent with the smells of street litter mixed with fresh rain. For the briefest of seconds, I forget why I'm here, too busy taking in the familiar sights and sounds from a lifetime ago. Reconnecting with the place I call home and letting it welcome me back into its concrete arms.

"Welcome to the Upper East Side," I whisper to myself as I pull up at Delaney Enterprises' underground parking lot. Paul had only been in this office a few weeks when I went AWOL. Yanking off one leather glove, I key Mom's date of birth into the door entry system, and the black metal gates slowly open.

I ride in and park up in the CEO space before switching the engine off. The silence is deafening. Taking off my helmet, I run my fingers through my hair. The adrenaline has worn off. Now I feel nauseous over what could have happened to us. I likely always will.

"What the fuck are you doing, Sarah? Are you insane?" I whisper with a sigh.

I'm about to hook up with a stranger, and I don't even know what he looks like. This isn't me. This isn't what I do. I'm not promiscuous. I never have been. The closest I've ever gotten to a one-night stand was with the Colombian, and look where that shit got me.

Is it because of what happened? Why do I feel the almost overwhelming need to do this? Have I put Ian on some sort of pedestal because he helped save us? The connection between us was immediate. But was it just a reaction to some weird rescuer syndrome?

I take my phone out of my pocket.

Sarah: *I'm not sure I can do this.*

He replies immediately.

Cillian: *You don't have to do anything you don't want to, Red.*
Sarah: *I think I see you as some sort of white knight.*
Cillian: *I can assure you there's not going to be any happily ever after with me. I'm a fucked-up person from a fucked-up family living a fucked-up life. Nice girls like you don't belong in my world.*
Sarah: *Who says I'm nice?*
Cillian: *This is no strings. It's the only way, sweetheart.*
Sarah: *I'll be at the meeting point in twenty minutes. Can we just talk?*
Cillian: *If all you want to do is talk, then I'm okay with that.*
Sarah: *Thank you. I think I just need some closure.*

THE BLINDFOLD TAM PUT ON ME AS SOON AS I GOT IN THE CAGE IS tight, likely to ensure no slippage. It's partially covering my ears, though, and as a result, I can hear my heart thrumming loudly at a million miles an hour.

It's the same vehicle as before. This time around, I find the vanilla smell and sound of classical music familiar and comforting.

"You can change your mind at any time." Tam speaks quietly. He's saying what he's been told to. What Ian thinks I need to hear. I feel caged in, even though this is my choice. I know I'm free to go. I know Ian won't harm me. Jaine assured me he won't, but the blindfold is making me feel uneasy. Why can't I see him? Know who he is? What difference does it make? Then again, I'm not prepared to reveal my identity either.

The cage comes to a standstill. Tam escorts me from the SUV and up some stairs. I hear a door open, and we walk forward into what must be a room.

"I'll let Ian know you're here."

I nod. Then I hear the door close behind him. My hands are sweaty. I feel panicked. I can't even pace the floor as I'll likely bang into something.

The door quietly opens and closes. He's here. I can feel him. I look in the direction of the sound. Can he hear my heart thudding? He must be able to. It's so fucking loud.

Then I smell him. Peppermint, cigarettes, and woodsy cologne. It should represent a hellacious combination, but instead, it's the best thing I've ever smelled. I want to inhale it into my lungs, trap it in my veins, but I don't. That would just be weird. This situation is fucked up enough as it is.

"You look good, Red."

Heat pools in my stomach the moment he speaks. I feel breathless. I can't reply. The ability to form words has temporarily escaped me. I know he's beside me now as his smell is more potent.

I feel drugged by it. I'm sure I can feel the heat of his body. Or is that just wishful thinking? His fingers curl around mine, and my whole body prickles with arousal and anticipation.

"Come sit with me."

His voice is quiet and reassuring. The Irish lilt is more defined than last time. Or maybe it's just the same. Is it the silence of this room? Is the stillness echoing the hypnotizing sound? It's the best thing I've ever heard.

I sit on what must be a sofa, and he sits down beside me, his thigh brushing against mine.

"I came on my hog."

There's a pause.

"So, you're a biker?"

I curse inwardly. He can't work out who I am. At least not before I tell Paul I'm back in town.

"Yeah."

"You someone's old lady, Red?"

I chuckle. "I'm surprised you know what an old lady is."

"I work with a couple of MCs."

I nod. *Fuck.*

"I'm not anyone's old lady, so don't worry."

"Good to know. Not sure I want an angry biker with a switch-blade turning up at my door."

I nod again. Shit. Does he know Paul?

"Which MCs do you work with?"

There's a pause.

"I can't tell you that, sweetheart."

In a way, I'm glad. If he'd mentioned the Scorpions, asked if I knew them, I'd have struggled to lie. Lying's a fool's game. My daddy always taught me that. It ties people in knots. Twist the truth if you need to, or don't answer. But never lie.

"So, what's your story, Red?" His voice is soft like a caress.

I fidget with the blindfold, and I feel him tense.

"Don't worry. I'm not going to take it off." I pause. "What do you want to know?"

"As little or as much as you're willing to tell me."

I run my hands down my leather pants, trying to wipe away the moisture. Where do I start? How much do I tell him?

"Well, I grew up in New York. My mom died giving birth to me, and I lost my daddy seven years ago." I pause as I choke back the lump that always forms in my throat when I say those words. He puts his hand over mine and gently squeezes.

"You got any brothers or sisters?"

"Um… I have a brother. He's thirty-two, so four years older than me."

"So, you're a youngster at twenty-eight?"

I smile. "How old are you, or is that classified information too?"

"I'm thirty-four."

"Ah… an old man." I snicker.

"And a bad man."

"Well, for the record, Jaine says you're a good man."

He chuckles. "That's kind of her. How do you know Jaine?"

"She's a friend of a friend."

"Classified?"

"Exactly."

"Touché. Why did you leave New York, Red?"

I exhale loudly. "Didn't get along with my brother and struggled to cope with losing my dad more than anything, I guess. So, I left and traveled around for a while. Visiting different countries. Eventually, I settled in Bolivia, working in a little community hospital. I watched people die and watched people live. I learned to accept death for what it is. A guaranteed part of life. I've come back hopefully older and wiser, having made the decision that I want to go to medical school."

"And you ended up getting trafficked in Mexico."

"Yeah."

"And then your friend spoke to Jaine, and she contacted me."

"Exactly."

"Then you got all pissy with me, gave my driver the slip, and now here we are."

"Yeah." I laugh softly.

"What is it you want from me, Red?"

I shrug. I feel warm all over and wet between my legs.

"I felt a connection. Not sure if it was just circumstance because of the shit going down at the time or whether it was something else. I'm guessing you felt it too, hence why you gave me your number and why we're both sitting here right now."

"Yeah, I felt it too." His finger gently strokes the back of my hand. "But I want to be upfront with you, sweetheart. If anything happens between us, it will never go anywhere. It's not going to be flowers and chocolates. There won't be any dates. No relationship. The most I can ever offer you is this. If it isn't enough for you, then I can ask my driver to take you back to the pick-up point now."

"Will I ever be able to see what you look like? Know who you are?"

"Maybe eventually. But I'd need to know everything about you beforehand. I'd need to be able to trust you. No woman I've been with has ever witnessed what I do first-hand. They may suspect, but that's it. You have. That changes things. My family wouldn't hesitate to kill you if you betrayed my trust. I'm just trying to keep you safe. Knowing who I am doesn't change things, though, Red. There's still no future for us."

I laugh. Conceited fucker.

"You say that like I'm going to fall in love with you or something."

"I'm saying it out loud to remind us both, not just you."

I nod. On the one hand, I should feel pleased. No strings sex is all I've ever wanted from men. Why do I suspect that with Ian it won't be enough, though? That it will never be enough? I should walk away. Run for my life. But I want to play with fire. To fan the flickering flame in my soul that he's ignited.

I want him to make me burn.

"Tell me what you want, Red." It's a whisper. His voice is smoky hot.

I lick my lips.

"I want you to kiss me."

CHAPTER FOURTEEN

SARAH

Upper East Side, New York

I'VE NEVER FELT SO FUCKING awkward. I asked Ian to kiss me, and several seconds later? Nothing. Doesn't he want to? He said he felt something too. Is he a lying asshole? Jesus, I sure know how to pick them. I feel disadvantaged because I can't see him. I can't look him in the eye to know for sure. Then again, I agreed to the blindfold. More fool me.

Seconds pass. Minutes. Hours.

I bite on my bottom lip, then hear him curse quietly.

Finally, his warm breath mingles with mine. He breathes out. I breathe in. I capture his air in my lungs. I want to keep it there forever.

"Are you sure, little Red? Because I really am the big bad wolf."

"Maybe one day you'll discover I'm just as bad as you." I whisper my response.

He chuckles softly, dragging his thumb across my bottom lip before pressing it against my mouth. I part my lips, allowing it to push past, then licking at the roughness with my tongue. I savor the salty taste on his skin before closing my mouth around it. He growls in approval as I suck and bite on him before pulling it free and rubbing the resultant wetness against my lips.

His tongue replaces his thumb as he licks across my bottom lip before sucking it in and biting down. Hard. I curse at the pain, my core immediately tightening. Large hands grip my waist, pulling me effortlessly across to straddle his slim hips as he claims total ownership of my mouth. Facial hair scratches my chin. And it's only when the metal bar collides with my teeth that I realize he has a piercing. Finding that even more of a turn-on, I can't hold back my groan.

Finally, the taste of peppermint and cigarettes is all fucking mine. I immediately feel possessive about it. I don't want anyone else tasting him.

I don't want to fucking share.

Unzipping my leather jacket, he pushes it from my shoulders, his hands immediately dropping to yank my tank top free from my jeans. He quickly pulls it over my head, then unclips my bra and discards it his mouth dropping to feast on each of my aching tips in turn. I discover his hair is long on top and shorter on the sides when I fist it in my hands as I arch my back and press my tits unashamedly against his face.

I want more of that wet, greedy mouth of his on my hot, needy flesh.

"Color?" I whisper as I run my hands through the longer strands before pressing my nose against his neck, inhaling the drug that is his woodsy cologne.

"Red. Auburn." He chuckles softly before biting down on my nipple. I curse at the pain and instinctively grind my pussy against his hard-on. His lips claim mine once more, his tongue stroking deep into my mouth while I rock rhythmically against his erection, my body now desperate for more.

I want to see him. To look at him. But I know I can't.

"Take off your jeans, Red." His voice is filled with lust. I'd give anything to see that deadly sin flicker in this bad boy's eyes. What color are they? I don't even know.

I stand, unzip each boot, and step out of them. My hand then reaches for the button of my leathers, then my zip. They drop to the floor, and I smile as I step out of them.

"Holy Mary and Joseph. I thought I said no panties. What the fuck are those?"

I snicker as I stand there in waist-high full black panties.

"You don't like them? Just for future reference, I don't like being told what to wear or what to do."

I'm not even aware he's moved to stand beside me until his arms snake around my waist, and he bites my neck in punishment.

"Oh, I'm looking forward to telling you exactly what to do, Red."

"And if I don't?" I say as I drag his tee over his head before running my hands over the smooth skin of his pecs.

"Disobedient red-haired girls will either be spanked or eaten by the big bad wolf."

A groan escapes me, and I press my thighs together at thoughts of the latter.

"You like the thought of me eating your pussy, Red?" he asks huskily as his hand drops down to cup me through my panties, rubbing my clit through the already soaked material.

His grip on my waist tightens as my legs grow weaker, and his mouth hovers over mine. I know he's watching me, watching my body's reactions to him. Is the light on? Off? I have no idea.

I'm grinding against his hand and clutching onto his shoulders as needy moans pass my lips. I should be embarrassed at how desperate I sound. I'm not. I'm almost at the pinnacle and nothing else matters. Then he stops.

"Not so fast, Red. I need you to come on my cock, sweetheart. You want that?"

I nod. I can't speak. There's no oxygen left in my brain as all my blood has rushed to my clit.

"Take your underwear off." It's an order not a request.

I slowly ease the black panties down my hips and past my thighs, stepping out of them when they fall to the floor. I can feel myself blush, aware I'm naked and that he can now see every inch of my body, including my bare pussy. I can't gauge his reaction. Does he like what he sees? I feel frustrated. Exposed. Vulnerable. I don't like this shit one little bit.

"Even with your olive skin, I can see that you're blushing right now." His hand gently strokes my cheek. "And I can see your freckles."

"Stop making fun of me," I hiss, suddenly feeling self-conscious. My temper flares at the unfairness of this one-sided situation. A situation that I allowed, so I have no one to blame but myself. I reach up, grab his hand, and push it away. I don't want him fucking laughing at me.

"Jesus, I'm not making fun of you, Red. You're beautiful. You're totally fucking perfect."

Before I can argue back, his mouth is on mine, his kiss deep and demanding. The time for talking is over, obviously, at least as far as he's concerned. His tongue collides with mine, and he meets the groan that rises from my throat with a growl of his own.

Lifting me into his arms, he lays me down, likely on a bed.

"Where are we?" The cool surface makes me shiver as it connects with my warm skin.

"Doesn't matter." His mouth covers mine again, his tongue filling my mouth to silence me as his upper body covers mine. My nipples pebble on contact with his hot flesh, and my fingertips move to trace his torso, which is bumped and ridged to sheer perfection on what I can tell is a lean, muscular body.

Spreading my thighs with his knee, he drops his hand to cup my pussy, running his talented fingertips along my drenched folds.

"There's no hiding how much you want me now, is there, Red?" He smirks against my lips.

"Conceited?" I feel my cheeks blaze again.

"Damn right." He thrusts two fingers inside me, curling them to connect with my sweet spot.

"Please, Ian." I'm begging now, my hips grinding against his hand as he drags them back and forth.

"You want me to let you come, Red?" he asks as he runs his tongue up my throat before nipping the skin with his teeth.

"Yes… please."

My body arches against his fingers as he continues his tortuous thrusting. Just as I'm reaching the edge again, he stops, causing me to groan loudly in frustration. He's such a fucking tease. He chuckles and leaves the bed. I can tell he's putting on a condom as I hear the foil wrapper tear. It's amazing how heightened your other senses become when your ability to see is removed.

The bed sinks beneath his weight once more as he uses his hips to spread my thighs farther apart before running the blunt head of his dick up and down my slick folds, then teasing my clit with it.

"Fuck," I groan as he rocks the full length of his cock against my pussy, and I feel just how big he is. I've never wanted anyone as much as I want him right now. "Please," I say again as his mouth torments my throat, his hips grinding against me over and over.

Tempting. Teasing. Torture.

“Tell me what you want, Red.” His lips hover over mine as his dick nudges against my entrance. So fucking close.

“I want you inside me,” I whisper.

He pushes my knees back toward the bed, and I gasp as he presses into me, forcing my inner walls to stretch to accommodate his massive dick.

“Fuck, you’re big.”

“I know.”

“And vain.”

“I know that too.”

Pulling out almost entirely, he angles his hips and slams back into me again, his cock connecting perfectly with my sweet spot. My legs immediately tense, the orgasm denied me twice before now clawing at the base of my spine.

“Come all over my cock, little Red. I want your sweet pussy to milk me dry.” His mouth is on my neck, giving me hickey after hickey. He grips my legs painfully, his thrusts alternating between short and fast and deep and slow as he plays me like a fucking pinball machine.

“Tilt your hips for me, sweetheart.” His whisper is hot against my ear, his sweat dripping deliciously onto my tits. I do as he asks and cry out when his dick bottoms out and bangs hard against my cervix. It’s tortuously painful. His mouth drops to silence me as his tongue fucks my mouth.

“You need to come for me, Red.” His voice is pained now. He’s close. Pulling one of my legs over his shoulder, he changes position again, and this time it’s even more perfect.

How many women has he fucked to fine-tune his craft? My entire body erupts with such an intensity of pleasure I struggle to breathe. I’m only partially aware of him roaring with his own release. My pussy is clenched so tightly around his cock its veins and ridges must be imprinted on my inner walls.

"Fuck. Fuck. Fuck," he curses as he pumps in and out of me in deep, steady strokes, filling the condom with his cum.

I lie there spent, taking his entire weight. Pinned under him, our bodies still connected, our sweat and breaths mingling, our hearts beating to the same loud, erratic rhythm, I realize I'm fucked in more ways than one.

CHAPTER FIFTEEN

CILLIAN

The Hudson Dusters' HQ, Manhattan, New York

"WHAT DID YOU FIND OUT, DYL?" I pull him to one side before we head into our weekly meeting with Da. I kept meaning to ask him, but between doing the wet work with Paddy and fucking Red every night for the past week, I've not had the time.

"About?"

"The property I sent the details of. Who owns it?"

"You're not going to like the answer, Cill." He stops and stares at me. Here we go. Mr. Doom and fucking Gloom. I'm sure he gets some sort of perverse pleasure out of giving me bad news.

"Just tell me."

"Delaney Enterprises."

I frown at him in disbelief. "Are you sure? It's in a shite location, and we both know how particular Razr is."

He shrugs. "They were the first two buildings he bought. Maybe he wanted to hold on to them for sentimental reasons."

The good mood I've been in this past week suddenly dissipates. It's been spoiled by the mention of one fucking name. Red's already admitted she's a biker. Was she involved with Razr in the past? Is she fucking him? Jesus, I can't be treading on his toes. Not if I want to live to see my thirty-fifth birthday with my throat still intact.

"Cheers, Dyl."

"Do you want to tell me what's going on, Cillian?"

I stare at my baby brother. His hair is way too short. He's also got his glasses on again. My guess is he doesn't even need them. He'll think they make him look more intelligent. They don't. They just make him look even more of a geeky, anti-social nerd. The type who spies on unsuspecting women through keyholes.

"Nothing, Dyl." It's been instilled in all of us never to mix business with pleasure, so I can't tell him I've been fucking one of the women we picked up during the trafficking incident. A woman I know fuck all about. A woman I'm becoming more and more obsessed with as she has a pussy with magical properties.

I EYE MY DA'S NEW TOY AS I TAKE MY SEAT WITH MY BROTHERS. It's a Newton's Cradle. Seemingly, Ma's fed up with paying for replacement paperweights. She should be grateful it's not medical bills for the heads he's been aiming them at. She seems to think this gadget will be therapeutic for him; to listen to the little silver balls as they bounce off each other. His blood pressure's risen, apparently. It's our fault, of course. All four of us can't do right for doing wrong. There are no favorites when it comes to apportioning blame. That shit's split evenly.

He sets the thing off with a smile on his face. By the end of the meeting, it'll be flung at someone's head.

"So, your ma and I have been talking." He's leaning back in his chair, eyeing us all one by one. Who is the Sword of Damocles going to fall on today? Who's going to be the loser in the O'Connell game of Russian roulette?

"Or should I say your ma's been talking to Cara."

His gaze fixes on me.

"Cara's more than a little upset that you've not been paying her any attention recently, Cillian."

He looks at my brothers in turn, issuing a silent threat so they know to be on his side and back him up should things get messy. "Your ma, Roisin…" He says her name like maybe we've forgotten who birthed us or something, "…is desperate for grandchildren, as you know. Plus, you all need to start generating Duster heirs. Now, we realize we'll have to wait for Paddy to produce offspring as he's still got a while to go before he gets wed to young Sophia, but there's nothing to say you can't take the vows with Cara, Cillian. It would make both families extremely happy. As you know, your ma already thinks of her as a daughter."

Aye, only because she can control and manipulate her.

Paddy mutters under his breath. He's still not happy about having to marry the teenager and hates being reminded of it. I can't say I blame him. He's still got a while to try to wangle himself out of the arrangements though. Time's still on his side.

I hear a thudding sound and realize it's my blood pounding through my ears. I need to argue my case without raising my voice. Sounds easy, but it's not when you have a volatile temper like me.

"Surely a bride should be found for our Eoin first, Da. He is the eldest, after all." Common sense tells me to try to body swerve the situation rather than outright refuse. At least initially. That's if I don't want to end up wearing the Newton's Cradle. I can feel my big brother's glare burning into the side of my head, but I don't look at him.

So what if I'm throwing him under a bus? It's nothing personal. This is all about survival.

Da nods and looks at me over the top of his glasses. "You're right, Cill. But the Ma Duster role is a difficult one to fill see, son. We need to be very selective about who's going to take over the reins of the O'Connell empire with our Eoin." He's staring at me now. Eoin doesn't need to come up with an excuse. Da's dug him out of the hole I tried to fling him in. Fucking gets off with everything that one does.

"Well, what about Dyl?"

Dad shakes his head and then wags the pointer finger at me. "Have you any idea how difficult it will be trying to find a woman who wants to stay in the house 24/7? Not that there's anything wrong with not wanting to go out if you're an old fella like me, but what young woman doesn't want to be taken out on the town for a turn?" I look at Dyl, and his cheeks are flushed. It's true, though. I love my baby brother, and it pains me to have to agree with Da, but our Dyl really needs to start getting out and meeting women.

For all I know, he might still be a fucking virgin.

He's got the looks, but not the confidence. He was molly-coddled way too much by Ma. If he didn't have a housekeeper, he'd probably survive on ramen noodles and live in his y-fronts.

"I don't want to marry Cara, Da." I say it how it is, then wait for the new gadget to connect with the side of my head. Thankfully, it doesn't.

"Let's mull it over for now, Cill. You're thirty-four, though. You need to be thinking about taking yourself a wife. Unfortunately, your ma won't wait for grandchildren forever, and apparently, Cara's only too happy to oblige."

I'll bet she fucking is.

"Noted, Da."

He looks at his pad. The one with no notes written in. The one he brings to every meeting so he can try to convince us he's not flying by the seat of his pants like the rest of us.

"Eoin, any news on this new pakhan, son? You were going to keep your ear to the ground. Those Russians are taking a while to decide. It's not like those fuckers to be selective."

"His name is Viktor Ivankov, Da. I've tasked our Dyl with finding out the intel on him. Background, family, etc."

"Good, son. Good. Let's assess him and see if he's someone we can do business with. Surely to fuck every Russian can't be a kiddie-fiddler. And you, Paddy? You were going to have a chat with Luc about these properties he's been buying up?"

"Aye, I did, Da. It turns out they were going for a song, and that's the only reason he bought them. No ill-intention towards the Scorpions or Paul Delaney meant. Luc has offered to speak to Razr direct to prevent any bad blood-forming. No one with a sound mind wants to get in his bad books."

Da nods. "You hear that, Cill? You're the main contact with both MCs, so you need to be letting Paul Delaney know that."

"Aye, I will do, Da."

"Now, boys." He's leaning back in his chair again, and it creaks in protest. "I have to say the way you handled those trafficked youngsters, making sure they were all returned to their parents safely, made me and your ma proud. As you know, we think of the Dusters as one big family, and all children are treated as if they're our own. Trafficked or not. I know many people played a part, some more than others, but you boys handled the situation and did so magnificently. I just wanted to let you know that your ma and I are proud of you all."

We look at each other, trying to take in the fact that Da's actually said something complimentary for once. I mean, Paddy did fuck all, and Dyl did very little, but who are Eoin and me to rock the boat?

"But…"

Here we go.

"…we need to find out who the other party is that's involved in this sick madness. This trafficking business. It can't only be the Russians as they've been out of action for a while now. Those heathens must be working with someone else, and I'll bet my bottom dollar that it's the Mexicans. We need to make a concerted effort to find out. As much as we helped one vehicle load, we can't be doing this sort of thing regularly or we'll start to draw attention to ourselves. This situation needs nipping in the bud, boys."

Da looks from face to face to see which of us is going to put our neck in the noose and take on this latest challenge.

Eoin clears his throat. "I have a contact who has the ear of someone in the top tier of La eMe, Da. Let me find out what they know."

"Excellent, Eoin, my lad. You can let us know what you unearth at the next meeting."

Da's pleased. We're pleased. The meeting's over, and no Newton's Cradles were harmed in the process.

Now I just need to have a word with Paul Delaney.

CHAPTER SIXTEEN

JAINE

Jaine's House, Rising, California

"Eoin."

"Jaine."

"What do you want?"

"Could you be any less charming?"

"Where you're concerned? Definitely, so don't tempt me. What the fuck do you want?"

"I did you a favor recently, did I not?"

"Yes, you did. Do you want a medal? Or is this something you're going to remind me of for the rest of my goddamn life?"

"No. I want one in return."

I exhale loudly. There's only one thing Eoin O'Connell could want from me. Intel on one of my fucking clients. Figures.

"Who is it, and what do you want to know?"

"Rodolfo Flores."

"What about him?"

"He's La eMe."

"Do you want to tell me something I don't already know?"

"Rumor has it the Mexicans are the silent partner in the trafficking business. The vehicle picked up Red and her little friend in Mexico City, after all. Now, I realize it's not their usual…."

"Bullshit. Utter bullshit," I spit out, rudely interrupting.

"You feel so strongly that they're not involved?"

"Everyone knows Mexicans abhor any wrongful acts against children. Mental, physical, or otherwise. They don't traffick—end of. I'm insulted on Rodolfo's behalf that you would even suggest such a thing. If you'd asked that question of him face to face, you'd be wearing his bullet between your eyes."

So, big brother Duster knows Rodolfo is my client. Well, what he doesn't need to know is that I only deal with his business affairs. I've made it clear to Rodolfo that I want no involvement in his illegal wrongdoings. I have enough outlaw clients as it is. Too fucking many, in fact, along with a plethora of bent politicians.

Rodolfo and I went to school together. We didn't speak the entire time we were there, or if we did, it was only ever in passing. He didn't talk to Ace, Jefferson, Emilia, or any others who used to hang around the clubhouse either.

Who said school days are the best days of your life? That fucker lied. Well, unless you excelled at sports or were good-looking, that is. Like me in those days, Rodolfo check marked neither box. We both wore glasses and had braces. We both had a rough time. We weren't popular. We both kept ourselves to ourselves for that reason—a pair of proverbial ugly ducklings.

It was only when he needed a lawyer in his twenties that he looked me up. It was around the time I started JAL. He showed up at my office quite the tall, tanned, and handsome hottie. I agreed to look after his property portfolio, among other things. All above board and nothing untoward unless I ever decided otherwise.

That aside, I don't even need to ask Rodolfo the question. Everyone in the outlaw world knows the Mexicans don't entertain kiddie fiddling.

Drugs. Check mark. Weapons. Check mark. Pedophilia and child abuse. Big red fucking cross.

"I wasn't trying to be insulting, Jaine, but we need to find out who this other party is. Now that the new pakhan's been announced, it'll be back to business as usual. Unless, of course, this one has more ethics than the last, which I very much doubt. The fact remains that while they were out of action, the trafficking still went on. The Dusters were able to help last time, but we can't make it a regular occurrence without drawing attention to ourselves, as you know. Even if we wanted to assist, our hands would most likely be tied."

In fairness to the pompous asshole, he does have a point. It was a mammoth undertaking intercepting and dealing with the vehicle, then returning the kids to their parents. They did well to keep it all low-key considering the numbers involved. It's only because they have reliable, trustworthy people and they run that Duster ship of theirs with military precision that they were able to pull it off. I need to calm the fuck down and accept the fact that Eoin O'Connell did me a favor. A huge one.

"Listen, I'll keep my ear to the ground. My gut feeling is the party concerned is having us deliberately look at the obvious. They want us to think it's an enemy when it'll transpire to be an ally. While we consider all suspects, it's best to keep quiet about my client list. I need to play my cards close to my chest in case we ever need these people."

"Enemy or ally, we need to catch them in the act. We can't go off all guns blazing then realize we've had The Exterminator put a bullet in the skull of an innocent third party."

I pause and take several deep breaths. Does this fucker think I'm an imbecile?

"I'm sure The Exterminator would review any intended hits before pulling any goddamn trigger, Eoin. He's a fucking professional. You should know that. From what I gather, you really like to use the sniper's services."

"He's the best. Why would the Dusters work with anyone else? When it comes to most things, we go big…."

"…or go home. I know. Irish used to say that all the time," I add quietly.

There's a pause.

"You miss him?" His voice turns soft, caring almost.

My turn to pause.

"Always will."

There's a deafening silence, both of us no doubt recalling what happened when Eoin paid me that surprise visit.

"Anyway, as I've said, I'll keep my eyes peeled and my ears to the ground. Like you, I want an end to this business. We'll never eradicate trafficking, but if we can stop them from transporting children, that will be a step in the right direction."

I grit my teeth, but it's only right and fair that I say what I'm about to.

"Thank you for helping them, Eoin." My voice is quiet, but the sincerity is there. My gratitude is heartfelt because it's deserved. Without the Dusters, I would have had nowhere to turn, and he could easily have vetoed my request as there was nothing for them to gain by helping.

"You're welcome. I hope if any future situations arise where you need the Dusters' input or assistance, you won't hesitate to ask."

"Thank you."

Another pause. A lengthier one. I find myself curious about what he's going to say next. What else is there to say?

"Jaine… this situation with Paddy. It was nothing personal. You do know that."

He sounds sympathetic. Well, I don't want his shitty excuses or his sympathy. I pause before I speak. I'm not a volatile person by nature, but I struggle when it comes to Eoin. This asshole makes my blood boil.

"I'm guessing your family deemed me unsuitable, which is their prerogative. I'm a biker. Even in the outlaw world, we're the lowest of the goddamn low."

"You're from the life. That would have been good enough for the O'Connells. The agreement with Luciano was unfortunately signed in blood, quite literally. If Padraig had told the family about you… if he'd told us of his intention to ask you to take the vows with him, then things might have ended differently."

I sigh frustratedly because he just doesn't get it.

"Eoin, listen, I know arranged marriages are common in the life. Me marrying Irish… that might never have been on the cards, regardless. I love him, but then I've loved him for years. We were together for three months when we were nineteen. In nine years, we never got back together. Do you know why we split up? He cheated on me. Would I ever have been able to forgive him for that and marry him? Only God himself knows the answer to that now. The decision was taken out of our hands.

"What pissed me off is that you took away the greatest of friends when you showed up that day. It was like what I wanted didn't matter. Like what *he* wanted didn't matter. Above all else, Irish was my fucking confidant. My sounding board. The someone I'd call day or night just to run something past. I spoke to him every single day. I mourn the loss of his friendship as much as I mourn the loss of my pop, and I'm sure your brother mourns our weird, dysfunctional relationship just as much. You took away something so special and showed zero remorse. You took away one of my reasons for living when I'd only just laid one of the others to rest. That's what was—what is—unforgivable."

I stop as tears threaten. I don't need to be showing emotional weakness. Not in front of him. Maybe I'd have ended the relationship with Irish anyway. Maybe I'd have had no other choice. Maybe he would have dug his heels in and refused to marry the Sicilian otherwise.

That should have been my decision, though. Not the Dusters'. Not Eoin's. Mine.

"Maybe we were a bit hasty, Jaine."

"Maybe you were, but what's done is done. We can't change the past."

"If it's any consolation, I'm sorry."

"That's no consolation at all. I meant what I said. One day, I will make your life as miserable as you made mine. You have my word on that."

Then I hang up.

CHAPTER SEVENTEEN

SARAH

The Delaney Home, Brightling, New York

STANDING at the entrance to the kitchen, I look around the all-white space that's brimming with out-of-date mod-cons and watch as my pocket-sized best friend dumps the bags of what she deems to be life's essentials on the kitchen counter. Milk, bread, cereal, fruit, and veg—shit like that.

She's mothering me. Feeding me. Treating me like I'm not a fully-fledged functioning adult. She tutted when I told her I'd been living on take-out. Mainly Chinese and all noodle-based, so not too unhealthy, or at least that's what I thought.

Apparently, I was wrong. Apparently, I'm also not a student. Ramen noodles or an equivalent is not proper food. Who knew?

She suddenly stops what she's doing and turns to frown at me over the top of her tiny round spectacles. Here we go. I'd know that school principal look anywhere, having been on the receiving end of it most of my life. She's about to launch into a lecture.

"I can't believe you still haven't told Paul you're back."

My eyes scan over her as she stands there with her hands on her hips, her brown hair tied up in a messy bun on top of her head. She's wearing black Daisy Dukes, flip flops, and an I <3 New York white crop top. I want to tell her that those are really for tourists, not for people who were born and grew up in the city itself. Then again, maybe she's just pleased to be back. Who the hell am I to judge?

For the past week, I haven't done anything apart from fuck Ian all night long, spending the days recuperating. For a thirty-four-year-old, he really does have stamina. Not that that's old, but still.

"I will when I'm ready, Laila." I roll my eyes inwardly. "I mean, it's been seven years. I need to work out how best to reintroduce myself to a sibling I now barely know and one who probably won't be pleased to hear I've returned. What's a few more days of sticking my head in the sand?"

"Don't be silly, Sarah. Of course he'll be glad you're back. He'll be upset you've been home all this time and you haven't contacted him!" She's unpacking the bags now and banging things about to emphasize just how displeased she is at my continual reluctance to contact Paul.

I roll my eyes outwardly this time before taking a seat at the breakfast bar. "Since when do you care about my brother's feelings? When we were young, he used to pull your pigtails so hard you cried. In fact, I'm sure he was still doing that shit when I left seven years ago and when you were actually at college."

When we left high school, Laila went to Columbia, choosing to major in computer science, much to the disgust of her parents. They're both world-renowned surgeons, and they wanted her to follow in their footsteps—a tall order for a girl who passes out at the first sign of blood more often than not. Laila came out to visit me in Bolivia after promising her parents she'd only stay for a month. One month turned into two years. Something else they weren't too happy about. I'm a bad influence in their eyes and always have been.

"He didn't really speak to me after you left. He seldom visited the house. Someone just came once a month to keep on top of things, but that was it."

She's upset. I mean, being home is bringing back a whole boat-load of emotional memories, and I've spilled more tears than I'd care to admit. But are Laila's tears over my dad, who I know she loved dearly, or over Paul, I wonder?

I walk over, put my arms around her shoulders, and rest my chin on top of her head. I know she hates when I do that, but it's at the perfect height. I can't help myself.

"I'll tell him. Pinkie promise." I hold it up, and she links it with hers. I hug the girl I've known my whole life and who's more like a sister than a friend.

"I'm also worried about you." She wraps her arms around my waist and stares up at me, her pretty green eyes sparkling with tears on her little pale, heart-shaped face. "This Ian you've been sleeping with. You don't know anything about him. You've never even seen what he looks like. It's not normal, Sarah. Don't you think it's like some sort of weird take on Stockholm Syndrome that you're suffering from? I mean, he makes you wear a blindfold, for goodness sake. Do you think he's a mobster or something? That he's someone of interest to the police? What if he's one of those terrifying O'Connell brothers?"

I laugh out loud—someone of interest to the police? Of course he will be. But most of the people I know would fall into that category, myself included. I retake my seat at the breakfast bar, resting my elbows on top.

"I doubt Ian is one of the O'Connells. They're all GQ model-like looking according to the images I've seen on the internet. Those boys are currently competing with my brother for the title of Manhattan's most eligible male, so they're not likely to ever look twice at little old me." I shrug. "I don't know what it is about Ian, though, but I really like him."

"How can you like someone you've never even seen? What if he's really unattractive or burned or scarred or something?"

I shrug again. "I'm not sure that would matter to me. Love is blind, or so they say."

She's staring at me open-mouthed, and it's only then I realize what I've said.

"Wow! Sarah! Are you falling in love with him?" She continues to stare before slowly starting to pack away the fridge items.

"Who knows? Maybe," I reply eventually, taking a bite out of a loose apple.

"What if he's married? What if he has a girlfriend? What if he has both?"

She has a point. I'm not naïve. Aside from the fantastic sex, I don't know anything about Ian. I mean, we talk, but it's about generic stuff. I know he's a Yankees fan like me. I know he has auburn hair and green eyes. I know he's never been to Ireland and that he's inherited that beautiful lilt of his from his folks. I know he doesn't like seafood. So, I do know stuff. Unimportant stuff, but stuff all the same.

I mean, he could be a mobster. He could be ugly. He could be married. He could be all of the above. I think I could cope with anything apart from the latter. I could never be with a cheat.

Always abide by the golden rule, my daddy used to say. *Do unto others as you would have them do unto you.* I wouldn't want someone to sleep with my boyfriend or husband.

"I'm pretty sure he hasn't got a wife or a girlfriend because I've seen him every night this week. That's why I'm shattered and surviving on take-out."

She grimaces. She wants to tell me I'm being promiscuous. That I should wait until I'm married like she's doing. I lost my virginity to Blaze when I was eighteen, so she's ten years too late for that lecture.

"So? He could have told her or them that he's working away? You met him on the docks. He could have a woman in every dock, like a sailor. You don't even know where you're meeting him. It could be anywhere in the Upper East Side. A drug den or a brothel or something else sinister."

I smirk inwardly. Does she not think I've already frequented those sorts of establishments? I'm the daughter of the president of an MC. I forget sometimes how innocent she is.

"Regardless, you can't just keep hooking up when there's no future in it. Is he ever going to reveal his identity to you? No. So how can it ever go anywhere? No good will come of this, Sarah."

"He said he would reveal himself to me."

She rolls her eyes. "When?"

"When he knows he can trust me."

"And for that to happen, you'd have to tell him who you are?"

"I guess."

"Which you don't want to do."

"No."

"Case in point. I think you should have your fun, see him once more, and then stop."

I stare at her. I mean, I'm not stupid. Far from it. I really should allow common sense to prevail. Everything she's saying is valid.

"Don't see him tonight. Let's stay in and watch Netflix like old times. I'll make us a nice healthy meal, and we can catch up on what's happened since we got back. Or at least I can tell you what's been happening in my life as you've spent all your time blindfolded in a bed." She rolls her eyes. Again.

I snicker.

"Let's do that, Laila. So you can see I'm not obsessed with the scarred mobster who lives in a brothel and is cheating on his wife, his girlfriend, and his harem of women with me."

She nods and continues to put the shopping away. She's satisfied she's got what she wanted—saving me from myself and Ian.

My burner phone vibrates.

She's staring at me again, and her hands are back on her hips. We both know who it is.

Cillian: *What time tonight, Red?*

"Tell him no, Sarah. You'll thank me one day."

Will I?

Sarah: *Sorry, I can't do tonight.*

There's a pause. Minutes go by. Laila is talking away, but I'm not listening. Why is he not replying?

Cillian: *Another time then, maybe.*

What does that even mean? Does that mean he doesn't want to see me again? How do I even reply to that? Did he word it so I can't?

My brain fills with regrets and my stomach sinks. I'm suddenly conscious I've dug myself into a hole where he's concerned. I've let this Irish stranger into my brain, and he's wormed his way into my heart too. He told me we have no future, even if he does reveal his identity.

No future, Sarah. What part of that don't you understand?

No good is going to come of this. Laila's right. But he's my addiction now. I crave him. I want to keep seeing him regardless of the consequences. I only pray I'm strong enough to pick up the pieces and move on with my life when this house of cards comes tumbling down around my ears.

CHAPTER EIGHTEEN

CILLIAN

The Subway, New York

"WHO STOLE YOUR SCONE?"

Our Paddy thinks he's fucking hilarious. We're on wet work, and it's one of our own. It's never a good day when you have to take out a brother, but Dean caved when under pressure and ratted us to the pigs, resulting in a handful of good men being sent on a five-year holiday to Rikers Island.

The guilty party is currently bound to a plastic chair in front of us.

"That's a Scottish saying, not an Irish one," I mutter. I've just wiped my blood-covered hands to read the message from Red saying she doesn't want to see me tonight. My guess is my face now reflects my mood.

"Scottish. Irish. Close enough." He smirks at me then turns his attention back to Dean, the smell in the air a clear indication that our grass has just shit himself.

"I know. I know. You just want it over with. You just want to die," Paddy singsongs as he walks back and forth in a pair of disposable coveralls, waving a blood-dripping switchblade and wearing his customary grin. "But why should you have instant relief when the men you've sent down will be slowly tortured on the inside at the hands of our enemies?"

"You." He slices into his torso.

"Got." Slice.

"Them." Slice.

"Five." Slice.

"Years." Slice

"Apiece." Slice.

"And that, Dean." He's waving the blade as he talks like he's conducting a fucking orchestra. "Means they will never get out of that hell hole alive. So, you've made five young women widows and fourteen wee ones orphans because you could not keep your big trap shut." With a flick of the blade, he slices Dean's mouth open from ear to ear. Even though he's barely conscious, Dean screams in agony.

Paddy stands back, then tilts his head to best admire his handiwork. It's all a bit Hannibal Lecter-like. Meanwhile, Dean's now trying desperately to hold on to his intestines which he's clutching in his hands to stop them from falling to the floor.

See, that's our Paddy's mark. Spilled guts. There isn't any doctor going to be able to piece Dean back together after Paddy's finished with him. Not that he'll live beyond today to tell any more fucking tales out of school.

Paddy holds out his hand, and I pass him the table salt. The fine shit that gets everywhere like sand and stings like a fucker on open wounds. He flicks the lid and sprinkles it all over Dean like he's dusting sugar over a cake. Dean screams loud enough to wake the dead then passes out, dropping his innards all over the floor.

Butter fingers.

Paddy throws water over him to wake him, then repeats the process. He'll do it all day until he takes his last breath. He'll make sure every last minute of Dean's life is filled with fucking pain. And hopefully remorse for betraying his kin, his peers, and The Hudson Dusters.

One hour later and Dean has gone to meet his maker. His penance for his betrayal? Losing his life in a way you wouldn't wish on your worst fucking enemy.

At the hands of our Paddy.

Dean leaves behind a widow and four young children. The Dusters will look after them, at least until the wife remarries. If she doesn't, she'll be looked after for life, and the kids will be too until they turn eighteen. His family won't know he betrayed us and let them down. They'll be told he died a hero.

"Deal with the clean-up, Tam." I motion my head towards the carnage Paddy's created, and Tam nods. We own several disused areas of the New York subway system. They're sealed, completely soundproof, and easy to hose down. They all have the facilities to turn bodies into soup or wrap them in concrete, depending on how long we have to destroy any physical evidence. By the end of today, there will be no trace of Dean in here. He won't be chucked in the river or turned into soup. His remains will be bagged up and placed in a casket. His family will be told it will need to remain closed for the funeral due to the injuries he sustained in his loyalty to the Dusters.

We're in the back of the SUV as Tam drives us to St. Peter's Church so we can confess our sins to old Father O'Reilly. Paddy and I decided long ago to confess as we went along, unlike Eoin and Dyl, who attend church every Sunday with Ma and Da and the majority of the Duster population. Our reason? Given we do most of the wet work these days, my and Paddy's sins are plentiful. Father O'Reilly only has so much time available on a Sunday and has many to cater to. So, we're doing him a favor. And we think he appreciates our drop-in policy. It means we never forget to seek forgiveness from The Almighty and be slapped on the wrist with our much-deserved penance.

"So, why are you being such a grumpy arse today?" Paddy's looking at me, his shoulder-length black hair still wet from the shower. Hippy hair, my da calls it. It would never have been allowed in his day, so he keeps reminding us. His da would have cuffed him round the ear for daring to wear his hair long like a girl.

"Nothing," I mutter.

"It isn't nothing, Cill. Is it a woman that's got your panties in a bunch?" He snickers.

"Mind your business, Paddy," I rasp, not in the mood.

"A problem shared?"

"Jesus Christ, do you ever give up?"

"Nope."

"Yes, it's a woman."

"Cara."

"No, not fucking Cara."

"Who then? Not the model or that other one?"

"No. It's none of them."

"You just going to keep me guessing?"

"It's one of the trafficked women. I've been fucking her."

He lets out a long whistle.

"Never mix business with pleasure, Cill. You know that. It never ends well for the innocent party."

"I know. I know. Tell me something I don't. There's just something about her, Paddy. She's… well, she's different."

"She's seen you at work. That means she can never know who you are."

"I realize that," I hiss.

"Unless, of course, she's from the life, and you're going to take the vows with her."

"I don't know anything about her apart from she's a biker. She's a friend of a friend of your Jaine's. It's awkward."

"My Jaine?"

"Let's be honest, in your eyes, she'll always be your Jaine."

He nods. We both know his heart will never let go of the MC chick.

"So, what are you going to do?"

"What can I do? I'm going to have to end it at some point."

"Why the long face today, then? When you don't have to finish it just yet?"

"She doesn't want to see me tonight. She's made other plans."

He snickers. I don't appreciate it, but it's nice to see him smiling, even if it's at my fucking expense.

"You're falling for her, Cill. Been there."

"What do you mean?"

"Jaine. When I first met her, I fell hook, line, and sinker. When she dumped me at nineteen, I was beside myself. It was the second-worst day of my fucking life. To this day, she's still the only woman I want. If any of the others told me they didn't want to see me for whatever reason, I'd not have been arsed. If Jaine told me that, I'd be huffing like you are and wondering what the fuck I'd done wrong. You're skating on thin ice, brother. My suggestion is to find out what you can about her. If she's involved in the life, great. If she's just a hanger-on and you still want to be with her, just let Ma and Da know. Be upfront. Don't do what I did and keep her a secret. That's how I ended up in an arranged marriage to a silly teenager." He sighs and runs his hands through his wet hair. "Then again, Jaine doesn't love me anyway. Never has, apparently. Hearing that was the worst day of my life. I pray for your sake your ending is better."

"Look, I hear what you're saying, but it's easier said than done when, aside from Jaine, the only person I can ask about her is Paul Delaney. From what I can gather, she has some sort of past with him."

"Shite."

"Yeah, shite. Listen, I'm sorry about Jaine, Paddy."

I put my hand on my baby brother's shoulder. His smile from earlier has vanished. I could kick myself for putting him back in a melancholy mood.

His phone vibrates. Taking it out of his pocket, he stares at the illuminated screen with a beaming smile. I've seen that smile before, and there's only one person who can put that on his face.

"Paddy, please tell me that's not who I think it is."

"I don't know who you could possibly mean." He winks at me.

We stare at each other.

"Are you messaging Jaine?"

"Nope. Our Dyl is messaging Jaine."

"Jesus Christ, Paddy. Are you pretending to be Dylan? Can't she tell?"

"Look, Cill, I'm admitting to nothing. I won't say anything about your situation if you don't say anything about mine or about what you suspect."

I stare at him. Has he gone fucking insane?

"Pinkie promise?" he adds, holding the digit out.

"What age are we again?" I stare at him, then shake my head and smile. "We're both royally fucked. You know that?"

He waggles the digit in my face.

"Pinkie fucking promise." I grab it with my own, and he laughs.

I ponder for a moment, thinking about both our situations as he types a response to his biker chick.

"Right now, I'll take anything I can get, Cill."

He's answering the question he knows I wanted to ask.

"Why?"

There's no pause or delay in his response. Again, he laughs, but this time it's forced.

"When you've nothing to lose, you've everything to gain."

CHAPTER NINETEEN

CILLIAN

Upper East Side, New York

TAM SHOWS Red inside the room, then closes the door quietly on his way out. I stand and stare at her. It feels like I haven't seen her in weeks, but it's only been forty-eight hours. The blindfold is black, and it's pressed firmly against her olive skin. Her pale red hair hangs down past her shoulders. She's wearing dark green cargo pants and a white tank top. Biker boots finish her look. Huge fuck-off monstrosities that could easily kick a door or a head in.

Red looks hot as fuck. The idea of watching her straddle that hog of hers is giving me a hard-on. Now I understand what Paddy was getting at. There's something dominatrix-like about these women, and combined with their complete lack of fear where we're concerned, they're the ultimate fucking dick-twitchers.

She's moving her head this way and that. No doubt trying to listen. To work out if I'm in the room or not. I can tell when she realizes I am as her nipples harden under her top and her breathing speeds up. How does she know I'm here, I wonder? I haven't made a fucking sound.

Scent. That sense will be heightened. Over-compensating for the lack of visual.

"Ian?" She bites her lip, and that tips me over the edge. In two strides, I've reached her and pushed her against the wall. My mouth claims hers, desperate to taste her. She groans, her hands reaching up to pull on my hair as my tongue strokes deep, needing to connect with hers.

I've fucking missed her. I can taste the same craving in her. She's missed me too. I know she has. I need to be inside her right fucking now.

I rip the top over her head. She's braless. I drop my hands to her tits, squeezing them roughly, her nipples forming into pebbled peaks as I continue to tongue fuck her mouth. She mewls her pleasure, a sound that makes my dick even harder.

"You taste like apples."

"That's healthy living for you," she murmurs against my lips.

I snicker. Yeah, and making out with a murderous mobster is healthy fucking living too. Her hand drops down to rub my dick through my jeans, and I curse.

She kicks off her boots as I unfasten the pants, and the loose material drops to the floor. No panties. I pull the condom from my pocket, my lips never leaving hers. Pushing my jeans off, I kick our clothing to the side before sheathing my rock-hard cock. I lift her off the floor and she wraps her legs around my waist as I sink my dick into her wet, welcoming heat.

"Fuck." I groan as her pussy walls tighten around me like a vice. "You feel fucking perfect, Red." I hang back before I move. I don't want to blow my load there and then. Seconds later, I pull out and slam back into her.

"Fuck me, Ian. Hard and fast," she begs.

She doesn't have to ask me twice. Lifting her legs over my elbows, I angle her hips so my dick's banging against her sweet spot. I drive in and out of her while my mouth bites and sucks on her neck, covering her in bruises for the world to see. Am I claiming ownership? Fuck knows. Maybe I am.

Definitely, I am.

Her nails are clawing my back. I curse at the sharp pain, punishing her in return with more ruthless fucking.

"Is that hard enough for you, Red?" I ask through gritted teeth.

"Fuck… yes!"

I look down and watch my dick drive into her, my thick length sheened with her slickness. It's the best visual I have ever seen in my entire fucking life. Her little pink pussy being drilled by my massive hard cock.

Her legs are shaking, and I know she's close now as she's panting in my ear and mumbling deliriously. I lift her slightly and thrust deeper, growling in satisfaction when her warm wetness covers me as she comes all over my cock, her pussy clenching around my dick, draining my balls dry.

I lean against her, panting. My weight is the only thing keeping her pinned to the wall as my legs are fucked. We stand there just holding on to each other before I eventually pull out and lower her feet to the floor.

Walking to the bathroom to deal with the condom, I take in the burst rubber.

"Fuck."

"I think I know what you're cursing at," she says quietly.

I wipe my dick with a clean cloth, then walk back through. She's standing where I left her, still leaning against the wall. Her legs are parted, and my cum is running down her thighs.

"The rubber broke, Red. I'll send Tam to the pharmacy now."

"No! Don't you dare ask him to go there."

"Why? It's not like he doesn't know we've been fucking."

Her cheeks go pink, and she bites her lip awkwardly. I can't help but smile. In some ways, she's so bold, and in others, she's so fucking innocent.

"I'll go… on my way back." She lifts her head defiantly.

I pause.

"It might be best if we address this problem now, Red."

She nods. I message Tam and tell him what we need. He'll be discrete. He's probably been in the situation himself before now. Shit happens.

"Lie on the bed and let me clean you up, sweetheart."

I guide her to the bed, and she lies on top and waits while I fetch a clean cloth.

"Spread your legs for me."

The sight of her pussy dripping with my cum is making me feel all kinds of possessive. I don't want to think of it dripping with any other fucker's seed. Not ever. I wipe her thighs, but I leave her pussy untouched. Raising my finger to circle her already sensitive clit, I watch as her body wriggles on the bed. I have a desperate need to fuck her and fill her with more of my cum.

"Red, I'm clean, so you don't need to worry about that."

She bites her lip. "Me too. I was checked a few months ago, and there hasn't been anyone since, apart from you."

"Seeing as we've already had the mishap, Red?"

"Yes."

"Yes, what?"

"Yes, you can fuck me bareback."

All the blood I have in my body immediately floods to my dick when she utters those magical words. This is a first for me. No rubber. My cock's never felt so big or so hard in my life.

Positioning myself between her thighs, I rub my leaking dick up and down her wet folds as I kiss her hard on the mouth, and then I thrust into her.

Her warmth sheaths me, my cock immediately coated in our mixed cum. She groans in appreciation, her legs anchoring around my hips, and I struggle to hold back from coming there and then. She feels so fucking good. Tight, warm, and so wet. Pushing her legs against her chest, I fuck her hard and fast, my dick sliding easily through her dripping folds. It doesn't take long before she's gripping around my cock as she comes again. I release inside her with a grunt, pushing my dick in as deep as I can so there's no part that isn't coated with my seed.

We lay there for seconds. Minutes. I don't know how long. I feel content with my deflated cock still inside her, her arms and legs wrapped around me and holding me close to her. Eventually, I lift myself off, pulling my dick out of her tender flesh. I kneel between her thighs and watch as my cum runs from her pussy onto the sheets.

"Fuck, that's a beautiful sight, Red."

She smirks as she drops her hand to dip it between her legs. Then, lifting a cum-covered finger, she sucks it into her mouth and licks it clean.

It's right then I realize I don't ever want to let her go.

She's fucking mine.

CHAPTER TWENTY

CILLIAN

Cillian's Apartment, Hudson Yards, New York

"I CAN'T MAKE it tonight, boys."

We're on a conference call. This is the second week in a row I've canceled poker night to be with Red.

"Jesus Christ. There has to be a pussy involved. The question is whose. Is it Cara?"

"Have I canceled before now, Eoin?"

"Never."

"Then it's not her. I've been fucking her since high school. I'm not telling you nosy fuckers who it is."

"Bear in mind Ma's got her heart set on you marrying Cara."

"Ma can mind her own fucking business. I can find my own wife."

"You, me, and Paddy can meet at mine if Cill can't make it?" Dylan interjects, sounding hopeful. No-one ever goes to his, as it's filled with screens, laptops, and computers all whirring away doing fuck knows what and looking at fuck knows who. I, for one, don't want to know what goes on within the confines of that apartment of his.

"Yeah, let's do that, Dyl," Paddy replies. No doubt he's agreed as he owes him big time. I'm guessing our resident computer guru is helping him with his secret mission. Those two always were thick as fucking thieves.

"Anyway, lads, I need to get off as I've some trash to take out before I can enjoy my evening. Paddy, I'll see you at the subway tomorrow."

ROISIN

Private Dining Room, Palace Hotel, Manhattan

I air kiss her on both cheeks.

"How are you, Cara? You're looking well. How's the family?"

We both take our seats. I ask the niceties to get them out of the way. I am interested in her family; I'm the matriarch of The Hudson Dusters, after all. I have to show an interest in my extended family. Cara knows that my interest in her right now, though, is to do with my immediate family. My blood family. My second eldest, Cillian.

It's two p.m. I order our usual.

Dry Martini for Cara. Bloody Mary for me.

She doesn't answer my question about her family. She knows why she's here.

"I haven't seen him for weeks, Roisin. I know he has two fuck buddies that he sees when I make myself unavailable, but it's neither of them that he's been spending time with."

"You've asked them directly?"

"Yes. We keep in contact to make sure his eyes don't go wandering elsewhere, you know?"

I nod.

Smart thinking. Maybe I don't give her enough credit at times.

"Cara, I need our Cillian married. Paddy's situation is settled, as you know. With Eoin, we need to wait because the girl for him needs to be a… shall we say… Bloody Mary." I smile and motion my head towards my untouched drink. She knows exactly what I mean. "But for Cillian, that's not quite as important, provided his bride is from the life and knows our ways. You know your ma Helen and I went to school together, and your da is Fergal's right-hand man. All of us always hoped you and our Cillian would get wed. That you would have done so by now."

She looks flustered. I know she loves my second eldest. She should have had him led down the aisle by his leaking cock before he got bored with her. Now it looks like she's got competition, and we've no idea who this new girl is. I don't like surprises. In my experience, most of them turn out to be something that needs to be permanently removed.

"I understand, Roisin. I've tried everything to get him to ask me, but nothing's worked."

I sigh. It pains me when I have to intervene in these matters.

"The next time you have sex with him, you do what you have to do." I take a sip of my spicy drink.

She's looking at me questioningly. I roll my eyes inwardly.

"You tamper with the condom, and you sheath his cock with it, Cara," I explain.

She frowns. "You mean trap him by deliberately getting pregnant?" She sounds shocked.

"That's exactly what I mean. He's Irish Catholic. If you're pregnant, he will have to marry you. If you achieve that, you'll seal your fate and his. Your parents will be happy. His parents will be happy, and we can get on with producing heirs to the Duster dynasty."

She smirks, as if pleased with the idea. She's thirty-two. She's not getting any younger, and she's invested most of her life in our Cill. It's now or never. It needs to be now. At my time of life, I don't need to be looking for a replacement.

"And from now on, you introduce yourself as his fiancée wherever you go, Cara." I open my handbag and take out a jewelry box. "It's on loan. Whatever you do, don't lose it. When he takes you to pick one for real, you can return it."

She opens the box and takes in the three-million-dollar pear-shaped diamond ring with wide eyes.

"Are you sure, Roisin? Cill will be annoyed if I do that, and I don't want to make him angry. You know what his temper's like."

"I have one to match, Cara. You leave our Cillian to me."

We make small talk, and eventually, she leaves, her drink untouched. It wasn't a sociable tete-a-tete. She knows that.

Cara's not perfect for my son. Far from it. The Almighty didn't grace her with much intelligence, which is why I have to spell everything out for her, and she's got no backbone whatsoever. But she's known to us, and she's safe. We have her loyalty and that of her family, and that's something money can't buy.

I take a cigarette out of my bag. This is a no-smoking establishment, but no one will dare tell me I can't smoke. I seldom do, but sometimes I feel the urge. I'm almost seventy. I'm not going to live forever. I call my driver.

"Liam."

"Yes, Mrs. O'Connell."

"I want you to follow Tam this evening. See if he picks anyone up and, if so, where he takes them. You call me immediately if you see anything."

"Will do, Mrs. O'Connell."

I light it up and inhale it deeply while taking in the ostentatious room with its gold, cream, and crystal décor. The price of each drink is three figures. Money buys silence. Cara and me? We were never here.

One by one, I need to get those boys of mine married off, and no one is going to stand in my way.

CILLIAN

Cillian's Apartment, Hudson Yards, New York

"Cillian."

He answers within three rings. Time to bite the fucking bullet.

"Razr. Just an update on the property situation. Our Paddy's spoken with Luc, and by all accounts, a colleague of his let him know the buildings in question were going for a song, hence why he bought them. He's asked the Dusters to assure you that there's nothing untoward behind the transactions. He's happy to speak to you directly to discuss."

There's a pause while the biker madman takes in what I've said.

"I still don't trust the Sicilian fucker, Cill. His old man was untrustworthy, and from experience, I know shit like that tends to run in the blood. I'll take on board what you're saying, but the Scorpions will be keeping a close eye on him. Discretely, of course. If he steps out of line, I'll slit his goddamn throat."

I rub my hand across my neck. Apparently, I do it subconsciously every time I speak to Razr. More so when he mentions putting his blade to work.

"Understood. We didn't expect anything less."

"I can't understand why you'd want to tie your family to theirs given what they did. Still, it's none of my business."

He's telling me something I've been asking myself. Da and Eoin must know what they're doing, though.

"Just one other thing, Razr."

Silence.

"I had my man drop two females off at a property a few weeks ago. We now know Delaney Enterprises owns that building and the one next door. The females entered through the front of one property and out via the rear of the other. My driver says there's an adjoining door between them with a keypad. Do you know anyone who would have that code? The Dusters don't want the girls for anything. We just want to get in touch to make sure they're safe."

Silence.

I give him the address.

More silence.

"I'll need to check who else has the code besides me, Cillian. I'll get back to you."

"Thank you."

He hangs up.

I've got a feeling Paul Delaney knows exactly who was in his building.

CHAPTER TWENTY-ONE

SARAH

Upper East Side, New York

I CURSE and yank on his hair as he bites down painfully on my nipple before sliding his dick home.

"Fuck." I groan as he fills me perfectly.

"Feel good, Red?" He chuckles against my throat before licking the length of my neck.

"So fucking good." His mouth claims mine, his tongue filling the space possessively as his hips grind against me, his dick pressing against my sweet spot with steady, languorous thrusts.

"Turn over, sweetheart," he whispers against my ear, biting the lobe hard before sucking the stinging flesh into his mouth.

Flipping over, I get on my hands and knees and push my ass in the air. One hand fists my hair, and he yanks my head back so he can kiss me hard on the mouth. The other drops to my pussy, and he runs his fingers up my wet folds before curling two inside. My core immediately tightens. He could make me come in seconds. He knows my body so well now. I grind against his hand, craving release.

"Don't you dare, Red. I want your cum all over my cock." His breath is hot in my ear. Removing his fingers, he pushes their wetness against my mouth, growling as I suck them clean, then he sinks his dick into me once more. My pussy welcomes his return, clenching tightly around him.

"Push against me, Red."

I do as he asks, arching my back, at the same time allowing him to go even deeper. Swearing, his grip on my hips tightens as he drives into me hard and fast, the sound of flesh slapping against flesh and our appreciative groans filling the room. His hand drops to rub my clit, and the orgasm explodes through my body. I press my face into the pillow to suffocate the sound as he roars with his own release, my contracting walls milking him dry.

He collapses on top of me. He knows I love the weight of his body on mine, pinning me down, crushing me. I groan in satisfaction as our hot, sweaty limbs entwine.

I love him. I know I do. What a fucking mess. I've fallen for someone, and I don't even know his real name or what he looks like.

He rolls onto his back briefly, then stands up from the bed to deal with the condom. Lying back down again, he pulls me against his chest, wrapping his arms tightly around me.

"I wish I could see your face."

He kisses me on the forehead. "So, tell me who you are, then."

"What difference will that make?"

"Well, if my family, more so my eldest brother, doesn't see you as a threat, then we can maybe do away with the blindfold."

"We still won't have any future, though."

I so fucking want a future with him.

"One step at a time, Red."

I sit up and pull my knees against my chest, hugging them to me. "It's just…"

"I know."

"You know what?"

"That you've got feelings for me."

"Conceited?"

"Damn straight, sweetheart." He chuckles as he runs his fingertips up and down my naked back.

"Do you…"

"Yes, Red. I have feelings for you too. So…" He pulls me back down beside him. "Let's do this slowly and see where it takes us. I'm willing to try if you are."

I kiss his neck and inhale his familiar woodsy scent that's now fused with sex and sweat—an intoxicating combination.

"There's just one person I need to let know I'm back, and then I'll tell you my real name."

He flips me over onto my back.

"Deal. So, tell me what else you'd like, Red." His peppermint breath mingles with mine as his body pins me down once more. I can already feel the pre-cum from his erection dampening my stomach, and my insides flip in anticipation. It seems we're insatiable when it comes to fucking each other.

"For you to be inside me," I whisper breathlessly.

"I thought you'd never ask." His smiling lips cover mine, and his tongue strokes deep inside my mouth, emulating precisely what his cock will be doing to my pussy any minute now.

We're interrupted by his phone. It's a ringtone I've never heard, so it must be his *actual* number and not his burner. His reaction emphasizes just that as he immediately gets off the bed to take the call. It must be important. Or at least the person calling is.

"Ma?"

He talks in grunts, not wanting me to decipher what's going on.

"I'll be there as soon as I can." He disconnects the call.

"I… I should go," I whisper. For some reason, I feel tears pricking my eyes when he doesn't try to stop me. A stark reminder that I'm just a casual hook-up, a dirty fucking secret, and that this is just some random room in a random building in the Upper East Side.

"I'm sorry, Red. It was my ma. Something's come up at work, and I need to take care of it."

"It's okay. I understand."

We both dress quickly. He's got somewhere to be, so I just need to be gone. I'm no longer wanted. Discarded. He pulls me against him and wraps his arms around me.

"We'll work something out, Red. I promise."

My heart fills with the hope that it's not just an empty promise.

The door opens and closes. As he leaves, he takes my hopes with him.

I wait.

Tam will come for me shortly, I'm sure

Minutes pass. I'm almost ready to rip the blindfold off and just leave, but I know I can't. I won't betray Ian's trust like that.

It's then I hear voices.

"You can't go in there." I recognize Tam's voice.

"I can go anywhere I damn well please." It's a woman's voice.

"Ian won't be happy about it."

She pauses and laughs.

"Oh, *Ian* is it."

The door opens. Then it's slammed shut. She's in the room with me as I can now smell her expensive billion-dollar an ounce perfume.

Vanilla notes. I fucking hate vanilla.

"So, this is where he's been spending his time and who he's been spending it with." The blindfold is ripped from my face, and I blink, quickly shielding my eyes as I struggle to focus with the room lights on.

I take in the woman in front of me. She's tall and slim. Strikingly beautiful. Her blonde hair hangs in waves to the middle of her back. Her face is pale, and her eyes are piercing blue. Her black trouser suit is designer and probably cost a small fortune. She eyes my biker attire with distaste like I'm a pauper. Little does she know my brother's one of the wealthiest men in Manhattan, and I'm not too shabbily off myself.

"Red. I might have guessed." She touches my hair, and I jerk my head away. "So, how long have you been fucking him?" She sneers.

Ignore what I said about beautiful. Her face is now twisted and grotesque, no doubt matching her ugly soul. She walks around the space looking at things, picking them up and putting them back down. I look around too. It's clearly a hotel room, extremely expensive but unfinished by the look of things, as the walls still need painting. I'm guessing it's not open to the general public yet.

"That's none of your fucking business," I reply defiantly.

"No? What about his family? Is it none of their business either?"

I don't reply.

"Well?" She turns and pushes me. I find myself wishing for the first time in seven years that I have a blade in my hand so I could cut her.

"He's a grown man. He doesn't need his family's permission to fuck someone."

She laughs in my face. “You have no idea who he is, do you? Who *they* are?”

My cheeks go red. I feel embarrassed. She’s right. I don’t. I suddenly feel like a fucking idiot for allowing myself to be drawn into this lunacy. A madness that I helped create.

“So, I guess you’re just some random hook-up. A fuck buddy. Well, you’re not the first, and you definitely won’t be the last. You’re just one in a long line.”

Her biting words describe exactly how I feel right now. I *am* a random hook-up. I’ll never be anything more. He’s already made that abundantly clear.

“He’s a good fuck? Ian, right?”

She laughs like it’s some private joke. Likely because he’s not called Ian at all. Jealousy ripples through me all the same. Jealousy over a man who is not mine and never will be. I can keep on lying to myself, but that’s my harsh, stinking reality.

It pisses me off that she knows who he is and I don’t. If I had a switchblade, she’d be dead right now. Cutting is way too tame for this bitch.

She turns and tries to stare me down, but I back down from no one.

“A word of warning. You need to stay away from him. He’s dangerous. His family’s dangerous.”

I glare at her. “You’re saying that like I don’t know what danger is.”

She laughs like I’ve told the funniest fucking joke in the world. “Trust me. You don’t know the meaning of the word. They’re in a different league.”

“And if I don’t?”

“You’re not one of those girls, are you? A mistress? A beck and call girl?”

“What do you mean?” I frown. “Ian’s single, isn’t he?”

She smirks. "Not sure what he's told you, but he's my fiancé."

I stare at her, and she stares smugly back.

"You're lying," I whisper.

She holds out her hand, and there on her finger is a diamond ring that will have cost millions of dollars.

I stare at it. Then back at her.

"Well, more fool you for putting up with a man who cheats on you," I hiss.

She glares at me. Fuck her. And him. He's made me feel like a fucking fool.

She hands me the blindfold. "You've been warned. If you don't want to end up at the bottom of the Hudson, stay away from Ian."

I take in the woman he's chosen to spend the rest of his life with. The woman who's been accepted by his family like I never will be. She smiles smugly again before leaving and closing the door. I can't breathe. I put the blindfold back on. I just want to blank this sorry episode out of my mind. Pretend like none of it ever happened.

What the fuck was I thinking? I feel dirty. Laila was right. It was never destined to end well. I need to stop seeing him.

Fuck feelings. I'll survive. I always fucking survive.

The door opens. "Red…" His tone is sympathetic. I don't want fucking pity. I hold my hand up to stop Tam from speaking further.

"Just drop me off, Tam."

"Sure thing."

"And, Tam?"

"Yes."

"Please don't say anything to Ian beforehand."

"Of course."

I switch my burner phone off, unsure if I'll ever switch it back on again. He has no other way of contacting me.

Asshole.

CHAPTER TWENTY-TWO

SARAH

The Delaney Home, Brightling, New York

I PARK in the driveway and walk to the door. I don't even notice the other hog parked up. The ride home went by in a blur. My mind is reeling. My heart is racing. Right now, I wish I'd never come back to New York.

Stepping inside the house, I switch on the lights and almost jump out of my skin when I take in the person sitting on the sofa.

"Paul," I whisper as I stare at my older brother before bursting into tears.

Twenty-Three Years Earlier (Age Five)

"And the mommy sits there, and the daddy sits there, and the brother…"

He kicks over my doll's house, causing all the pieces to tumble to the floor.

I try not to cry. It's not the first time. It won't be the last. I'll just have to ask Daddy to stick the broken parts back together again. Tell him that I knocked it over by accident, again.

Paul's face is red and angry. He looks just like my daddy, but mean and nasty. My daddy never looks at me like that. Like he hates me.

Is he going to hit me?

My eyes fill with tears, and my bottom lip trembles.

I know what he's going to say.

It's my fault. It's all my fault.

"There is no mommy," he says venomously. "Why is there no mommy, Sarah?"

Tears spill down my cheeks.

"Because I killed her," I whisper as guilt floods me. I pick at the hem of my little lemon sundress, not making eye contact.

"That's right. Because you killed her."

I nod, accepting that it was my fault, even though there was nothing I could have done to change it.

"If you hadn't been born, she'd still be here."

I nod again. I can't hold back the silent tears, but I'm not going to sob.

"Who killed Mommy, Sarah?"

Then the sobs burst free, and more tears spill down my cheeks.

"Say it!" he screams.

Present Day

The memories and emotions of the first twenty-one years of my life hit me like a sucker punch as I take in my brother. My childhood bully. The monster from my fucking nightmares.

"I killed her. I killed her." I automatically sink to my knees as the familiar sobs wrack my body while I tell him what he wants to hear. What he needs to hear. Because he has to blame someone for his loss. He has to pass on the pain he's going through. He can't just bear it like the rest of us fucking have to.

He grabs me by my shoulders and yanks me from the floor into his arms. I raise my hand to shield my face. Is he going to hit me? He never has before, but I've always felt threatened somehow because his fury was almost tangible way back then.

"You didn't fucking kill her, Sarah." His whispered voice is soft.

Is that sadness I hear? Regret? Is it over Mom? Is it over how he treated me? Over the mental anguish he inflicted? The invisible scars he carved into my soul; no physical blade necessary. Scars I will have to carry always.

I cry until I'm hoarse. Until my chest hurts, my throat's raw, and my eyes sting. I cry, and my big brother does his best to soothe me. I cry for the mom I never got to meet. I cry for the daddy I could have saved. I cry for the sibling that never truly was. And I cry for Ian. An invisible man that maybe I could have been happy with.

Then I cry for myself. I'm not proud of the fact that there are tears of self-pity in there. Self-pity is for fools. Frowned upon when you come from the life. I cry them all the same. I feel entitled after the day from hell I've had.

Eventually, the sobs subside. Paul leads me to the sofa, sits us down, and pulls me to his chest before wrapping his arms around me. Playing with my hair, he kisses the top of my head. He doesn't speak. He'll wait for me to be ready, I'm sure.

What do I say to the boy, now man, who made my childhood a fucking misery? Who mentally tortured me every waking moment for something I had no control over? What do I say to the only kin I have? To the person who hated me. Probably hates me still. Who blamed me for everything wrong in his life, all because he didn't have a mother? Then didn't have a father.

Did he forget that I didn't have them either?

"I shouldn't have come back, Paul. I'm so sorry," I whisper sob.

I'm opening up old wounds—painful memories. Neither of us needs to regurgitate any of that shit.

He grips the top of my arms and pulls me back so I'm facing him. It's then I see his red-rimmed eyes. The tears that match my own. I've never seen Paul cry. Not even at my father's funeral. Am I glad he's feeling guilty?

Yes, I think I am.

"Don't you ever say that. I'm so fucking glad you're back. I've missed you so much, Sarah. I just need to know one thing."

I nod and watch as a silent tear slides down his cheek. I wipe it off, and he closes his eyes.

"Did you run away because of me?" His voice is quiet.

He already knows the answer. He just wants to hear it. For me to admit it out loud. Why? So he can feel guilty? Have regrets? Punish himself? What good will any of it do?

Does he want absolution? Does he seek redemption?

I'm not sure I can give him either. Not yet. Maybe in time. My childhood was traumatic because of him. What I can give him right now is my answer. My honesty. He deserves nothing less.

"Yes. In the main."

His eyes screw up in pain. Does he feel remorse? Or is it self-pity?

"I'm so fucking sorry for everything I said and did. For fucking everything up. I just hope one day you'll forgive me for the pain I inflicted and the damage I caused. For being the reason you ran away."

He pulls me against him again, and I let him. I embrace the brother I never really had, and I say a silent prayer that maybe now we're both older, we can have some semblance of a relationship.

When we're all cried out, we talk. Probably for the first time ever.

There will always be bitter memories, moments of frustration and blame, name-calling and lashing out. What happened in the past can't ever be forgotten. Forgiveness is the only path available to us now, and we agree to start on that slow journey together in the hope that one day we can find some inner peace.

"So, you left the house as it was?" I look around the room. At the heavy dark brown furniture set against the cream-colored background. At the photographs covering most surfaces. Images of Mom or Daddy or of happy times. Not that there were many of those. At least not if Paul was involved. He hated the world and everyone in it, and he liked to make it known to all around him. If he was suffering, we all had to suffer.

I stare at my brother. He stayed over last night in his childhood bedroom. We talked until the early hours. He's wearing grey sweatpants, his upper half on display. He looks almost normal. A tattoo of the Iron Scorpions' crest covers most of his back, reminding me of exactly who he is. He has so many tattoos. One for Mom. One for Dad.

Over his heart, it says *Sarah*.

My eyes fill with tears, and I blink them back. Maybe I should have come back sooner. We've lost so much time. Then again, I think we both needed to journey apart for a little while to come to terms with our past. We needed to bury the past to move on with the future.

"Didn't seem much point in changing anything. I was never

going to live here. Figured you'd want to see it looking the same if you ever came back."

I watch as he makes coffee. He's domesticated. Someone's been a good influence on him. One that's helped him control his inner demon and his rage. And I think I know who that person is. I'm only sad things didn't work out for them.

I nod.

In a way, I'm glad he made that decision. To leave things unchanged. It was comforting to come back to something familiar.

"How is everyone? Bomb? Blaze? All the other brothers?"

"Bomb's dead."

I look at him in surprise.

He narrows his eyes at me. "A while back, he betrayed the woman I was seeing at the time. What he did was unforgivable. He gave me no option."

"Ah."

I don't need to ask how he died. Paul will have killed him personally. His childhood best friend. Gone. Just like that. His throat slit ear to ear. Sister or not, I know he'd do the same to me in a heartbeat if I was disloyal to him or the club.

"Jaine? Right?"

He frowns at me and stops what he's doing. "How the fuck do you know Jaine?"

"On my way back from Bolivia, we were picked up by traffickers. Laila and me."

"You were what?" He throws the cup he's holding across the room, and it smashes against the wall facing. "Why didn't you call me?"

"You know why, Paul," I say quietly.

He doesn't speak. Minutes pass. He's trying to rein in Razr. He ignores the shattered cup. Taking another from the cupboard, he continues to make our drinks.

Eventually, he walks across and places them on the table in front of us before sitting down and grabbing my wrist, causing me to grimace in pain.

"If you're ever in any kind of trouble, you call me. If anyone lays a goddamn hand on you or upsets you, they'll feel my fucking blade, Sarah. Nothing must happen to you. Nothing. Understood?"

"Understood, Paul," I whisper, surprised that he cares so much after the abuse he inflicted on me during our childhood.

I look at my wrist, and he looks at it too. He can tell I don't appreciate his inability to control his temper. He closes his eyes as though disappointed with himself, then lets it go, rubbing gently at the purple marks his fingers left behind.

"You still see Dr. Crabtree?"

He leans back on the sofa and runs his hand through his hair.

"No." He sighs. "Didn't need to when I was with Jaine. She always knew how to keep me sane."

"Well, now you're no longer together, maybe you need to reconsider that decision. You know you need help controlling your anger."

"Maybe," he whispers, his gaze directed toward the window. "So, Jaine."

"Well, after I killed the driver…."

"You killed the fucking driver? Jesus Christ, you had to kill someone?" He's glaring at me, his eyes wild. I've set him off again. He's volatile by nature. Shit, we both are. But he struggled with his demon after losing Mom, whereas I didn't. How could I struggle with the loss of someone I'd never even met?

I put my hand over his as it starts twitching. His jaw is clenching and unclenching, and the vein in his neck is pulsing as he tries to calm himself down. I keep my voice slow and steady.

There's no point poking a bear.

"I had to. There were dozens of kids in the vehicle. I needed to do something to get them safe." I'm sure I see a flash of pride in his green eyes. Eyes that look just like my daddy's.

Most family members would be proud if you graduated or got a great new job. My brother's pleased because I committed murder for the greater good. Go figure.

"Anyway, so, I contacted a friend from school, and she put me in contact with Jaine. She arranged for someone to meet us on the other side. They handled everything."

"Who were they?"

"I don't know. They wanted their identity kept secret, so Jaine wouldn't say." He must already suspect who this third party is since he knows I'm back. I see him file a mental note on it. He'll want to be sure so he can pay them back, most likely. He won't want to feel obligated to anyone, even if it's my debt and not his.

Maybe he'll know Ian. Not that it matters as Ian's fucking engaged and the relationship's serious given the size of the rock on his fiancée's finger.

"How long ago was that?"

"Weeks ago."

"Were you ever going to tell me you were back, Sarah?" His voice sounds pained, and his hand-twitching intensifies. He wants his blade. Not because he wants to use it. He just needs to flick it back and forth. It's something he does when he gets wound up to calm himself down.

"Yes. I just needed time."

"So, what have you been doing?"

I shrug. "Nothing."

"You've been doing nothing?" I can hear the anger in his tone now. I forgot how much of a madman my brother truly is. "Don't fucking lie to me, Sarah." He runs his hands through his hair frustratedly. Paul hates lies. Deceit of any kind. Everything is truth and loyalty with him.

"Okay, so I met a guy."

"I want to meet this guy," he rasps.

"No need."

"Why?"

"It's over between us."

"What did he do?"

"He had a fiancée. Didn't tell me."

"I'm going to slit his goddamn throat for messing you around." His blade is in his hand now. It must have been in his pocket the whole damn time.

"Paul. You can't live my life for me." I roll my eyes frustratedly.

"No, I can't, but I can kill anyone who hurts my baby sister."

"In case you hadn't noticed, I'm not a baby anymore. I'm twenty-eight years old."

"You'll always be my baby sister. Anyone who hurts you, hurts me, and anyone who hurts me will pay the goddamn price."

"If you just threaten to kill everyone who causes me pain, then I can't ever be honest with you. You decide what it is you want."

He doesn't reply. He just flicks his knife back and forth. I change the subject.

"What happened with you and Jaine?"

"Turns out she doesn't love me. She's back with her childhood sweetheart."

"In California?"

"Yeah."

"I really like her."

"Makes two of us."

"You love her still?"

"Yeah. Probably always will." His voice breaks ever so slightly.

"You going to give her shit for not telling you about me?"

"Yeah."

"Paul!"

"Damn it, Sarah! She should have told me what was going on. You could have been fucking hurt."

"I asked her not to."

"I realize that, but…."

"But nothing. I asked her not to. She respected my wishes. She pretty much saved my life and everyone else's. You should be grateful she was there for me, not thinking about how much shit you're going to give her."

He flicks his knife again like it's some sort of serial killer's soother. Still, when it's in his hand, he's way more relaxed.

"So, Laila's back?"

"Why do you want to know?"

He shrugs. "Just asking."

"You going to pull her hair and make her cry again?" I smile.

"Maybe."

That answer causes both of us to snicker.

CHAPTER TWENTY-THREE

JAINE

Jaine's House, Rising, California

"Stop yelling at me!"

I can hear the heavy breathing on the other end of the line as he tries to rein in his insane alter ego.

"You know I'd never have let anything happen to her, Razr. So, you calling me up, giving me all sorts of crap, and threatening me with violence is neither welcomed nor appreciated. Now fuck off."

I disconnect the call.

Asshole.

Ten minutes later, my phone rings. I answer, knowing he'll have used the time to calm down.

"I'm sorry, Jaine."

"So you fucking should be. It was her call, Delaney. She's a big girl. It was clear to me she could look after herself since she'd already killed the driver and taken control of a big-ass truck. Some of us women can look after ourselves without male intervention. I first told you that years ago, and I'm telling you that again. Stop being such a goddamn chauvinist. Anyway, how did you find out she was back?"

"Cillian called me. He told me he dropped two girls off at one of my properties. It was the first building I ever bought. Apparently, the girls gave his guys the slip as they knew the code to get into the adjoining building, which I also own, and then they vanished."

"And only you and Sarah knew it."

"Exactly. So, the Dusters were the help?"

"Yes, and that's strictly between you and me. They want to be silent in all of this. They also don't want it to become a habit. We need to find out who's working with the goddamn Bratva."

"Do I need to pay them back? The Dusters?"

"No need. I'm going to write off the debt with a free hit provided I can do it while I'm in town."

"Anyone I know?"

"I'll keep you posted so you can add the name to The Exterminator's logbook."

Padraig: *So, a free hit? What for?*
Jaine: *To pay off the trafficking debt.*
Padraig: *I didn't realize it was a debt.*
Jaine: *Eoin seems to think it created an owing. He's already used it as an opportunity to ask questions. I'm not prepared to be interrogated or give him intel on any of my clients.*
Padraig: *He's manipulative.*
Jaine: *He's an asshole, Dyl.*
Padraig: *He's not that bad.*
Jaine: *Are you joking? After what he fucking did?*

Padraig: *Okay, don't get your panties in a bunch.*
Jaine: *What's got into you? First, my hot dog legs and now my panties. Where's your mind at these days? Should I be worried that I'm starring in your fantasies?*
Padraig: *Well…?*
Jaine: *Seriously? We're actually having this conversation?*
Padraig: *Paddy and I could compare notes.*
Jaine: *This is all kinds of wrong, you know that? Have you banged your head? Where's the real Dylan? The one that's all prim and proper and most likely still a virgin?*
Padraig: *I've had women. I've even been in love before. I still am, in fact.*
Jaine: *With your hand?*
Padraig: *You should have been a comedian. No. With a real live woman.*
Jaine: *I'm intrigued. Was it a poster? A centerfold in Playboy? Someone on TV?*
Padraig: *I don't live that much of a sheltered life.*
Jaine: *No? I've Face-timed you before. You spend your time watching screens, looking at buildings, and spying on people. Is it someone in one of the Duster properties? Like in that old Sliver film? Do you have your very own Sharon Stone tucked away somewhere?*
Padraig: *You're not being very kind.*
Jaine: *LOL. Sorry. I'm only messing. So, this woman. Tell me about her.*
Padraig: *You really want to know?*
Jaine: *Why wouldn't I? I'd love to know all about the woman who captured the heart of Dylan 'Batman' O'Connell.*
Padraig: *Well, she's tall, slim, blonde, and beautiful.*

Jaine: *She sounds like a cliché? Is she make-believe? A Disney princess maybe?*
Padraig: *Jaine!*
Jaine: *LOL. Go on. What age is she.*
Padraig: *She's my age. Twenty-eight.*
Jaine: *You're twenty-nine. It's Irish who's twenty-eight.*
Padraig: *I meant twenty-nine.*
Jaine: *And what does she do?*
Padraig: *Same as me.*
Jaine: *And where did you meet.*
Padraig: *College.*
Jaine: *You studied online though?*

There's a pause.

Padraig: *I met her online.*
Jaine: *Have you slept with her? Sorry, you don't have to answer that.*
Padraig: *Yes, but nowhere near enough times. Even if I slept with her every day until the day I died, it would never be enough.*
Jaine: *So, you're in love with her?*
Padraig: *Yes.*
Jaine: *So, what's wrong? Why can't you be with her?*
Padraig: *She used to love me. Now she says she doesn't.*
Jaine: *Seriously? You can't just switch shit like that off. I should know. Did she tell you that face to face?*
Padraig: *No. She messaged me.*
Jaine: *Really? That's not something you'd just message. Not without good reason.*
Padraig: *What do you think I should do?*
Jaine: *The eyes are the windows to the soul. Take my word*

for it. Ask her if she loves you but do it face to face. I think she's lying. Something's not stacking up.

Minutes pass. Has he gone and not said goodbye? He's probably engrossed in those screens of his, watching his Sharon Stone equivalent in the shower.

Jaine: *You still there, Dyl?*
Padraig: *Yes, I'm still here.*
Jaine: *So, heart to heart over. Find out who old Fergal wants me to use his freebie on. Provided it's doable in the timeframe, this one's on the house.*
Padraig: *Will do, and thanks for the advice.*
Jaine: *Anytime, Batman. Love, Robin.*

Jaine: So, *Delaney now knows.*
Sarah: *Yeah. He's been flicking that blade of his back and forth ever since I told him.*
Jaine: *He's just given me an earful. I hung up on the asshole.*
Sarah: *I asked him not to do that.*
Jaine: *You think he ever listens to a female? He's a chauvinist, remember?*
Sarah: *I know. Still. I can see the changes in him. He's even partially domesticated.*
Jaine: *LOL. Listen, there are two sides to your brother. Delaney's a good man. Razr's full of anger and highly volatile. I just try to keep on the right side. I also never took any shit from him. You just need to give him time.*

Sarah: *I'm so sorry you guys didn't work out. You were good for him.*
Jaine: *Thank you. I loved him, but I wasn't* in *love with him. He deserved more than I could offer.*
Sarah: *He still loves you, you know?*
Jaine: *I know, but I don't encourage it or lead him on. Eventually, he'll find the right woman for him.*
Sarah: *You still coming to Manhattan?*
Jaine: *Yeah. I'm just making the final arrangements now. Remind Delaney that he agreed to go to the function and that he'll need a plus one. There are a few clients of mine attending that he wanted me to introduce him to. Our conversation this morning wasn't the ideal time to discuss it. He can't go with me as I'll be taking Cherry. I need to introduce her around. She's agreed to hold the reins to my company while I'm out of town. In fact, just thinking, maybe you could go with him?*
Sarah: *I'm not sure.*
Jaine: *It'd be an excellent way to reintroduce yourself back into New York society. In my experience, it's best to confront wagging tongues and speculation head-on.*
Sarah: *You know what? You have a point. Let me speak to Paul.*
Jaine: *You do that. I'm glad you're back. He's missed you. He needs you in his life.*
Sarah: *I'm glad to be back, and I've missed him too. Oh, and one other thing.*
Jaine: *Yes?*
Sarah: *Ian. If he asks anything about me, please don't tell him.*
Jaine: *Can I ask why? Now that Paul knows you're back, does it need to be a secret?*

Sarah: *Let's just say he's an asshole, but I'll explain all when I see you.*
Jaine: *No worries. Your secret's safe with me.*

I'M GUESSING IF SHE'S REFERRING TO HIM AS IAN, SHE STILL doesn't know he's Cillian O'Connell.

CHAPTER TWENTY-FOUR

CILLIAN

Cillian's Apartment, Hudson Yards, New York

"WHAT DO you mean you can't tell me who she is?" My voice is more threatening than I intended it to be.

This is the first time I've ever called Jaine Jones, and the first time I've ever asked anything of her. Jaine usually deals with our Eoin, so I'm surprised she even answered the phone to an unknown number. She had the sense to wait for me to speak first, mind you.

"Cillian, you didn't want your identity revealed and vice versa for her. She didn't want you to know who she was either." She ignores my tone and keeps hers calm.

"So, you won't tell me?"

"No. I won't. Unless Red agrees that it's okay for me to do so, I won't tell you. Would you thank me if I just outed your identity? Anyway, why? What have you done that she won't speak to you?"

"It's not what I've done. It's what my ma's done." I huff.

"I don't like the sound of that. Have you been sleeping with her? If so, how the fuck did you manage that without revealing who you are?"

"Blindfold."

"Jesus Christ. Look, I don't want to know any more. It's none of my business. I'll ask her if she wants me to do the big reveal. If she says no, then it's a no. I won't betray her confidence, same as I won't betray yours."

"Surely you should have more loyalty to the Dusters than to some victim of trafficking."

"Firstly, she's not a victim—she's a survivor. Secondly, my word is my word no matter who it's given to."

My brothers are right. Jaine's not afraid to stand up to a Duster. I have to admire her for that. Not many would be so brave.

"Ask her, Jaine. Please."

"Why can't you just ask her yourself?"

"She won't speak to me or reply to any messages."

"Well, she did mention that you're an asshole."

"Fucking great." I huff again.

There's a pause.

"I'll call her and let you know, Cillian."

"One last thing."

"Yes?"

"Given what you know about my family, would she be a good match for me?"

She doesn't even hesitate. "Yes."

"Thank you. I just needed to be sure."

"You're welcome."

The O'Connell Home, Darling, New York

"Wait for me, Tam. I've no idea how long I'll be. Could be five minutes. Could be five hours."

He nods. I pay the fucker a fortune so he can wait five days if needs be.

I step out of the SUV and take in my family home. It's ostentatious. A mini-mansion with twenty bedrooms and fuck knows how many other rooms. There's a safe space underneath covering the same footprint as the house itself. We could survive an apocalypse in there. Having to put up with that lot in forced proximity for an extended time, though? Maybe the alternative would be better.

The building's over-the-top appearance is finished with water fountains and landscaped gardens. The only blight is the security system—cameras at every turn and electrified everything, all coordinated by our Dylan. There's only so much you can do to beautify that shite.

It's like Fort fucking Knox.

I usually only go home on the last Sunday of every month or when it's a special occasion or a Holy day in the calendar. All my brothers go then so Ma can make full use of the kitchen and make a show of things by producing countless meals, each one crammed full of potatoes so we can cling on to our Irish roots by filling our guts with starchy carbs before spending the next week detoxifying.

My ma and da like to believe they're God-fearing Catholics, but in reality, they flick the middle finger up to the Father, the Son, and the Holy Spirit, to Moses himself, and to the majority of the Commandments. They then think by going to church every Sunday to take their penance on the chin and donating shit loads to church causes that The Almighty will still see fit to instruct Saint Peter to let them in those pearly gates. He won't. They're kidding themselves on if they think he will. Still. Who am I to argue? They have their faith, and like many others, they need that to cling to.

I open the door and take in the gold flock-papered walls laden with photos of my brothers and me. My da's parents moved to Hell's Kitchen from Dublin when he was twelve years old. It was his da's destiny to take over the Duster reins as it was his and as it will be our Eoin's. When his folks passed, his siblings, Mick and Ruairi, moved back to Ireland along with their wives, my plethora of cousins, and a multitude of grandkids. They handle the shipping of the weapons to us here in the US. There's a whole wall dedicated to their photos. Ma frames and hangs up every single one that's sent to her.

Unlike Da, she was an only child, and her parents moved here when she was eight in the hope of giving her a better future. Did they succeed? Some might say not. Still, she and Da are happy. And now? She wants grandkids. At her time of life, she's desperate for them. I understand. She wants us all married off, but I will not be told who to wed. Paddy was given no choice. Now he's miserable as sin most of the time. Or at least, he was. He was in a cell when his life was signed away. He had no say in it. It's a shame, as I think Jaine would have been a good match for him. If she loved him that is. Apparently she doesn't.

"Is that you, Cill?" Da shouts from his office, which is just off the front door. He's not being nosy having it there, he's just keeping Ma safe. He has an arsenal of weapons in that room. Makes sense. We have a lot of enemies.

"Aye, Da," I shout back. I called in advance to let them know I'd be dropping by. I make my way through into the most used of the family rooms. It's a comfy space, all neutral colors with a massive TV hanging from the wall and two large black leather sectionals to lounge on.

Not a minute later, he appears. Unlike when we meet at the office, he's wearing grey slacks and a black button-down. He looks like any typical almost seventy-year-old. It's only when you look into his piercing blue eyes that you see the atrocities he's committed reflected in them. His glasses are perched on the end of his nose, and he looks at me over the top of them.

"Before your ma comes down, son, I just want to say thank you for taking care of the Dean situation. I'm still astounded the boy thought he could get away with such disloyalty. Have you heard that one of our lot has already been attacked and killed in Rikers? A wife and three kids under five he's left behind." He shakes his head. "It's a bloody shame."

"Well, we create a lot of widows and orphans in this game, Da. They know what they're getting into when they join the Duster ranks."

"Aye, you're right, Cill. You're right."

"Anyway, it was our Paddy who dealt with it, so it's him you need to thank. You know how he is. He spilled Dean's guts for spilling his guts. He also made him suffer until the very end like he knew our guys would be made to do on the inside."

"Aye, he's a good lad is our Paddy. Not sure what's changed, but I've been happy to see a smile back on his face these past few weeks. I was worried we were going to lose him to the drink. Anyway, it's Dean's funeral on Tuesday. I've already given your apologies to his family. I'll do the same for Padraig now I know what happened."

I nod.

"I've given your ma a shout, so she should be through shortly." He shuffles from side to side. He knows exactly why I'm here. She must have told him.

Turning to stare out the window, it's not long before I hear mumbling. They're probably thinking about how best to approach this. The fact that Ma's stepped way over the fucking line this time.

"Cillian," she says softly.

I turn around and take in Roisin O'Connell. My ma. A tiny woman at just over five feet. Her auburn hair's now almost entirely grey, like Da's. She's still a beautiful woman. Elegant. All twinsets and pearls on the outside. Her appearance perfectly disguises the bloodthirsty demon hidden underneath. Inside, she has a soul as black as the rest of us. She's ended dozens in her time, so not a vast number. The way she kills them, though. She burns the fuckers. Sets fire to various parts of them. If they've stolen, it's their hands. If they've raped, it's their dick. If they've lied, it's their tongue. She'll extinguish the flames, then relight, typically until the appendage is burnt to a crisp and ready to drop off. When she's satisfied they've suffered enough, she douses them in petrol and throws the final match.

"Ma."

She's linked her arm with Da's. It's clear she's nervous and wants his moral support.

"You know why I'm here?"

She nods, and I watch as they both take a seat on one of the sectionals.

"Explain to me why you did what you did, please." I try to keep calm. We're both hot-headed, but we both also realize shouting and bawling never gets either of us anywhere.

"Cara came to me, Cillian. Said she hadn't seen you in weeks. She thought maybe there was someone else. Asked if I'd find out." She glances at Da, but he keeps his eyes on me. "I had Liam follow Tam. He saw the girl being taken into the new hotel that's opening soon."

"Right, and what happened next?" I lean my backside against the window ledge and fold my arms.

"I called you and said I needed a hand with a problem."

"*Was* there a problem, Ma?"

"No, there wasn't." She has the decency to look sheepish, at least.

"What happened then?"

"Cara went in and confronted the girl."

"What did she tell her?"

"That she's your fiancée, that you're cheating on her, and that she needs to back off."

"Did she threaten her?"

"I believe she did."

"Did she tell her who I am?"

"No. She kept up the pretense that you're called Ian."

"What happened next?"

"Cara left. I'm guessing the girl must have left straight after."

Silence. One minute. Five. Ten. I run my hands through my hair, struggling to speak without lashing out.

"Why?"

I watch as tears prick my mother's eyes. I know they're not crocodile ones; they're heartfelt.

"We've all always hoped you'd take the vows with Cara. She's a good girl. Beautiful. Loyal. She's had you on a pedestal your whole life. You know how much she loves you, Cill. To tie our two families together would be a good thing for everyone…"

"But I don't love her, Ma. I never have, and I never will." I interject as I rub my hand over my forehead in frustration.

"You'd grow to love her, son. Look at me and your da. Ours was an arranged marriage, and we grew to love each other. Didn't we, Fergal?"

Dad smiles at her. Would I love to have what they have? Fucking right I would. But I could never have that with Cara. I've known her too long. The thought of spending the next fifty years of my life with her… I'd sooner make my own concrete shoes and fling myself in the Hudson.

"Look, Ma…"

"Cillian, just tell me you'll consider her, and I'll be happy with that for now."

"Of course I'll consider her." I tell her what she needs to hear.

"Me and your da, we're in the winter of our lives. We want to see our boys happily married. We want grandbabies running around our feet. It's not too much to ask now, is it?"

"No, Ma."

"I mean, do we even know anything about the girl you were sleeping with? She might just be a gold-digger or, even worse, a heroin addict."

"Jesus Christ, she's neither of those things." I exhale loudly.

"Do you know that for sure, Cillian?"

"I have it on very good authority that she's not, Ma."

"On who's good authority?" She's sitting upright now. She's looking to pick a fight. Or at least get Da on side and get him to issue an order condemning me to a lifetime with Cara.

"Jaine Jones."

She tsks me. "She was that biker woman who was sniffing around our Paddy, wasn't she? What does a biker know when she's probably a gold-digger or a heroin addict herself?" Her voice is smug. She looks at Da for back-up.

"Ma, you're skating on very thin ice," I say.

"Well, everyone knows bikers can't be trusted. Heathens, the lot of them."

"Ma…"

"Look, the pair of you." Da has reached the end of his tether. His tone is cutting. "I've listened to what both of you have to say. Now, Roisin, Cillian has agreed to consider Cara, so you've got what you wanted. Cillian, if you don't find a suitable alternative within the next three months, then your engagement to Cara will be announced. Your ma's right. If it's left up to you boys, you'll all remain single. We need to be creating the next generation of Dusters before you lot get any older. You boys know that. Now, that's my final decision on that matter." He holds up his hand as Ma attempts to speak. "Roisin, Cillian also has a valid point. There's no need to start saying unkind things about the bikers. You know we rely on them for transport and the like. They also give us access to The Exterminator, and his services have been invaluable. The bikers are our allies, not our enemies, and it's best we don't forget that. Jaine Jones was the old lady of Paul Delaney for four years. Delaney is no fool, so with that in mind, I trust her words. Until they betray us, we treat them like brothers."

Ma purses her lips. Da will pay for not taking her side. He'll likely have to make his own dinner, wash his own underpants, and fend for himself for the next two weeks as a penance.

I stand up to leave, and they escort me to the door.

"So, you'll consider Cara?" Ma's voice is pleading as she hugs me tightly, kissing me on both cheeks.

"I said I would, Ma, and I will, but don't get your hopes up," I mumble, knowing full well I have no intention of ever taking Cara as my bride.

I turn, about to leave.

"Oh, Cill. Before you go, I've heard Leoluca is having a shindig in a few weeks, and there's going to be a lot of well-to-do people present. I'd expect an invitation will be forthcoming for the Dusters, even though we don't work together. At least not yet, anyway. It may be an idea for you and Cara to attend. I've mentioned it to Eoin also. He can take that secretary of his that he's fucking."

"Fergal!" Ma elbows him in the ribs and glares at him.

"Sorry, Roisin." He rubs the sore spot. "I'm told Paddy can't go as he's got other plans. And, well, Dyl." He shrugs, knowing there's no point even going there.

I roll my eyes. Black tie functions aren't really my thing, but I've heard good things about Leoluca, so maybe I'll make an exception.

"I'll think about it, Da." I raise my hand in farewell and get back in the SUV fifty-five minutes after I got out of it.

"Get me the fuck out of here, Tam."

He chuckles. "No worries, Cill."

I now have to get Red to talk to me, find out who she is, and then convince her to marry me, all inside three months.

CHAPTER TWENTY-FIVE

SARAH

The Delaney Home, Brightling, New York

"I DON'T WANT him to know who I am!" I hiss.

"I said I'd ask. So that's what I'm doing. I'll pass the message on." Jaine ignores my pissed-off tone.

"Sorry."

"For what?"

"Almost taking your head off."

"Don't worry about it. I was with your brother for four years. I'm used to short tempers. If it gets too much, I'll put the phone down on you, same as I do him."

I snicker. "So, Ian wants to know who I am?"

"Yes. I also know you guys have been sleeping together."

"He told you that?"

"Not in so many words, but he didn't deny it when I asked, and then he mentioned a blindfold."

"Did he also mention his blonde bimbo of a fiancée came into the room after he'd been called away on urgent business, flouted her gazillion-dollar engagement ring in my face, then told me to back off or I'd find myself at the bottom of the Hudson?"

"There's no way Ian's engaged. I speak to his brothers all the time. I'd know. Unless it's a recently arranged thing."

"What, like an arranged marriage?"

"Yes. It's common in certain influential families. Keep your friends close and your enemies closer and all that. You can't get much closer than taking the vows with them."

"Wow. I'm surprised that still goes on."

"Trust me, it does."

"Well, this woman was wearing a rock, and it was the genuine article, so she's most definitely engaged to him or wants to be."

"There are a lot of women who could fall into the latter category. He's quite the catch. I'm sure many of Manhattan's socialites would love to be Ian's bride."

"So, just how good-looking is he?"

She chuckles. "Extremely. All the brothers are."

"His 'girlfriend' said his family is dangerous with a capital D."

"They are."

"You know them well?"

"Yes."

"What should I do?"

"I can't tell you that, Sarah. Do you like him? Love him even?"

"I like him… a lot."

She exhales loudly. "They get under your skin for sure."

"You sound like you've been on the receiving end of it yourself?"

There's a pause

"You could say that."

Her tone is both defeated and abrupt. It's clear it's something she doesn't wish to talk about.

"Anyway, you need to decide, Sarah. Have you contacted him since you left the hotel? Or vice versa?"

I bite my lip. "I switched off the phone, and I haven't turned it back on since."

"Switch it on. Read the messages. Listen to the voicemails if there are any. See what he has to say. Don't not listen. I've been there and done that and had a whole ton of regrets as a result."

I LIE IN MY CHILDHOOD BEDROOM. IT'S A COMFORTING SPACE EVEN after all this time, with its rock-god poster-covered walls contrasting on a pale pink background. Every surface is scattered with photos of Laila and me through the years, among a plethora of cuddly toys.

I take the burner phone out of my bedside drawer.

"Let's find out what the asshole's got to say for himself," I mumble.

I switch it on, and it immediately springs to life, flashing like a one-armed bandit announcing I've hit the jackpot. Yeah, right. More like I've scooped the fucking booby prize.

There are no voicemails. He probably thinks I'd try to use voice recognition software to work out who he is. He's arrogant enough to think I'd go to such extreme lengths.

Cillian: *Tam told me what happened. It's not what you think.*
Cillian: *Do you really believe I'd treat you like that?*
Cillian: *I need to speak to you urgently, Red.*
Cillian: *Don't hang a man before he's had the chance to say his piece, sweetheart.*
Cillian: *Quit running from me.*

Cillian: *Tell me who you are, Red?*

I stare at the handset. At the messages. At the final one. Why the fuck should I be the one to tell him who I am? Why can't he be the one to spill his guts? He's the one with women hidden in his closet. How many more? One in every dock, Laila said, and she's probably right. On top of his harem, he's also got a fiancée who's sporting a rock the size of Gibraltar on her ring finger and who seems perfectly happy to put up with his philandering ways.

Well, not me. I'm no one's fucking doormat. I'm way better than that.

Sarah: *Your fiancée threatened to have me thrown in the Hudson.*

He's typing.

Cillian: *She's not my fiancée.*
Sarah: *So, you haven't fucked her?*
Cillian: *I've fucked a lot of women, Red.*
Sarah: *Her ring was mighty impressive.*
Cillian: *I wouldn't know.*
Sarah: *Don't lie to me.*
Cillian: *I'm not lying. Meet with me. Let me explain.*
Sarah: *No. You know what will happen if we meet up.*
Cillian: *We can always talk afterward.*
Sarah: *You're just using me for sex.*
Cillian: *I can have pretty much any woman I want if that was all I was chasing.*
Sarah: *That's just as well because this one's not interested.*
Cillian: *You're only lying to yourself, Red.*
Sarah: *My name isn't Red.*

Cillian: *I know it's not.*

Sarah: *Do you know what it is?*

Cillian: *No. Do you want to tell me?*

Sarah: *You tell me yours first.*

Cillian: *You know I can't do that. You're asking for the one thing I can't give.*

Sarah: *You can't give me a relationship either. Guess we've reached a stalemate.*

Cillian: *It's your call.*

Sarah: *Yes, it is. Goodbye, Ian.*

He's typing. Then he's not.

I watch. I wait. I watch. I wait. No new messages appear. What does fucking appear is a lump in my throat, which I swallow down. He's not worth it. Lying fucker. It's better this way. I need to restart my life, sign up for classes, get to know my brother all over again. I don't have time to play guessing games with Ian, blindfolded or otherwise. Everything until now has been on his terms. After being threatened by the blonde, it now has to be on mine. I'm worth more. It's about time he realizes that.

I open the bedside drawer, place the phone back inside, then close it before exaggeratedly dusting my hands.

CILLIAN

Cillian's Apartment, Hudson Yards, New York

I stare at my phone. Have I just been dumped? I've just been fucking dumped. Well. Sort of.

"Paddy."

"Aye, Cill?"

"She's told me she doesn't want to see me anymore."

He laughs for a solid minute. Not sure why because it's not even remotely fucking funny.

"Sorry, Cill. I know I should be more sympathetic. Why, for fuck's sake?"

"Cara confronted her. Told her we were engaged or something and then flashed some massive rock she was wearing on her finger."

"Ma?"

"Ma."

"What are you going to do?"

"What can I do?"

"Jaine won't tell you who she is?"

"Not a chance."

"Maybe you'll just have to chalk this one up to experience, brother."

"Can't do that, Paddy. I've agreed with Da that he can announce my engagement to Cara in three months if I don't find an alternative bride."

"Shite. And you'd be prepared to take the vows with this girl?"

"Aye, Paddy. I would."

"Well, we'd best try to find her, then."

PADRAIG

Padraig's Apartment, Hudson Yards, New York

Padraig: *You there?*

Jaine: *As far as I know, Dyl.*

I snicker to myself at the familiar dry sense of humor I've missed so fucking much. God I love this girl.

Padraig: *Can I ask a gigantic favor?*

Jaine: *As long as it's not for a pic of my legs, my panties, or anything else.*
Padraig: *Nothing inappropriate, darlin'.*
Jaine: *Spit it out, then.*
Padraig: *This trafficked woman our Cill's been seeing.*
Jaine: *What about her?*
Padraig: *Mind telling me who she is?*
Jaine: *I can't do that.*
Padraig: *Surely, if she's not from the life, it's not a big deal.*
Jaine: *It wouldn't matter if she were Santa's little helper. I gave my word. Anyway, who said she isn't from the life?*
Padraig: *She's from the life? A good match for him?*
Jaine: *I'd say so, yes.*
Padraig: *Shame. She's dumped him.*
Jaine: *Sorry to hear that.*
Padraig: *Not as sorry as he is. He's smitten with her. He's threatening to marry her if she'll have him.*
Jaine: *Fuck me... not literally.*
Padraig: *Tempting offer.*
Jaine: *It wasn't an invitation, weirdo.*
Padraig: *So, I can't persuade you to reveal who she is?*
Jaine: *No, sorry.*
Padraig: *It's just my da's threatening to announce his engagement to Cara in three months if he doesn't find an alternative and he really likes this girl.*
Jaine: *Stop trying to coerce me. I gave her my word.*
Jaine: *So, Cara is the girl who threatened her?*
Padraig: *Yes. She's been in love with our Cill for years, but he's never made any commitment to her. Ma wants grand-children and future Duster heirs. She's fed up waiting, so she's forcing Da's hand and pushing him to force Cill's. Cara is known to the family, so she's a safe pair of hands for*

our Cill's dick, but not sure that's what he wants for the rest of his life.

Jaine: *TMI. I don't need to be having a conversation about your brother's dick.*

Jaine: *Listen, I know my contact likes him too, but I'm a biker. A sniper. I'm not fucking Cupid. I fire bullets, not arrows.*

Padraig: *But what if they're soulmates?*

Jaine: *Sometimes fate has a way of fucking you over.*

Padraig: *What do you mean?*

Jaine: *You even have to ask?*

Padraig: *Look, if you think she's right for him, I'll take your word for it. So how do we get them in front of each other?*

Jaine: *He'll meet her without a blindfold?*

Padraig: *He's been making her wear one of those?*

Jaine: *Yup.*

Padraig: *Fuck me.*

Jaine: *Let me just add 'not literally' right there for you.*

Padraig: *Spoilsport.*

Padraig: *Is there anything you can do? He'll be forever grateful. They might even name their first wee one after you. Although my ma and da might object since it would be their first grandchild.*

There's a pause—a lengthy one.

Padraig: *Jaine, have I said something to upset you?*

I frown at my phone. I've touched a nerve. Said something I shouldn't have. I know this woman inside out. In some ways, even better than she knows herself. For the life of me, I've no clue what it is, but something triggered her.

Jaine: *Is he going to Leoluca's function?*

I wait and wait and wait, and finally, she replies, completely dodging the question. Did I say something wrong? Yes, I did, and she has no intention of telling me what that something was.

I want to fucking know.

Padraig: *Let me check.*

After dropping a message to our Cill, I text back.

Padraig: *He'll be going, yes, and he's taking Cara with him, no doubt in preparation for the big engagement announcement.*
Jaine: *Then I'll be there to witness the scene unfold as my 'trafficked survivor' will also be attending.*
Padraig: *So, we'll have the equivalent of the Big Bang Hudson Duster style?*
Jaine: *Yup. Why don't you come along and we can watch the fireworks together?*
Padraig: *Maybe. We'll see.*
Jaine: *You're starting to give me a complex. Are you avoiding me for some reason?*
Padraig: *Not at all, darlin'. It's just you know I'm not the sociable sort.*

CHAPTER TWENTY-SIX

SARAH

The Iron Scorpions' Clubhouse, Brightling, New York

I TAKE in my former home away from home. So many memories. Some good. Some bad. Most left scars for life.

From the outside, the Iron Scorpions' clubhouse still looks like a prison. Set in around sixty acres of nothingness, the exterior of the two-story building is depressingly grey with windows covered in bulletproof metal, and with bars over the top, just for good measure. Metal railings surround the perimeter, and there's only one way in or out. The top of the fencing is electrified and finished with barbed wire, and there's CCTV everywhere.

Not sure why anyone would want to break in, and trust me, if they don't want you leaving, then you're going nowhere.

I turn and smile at my ex-boyfriend, my *first* proper boyfriend, taking in his long wavy blonde hair and piercing blue gaze. The years have been kind to him. He's a handsome man. Tall, lean, with muscles in all the right places, and inked to perfection. We might have stayed together if, after six months, he hadn't stuck his dick in a cum slut. That appendage was never getting anywhere near my pussy again after that. I've seen where some of those women have been and who they've been fucked by. I loved him. Or at least I thought I did.

Now I know I didn't. It was puppy love—that rose-tinted spectacles, first love bullshit.

These days, all I see when I close my eyes is a stranger with auburn hair and green eyes. A man whose face I have to imagine as I've never seen it and never will. A man whose voice claws at my brain, that soft, unforgettable Irish lilt haunting both my night and my daydreams.

"Thanks for picking us up, Blaze."

He collected us in a cage, as I've only got my hog at home. By all accounts, he's dating Cherry Avery now, my old school friend. What are the chances? Cherry's family is old money and worth fortunes. She'd have been expected to marry a professionally-educated billionaire in line with family tradition, but I guess when she met Jaine, she found herself on that slippery slope down to biker territory. Once you hit rock bottom in this world, there's no way you're ever clawing your way back out. Forever tainted. Forever stained. This shit becomes engraved on your soul.

Her folks must be so fucking proud.

"It's good to have you back, Sarah. We've missed having you around." His hand covers mine, and he squeezes it gently. It feels strange. But then, being back here feels the same. Do I still belong? Time will tell, I guess. This was my life. My extended family. Everything I knew. These past seven years, I've lived differently, though. I'm not the same Sarah I was back then.

I squeeze his fingers in silent response.

"You ready to go inside, Laila?"

I turn in my seat to look back at my little friend. She's only been here a few times. Her parents were never keen on her frequenting this place, what with all the sexual shenanigans and debauchery that goes on.

After high school, she went to college, whereas I just pondered over my future. I'm glad I did in some ways, as it allowed me to spend so much more time with my daddy.

"Is it safe?" she whispers in my ear. Blaze can hear every word. I snicker as he tries to suppress a smile.

"Oh, it's safe. I mean, it's only ten a.m.. The real shit doesn't start until at least midday."

She looks thoughtful, digesting what I've said like it's a fact. Like shit going off around here is so regimented you could synchronize your watch to it.

"Okay, so we have two hours."

I run my hand down my face, trying to stop my lips curving upwards as one of the young prospects opens the gates to let us in. Blaze lowers the window.

"Jamie, this here is Sarah and her friend, Laila. Sarah is Razr's baby sister, so you bear that in mind before you open your mouth and let that belly of yours rumble with any inappropriate remarks."

Jamie smirks, running his hands up and down the seams of his cut. He's going to be a heartbreaker for sure, with his long wavy black hair and baby blue eyes.

"It's nice to meet you, Sarah. Laila." He nods at us.

"Good to meet you, Jamie, and don't you pay Blaze here any attention. I'm a big girl, so I'm sure I can handle your cussing little mouth. And those smutty thoughts going on in that head of yours right now that involve me? Well, I can assure you I've done every single one of those positions and then some. Many of them with Jackson here."

I motion my head at Blaze. Jamie's smirk widens, staying in

place even when Blaze draws him a warning glare before driving us into the compound.

"I can't believe you just said that, Sarah." Laila sounds shocked as she looks between Blaze and me.

I shrug and smile at Blaze. "Jackson here took my virginity. Isn't anything going to change that fact."

THE SILENCE IS DEAFENING WHEN WE WALK INTO THE CLUBHOUSE. The walls are still the same white, contrasting against the gunmetal grey tables, chairs, and bulletproof bar. The floor's still black with an easy wipe finish.

I'm sure word will have spread by now that the prodigal former president's daughter has returned. The one who abandoned the club. The one who should have stayed and helped her brother. The one who killed her momma by being born and let her dad bleed to death in her arms.

In an instant, I'm surrounded by smiling, welcoming faces. None of them are accusing or silently blaming. Reality dawns on me that the shit I have rattling around in my brain, the guilt I have that tries its damndest to eat me alive most days, is all in my head. It's my conscience working against me and trying to tear me apart for shit I had no control over.

I touch my face, and my cheeks are wet. I'm crying as I take in these people from my youth. Familiar faces from my past. Older, more scarred, and wearing more of life's experiences, but still the same. My extended family. My life and theirs will always be connected, no matter the time or distance. I realize that now. None of us will ever escape the life because the same outlaw blood courses through all our veins.

It's then I see her. She's shuffling from foot to foot. She's dressed professionally in a grey business suit matched with stiletto heels.

I finish up with the hugs and kisses from the people who are once again part of my future, then I walk over to her. Without her help, would I even be here right now?

"Well, if it isn't Cherry Avery."

I wrap my arms around her shoulders, giving her no time to refuse or accept my tactile gesture. She stiffens slightly. I know why. So, I deal with the elephant in the room right away. The one that's standing protectively beside her.

"So, what's this I hear you're fucking my ex-boyfriend?" She frowns and bites her lip nervously. They're poutier than they used to be, so she's obviously had them surgically enhanced. I cast my eyes over her long crimson hair. Hair that was blonde at school. She still has the same flawless creamy skin and bright blue eyes on that perfect heart-shaped face of hers. She's beautiful, all hourglass perfection in a compact five-foot-five body, with long legs, massive tits, and a perky butt.

"I'll let you into a little secret, Cherry." I pretend to whisper in her ear, keeping it loud enough for Blaze to hear. "I taught him everything he knows, including how to treat a woman right. So, if he ever does you a disservice, you let me know, and I'll whoop his ass personally." I wink at Blaze, who smirks in response.

Cherry's beaming. Her face is full of relief as she looks up at Blaze, who kisses her softly on the side of the head. Shit, he really does love her.

"Where's Paul?"

I shrug at Laila. "Probably in his office planning a run or something. Why don't you go find him?"

RAZR

A mixture of saliva and pre-cum runs down my cock, and she gags as I thrust deep, the tip touching the back of her throat. I fist her blonde hair in my hand, holding her head in place as I continue to fuck her mouth hard. Her hand tightens on my base, stopping me from going too far. My eyes drift over her face as she stares up at me, her lips stretched around my dick. She's an attractive enough girl with nice skin and pretty blue eyes, but she wears way too much make-up and coats herself in cheap, sickly perfume.

She's no Jaine. This mouth wasn't made for sucking me off like hers was, but beggars can't be choosers. I just need a receptacle to empty my balls, and Bailey's always first in line and eager to please with that little hot vacuum of a mouth of hers.

"I need you to take me deeper, sweetheart."

My balls are starting to tighten as I get closer. I grip her hair as my orgasm claws at the base of my spine.

"Fuck." I curse as the first shot of cum hits the back of her throat.

"Paul, are you in there?" My office door is thrown open moments later.

Bailey turns around, my cum dripping down her chin, her hand wrapped around my still rock-hard shaft, and I'm leaning back in my chair with my jeans at my ankles.

My eyes immediately connect with pretty green ones wrapped in tiny round spectacles. Her mouth is agape as she stands at the doorway dressed in a little pink tank top and white jean shorts, looking like an adult, only smaller.

Laila.

Her face flits from mine to Bailey's, and then she stares at my dick.

Laila's not from the life. She hides nothing. She doesn't know how to. I watch as her cheeks immediately flush with color and her emotions flood across her face, each of them clear as day. Embarrassment, confusion, regret, pain. A whole plethora of the fuckers.

"You're a bit too late to join in, girlfriend." Bailey smirks at her while licking my cum from her lips.

"Laila. What the hell are you doing here? What the fuck?" I push Bailey back, then stand and yank up my jeans. The door slams shut, and I hear her run down the corridor.

"Fuck." I growl as I drag my hand through my hair and fasten my fly.

My strides are long as I follow her past the bar area. I'm aware everyone's wondering what the fuck's going on. Sarah goes to open her mouth, but I hold my hand up to silence her. Now is not the time.

When I reach the steps of the clubhouse entrance, I stop to look around. It's then I see her disappearing around the back of the building.

I follow her. I'm not sure what I'm going to say or do, but it's not sitting right with me that I've made Laila cry. I haven't seen her in years. I need to fix this shit somehow.

When I turn the corner, she's sitting on a rickety old bench, sobbing. I walk over slowly. I know I'm a scary motherfucker, but Laila knows me. Has done ever since I was a boy. She won't be scared. Her brown hair's tied up messily, and I watch as she pushes her spectacles up to the top of her head then wipes her hands across her cheeks. She looks up at me, her green eyes sparkling with tears before fixing her gaze on the ground, her arms crossed almost defensively in front of her. I take a seat beside her, my bulk talking up most of the bench. She shifts across, but my thigh is still touching hers.

"I'm sorry you had to witness that, Laila. I wasn't expecting you to walk in," I mumble. I'm aware my fingers are flicking an imaginary blade, but I can't stop myself. She knows me well enough to know that's just part of who I am.

"It was supposed to be a surprise."

"Well, it sure as hell was that."

"I'm the one who should be apologizing. It's all my fault. I should have knocked, not just barged in. I'm such a fudging idiot."

I rub my hand across my mouth, trying not to smirk. I forget she doesn't like to use cuss words.

"Still, there's a time and a place for that sort of thing," I say. "And it's not mid-morning and in my office."

We sit there in silence for a bit.

"I feel like such an idiot. I mean, if you weren't with everyone else, I should have known you were off having oral sex or something."

This time, I can't hold back my snicker.

She turns to stare at me, her pointed chin raised in defiance, her lips pouty. My gaze drops to them. I wonder what they'd taste like. What she'd taste like.

"Are you making fun of me, Paul Delaney?"

I hold my hands up in mock surrender and shake my head. "Not at all. It's just… most folks tend to say blow job. Your wording took me by surprise is all."

"Not as much as me barging in the middle of the event then staring at your… you know… your thing."

I laugh out loud. Fuck me. I haven't laughed in so fucking long.

"My dick, Laila. You can say the word dick."

"I meant to say penis, not thing. Your penis."

"Okay, my penis."

"I've seen your penis."

"Yup. You have."

"What are you guys doing back here? You been pulling Laila's pigtails for old time's sake, Paul?" I turn to look at my sister, who's followed us to no doubt find out what the fuck is going on and why her best friend's crying.

"Laila witnessed something she shouldn't have, and I was just coming out here to apologize."

She leans against the edge of the bench, looking between us both, her eyes narrowed.

"And what did she see exactly?"

"I saw someone giving Paul oral sex… I mean a… a."

"A blow job, Laila. You can say the damn words, baby girl."

"Yes. One of those. It wasn't his fault or the girl who was carrying out the... you know… act. I just barged straight in like the fudging idiot that I am." She slides her glasses back into place as her cheeks redden once more.

"So, you saw my brother's cock? Is that what you're telling me, Laila?"

"His penis, yeah." She nods.

Sarah snickers. "Jesus, it's no big deal. I mean, there has to be a first time for everything."

"What do you mean?" I frown at her. Is she getting at what I think she is?

"It's the first time our little Laila will have seen a fully functioning dick."

"Sarah!" Laila yells, drawing my sister the dirtiest look she can muster, which isn't really one at all, before standing and storming off. At least she's angry now as opposed to upset.

My sister curses herself, then takes Laila's place on the bench.

"I shouldn't have said that."

"Nope, you shouldn't have. So, Laila's a virgin."

"Yeah. No sex before marriage, that kind of thing."

"Shit."

"Yeah, shit."

"Before I go after her, Paul, a word of warning."

I look at her. She looks just like our mom, but with Dad's hair coloring. A unique mix that makes my little sister striking to look at.

"I think she's still got a crush on you. I think that's why she reacted so badly to what she saw. I sort of suspected it recently, but you know, with the tears and stuff. Well, it seems to confirm exactly what I thought."

I nod. "Good to know, Sarah." Or maybe not so good to fucking know. Kissing me on the cheek, she takes off after her friend.

A born-again Christian and the prez of a one percent club? I'm sure The Almighty would strike me down if I so much as even thought about putting my murderous hands on that innocent little body of hers.

The trouble is, that's just about all I can think of doing right now. I stare at the sky and wait for the goddamn lightning strike.

Thankfully, it doesn't happen.

CHAPTER TWENTY-SEVEN

SARAH

The Delaney Home, Brightling, New York

"LAILA, I have to go to this fancy event next week. You want to dress up and go with Paul and me?"

We're watching the classic *Thelma and Louise* on Netflix and eating popcorn. Separate bowls. I like mine salted, and Laila likes hers sweet. I throw my final piece in the air and catch it in my mouth. I tried to make it last as long as I could, but mine is now all gone while she's barely scratched the surface of hers. Even though it's coated in sugar and drizzled in caramel, I'd still eat it. I seem to be constantly fucking hungry these days.

She doesn't answer. I point at the bowl. "You eating that?"

She rolls her eyes at me, huffs loudly to let me know I'm being annoying, then passes it across.

"So?"

"I can't."

"My daddy always said there's no such word as can't."

"I'm too embarrassed."

"Because you saw my brother's cock?"

Ever since the grand unveiling of Paul's dick, she's avoided him like the plague. I think it's totally hilarious.

"His penis."

"Lots of women have seen his penis, I'd imagine."

"I don't want to know about them."

"Why don't you want to know about them? You got a thing for my brother?"

"Yeah."

She just comes right out with it. I turn and stare at her. "Why the hell have you never said anything?"

"I've always liked him. You know that. I just like him even more now."

"I thought it was just a childhood crush. So you like him *like that*?"

She shrugs. "Yeah, I like him *like that*."

"You do realize that's a match made in hell right there?"

"I realize that."

"I mean, he's done a lot of very bad things. He's a very bad man. There's no way he's ever getting into heaven, no matter how much you pray to The Almighty for his condemned soul."

"I know."

"He'd also definitely the type to want to try before he buys."

"What do you mean?"

She's staring at me now. How the fuck can she not know what that means?

"It means that he's not going to be prepared to wait until he marries you, if indeed he ever asks for your hand, before he expects to fuck you, Laila."

"Sarah!" She whacks me with a cushion.

"What? It's true? My brother is not going to abstain from sex, so you might as well face facts. You'd have to be way more flexible with that pussy of yours if you want to catch his attention."

There's no response.

"So, do you want to go? We could get you a sexy new dress, so Paul stares at you all evening?"

"Yeah, okay."

I snicker. "I'll let Jaine know there'll be three of us, then."

DYLAN

Dylan's Apartment, Hudson Yards, New York

"Dyl, sorry for calling, but I'm just trying to coordinate my movements for next week. Do you want to meet up or not?"

"Jaine… sorry you've lost me."

"Leoluca's function. I messaged you twice to ask if you wanted to go or if you wanted to meet up while I'm in Manhattan. Aside from some seriously random comments about hot dog legs, panties, and about the woman you're in love with, you haven't given me a direct answer. Speak now or forever hold your peace."

I'm going to kill our Paddy.

"Um… I'm in the middle of something right now. Can I call you back?"

"Jesus Christ, Dyl. It's a simple question needing a simple yes or no answer."

"I'll come back to you, Jaine."

"Oh and, Dyl?"

"Yes?"

"I'll need a name."

"For?"

"The freebie hit."

"Jaine, I'll have to get back to you."

Make that twice. Sibling or not, I am going to kill our Paddy twice.

"You've put me right in the middle, Padraig." I'm aware I sound pissed off and that's because I am.

"Of what?"

"Of your web of deceit. Jaine's asking me questions. Questions she's apparently asked you and not had a reply to. She's also mentioned hot dog legs, panties, and girlfriends."

He snickers. It's not funny.

"What's she asking?"

"If you're going to Leoluca's function, which I'm not, and you're not going either."

"I wasn't going to."

"Really?"

"Nope."

"Because if you do anything stupid like that and our Eoin finds out, you'll be toast."

"Noted."

"She also mentioned a free hit."

"Shite. I forgot about that."

"Send me the screen-grab of all of your conversations, please."

"Now?"

"Right now, Paddy, or I'm taking the message forwarding off. Jaine thinks she's talking to me, and apparently, my tone's gotten inappropriate. I don't want to know what she must be thinking of me."

"She's probably wondering where you found a personality and sense of humor."

"Very funny. From now on, the messages will be coming to me too, real time."

"I've got nothing to hide, brother."

I exhale. "I'll let Eoin know about the free hit. He'll probably want to speak to her directly about that."

EOIN

Eoin's Apartment, Hudson Yards, New York

"To what do I owe the pleasure, Eoin? Why is Mr. High and Mighty Duster deigning to call me?"

"How are you, Jaine?" I smile as she hisses like a viper at me down the phone.

"Like you care."

"Why are we being offered a free hit?"

"Because, Eoin, I refuse to be subjected to any more interrogations about any of my clients. I don't appreciate it, and they won't either. I paid The Exterminator personally. This will wipe the trafficking slate clean."

"What if I don't want it wiped clean?"

"Tough. Take it or leave it."

I sigh in frustration. I don't want the slate wiped. I want her intel on her clients as and when I need it. I also want to keep talking to her. She's abusive and foul-mouthed, but I'm getting quite used to that. I'm enjoying the repartee with Jaine and that ballsy, quick-witted mouth of hers.

She's not afraid of me. It's intriguing.

"Sorry, but I don't want the slate wiped, Jaine."

"I'm not passing you any more information on my clients, Eoin. Take the hit in return for my gratitude. If you don't, then that's your call. Then you leave empty-handed."

"We can discuss the matter next week when you're in Manhattan."

"I have no free time. I'm all booked up with appointments."

"I won't take up much of your valuable time, Jaine."

"I'm..."

I disconnect the call before she can tell me to fuck off. Because she will.

You will meet with me next week, Miss Jones, whether you want to or not.

Jaine: *You're an asshole, but then you already know that.*
Eoin: *Charming.*
Jaine: *I do my best. Listen, I really have no time to meet as it's a flying visit, so the best I can offer is an introduction. If there are any of my clients on the guest list that you wish to meet, then I can make that happen. It's up to you what business you do with them after that. It's my final offer. Take it or leave it.*

I pause. It's a good offer.

Eoin: *I'll take it. And a dance.*
Jaine: *Are you fucking serious right now?*
Eoin: *Totally.*
Jaine: *Jesus Christ.*
Eoin: *He has nothing to do with it. Introductions, one dance, and the trafficking slate is wiped clean.*
Jaine: *Agreed. See you next week.*

CHAPTER TWENTY-EIGHT

EOIN

The Meeting Rooms, New York

"HAVE you seen what she's wearing?" Candice and Cara are whispering loudly about the gowns the other women present have on, both of them snickering at any unfortunate soul that isn't deemed perfectly formed or perfectly dressed in their judgmental eyes.

I glance at my PA, one of the women I routinely sleep with. Why several? It's easier than getting involved, more so when I can't commit to anyone. Each knows the others exist, so none expect or receive any preferential treatment.

None of them will ever be Ma Duster.

Candice is tall and willowy with creamy skin, dark hair, and large hazel eyes. She's beautiful. Exactly my type.

Or at least what my type used to be. I seem to have a preference for green-eyed blondes these days.

Candice is decorative arm candy in the main. I'm not saying she's not intelligent; far from it. She is. Both her parents are politicians. But she's not my equal. I've never met anyone who is.

Until now. Apart from *her*.

The venue is ostentatious, bordering on vulgar with its crystal chandeliers, sweeping staircases, and everything finished in marble or gilded gold. Still, it's the best Manhattan has to offer. To book this venue, you need to be of suitable breeding. Even if you could afford it ten times over, the management would still look down their nose at you and turn you away if you don't have the right background. They want the place filled with Manhattan's royalty, not its riffraff, regardless of your net worth.

Tonight, it's filled with mobsters, mafioso, bent politicians, and the upper echelons of the business world. In simple terms, the people in the city who matter. All dressed up in tuxedos, of course, and with only the most dazzling of partners on their arms. Outward appearances are everything. Everyone will be assessing who uses which tailor. Mine is the best money can buy. When you're the heir to The Hudson Dusters, you have to look the part. Play the part. Know the game inside out.

No one understands it better than me. I've been learning my craft for thirty-six years.

Waiters strut around like little soldiers, with glasses of champagne balanced precariously on solid silver serving trays. The price to attend tonight? Nothing, save the opportunity cost. Leoluca is a billionaire. High in the ranks of the Sicilian mafia and perhaps even vying for the position of Don. The cost of this evening will likely be written off through his petty cash account, as the amount will be deemed insignificant.

His accountant will be as good as his lawyer, I'm sure.

And speaking of lawyers.

“Jaine.” I watch as Leoluca makes his way up the stairs to greet her.

“Leo.” She holds her arms out to him, speaking to him in fluent Italian, and the smile on each of their faces is genuine. They’ve known each other for a long time going by the intel we’ve unearthed. Nothing untoward. No romantic entanglement. Purely business. She kisses him on both cheeks before he takes her hand and walks her down the stairs, his colleague escorting her red-haired friend—the woman who will handle her business affairs for the foreseeable future, I’m told.

I stare at *her*. It’s impossible not to. She’s poised and collected, self-assured and confident. She’s also fucking beautiful. Bright green eyes on a heart-shaped face with an upturned nose and pouty lips. All of that flattered by her natural long blonde hair, which she’s wearing straight down her back. Her dress is gold sequined. Halter-necked with an open back. It’s not tight. It’s been designed to simply flow as she walks, drawing attention to her slim shape and long legs. It’s like she’s been gift-wrapped.

For me.

She’s had nothing enhanced. She looks after what God gave her, and she does so exceptionally well. Tall, some may say too slim. Not that she cares what people think. I love that she doesn’t give a fuck.

“You’re drooling, Eoin.” Cillian whispers, interrupting my thoughts.

I look at my brother. He’s scrubbed up well. He’s not been himself these past few weeks. Not since Da’s threatened to marry him off to Cara. There’s something else going on, but I’m not party to it. I have my suspicions that it’s to do with Red, but I’ll keep my nose out unless I have to intervene.

“I didn’t think it was that obvious, Cill.” I mumble, taking a sip of champagne, my eyes continuing to focus on Jaine.

"You're skating on thin ice, brother." He warns.

"Why do you say that?"

"In case you've forgotten, our Padraig's in love with her. If he finds out you're drooling over the love of his life, there'll be hell to pay."

"A man can look, Cill."

"Aye, he can, but don't fucking try to touch her."

I nod. I'm aware she's in love with my brother and he her. But he's engaged, whereas I'm not. She check marks every box.

Every. Single. One.

We chat with other attendees, but all the while, I watch her. She flits from one person to the next, working the room and captivating the other guests with her smile and conversation. No swear words. She saves that potty-mouth just for me. I like that it's only me on the receiving end of that barbed tongue of hers.

"Look at her. She's got no shape whatsoever." Cara and Candice have moved on to scrutinize Jaine. They both must realize they pale in comparison. Everyone else in the room does.

JAINE

The asshole's been staring at me all night.

Eoin fucking O'Connell.

Probably because he wants me to do his introductions. I do the rounds with Cherry first. That's my priority. I've got my own business empire to run, and I need her to slide her shapely little legs under my desk, willing or otherwise, before I high-tail it back to California and safety.

It's a nice venue. A bit too pretentious for my biker blood, but my clients are wealthy. They want to be surrounded by the best money can buy, which is their prerogative. There are trillions of dollars in the room this evening. Billionaire city. Most of it earned illegally, hence why they employ me to stop them from paying an unscheduled visit to Rikers Island. My services don't come cheap, but it's a drop in the ocean when compared to each net worth.

I finally make eye contact with him. I only pray I have the fortitude to put up with his arrogant ass without wanting to shoot the fucker between those Irish eyes of his. I look at the gold-gilded clock. Vulgar and then some.

A bit like him.

Delaney, Sarah, and Laila are running late. I'm expecting them to arrive within the next half hour. Hopefully, that's enough time to deal with the eldest O'Connell before it all kicks off between Sarah and Cillian.

If they love each other, it will all sort itself out, I'm sure. I have zero qualms about either of them finding out who the other is. They're a match made in hell. In this life, that means they're perfect for each other.

I walk towards him, and I'm conscious that his eyes are drifting over every inch of me. He's looking at me like he wants to fuck me. Normally, I'd rejoice in that. If a man thinks of you with his leaking cock, it gives you the upper hand.

I don't want him looking at me like that, though. I don't like it. Maybe because I don't like him. And the fact that he's Irish's brother.

My eyes drift to Cillian, and he smiles. They then drift to the women standing with them. Their fuck buddies, for want of a better description. Both are extremely beautiful, I'll give them that. The blonde beside Cill must be Cara, the one who threatened Sarah. She's in for a goddamn rude awakening shortly.

The other? The dark-haired one? Eoin's bit of skirt, or at least one of them. He'll have a harem, the pompous prick.

They're whispering between themselves, sniggering. About me, no doubt. I learned a long time ago to ignore bitches.

"Eoin." I hold out my hand to him, but he ignores it and leans in to kiss me on both cheeks. His scent wraps around me, taking me back to the day when he fucked with my life. To when he took my Irish from me. I bite my tongue. I don't want to say anything negative in front of Cillian or these two women. I'll save my sarcasm and cussing for later.

"Jaine. You look beautiful."

I can tell he means it, and my cheeks immediately flood with warmth. I don't want to react to this goddamn fucker, but I can't seem to stop myself at his words.

"Thank you." I smile politely, then turn to look at his brother.

"It's good to see you again, Cillian." I shake his hand politely. "Would you introduce me to your partners, please?" I say partners, but we all know these ladies are not that, despite being desperate to be.

"This is Candice, my PA." Eoin undertakes the necessary introductions.

I take in the willowy brunette in the long cream silk dress. It's a bit too clingy and looks more like a nightdress, but who am I to judge if she wants the room to see her nipples?

"And this is Cara, a family friend."

Who's about to get her head kicked in by Paul Delaney's little sister.

I take in the blonde wearing a long black gown with her cleavage hanging over the top. Cillian's obviously a tits man. This woman will have learned long ago how to dress to impress the man she set her sights on.

"Candice, Cara. This is Jaine Jones."

They stare at me. I can see Candice's head whirring. She's trying to place me, remember where she's heard my name.

"Aren't you the one who had a thing with Padraig?"

I stare at her. My face reflects nothing, and definitely not the fact that I want to snap her scrawny neck for even mentioning his name.

"I'm not sure what you mean by *thing*, but Padraig is my ex-boyfriend, yes," I reply.

"You must have been so disappointed when his engagement to Sophia was announced. He really is quite the catch." She's trying to make me react, but it won't work.

"Not at all." I smile warmly. "I was one of the first to offer my congratulations to the happy couple, don't you recall, Eoin?" I look at him pointedly before smiling at Candice once more. "I'm sure they'll be very happy together."

I move straight on.

"Eoin, you had some people you wished to be introduced to?" I offer. "Unfortunately, Senator Bidewell has been delayed, but Leo informs me that we expect him to arrive shortly. Will it be just you, or am I to introduce all of your party? Your partner, perhaps?" I ask, my gaze focusing on his arm candy.

"Just me, Jaine."

Candice glowers at me as Eoin offers his arm for me to take. Not that I want to touch him, but it would be rude to refuse. Plus, it's almost like flicking the bird at her, and that bitch deserves it.

Suck it up, sweetheart.

CHAPTER TWENTY-NINE

JAINE

The Meeting Rooms, New York

"Rodolfo." My childhood friend greets me with a kiss on each cheek, and I smile warmly up at him. A very appealing exterior now shrouds the other ugly duckling from my youth. My male counterpart has tall, tanned, and handsome down to a fine art these days. He's still single. Probably making up for the barren school years when girls wouldn't look at him once, let alone twice.

I made him aware in advance that Eoin wanted an introduction, and he's more than happy to oblige. The Irish have only sold once in the past to La eMe and by all accounts, the Mexicans were pleased with the quality. An established alliance could be mutually beneficial, so it makes complete business sense. Provided they keep me out of their outlaw dealings, they can do as they goddamn please.

I speak to him in fluent Spanish, explaining that I'll come back to collect Eoin in around ten minutes. I can't spare any more time than that.

"I will ensure we have concluded matters by then, Jaine. Mr. O'Connell and I can always arrange to reconnect at a time and date to suit both parties."

I nod and turn my attention back to Eoin.

"Fluent in both Spanish and Italian?" He raises an eyebrow, obviously impressed.

"And French." I smile. Okay, maybe it's a little too smugly. "I have a wide client base. It pays to understand what people are saying, more so when they don't realize. I'm more than just a pretty face, you know. You really didn't do your homework where I'm concerned, did you?" I smirk, and he frowns.

He knows it's true. Never underestimate your allies or your enemies. In this game, they could be a friend one day, a foe the next. I reckon old Eoin only scraped the surface with me as I'm a female biker. He thought I was only ever destined to be someone's old lady.

No knowledge. No power. So, no threat. Little did he fucking know. Arrogant fool. My guess is he'll never make the same mistake again.

I stand to the side, taking five minutes to myself to watch couples dance. The music is mainstream but played in a classical way.

"How are you, Jaine?"

I don't need to turn around to know who the voice belongs to. A smirk crosses my face as I glance up at one of my favorite sparring partners.

"Well, if it isn't Detective Gabriel Prescott. It's good to see you, Gabe. I'm doing well." It's an evening for double kisses all around as he greets me in the same fashion, his hand skimming my ass at the same time. Same old Gabe. Copping a goddamn feel whenever he can and always up for close inspection of any available cleavage.

"You in New York on a flying visit?"

I nod. "Yes. I'm handing over my business reins for now to my colleague." I motion my head towards Cherry. "Be gentle with her, please."

"I'll do my best, Jaine. You'll be missed around NYPD. The place won't be the same without the angry echo of your stilettos." He exhales like my leaving is a huge inconvenience for him.

I snicker. "You're a shit liar, Gabe."

He shakes his head. "No. I mean it. In our game, we get used to the roles we play. It becomes a dance of mutual respect. The synergy gets disrupted when someone new gets introduced. You know that as well as I do."

He's right. If he left, I'd have to learn the ropes with someone else. Figure out new boundaries and test them. It's a long and arduous pull and push process. It's definitely better the devil you know.

"Jaine." I look up, and Eoin's looming over me. I know what the asshole wants. I never agreed to introduce him to Gabe, but it would be rude not to since he seems to have concluded his *business talk* with Rodolfo, and he's standing right beside us. He probably made his excuses the moment he saw me with Prescott. Everyone wants pigs on their side if they can get them. Life can be so much easier when they work with you rather than against you.

"Eoin, this is Detective Gabriel Prescott from NYPD. Gabe, this is Eoin O'Connell. I'm sure you've both heard of each other. Eoin is a… business acquaintance."

I realize I'm stretching it. I'm sure Gabe realizes it too. But I need to introduce the asshole as something. Not sure he'd appreciate being introduced as the bane of my goddamn life.

I nod at Gabe. "I'll leave you to it."

"Take care of yourself, Jaine, and don't stay away too long," Prescott shouts after me.

"I'll be back before you know it, Detective, and I'm sure you can't wait." I laugh as I walk away. I'm well aware both sets of eyes are trained on my ass as I leave them to talk. Again, I don't want to know what they're discussing. If I don't hear it, I'm not aware of it, and no one can call me out on it.

When they're done, I introduce Eoin to Leo, the billionaire holding the event. He's another client of old who approached me immediately after I started representing the Iron Scorpions. Like Delaney, I deal with *all* Leo's affairs, both legal and otherwise.

Another very eligible single man, Leo plays the field. A lot. I watch them as they chat. They could be brothers, although Eoin has the pale Celtic skin of the Irish to Leo's golden Italian tan, and Leo wears his black hair slightly too long.

Leo laughs exaggeratedly, and Eoin smirks and mumbles something in his ear. Both of them turn to stare at me. I smile politely. Eoin murmurs something else in Leo's ear and smirks again.

It'll be something borderline derogatory. Asshole.

When Lawrence Bidewell finally arrives with his wife Susan five minutes later, I make the final introduction. Lawrence is in his early fifties and is a decent politician as far as that lot go. He's destined for great things. Unlike some, his policies have always been realistic. Susan insists we meet for lunch before I head back to California, and I can hardly refuse. Something else I have to squeeze into an already packed schedule.

"You agreed to dance with me."

Introductions over, it's the final pre-agreed transaction.

"You're really going to make me go through with this?"

"If you want the trafficking debt written off." He raises an eyebrow at me.

Eoin leads me to the middle of the floor. I'm conscious we're being watched by the room, but more so by the lovely Candice.

"Your PA with benefits doesn't look too impressed." I place my hand on his shoulder, and his other clasps mine. It feels intimate. Way too intimate, especially when he snakes his arm around my waist and pulls my front against his.

He leans over and whispers in my ear. "That's because we contrast each other magnificently."

I laugh. "It's more likely because she sees herself as the future Ma Duster and she thinks I'm competition, which I'm most definitely not."

I look up, and his aquamarine eyes bore down into mine.

"Why are you looking at me like you want to fuck me, Eoin?"

"Because I do want to fuck you, Jaine." It's said matter of factly. There's no hesitation whatsoever.

"That's completely inappropriate," I mutter. I try to pull away, but his grip is vice-like.

"Don't create a scene. I'm only answering the question you asked."

"You could have lied."

"You could have chosen not to pose it in the first place. I'm sure there are a lot of men who look at you like they want to fuck you, Miss Jones."

Once the song ends, I excuse myself and leave the asshole standing in the middle of the dance floor.

SARAH

Jaine: *Where are you?*

Sarah: *We'll be there in ten minutes. I had to make a quick stop at the pharmacy—headache from hell.*

I'm lying. I'm late, and there's no time like the present for taking a pregnancy test. As soon as I suspected I might be. I needed to know. I have zero patience. Especially when it comes to life-changing fucking events.

Jaine: *I'll come and meet you at the entrance.*

I fidget with the split on my long green gown, my gaze shifting from Paul to Laila. I seldom dress up. Jeans or shorts all the way for me. My only girlie weakness is stiletto heels. The higher the better.

All the better for murdering assholes with.

The cage pulls to a standstill. My brother gets out on the sidewalk, then offers his hand to help us exit the black bullet-proof SUV. He looks handsome in his tux with his long hair tied back. On the outside, you'd never know he's a mass murderer with zero conscience over the countless lives he's ended. Then again, this evening, this place will be filled with ruthless killers, all impersonating bonafide businesspeople.

Laila looks good in a simple black cocktail dress with her hair straightened. She looks like a grown-up. Still pint-sized, but a certified adult all the same. Like me, she's wearing minimal make-up, and she's opted for contact lenses instead of spectacles.

My attention is caught by the woman standing at the door. I know straight away that it's Jaine Jones, based on Paul's description alone. Plus, she seems to emit an aura.

Don't fuck with me or else.

"Delaney."

He pulls her to him, and she smiles. Her expression is filled with love and tenderness. A lump forms in my throat at how my big brother *almost* had the woman of his dreams and the life he apparently desperately craves. Who knew he wanted to be a husband and a father?

I want all of that for him and more.

"Hey, baby," he replies, visibly breathing her in. His whole body relaxes when she's in his arms. It's like she's absorbing his pain and madness so he can see and think clearly, even if it's just a temporary respite.

It's so obvious he loves her, but it's not reciprocated as she tries to separate their bodies and put a more respectable distance between them. Jaine loves him, but not in the same way. I look at Laila, and she's staring at them, watching closely as my brother kisses Jaine on the forehead.

Jaine then turns to look at me.

"Sarah… or should I call you Red?" She smiles warmly, and I walk over and wrap my arms around her. I feel like I've known her my whole life. Sometimes you just know when you're meeting someone who's going to change your entire world. She's already changed it.

"It's so good to meet you finally, Jaine."

She squeezes me, then turns her attention to my friend. "And you must be Laila."

Laila's smile is half-hearted, so Jaine just holds out her hand, which Laila shakes.

I link arms with Jaine and watch as Paul offers his to Laila. She takes it before looking up at him.

"Shall we?" Jaine offers.

I nod. "Let's let everyone know Sarah Sanders Delaney is back in town."

Jaine squeezes my hand, and I look at her.

"I hope tonight works out for the best, Sarah." The words are so quietly spoken I'm not sure she meant to say them aloud.

I frown at her, but she gives nothing away.

CHAPTER THIRTY

SARAH

The Meeting Rooms, New York

INSIDE, I'm almost blinded by lights reflecting off crystal. This place is over the top and then some. It's like something from *Gone with The Wind* with its chandeliers and sweeping staircases. Apparently, it's the only place deemed worthy of Manhattan's royalty these days. Given that status, the owner must be raking it in. He can charge whatever the fuck he likes. Money is no object to these people. It's something they all have in droves.

I smooth my hands down my dress. It's not too fitted. It more graces my curves while discreetly emphasizing my cleavage. My hair is straight down my back. I look good. I know I do. My unique coloring is already attracting unwanted male attention. Then again, there are a lot of people who will want to see with their own eyes the living proof that Paul Delaney's little sister is back. My brother is a big fish in this relatively small pond.

"Jaine, I just need to visit the restroom."

She nods. "No worries. I'll quickly introduce Delaney to Leo."

Grabbing Laila's arm, I drag her with me. I need some moral support while I pee on a fucking stick.

"SARAH, I CAN'T BELIEVE YOU MIGHT BE PREGNANT."

I press my pointer finger to my lips to gesture for her to be quiet, but the restroom appears to be empty, thankfully.

"You and me both, but as I'm eating enough to feed a small village and my period's late, I guess I'd better rule it out."

Who knew the morning after pill could fail? Maybe I'm worrying about nothing. Hopefully I am. A single mom at twenty-eight to a man I don't even know. You couldn't make this shit up.

"But you don't even know who Ian is."

I roll my eyes at her blatantly obvious observation. "Tell me something I don't know."

"Will you tell him?"

"I don't know what the fuck I'll do. Let's just find out first, shall we?"

Deed done, we stand there and wait.

"It's been a minute, Sarah." She's in one of her stating the obvious moods.

"I know."

"Well?"

"I don't want to look."

"You have to."

"I know I fucking have to, Laila, but it doesn't mean I want to."

"Do you want me to look for you?"

"Yes. You look, and don't you dare mess around. You just say that shit how it is."

I watch as my little friend looks at the result.

“Well?”

“Oh my God, Sarah. You're pregnant.”

“Give me that.” I snatch the test out of her hand and stare at it. My blood runs cold. She’s right. It’s no fucking game.

Pregnant. Fuck me. If it’s from when the rubber broke, I must be around four weeks.

My brother will kill me. And him, if he ever finds out who he is.

I stare at my reflection in the full-length mirror, pulling my dress against my stomach. Of course, there’s nothing to see. It’ll be the size of a grain of rice or something stupid like that.

“Are you going to keep it?”

“Jesus Christ, Laila. I’m Catholic. I don’t have any choice. Anyway, we need to go. Jaine’s waiting for us.”

“Are you keeping the test result?” She stares at it in my hand like it’s about to explode. Then, when I lift it, she shrinks back like pregnancy’s contagious or something.

“Of course not.”

I roll my eyes, walk back into the stall, and put it in the trash can.

JAINE

I watch as Sarah leaves the restroom. She looks shell-shocked. Has something happened? I turn to look at Delaney, but he’s facing the other way and chatting with Leo and Cherry. I really don’t want to interrupt.

“Are you okay?” I look at her, and she smiles, but it’s clearly forced.

“Yeah, I’m fine.”

“You sure?”

“Yeah, I’ve just got a bit of a headache.”

"Do you want to leave? I can do the rounds with Delaney." I motion my head towards him.

"I'll be fine, Jaine," she snaps.

If it were anyone else, I'd have gladly torn them a new asshole for speaking to me like that, but I realize with Sarah that it's unintentional. Something's got her spooked, so I'm willing to make an exception. Over her shoulder, I see Cara leaving the restroom. Did she have a run-in with her while she was in there? The blonde bitch looks smug as fuck. Maybe I should abandon the introduction I had in mind for Sarah if she's not feeling up to it. Not sure when I'll get another opportunity to introduce her to Cillian O'Connell, though, as it's not often he frequents functions, plus I'm going to be back in California soon.

"There are some people I wanted you to meet, Sarah, but if you're not feeling up to it."

"Honestly, Jaine. I'm fine, and I'm sorry for snapping."

I switch my attention to her little friend. "You want to meet these people, Laila?"

She stares at me. She has to be all of five feet, and, Jesus Christ, she even radiates goddamn innocence if that's possible.

"Are they dangerous?"

"Extremely so."

"I think I'll wait with Paul."

SARAH

I look at Jaine. I'm sorry I had to lie to her, but I'm still coming to terms with the fact that I'm carrying Ian's baby. I'm not sure I'm ready to share that news nugget yet.

Jaine turns to escort me to whoever I need to meet, then she freezes. I look in the direction she's staring. There's an extremely handsome man on the stairs smiling down at her, his hand gracing the waist of a perfect-looking woman. She's petite, her long black hair hanging like silk down to her mid-back. Everything she wears, she wears well. Her mama no doubt taught her everything she knows.

Lucky her.

"Sophia," Jaine whispers to herself. I can feel the tension in her body, which surprises me as scum like us are good at hiding that sort of shit. My gut's telling me there's more to Jaine than meets the eye, and it's seldom wrong.

"Let's get this over with." Rather than avoid the couple, we walk in their direction. "For your information, Sarah, Luc is the current don of the Sicilian mafia. He's also a goddamn asshole. Sophia is his teenage sister."

"Luc. How are you?" She air kisses him on both cheeks, her off-kilter moment now well and truly hidden.

"Jaine, you look resplendent as usual, and despite all the kind words I say, still, you will not give me your number." The handsome Sicilian, who looks to be our age, is wagging a manicured finger at her. His hands look soft so he obviously doesn't roll his sleeves up and get them dirty. His black hair is slightly longer than the norm and is tied back at the nape of his neck. He's wearing perfectly trimmed designer stubble on a face that could easily grace the cover of any magazine. Jaine smiles at him politely but doesn't respond.

"Sophia, it's been a long time." She moves her attention to the young woman who looks her up and down like she's competition.

"Jaine, it's nice to meet you again. I'm so sorry for stealing Padraig from you. I hope there are no hard feelings." Her voice is smug.

Who the fuck is Padraig? Will someone please tell me what the fuck is going on?

"None whatsoever. I'm aware that arranged marriages are

common, I fully understand that. I only hope Padraig grows to love you as much as he did me."

The young girl glowers at her, and her brother doesn't look very pleased with the remark either. Jaine just smiles saccharinely sweetly at them both.

"Anyway, where are my manners? Sarah, this is Luciano and Sophia Ruocco. Luc, Sophia, this is Sarah Delaney, Paul's younger sister."

The Sicilian stares at me like I'm a piece of meat, and I instantly want to club him with my shoe. Realizing that, Jaine quickly interrupts.

"If you'll excuse us. I have someone Sarah actually does need to meet." A snub and then some. Middle finger duly flicked, we walk away.

"Asshole." We both whisper it at the same time and immediately start to giggle. Unfortunately, Jaine's amusement soon fades.

"Sarah, listen, what I'm about to do, I'm doing for all the right reasons. Just remember that."

I nod, intrigued.

We cross the floor, and that's when I see who I know to be two of the O'Connell brothers. The Irish mobsters. And what a fine-looking pair they are. The images online don't do them anywhere near enough justice. The older, dark-haired one is staring at Jaine like he wants to eat her alive, regurgitate her, then do it all over again. Man, oh man, is he handsome. Tall and perfectly formed, with an air of power and destruction emanating from him so tangible you can feel it flood the room. I guess the rumors are true about these bad boys. My eyes flick to the other. The redhead. He's slightly shorter and much leaner than his brother. Auburn hair glints under the lights, and green eyes sparkle on a angular face that's caressed with just the right amount of facial hair. I feel myself getting wet, which is never good when you're not wearing panties, but I do love me a redhead, and this guy does not disappoint. He's probably the best-looking example of one I have ever seen in my life.

My eyes connect with his, and I feel like I've come home. Do I know him? I don't think we've ever met. He's looking at me like he's seen a ghost.

We stand in front of them, and I find myself wondering why they're here without lady friends. They're way too good-looking to be short of female company. I'm sure they could have their choice of any woman in Manhattan.

Unlike me. Who's going to want a twenty-eight-year-old pregnant woman who doesn't even know who the father of her child is?

I find myself stealing glances at him. My cheeks redden when, time after time, he catches me doing so. Fucking great.

"Sarah, I'd like you to meet Eoin and Cillian O'Connell."

Jaine's staring at Cillian.

"Cillian, I'd like you to meet Sarah Delaney, Paul Delaney's baby sister."

He jerks his head up. He looks shocked, and then the hint of a smile makes his mouth curve upwards.

Is there some sort of private joke going on?

"It's nice to meet you, Sarah." Eoin's voice is deep, dark, and dangerous, perfectly matching his demeanor. He shakes my hand professionally, then looks between his brother and me. Cillian smiles at me, then grips my arms and kisses me on both cheeks. The familiar scent of peppermint, cigarettes, and woodsy cologne immediately envelopes me.

Cillian.

Ian.

I fucking get it.

My Irishman?

The man from my dreams?

My baby daddy?

I walk backward. Scratch that, I stumble back, almost falling on my ass. I must look like a rabbit that's been caught in the headlights as my gaze flicks from Ian to Jaine. She smiles. So, Jaine planned this. I don't know whether to feel pleased or fucked off.

So what if I'm allowed to see him in the flesh? It means nothing, right? He said even if I saw him, we have no future. I stare at him. He stares at me. I can't breathe. I can't speak. But I so want him to speak. I want to hear that beautiful Irish lilt of his. I want to hear his words so I can be sure that it's really him.

He smirks. I'm sure I've heard that smirk. I know I've felt those green eyes of his laughing at me before now. My gaze drops to his mouth. My mind goes over all the places it's been on my body. All the magical things that tongue of his can do. As if on command, he licks his lips, and I see the piercing. That beautiful, incredible piercing. And his hair, red, vibrant, and thick. How many times have I fisted it in my hands as he's fucked me into oblivion?

My eyes drop to connect with his. They've darkened. It's like he can read my mind. He knows where my thoughts are going.

Maybe we can have a future. Why else would Jaine go out of her way to introduce us? Maybe being Paul's sister means I'm a match. That I'm enough of a fuck-up to survive in his Duster world.

I hear giggling. My head swings around in its direction, and then I see her. The blonde. Her tits are hanging over the top of her dress. My gaze drops to her hand, and I take in the absent diamond rock. Was he telling me the truth? Just because she's not wearing it doesn't mean they're not engaged. I mean, he's brought her to this event, hasn't he?

"What's she doing here?" The blonde scowls at me, wrapping her arms around him. My Ian. The man I now know to be Cillian O'Connell, the second eldest son in the Irish mob ranks. He doesn't stop her. That pisses me off.

"I have a name, bitch," I hiss at her. My fists clench at my sides.

The dark-haired woman stares down her nose at me, then at Jaine.

"Let me handle this, Cara." She puts her hand on the blonde's arm and smiles politely before switching her gaze back to me. "My, my, Jaine. Some would surely question the friends you keep. Do you find them in the gutter? This one has a mouth on her that, quite frankly, belongs there."

I rock on my feet, ready to hurl myself at her.

"Now is not the time, Sarah," Jaine whispers. She grips my blade hand and squeezes, calming me down like she does my brother.

"Not at all. Candice, is it? I'm struggling to remember your name. Most of the people in this room are business acquaintances and friends of mine. Some of us aspire to be more than PAs with benefits, so I tend to mix in circles higher than most. I'm sure my contacts would love to hear your remark that they belong in the gutter with Sarah Delaney. Sarah's the younger sister of Paul Delaney, who I'm sure both of you will have heard of in your socialite circles as being Manhattan's most eligible bachelor. Present company excluded, of course."

Jaine looks between Cillian and Eoin. Eoin's blatantly admiring her. Candice is glowering at her as a result. Jaine's aware of his attention, but she's clearly not interested. Something's going on there, and I need to know what it is. Cillian doesn't make eye contact with her. He's just staring at me.

Watching. Waiting. For what?

The trouble is, I have no idea how to react or what the fuck to do. I suddenly want the reassurance of my blindfold so I don't feel so exposed. I look at the blonde and venom burns my veins.

I do know one thing I'm going to do. I walk over to Cara. I

remove her hands from Cillian as I stare at him, daring him to say something.

"I don't know where we go from here, but while I figure shit out, I don't want any other woman's hands on you. Am I making myself clear enough about that, Cillian O'Connell? If I see anyone touching you or you touching them, you'll both answer to my blade."

He smiles at me. I've got a feeling he likes my threat and my possessive tone. He likes the fact that I'm staking my claim on him. I can feel the dormant energy fire up between us, and I almost growl out loud. I'm so fucking wet. He'll know that. My hands are itching again, but to touch him this time, not for any other reason. They want to be unleashed on that hot Irish body of his.

But he's not having me that easily. I refuse to simply cave in. This time, it's on my terms. If he wants me, he can do the chasing.

I spin around and walk off.

"Red." It's a warning.

I smirk. I know he's following me.

CHAPTER THIRTY-ONE

CILLIAN

The Meeting Rooms, New York

Fuck. She marches off pretty much like she did the first night I met her, her hair trailing behind her like fucking Medusa. Now? I can clearly see the perfection in front of my eyes. She's mine. No one else's. Like she laid claim on me, I'll lay claim on her in every way. Before the week is out, she'll be my bride.

Fuck the Dusters. Fuck Razr.

I want my seed in her. Her carrying my offspring. I want that right now. More than anything. I want that rebellious mouth of hers screaming my name every time I fuck her into oblivion. Then I want to shut her the fuck up by ramming my dick down her throat and filling her with my cum at both ends. She's my perfect match. No one else will ever touch her again. My blood pounds in my brain possessively at the very thought of any other fucker going anywhere near her. My eyes trail up and down her retreating figure as she storms across the room.

From now on, every minute of every day, we'll be together, even if I have to tie her the fuck down.

She enters the ladies' restroom. I follow her in and immediately switch the light off. We're plunged into darkness. Familiarity. Reassurance. She needs it. I know she does. I can feel the energy palpitate between us.

"Red."

"I'm not called Red."

"I'm not called Ian."

The room pulses. I can hear her subtle movements, smell her scent, almost smell her arousal, for fuck's sake.

"I never cheated on you," I whisper.

"You can't cheat on someone if you're not together."

"You laid claim on me and we're not together."

"I won't have you make a fool of me."

"It was never my intention."

"She fucking threatened me."

"She did, but I was never with her. My parents want me married."

"So, you're going to marry her?"

"I never said that."

I walk across. Her body is calling out for mine. I can feel the invisible connection.

"Red?" I snake my arms around her waist, and she lifts her head so our breaths can mingle. She breathes out. I breathe in, capturing her in my lungs.

"Cillian." She says my name, and I swear to God the sound of it leaving her lips is the best single thing I have ever heard in my entire fucking life. Better than a choir of angels. I only need one. This fallen one.

"Sarah," I whisper.

Her lips cover mine, and her tongue forces itself into my mouth. I growl as my hands fist her hair, then I eat her alive.

Mine. Mine. Fucking. Mine.

She tastes of apples. Still, on the healthy living regime, I take it. Well, now she's just signed a deal with Lucifer himself, so it's time to get off that fucking roundabout.

My tongue strokes deep into her mouth, claiming every fucking inch of her. She groans against my lips, and the sound that leaves me in response is barely human. I want to fuck her into next week. Right here. Right now.

But first, I need to ask for her hand from her bloodthirsty fucking brother.

I hold her close but I keep my hands respectable. She'll be my bride. We'll wait until our wedding night before we take things any further now. Everything needs to be proper. I need to show respect to the woman who's going to be my wife and the mother of my children. We'll have all the time in the world to fuck. The rest of our lives.

"Fuck me, Cillian."

"No." I laugh against her mouth.

Like the hothead she is, she pushes me away so hard I bang into the wall. She's taken that as a rejection. Like I don't want her.

The door opens.

"Get out." I hiss at the intruder. Now is not the fucking time.

"I need to speak to you, Cill." It's Cara.

"Not now."

"It's important."

I run my hands through my hair. "What the fuck can be that important that you have to follow me in here? Can't you see I'm busy?"

"I'm pregnant. I found out tonight. I just needed you to know. I've already told Roisin."

"You did fucking what?"

"I told your ma."

The door opens, and light filters in briefly, then it closes.

This time, I know it's Red who's left.

She knows what this means.

We both do.

CHAPTER THIRTY-TWO

SARAH

The Meeting Rooms, New York

FUCKING Irish mobster Duster lying asshole.

I can raise a baby on my own. How difficult can it be? Feed them, change diapers—nothing to it.

I don't need you. Fuck. You.

After storming out of the restroom, I straighten my dress, then immediately search for Jaine. There's no point trying to find Laila. She'll be following Paul around like a little lost puppy, plus she'll just look at me all disapprovingly with her hands on her hips while wearing her, *I told you so. It serves you right for being promiscuous* face. It really doesn't help. The damage is already done.

I need to speak to someone who can give me advice. Someone who'll be understanding about my predicament. Someone who won't be judgmental.

I can't get enough oxygen into my body. I'm about to start

hyperventilating. I feel like I'm going to pass out. How can a shitty situation go from bad to worse? Because it's my life, that's why. If shit's going to happen to anyone, that crap's going to stick to me.

I want to cut that bitch Cara so bad. Slice the smirk off that smug face of hers because she's won. And her timing was fucking perfect.

My blade hand is twitching, and I'm contemplating cutting her when I slam into a huge human wall, causing me to look up.

Do I look shocked? I must look shocked. What are the fucking chances?

It's him. The nameless smoking hot guy. He's still nameless. Still smoking hot. Even hotter in his tuxedo.

My shitty situation has just taken a turn for the worse. This night is not going to end well.

His face floods with recognition, then he grabs my wrist. "Ah. If it isn't my little American friend. We meet again." So much for not speaking English. Lying bastard. His musky cologne envelopes me like it did in that dingy little bar in Mexico City.

"Fuck off, you trafficking asshole. I'm going to turn you over to the pigs. This place is teeming with the fuckers," I seethe.

I try to walk away, but his vice-like grip tightens. "Not so fast. Rumor has it you're the one responsible for costing me the best part of a million dollars. We should take this outside. I think we should discuss how you're going to repay me, don't you?" he hisses, spraying saliva over my face.

Ugh. How could I ever have thought he was hot? I wipe it off with the back of my other hand.

"I'm going nowhere with you, asshole."

"Outside." He bends my wrist back so far it almost fucking snaps.

"I'll scream the place down."

"I'll cut you before you can even make a sound." It's then I feel the blade against my side. This asshole means business. I'm fucked if I scream and fucked if I don't.

I weigh up my options. If I go quietly, at least I'll still have an opportunity to run later. I can't run if I'm dead with a knife jutting from between my ribs.

Plus, it's not just me anymore. I rub my hand discretely over my stomach. There's two of us now, and I'm all this little one's got since their daddy is a prize asshole who can't keep his dick in his pants.

I stop struggling and go quietly, letting my Colombian buddy lead me outside and praying that someone sees us leave.

"Bring the car around." He's on the phone to someone. It can't be Mario as that fucker's swimming with the fishes at the bottom of the Hudson, courtesy of Cillian O'Connell.

Tears prick my eyes. His fiancée is pregnant. His family knows. They'll be married quicker than you can say Jack fucking Robinson, meanwhile, I'll be the one left holding the *other* baby. The one born outside of wedlock. The child that will always be on the outside looking in. Never quite belonging or fitting anywhere.

The bastard.

If I get out of this situation alive, which I have every fucking intention of doing, no one is hurting my baby.

Not now. Not ever.

We stand on the stairway in front of the building. I guess we look just like any other young couple stepping outside to take in the night air. I don't even know what time it is. Ten p.m., maybe? There's a clear sky, so the temperature's frigid.

"Sarah?"

I jerk my head up. It's Jaine. She walks slowly towards us, staring at my nameless friend.

"Who the fuck are you, asshole? You take your goddamn hands off her." She points at where he's gripping my wrist.

"You step any closer and I'll stick her with this knife." He warns quietly.

She stops when she sees the moonlight glinting off the piece of shiny metal. "What do you want with her?"

"She owes me."

"For what?"

"She cost me just under a million bucks. It's payback time."

"Are you the trafficker?"

"If I answer that, pretty lady, then you're going to have to come along for the ride."

"I asked you if you're the goddamn trafficker." She hisses right in his face like she has some sort of death wish.

"You could say that."

She smirks at him. I can almost feel the venom spike in her veins. "Then count me in, you filthy piece of scum."

"Jaine, what the fuck are you doing? Get back inside." On the one hand, I want her to save herself, but on the other, I want her to come with me.

Not that I'd ever admit it to anyone, but I'm scared. I feel out of my depth, more so after the night I've just had.

She laughs. "It's way too late for that now, Sarah. Plus, how much of a friend would I be if I let you go on this magical mystery tour all on your lonesome? No, babe. Count me in."

A black SUV appears, and we're bundled inside, our hands quickly tied behind our backs.

"Take them to the holding area." My nameless friend instructs the driver before getting in.

Shit. That sounds temporary. Where to after that?

I doubt it's fucking Disneyland.

The cage takes off. The Colombian sits in the front, talking on the phone.

"So, this guy is the scum who picked you up in Mexico?"

"Yeah, the guy who drugged us. Listen, I'm sorry for dragging you into this shit."

"Don't worry about it, Sarah. This isn't my first rodeo. I appear to have a *please abduct me* sign on my forehead. Anyway, let's keep our conversation quiet for now."

I guess that means we sit in silence. Makes sense. They're no doubt listening to every fucking word.

CHAPTER THIRTY-THREE

SARAH

Unknown Location

The vehicle comes to a standstill.

My Colombian buddy yanks me from the cage while the driver escorts Jaine. We're not blindfolded or anything. I guess that means we're not expected to leave this place alive. Dead people can't talk. Well, I didn't survive the first time around to die now.

"Watch where you're putting your feet, asshole."

I turn to see what the drama is, and the goon who was driving has trodden on Jaine's gown. It was floor length. Now, it's in tatters and ripped right up to mid-thigh.

We're ushered inside a rusty tin-roofed warehouse. On the surface, it appears to be abandoned as the windows are smashed and boarded up. There's no sign of life or movement of any kind. I have no idea where we are. We were driving for around an hour, so we could be anywhere within a sixty-mile radius of Manhattan. How the hell is anyone supposed to find us, let alone rescue us?

That means we'll just have to save ourselves.

After being led down several corridors, we're eventually shoved into a sparsely furnished room. There's a filth-covered toilet and two foldable beds. The mattresses leave a lot to be desired. The marks they bear look like the dried stains of the fluids representing the end of someone's life. Several lives, in fact. We'll be sleeping on the floor, then. That's if we get to sleep at all.

"Can you untie us?"

"Sorry, blondie. I can't do that," my nameless friend replies to Jaine.

"Why not? What are two women going to do? It's not like we can escape."

He nods in my direction. "Your ginger friend can't be trusted."

"Hey! Strawberry blonde, asshole."

Jaine nods at her bindings. "So, untie me and leave her."

"And you won't remove hers as soon as we're gone?"

"What if we need to use the bathroom?"

"I'm sure you can figure something out."

They leave, and we're still bound. I perch my ass on the side of one of the beds while Jaine paces the floor.

"Well, this is cozy."

Jaine finally sits on the other. She doesn't seem fazed that it's covered in stains. I guess when you're facing certain death, stuff like that is the least of your worries.

"We need to get these bindings off." She mutters.

"No shit. Tell me something I don't already know."

She swears almost silently then pauses before she speaks. "Your smart mouth's going to land you in trouble one of these days, Sarah."

She's right. I know she is. One day, my inability to keep my mouth closed will likely get me or someone else killed.

I stare at the bland room with its easy-to-hose-down grey concrete floor and walls. The paint on the back of the off-white door is scratched, probably as some poor fucker has tried to claw their way out.

We sit there—I don't know for how long—just looking around. Both of us searching for any potential murder weapons since they've taken our shoes.

I decide we need something to pass the time.

"Conversation. That's what we need."

"Are you for real?"

I ignore her lack of enthusiasm and carry on regardless. It's not like we've got anything better to do.

"So, tell me about you. Tell me about Jaine Jones. The love of my big brother's life."

I watch as she feels over the metal edges of the bed. She pauses, running her fingertips up and down a particular section. She then sits down and begins to drag her bindings over and over what must be a rough spot. Given the thickness of the rope, it will take a lifetime for it to cut through, but we're not going anywhere any time soon. And it's not like there are any other options available to us.

"What do you want to know?"

"Whatever you want to tell me." I shrug.

"Well, before I start spilling my guts like this is the last supper but without the goddamn meal, this conversation goes no further. Not even Laila. Not even Delaney. Understood?"

"Understood."

She starts talking. About her past, about Ace, and I lie back on the stained mattress, and I listen.

"So, you have no siblings or anything like that?"

"None that I'm aware of."

"Who's Padraig? The dark-haired girl at the function this evening mentioned him. She said she hoped there were no hard feelings."

"Maybe you should have been the lawyer and not me, Sarah."

Her tone has changed. Regret. Annoyance. Frustration. There's a whole bag of emotions in there rolled into one.

"Anyway, enough about me. It's your turn."

I watch as she continues to run her bindings methodically over the section of bed and I tell her my own story. Not that there's much to tell.

"I left New York and traveled around before settling in La Paz, Bolivia. I worked in a little village hospital, learning how to stop people from dying from preventable deaths like bleeding out. I decided I wanted to make a career of it and study medicine. Laila and I were heading back when we got picked up by traffickers. You know—the nameless smoking hot guy. You know the rest."

She nods, straightening her legs out in front of her. She grimaces as the movement causes her to pull on the bindings. Given the friction she has to create, they must be cutting into her wrists. I guess it's best we keep talking to take her mind off it. Her getting those off might be the only chance we've got of getting out of here alive.

"So, Padraig."

"Fuck me." She rolls her eyes.

I give her a minute. She's probably hoping I'll change the subject. I don't.

With an exaggerated exhale she starts talking. "Padraig O'Connell is the son of Fergal and Roisin O'Connell, the matriarch and patriarch of The Hudson Dusters in New York."

"So, he's Cillian's brother?"

"Yes. The youngest of the four."

She sighs. It's clear she'd rather not expand further, so she doesn't go on.

"Hey, we might never get out of here alive, so I'd like to know."

She reluctantly starts to talk further. About how they met. About him cheating on her.

"So, while me, Ace, and Irish were being held by the Bratva, his family entered him into an arranged marriage with Sophia Ruocco. The dark-haired girl from tonight. Signed in blood, apparently. No way out of it."

"You wanted to marry him. You love him?"

She shrugs. "I love Irish and Ace. I wanted them both. But the decision was taken out of my hands. Eoin said if Irish thought there was a chance with me, he wouldn't go through with the wedding, so I left New York not long after."

"Why did you need to leave, though?"

"To distance myself from Irish. To be with Ace. His life is in California. Aside from JAL, there was nothing keeping me in Manhattan, so I went home."

That's not the only reason. I can sense she's holding something back. I want to know what the fuck that something is.

"Stop that brain of yours whirring now, Sarah. That's all you're getting. There are things it's safer for you not to know about me."

We sit quietly for a while. I have no idea how long. Minutes. Hours. The only sound is the relentless scratching of the bindings against the bed.

"Paul will be tearing apart Manhattan looking for us." I break the silence.

"Yup."

"Why did you set Cillian and me up like that tonight?"

"Honestly? I could tell your feelings for each other ran deep, so I agreed with Dylan that I would try to get you face to face. I didn't want either of you to have any regrets, and if Cillian doesn't find a suitable alternative within three months, his engagement to Cara is going to be announced."

Tears prick my eyes as I think back on what took place earlier this evening. Just when things looked like they'd all map out, shit happens. Story of my fucking life.

"It's going to be announced anyway," I say with a sigh. "Cara's pregnant."

For the first time this evening, she stops her rubbing.

"You're shitting me?"

I shake my head. "Nope. She came into the restroom and smugly announced it. I was on my way to tell you when I bumped into our Colombian friend."

"Sarah, I'm so sorry. I know you like him."

I don't reply. What's there to say? No point denying it, as it was obvious to everyone around us this evening just how much.

"If it helps, he likes you too. Enough to ask you to take the vows with him, hence my intervention."

I laugh. "Only to escape a lifetime with her."

She shakes her head. "No. I have a feeling even if she wasn't in the picture, it wouldn't have been long before you would have been Mrs. Cillian O'Connell. These Irishman are extremely possessive. When they fix their sights on who and what they want, they refuse to let go."

"The reason you had to leave New York."

"Exactly." She snickers, then starts rubbing her bindings again.

"You do know that the eldest O'Connell has set his sights on you too, don't you?"

She grimaces. "Yes, I realize that. He made me end things with his brother, and then he tried to make a move on me himself. That's the type of selfish asshole he is. It's not about love or family for him. It's all about power and being more successful than his peers."

"So, you'd never consider him?"

"I'd rather shoot myself in the head. Anyway, I'm with Ace."

"I need to meet him."

"Yup, you do. He's not as outgoing as Irish. Ace's soul runs deep."

"You love him?"

"Left my hometown for ten years because I couldn't bear the thought of seeing him with someone else. That's how much I love him."

"Maybe things worked out for the best, then."

"Maybe."

"I guess Eoin was only doing what he was tasked to do by his daddy."

"Most likely. But he showed no remorse. He got rid of me like he was taking out the trash and broke his brother and me into pieces in the process. Shit like that is unforgivable."

I nod. She has a point. There's a right and a wrong way of doing things, and I guess Eoin went about it all the latter. I think this is more than just power for him now, though. He looks at Jaine the way Cillian looks at me. Like he wants to eat her alive. She's right. They are possessive. It's like they'd kill another man for even daring to glance at us.

It's hot as fuck to be wanted that much.

Or at least, it was. Now, Cara's pregnant. It's game over. Even if I announce my news, she's already been chosen in advance as the perfect match by the family. They may even try to take my baby away from me, so it's best I keep quiet about my condition.

I lie on my side on the smelly old mattress, and I drift off while Jaine continues her relentless quest against her bindings.

CHAPTER THIRTY-FOUR

CILLIAN

The Meeting Rooms, New York

I KNOW murderous bastards like me don't deserve anything good in life. We're not entitled to any happiness for all the atrocities we commit. For all the pain and suffering we inflict on others, whether deserved or not. But to be handed the love of my life only to have her whipped out from under my nose and replaced with Cara. The Almighty really does have it in for me.

Here's your penance, son—purgatory on Earth for the rest of your days.

Cara and I haven't slept together in weeks. Since way before Red. How is she only finding out she's fucking pregnant now?

We've always been extremely careful. There's never been a burst rubber like there was with Sarah.

My ma has tried to call me, but I've ignored her. I'll deal with the fallout tomorrow. I haven't got it in me to listen to her explain what I already know. That I've made my bed and I must lie in it. With Cara. For the rest of my fucking life.

For now, I just want to lick my wounds in peace.

"Cill, what's going on?"

"Tell me what you've managed to work out so far, Eoin."

"That you've been fucking Paul Delaney's sister. That you're in love with Paul Delaney's sister. You looked happy one minute, and now you look miserable as sin."

I look at him. The future Irish fucking king. See, shit like this would never happen to him. God's too scared of Eoin O'Connell to ever piss on his parade.

"Cara's pregnant."

"Shite."

"Exactly."

"And now you'll have to take the vows with her. Meanwhile, the beautiful Red will be off bending the ear of her big murderous older brother, telling him how you've fucked her over and broken her biker heart. Twice."

"You're not helping the situation, Eoin."

"Just saying it how it is. So, what's next?"

"Well, for now, I'm just trying to avoid Ma's calls while I get my head around it."

"Sensible. Where's Red?"

"I've not seen her since she left the restroom. Probably discussing with Razr how many pieces to dice me into before they feed me to the fucking fishes."

"Maybe she's with Jaine. I haven't seen her since around then either."

"That was over an hour ago."

The hairs on my neck immediately stand on end. My gut's telling me something's going down, and it's seldom wrong.

"Something's not right, Eoin. I can feel that shite in my bones."

He nods. Maybe he's experiencing the same premonition.

"Listen, we tell Paul Delaney we can't find Jaine. That maybe Red's with her. You don't mention what's going on between you and his baby sister. We'll deal with that shitshow after we find them."

"What if we don't?"

"We will, Cill. I've got a feeling Jaine Jones knows exactly how to look after herself, and I've got a feeling your Red's not too far behind her in the survival stakes given how she handled the trafficking situation."

"WHAT THE FUCK DO YOU MEAN JAINE'S MISSING? AND WHERE THE hell is my goddamn sister?"

We're in the male restroom with Paul Delaney. His blade's in his hand, and he's flicking it back and forth.

"We haven't seen them for over an hour. They may be around somewhere, but it's not like Jaine to disappear. We just thought we should make you aware," Eoin replies.

"It's like my sister to disappear, though. That's what you're saying. Because she disappeared for years. Are you suggesting this is somehow my fault?" The madman raises himself to his full height and is now right in our Eoin's face. They'd both best tread carefully. Things might not end well for Manhattan if two of the most evil bastards in the city come to blows.

I put a hand between them. "Razr, Eoin. No one's saying anything about anyone. We need to find them. Let's focus on that."

It's me that'll be coming to blows with Razr when he finds out I've been fucking his baby sister behind his back, and to rub salt in his wounds, I can't even make an honest woman out of her. I now have to wed someone else. I rub my hand across my neck, grateful it's still intact, at least for now.

They stare at each other, neither wanting to break eye contact first. They'll be pissing up the wall next. This will not do well for business.

"Lads." They both turn to look at me. "If you want to take each other on, that's fine, but do it after we've found the girls."

Razr turns and punches the over-sink mirror. It shatters. His knuckles immediately start pissing blood all over the expensive white restroom finish. I pass him a hand towel but say nothing.

The two people he loves most in the world may have been taken. If they have then fuck knows by who, and fuck knows to where. He's only just got his sister back. I fully understand his frustration.

I also know next time he punches something, it'll be my fucking face.

He takes a small phone out of his inside pocket. It's plain. Black. Nothing fancy. Clearly a burner.

"Sarah carries a burner on her?" I look at him.

He shakes his head. "Jaine."

"Why?"

"That's none of your goddamn business."

I know when it's time to shut my mouth and stop asking questions, and that's right about now. I may be a Duster, but even I'm not brave enough to poke a fucking Razr bear.

CHAPTER THIRTY-FIVE

JAINE

Unknown Location

MY WRISTS ARE KILLING ME, and I know they'll be red raw. I hiss in pain as I adjust my angle briefly. Slowly but surely, the rope is thinning.

Just not quickly enough.

I know we're running out of time. I've pretty much told Sarah my entire life story to take her mind off our predicament. While she's a ballsy little fucker with that mouth of hers, she's not well-rounded with experience when it comes to *the life*. Based on the conditions we're being kept in, the lack of food, water, and hygiene, I know our Colombian friends don't intend to keep us around for very long. They won't traffick us as we're way too recognizable, so that means we're destined to be killed, and my guess is it will happen before morning. To keep us alive beyond means they'll have to start looking after us like human pets. They won't. They may not know who our ties are, but they know who the attendees were at tonight's function. Each one a high ranker and heavily involved in the outlaw life. They need to get rid of the evidence and fast.

I need to get us out of here alive. I have a life growing in my belly, and I'll be damned if he or she is never going to get the chance to take their first breath. It may be a shit existence in a shit world, but it's life all the same, and they deserve their chance at it, the same as the rest of us.

I bite back the pain and increase my efforts.

Whether they're an MC baby or a Duster, they have a life mapped out. A future. A ready-made family. It's my job to get them to their starting point, and that I will fucking do. Same with Sarah. Delaney's already a broken man. What would it do to him if anything happened to his baby sister? It doesn't bear thinking about. His demon would eat him alive from the inside out. I can't allow that to happen.

I grit my teeth and speed up my movements. Scarred wrists? Better than being dead.

I pray that Sarah stays asleep. She's digging way too much, and I don't want to be giving any more answers than I already have.

She stirs not long later. Beads of sweat lace my forehead. I feel nauseous. I want to lie on the bed and sleep, but I can't because time is running out.

Tick fucking tock.

"How long have I been out?" Sarah yawns and then attempts to stretch, frowning when she remembers her hands are bound. She doesn't wait for any response. "You almost freed yet?" She motions her head towards my hands.

"I hope so, Sarah."

I'd ask her to pray, but that might cause her to panic. So, I do it. Silently. I pray to the Father, the Son, and the Holy goddamn Spirit that we make it out of this shitshow alive. If he can't forgive me for my worldly sins, he surely can at least show mercy to the innocent life I'm carrying inside me.

Footsteps. Can I hear footsteps? Shit. If they've brought food, we could be safe, for now at least. But, if their hands are empty, then it's game over.

I tug at my bindings, but they still hold fast.

Fuck. Is this it? Tears prick my eyes.

Fucking hormones.

Ace. Irish. I love them both so much.

My unborn baby. Are they destined never to take their first breath in this godforsaken world?

Sarah can sense my panic now, and she starts to yank at her own bindings.

"Jaine, you're scaring me," she whimpers, her eyes huge on her face.

I've let her down. Let Delaney down. This will destroy him. He'll never fucking survive it.

I look at her, my face full of regret.

"Jaine, we need to get out of here. I'm pregnant."

I stare at her. Hear the words coming from her lips—the huge admission.

"That makes two of us," I whisper.

There could be two Hudson Duster babies in this room. Our babies could be cousins. Not that Sarah will know that. She'll surely assume the baby in my belly is Ace's.

I stare at her. This is not over until the fat lady sings, and I'm not hearing any soprano vocals quite yet. I can't rub my bindings any more as it will only draw attention to what I've been doing.

The door opens. It's the driver. I look at his hands, and he's wearing gloves. I swallow. This really is it. He's come to get dispose of the walking talking evidence. I wonder why the other guy isn't doing the honors. He probably doesn't want to get his hands dirty. Or maybe it's because we're women.

It takes a special sort to murder a woman in cold blood, even in this life.

He walks towards Sarah, and she shuffles backward on the bed away from him. What's the point? It's just delaying the inevitable. In a room that can barely hold two foldable beds and a shit-filled toilet, there's nowhere to run or hide.

"Jaine." She sobs, her gaze dropping to his hands as he pulls up his black leather gloves. Killer gloves. How many lives has he ended while wearing those? Tears of fear roll down her cheeks as she stares up at him. Both of us have been through so much in our twenty-eight years, and it's going to end here? Now? Today? In a room where the walls still hold on to the screams of those murdered before us. We're just another two in a long line. Quickly silenced, our souls then handed over to Lucifer himself.

He's looming over Sarah now. His hands are reaching out. He's a silent killer. No words. He's focused on one thing, and that's strangling the life out of her. Then me.

She stares up at him and shakes her head. One final silent plea. Trying to appeal to his better nature. To reach his humane side. There is none. He doesn't have one. This is all in a day's work for him. Like me when I take out the trash. At least my victims are deserved. Then again, maybe we are too. We've both taken a life. An eye for an eye and all that.

He wraps his hands around her throat. My thought drifts to the baby in my belly. I'm over twenty weeks now. I finally have a tiny, rounded tummy. I want to touch it. Can they sense what's about to happen? To me? To them? I want to comfort him or her. Let them know everything will be okay. That I'll always be with them in this life and the next.

Together always.

Then I think of my beautiful boy. My Ace. We lost so many years. So much wasted time. Does he know how much I love him? Yes. Finally, he does. I show him or tell him every day. As often as I can.

And then I think of my Irish, and a single tear spills. He thinks I don't love him. That I never have. But I do. I love him so fucking much. My heart beats in time with his, and I miss him.

Oh, God, how I miss my fucking Irish.

I need him to know that. That I love him. One day, I need to be able to rewind what I said. Take it all back. I need to be able to tell him how much I care. Always have. Always will. I'm not sure it's even possible to put unquantifiable shit like that into words. But I need the chance to try.

Adrenaline spikes through me. I watch as the fucker throttles Sarah Delaney. She can't even fight back with her bound hands.

With every ounce of strength and determination in my body, I pull against the bindings. I can feel them rip and tear at my flesh. I can feel the blood running down my wrists. My lifeblood. It keeps me alive, and it's pumping in my heart, urging me to fight for life. For all four of our fucking lives.

I pull, and I pull, and they snap.

I pounce at the fucker with his hands wrapped around her throat, squeezing the life out of her.

I roar as I grab his head in my arms, pulling it backward and twisting with every bit of strength in me at the same time. Relief floods through me when I hear the snap and he collapses on the bed.

"Take that, you goddamn motherfucker!" I scream at him as I throw him on the floor. He's paralyzed. Dead? Maybe not. But he won't be standing again any time soon. Or ever again.

"Sarah."

She's gasping for air. I wrap my arms around her as she sobs. It's a heart-breaking sound. She looked death in the eye, touched souls with the devil briefly, and survived. We've survived. For now, at least.

"Sarah. Stay with me. We're not out of the woods yet, babe."

I give her a gentle shake. We've got the other goon to worry about, and we have no idea where he is or when he's going to show up. We probably have very little time.

"Sarah." I slap her hard across the face. The sobbing stops, and she stares up at me in shock. It's then we both notice my wrists; the destruction caused by the bindings. The exposed raw flesh. Still, I'm fucking alive. *We're* alive. It's a small price to pay.

I check for a pulse on the driver, but he's dead. I search his pockets, but there are no weapons. Fuck. We have no way of defending ourselves except for my hands, and I'm not sure how useful they'll be now.

Surprising a victim from behind and snapping their neck is one thing. I very much doubt the other guy is going to let me just walk up and repeat the process without fighting back.

"Let's get him behind the door so he can't be seen when it's opened." I untie her bindings, and she rubs her hands across the indents on her wrists.

"You saved my life… again," she whispers in disbelief, staring at me.

"Yes, but we don't have time to dissect that now," I reply, trying to deal with the corpse on my own.

I reach my hand up under my dress.

"What are you doing?" She frowns at me.

I pull the burner phone free from the pouch that's tied around the top of my thigh, and I switch on the location finder. Delaney will know just by me switching the finder on not to message and not to call. He'll just locate us. We don't need the phone vibrating or ringing at an inopportune time.

"Why do you have a burner phone?"

"Because I'm a very bad person."

"What do you do that makes you bad?"

"I could tell you that, but then I'd have to kill you, and your brother would never forgive me, so it's best you don't know."

"Who does it connect to?"

"Delaney. And before you ask, he won't betray my confidence as to why I need to carry one at all times."

She leaves it there. No doubt we'll pick this conversation back up at some point, but now is not the time.

I glance around the room, trying to find something. Anything. I finally manage to pull off a section of the metal bed frame. Will it offer enough as a weapon? For me to be able to at least knock a fucker out? We'd best hope so, as I imagine the other goon will show up way before Delaney arrives.

My guess is he's already here.

CHAPTER THIRTY-SIX

SARAH

Unknown Location

I WATCH as she yanks a piece of metal clean off the bed frame. Jaine looks all slim and elegant, but she's lethal. She snapped a man's fucking neck like a twig, and now she's twisting metal with her bare hands.

She looks at me and smiles. "Years of MMA training. My pop always told me I'd be thankful for it one day, and that day is today."

Her gaze drops to my neck and I reach up my hand and touch it, grimacing at the pain. It'll be bruised, I'm sure. My life flashed in front of my eyes as the fucker squeezed my throat. It wasn't painful then. I was simply drifting off to sleep.

"You're pregnant."

She stops what she's doing briefly and stares at me. She's ripped off more sections of her dress and bound her wrists with them, but the blood is still seeping through and dripping on the floor.

"Yes."

"Is it Ace's?"

"Don't pry, Sarah." Her tone is laced with warning.

"Well, mine is definitely Cillian O'Connell's." I lighten the now darkened mood.

It works. She chuckles.

"I didn't doubt it. You don't strike me as the promiscuous sort."

"You're not either."

"Nope."

"It's not Paul's, is it?"

She straightens up. My continual question-asking is clearly driving her mad. She's probably going to kill me with that piece of metal if I don't stop.

"No, it's not Delaney's."

"Sorry for all the questions. It's just for some reason it feels easy to talk to you about this sort of shit."

"It's just heightened emotions, Sarah. That's all. Don't share something you may later regret."

"So, you won't tell me?" Still I persevere.

"No. There are some things it's better not to know. If you do ever end up with Cillian, I wouldn't want for you to have to keep secrets from him. So, no, I can't tell you."

"Padraig," I whisper. Why else would I need to keep it a secret from Cillian?

"Sarah!" It's a warning to back the fuck off. To stop asking questions about that cub in her belly. I know now, though. That there are potentially two baby daddies, and that's the other reason she's left Manhattan.

"What's he like?"

"Irish?" She smiles. I watch as she re-positions the dead guy behind the door so he's not interfering with it opening. Her weapon —the section of bed—is lying on the filthy mattress. She's organized. She's done shit like this before. Many times. That much is obvious.

"Yeah. Padraig O'Connell."

"Funny. Smart. Possessive. Handsome and then some."

"I've seen pics of him online with the others. I didn't know who Sophia was talking about due to the name pronunciation. He's definitely the best looking of the O'Connells."

She laughs. "He wasn't as handsome when I first met him. He was gangly and still growing into himself. But the cheek that came out of that goddamn mouth of his. He made me laugh every day. Still does… did." Her face clouds over.

"And Ace? What's he like?"

"Deep. Thoughtful. The most unselfish man I've ever met. Sinfully handsome."

"You happy with him?"

"Yup. My first love." She quickly changes the subject. "Anyway, what are you going to do when we get out of here?" I realize she's deliberately said *when* and not *if.* She's right. Now we're unbound, we have more of a chance with two against one. Plus, my brother will be on his way.

"I don't know. I mean, Cillian's going to be married off to Cara. She's already pre-approved. Not sure what I can do about that."

"It's not over until it's over, Sarah. Never give up on what you want."

We sit in silence, pondering our own thoughts. It's then I hear the footsteps.

How long has it been? Fifteen, twenty minutes since the last fucker had his neck snapped?

I lie on the bed with my hands behind me and my eyes closed, pretending to be dead. It's not difficult. I almost was. Shit like that will always come easy to me now.

Jaine stands behind the door, almost on top of the dead guy. It seems to take an age before the live one finally opens it.

I keep my eyes closed, but I can almost hear the swinging piece of metal parting the air and the thunk sound as it connects with the asshole's skull. I open my eyes to see the nameless smoking hot guy collapse to the floor in a heap.

"He's not dead, Sarah, so let's tie him up. Quickly, pass me the ropes."

We truss him up like a festive turkey using our discarded ropes, and Jaine uses the final piece to tie her hair back. Hair that's covered in blood from her wounds and from the spattering created when the metal bar connected with this fucker's head.

She leaves him on the floor. We both lie on our beds and stare at the ceiling. Stained mattresses? Who cares? The time for talking is also over. Now, we wait for the cavalry to arrive.

CILLIAN

It's a disused warehouse in Lettling, around an hour's drive outside the city. It looks empty. There are no lights on. There's a black SUV parked up outside. Empty too, but the hood's still warm, so it's been used fairly recently.

Razr grips the burner phone in his hand. It's brought us here. To them. Are we too late? Fuck, I hope not.

Not that it makes any difference. Red will never be mine. My life's now mapped out. Cara showed me the test, and it's positive. She's delighted. I'm sure my ma is too. I'll have a ball and chain attached to my ankle within the month, most likely, and there's not a damn thing I can do about it. As practicing Irish Catholics, if we get a girl pregnant, it's game over.

Eoin and I are armed with Glocks. Razr with his blade. Tam and the others are close by, ready to provide back-up if needed. We thought it best not to draw attention to ourselves by turning up en masse in case they just decided to kill the girls and then make off.

We head inside the building. There's not a sound, just lots of corridors. Razr follows his phone. It's then we see the thin line of a dull light at the bottom of the doorway ahead.

"Cill, you kick the door in, and I'll scan the room before we enter. Razr, you stand back. We'll go first as we have firearms."

Razr nods at Eoin.

I kick the door, and it bounces back and hits off something or someone.

The first thing I see is Jaine. She's standing there with a piece of metal in her hand, raised above her like she's about to use one of our heads to hit a home run for the Yankees. I'm just grateful she didn't swing for mine.

"Cillian," she whispers as she lowers the metal bar. I'm not stupid enough to even attempt to prise that makeshift weapon off her.

I can see the goon behind her unconscious on the floor. He's not dead. He's been bound in blood-covered ropes. He's had a come-to-Jesus moment with that bar, that's for fucking sure.

We walk into the room, lowering our weapons as we do. It's then I see her sitting on the other bed. Her throat's red. It'll be covered in bruises tomorrow. Someone's tried to take her life today. I growl at the sight. I'm not sure if it's outwardly or not. Jaine stares at me, which gives me my answer. I'm going to fucking kill whoever it was that dared lay a finger on her.

"Sarah." Razr pushes past me and rushes to his sister's side, enveloping her in his arms. He's crying. She's crying. It's taking everything in me not to cry at the mess both these women are in too, and all this in just a few short hours.

It would only ever be in extreme circumstances that the Dusters would harm a female.

"Paul. He… he tried to strangle me." She points at the dead guy behind the door.

"What the fuck happened to him?" Eoin asks as he eyeballs the stiff.

"Jaine happened. She… she snapped his neck."

I look at Eoin. I see the respect grow in his gaze as he looks admiringly at Jaine. Even more admiringly, if that's possible. This is dangerous territory. Our Paddy is almost as insane as Razr. If he saw how possessively our eldest brother was looking at Jaine, like she belongs to him, he'd gut him, blood or not.

Her dress is ripped to shreds, and it's now halfway up her thighs, and her wrists have the same material wrapped around them. She's obviously fucked them up as the temporary bandages are soaked with blood, and it's dripping on the floor. She's splattered in blood too. My guess is her own as well as that of the unconscious goon.

She's taken care of business today. She's also saved Sarah Delaney's life, and for that, I'll be forever indebted to her.

Jaine's tied her hair back with rope. It's the only reason I see it. It's then I know that something's gone down, and I've not been party to the whole fucking story.

See, our Paddy used to bang on about the A tattooed behind her left ear. Her declaration of love for Ace. From where I'm standing, Jaine now has an I tattooed behind her right ear. For Irish? She didn't have that last time I saw her. I was under the impression she didn't love our Padraig, that she never had, so why the new tattoo? I look at Eoin, and I know he's clocked it too.

Jaine's bold declaration of love for our baby brother.

CHAPTER THIRTY-SEVEN

EOIN

Unknown Location

I TAKE in the little spitfire in front of me. Her gown is ripped to shreds, and her wrists are pissing blood. Thankfully, she's lowered the piece of metal she looked like she was about to cave our Cill's head in with. I know she's watching me as I take in the body behind the door. To gauge my reaction. To garner whether I'm impressed or not.

Of course I am. She killed a man twice her size with her bare hands.

She eventually puts down the makeshift weapon. No one in their right mind would ever have attempted to wrestle it from her grasp. Unless they had a death wish, of course.

"Jaine, we need to take you to have those wrists looked at. We have doctors and surgeons on standby."

There are no arguments from her. Instead, she simply nods and accepts my offer. She's not stupid. She knows they need to be dealt with by a professional. A band-aid will not suffice when her wrists are likely exposed flesh underneath those scraps of material.

I watch as Razr storms across to the swine on the ground.

"Who is this?" He points his blade at him.

"The trafficker," Jaine replies.

"The one who trafficked my sister?" He kicks him hard in the ribs before Jaine even has a chance to reply. The semi-conscious man curls up into the fetal position, groaning in agony.

"Yes." She rolls her eyes at him.

"I'm going to slit his goddamn throat." Razr moves to reach down for him.

"You're going to leave him the fuck alone, Delaney," she hisses as she presses her hand flat against his chest.

He stops in his tracks. I never thought I'd see the day when anyone would be able to control this insane biker, but she can. And with relative ease.

He glares at her and tries to stare her down. She never breaks eye contact with him and stands her ground. It's as if she's daring him to push her too far. What would happen if he did, I wonder?

"If anyone's going to slit his throat, it should be Sarah or Laila. They should be offered first refusal. But not today. That's not a decision Sarah can make today." She motions her head towards his sister, and he turns to look at the girl who's still in a state of shock having gone toe to toe with the grim reaper himself.

Jaine's right. She's not capable of making that decision today.

He covers the hand Jaine has pressed against his chest with his own and nods in acceptance. A feeling I've never experienced in my life before now surges through me. Possessiveness. Jealousy. I don't want him touching her.

She's fucking mine.

"Cill, call Tam and tell him to get the others here. We need this problem handled now. Let's get this situation transported to the subway. Also, make arrangements for the medical team to meet us there. I'm not sure which one we'll need, so have them all attend." He glares at me, likely to work out why I'm barking orders at him. Then he looks at Jaine and Razr. Their almost intimate pose. It doesn't take a rocket scientist to work out why I'm in such a foul mood.

He gets on his phone. His gaze rests on Sarah as he makes the necessary arrangements, but she refuses to make eye contact with him. Who can blame her? He's now betrothed to someone else. Well, as good as.

When news of their little tryst gets out, he'd best hope Paul Delaney is in a much better frame of mind than he is now.

I STARE AT HER WRISTS. THE WRAPS HAVE BEEN TAKEN OFF, AND THE nurse has cleaned them up. The doctor is frowning at them. He's one of the best surgeons in New York, and we have him on retainer, so he's available at all times. We pay handsomely for the privilege. Both wrists are bad, but one is almost to the bone. How she didn't pass out from the pain is beyond me. She'll be scarred for life.

"You really need a skin graft."

"What, and disfigure another part of my goddamn body? No, thanks, Doc. Just stitch them up."

She's lying on a temporary bed in a makeshift cubicle, staring at the ceiling.

With the speed and agility of a cobra, she suddenly grabs him by the collar and yanks his face down until it's almost touching hers. "And there must be no restriction of movement. You got that? Zero. So, if you have to do any of that skin stretching shit beforehand to make sure everything is one hundred percent back to normal afterward, then you do it."

"But the scarring...."

"Don't you worry about it, Doc. I won't hunt you down if it's not picture-postcard pretty when you're done. I'm not bothered about what it looks like. I'm not a vain sort of girl."

The doctor is huffing and puffing like an old woman, shuffling from foot to foot. He's not old. He's barely thirty and at the top of his game. Boyishly handsome is how Candice would describe him. He's obviously not pleased with Jaine's recommendations. He likely takes pride in his work. She smirks at him. He can obviously read the underlying threat it contains as the color drains from his face, and he coughs nervously.

"We can stitch this one. He points to her right arm. The other, we'll stretch the skin beforehand as the wound is almost to the bone. The positive is it will allow us to leave the area open. If there's any sign of infection, it will allow us to treat it quickly. You'll need to stay local for the next ten days or so, as both wrists will have to be heavily bandaged in the short term. Your movements will be restricted, so you may need help with certain things around the home."

She visibly rolls her eyes at that, and his face pales further. He knows he's told her something she doesn't want to hear. She wants to head back to California. Away from all this shite. Away from me.

I intervene.

"I'm sure Miss Jones can stay in New York for the next ten days, Dr. Kelly. That won't be a problem." I answer on her behalf, and she glares at me. My dick twitches in response. I don't think I've ever wanted a woman as much as I want her. She's sitting there in a blood-splattered gown with her wrists ripped apart, her hair a mess, and still looking like she could take on the world single-handedly. I don't think I've ever seen anything more beautiful in my entire life.

"I can answer for myself, Eoin. Don't you be pulling any of that chauvinistic shit with me."

I smirk at that barbed tongue of hers.

The doctor looks between us. I can tell he just wants to be out of here. He doesn't like being piggy in the middle of whatever the fuck this is. He has the sense to know it's not a safe place to be.

"I'll just get everything prepped." He sidles away, leaving me alone with her.

"So, you snapped his neck." She knows I'm referring to the body at the warehouse.

"It was an easy thing to do when he was facing the other way."

"It still wouldn't have been that easy."

She shrugs. "I've trained in MMA since I was in my teens. What can I say? I learned a lot."

"I'm impressed."

"I'll bet you are."

My gaze drifts to the I tattoo scrolled behind her ear. She lifts her head defiantly as I take it in.

"I for…"

"Are we playing eye-spy? You know who it's for."

"Why?"

"You can separate us, but you'll never change how I feel about him."

"You're with Ace."

"And?"

"You love both of them?"

"Yes."

"Isn't that…"

"Unconventional. Yes. So, sue me."

"Not sure it would be a good idea to try to sue a lawyer."

A smile crosses her face fleetingly, which she tries to suppress. I smirk in response.

"If you haven't anywhere to stay where you can be looked after, I'd be happy to put you up in my apartment."

"Thank you, but I can stay at my own apartment. I'm sure Sarah can help me out."

"I'm sure she can. She owes you her life."

"It's payback for when Delaney saved your brother and me."

I nod. She's right. Razr did save them, along with Ace, when they were held by the Bratva, likely using the same trick they used this time around.

"Why do you carry a burner?"

"That's my business."

"Maybe I should make it mine to find out."

"And maybe you should keep your nose out. That's if you don't want the discovery to see it blown off your face."

"I'm intrigued."

"I'm glad. Stay that way. It's better than being dead, I assure you."

"Are you threatening me?"

"I'm not stupid enough to threaten a Duster, Eoin. But let's just say any digging in that area might see you and me ending up on a promise, and not the kind you were hoping for."

The doctor comes back into the room, along with the nurse, so we have to leave it there for now.

We stare at each other. She knows I will make it my life's fucking mission to find out what she's hiding, so I hope she's covered her tracks well.

CHAPTER THIRTY-EIGHT

CILLIAN

The Subway, New York

Our Paddy is alternating between pacing the floor and stopping and fisting his hair in his hands. Ever since he saw the images of Jaine's wrists, he's struggled to stop his inner Hannibal Lecter taking control. He doesn't want to do the flesh-eating part. He just wants to intricately carve this fucker up in the slowest and most painful way possible, then stand back and admire his art. Then he wants to take an image of his masterpiece and send it to Jaine.

His revenge on her behalf.

The ultimate declaration of *his* love for *her*.

He can't do that, though. He's been told he can't end this fucker. That's what's tearing him apart and has him yanking at his hair. His inner beast is howling to get out. This swine scarred his woman for life. He scarred mine for life mentally too. We both want our revenge, but it's not ours to have.

Jaine's already told us in no uncertain terms that the fucker must die at the hands of Sarah or Laila. If they choose not to end him, only then will it be a toss-up between the rest of us.

If the women decline, it'll be like a pack of rabid dogs with a single bone. Paddy will rig it somehow, so it's him who gets to end the fucker. Then he'll act all innocent, like it was some sort of fluke. Then again, he really does have all the luck of the Irish.

Well, apart from when it comes to Jaine. She loves him. He loves her. For some reason, my big brother and my da didn't deem that enough to allow them to be together.

Same as me loving Red and her loving me won't be enough either. Not with Cara carrying a baby Duster.

Outlaw politics comes first. Always.

The Colombian's now conscious. From the second he opened his eyes, Paddy's been dicing him up. Making his life a living hell. Chopping digits off, hacking off flesh. This fella's being treated like a stuck pig. I'm surprised he can scream any louder, but he always manages to impress by raising it an octave or two every single time. I'm sure my baby brother would happily seal off his cries with a rosy red apple and offer him up to Lucifer on a silver platter, along with a goblet of fresh blood to wash it all down.

I stare at him, and he smirks at me defiantly. I slap him hard across the mouth, and he spits out the resultant blood. His wrists are tied to the chair arms, his ankles to its legs. He's only wearing jeans, and his exposed torso has already been hacked to pieces by Paddy. He's covered in blood, dried and fresh, the side of his head swollen magnificently from when Jaine clubbed him across the dome with the metal bar. The dead-man-walking has six fingers left. Four, on one hand, two on the other. No thumbs. He still hasn't uttered a word about who's behind this trafficking business. My guess is, he won't. He'll be a high ranker. Likely with a wife and children at home. There's no way he'll betray his family—blood or otherwise.

"Paddy, he's not going to talk."

"I fucking know that, Cill, but I still want him to suffer."

"I know you do, but we need to leave something for the girls. It's their right."

"I know. I know. But what he did to Jaine. She'll be scarred for life."

"She's a big girl, Paddy. She's fully aware of the risks we face in this life."

He drops his head to his hands. No doubt his inner demons are arguing with each other in that fucked-up headspace of his.

He growls, reaches out, and slices the Colombian's ear clean off. The swine screams in pain. Paddy laughs in his face before firing up a blowtorch and sealing the wound. The smell of burnt flesh fills the air. Soon, it will be the smell of death.

Blood, shit, piss, and fear.

"Get Razr to bring the women in before I wind up ending him myself."

Paddy stares at the wall. He knows it's only Sarah and Laila. Jaine won't be present today. Not with him here.

Eoin would never permit it. And what he says goes.

Usually, we would never allow anyone inside our inner sanctum, but these are exceptional circumstances. The Dusters, the Angels, and the Scorpions have all been affected by this blanket of evilness. We trust each other enough to know that the other parties present won't betray us. It would be a death sentence; outlaw war.

On this matter alone, we'll stand united.

Both brothers and sisters in arms.

Razr storms into the room, his expression borderline psycho. Then again, what's new there? He stops and stares at the fucker who's been partially diced by our Paddy. A large silver kidney tray on a wheelable trolley holds the appendages that have been hacked off so far. All as painfully as possible, with the aftermath either sealed with fire or table salt.

Razr looks impressed as Paddy stands beside him. They both tilt their heads, pointing at the wounds inflicted like they're in The Louvre studying the Mona Lisa. It's surprising how alike they are.

"Razr, are the girls up for doing what needs to be done?"

He turns to look at me. In truth, he seems a bit pissed off that I'm interrupting his conversation with our Paddy.

"Sarah will. I'm not sure Laila's got a kill in her."

"Shall we let them in and leave them to it? We can give them, say, half an hour, and if they can't hack it, then we can finish the job."

He nods.

Adrenaline spikes through me when she walks in. Red. She's wearing skinny black jeans, a black tank top, and a biker jacket. Her boots are those giant monstrosities. Jesus Christ, today might be neither the time nor the place for such thoughts, but I wish I'd fucked her wearing them when I had the chance.

Her hair's hanging straight down her back. She looks at me, her eyes scanning me briefly. She looks fucked. The dark circles under her eyes have likely been caused by the lack of oxygen when the goon tried to throttle her. His fingerprints are dotted around her neck in large purple bruises.

I want to wrap my arms around her, but now's not the time with her brother only feet away. I want to live to see another day, and his alter-ego won't need much persuasion to end my life right here and now and to hell with the consequences.

"Cillian." She acknowledges me.

"Sarah," I reply. I motion my head towards my brother. "This is our Paddy."

She turns and takes in my younger sibling. I've got a feeling she'll know all about what's gone on between him and Jaine. Sometimes when you're held captive, you let your mouth run away with you and talk about things you wouldn't normally. I'm pretty sure they've been comparing Duster notes.

"It's nice to meet you, Paddy." She smiles at him warmly. "I've heard a lot about you from… from..."

"From Jaine. You can say her name. I promise I won't burst into tears then wail into the crook of my elbow." He smiles his cheeky chappy grin, which contrasts with the blood-dripping blade he's clutching in his hand.

"Yes, from Jaine." She laughs.

"All good things, I hope?"

"Like you wouldn't believe."

He chuckles. "I'm sure there were some unkind remarks that came out of that smart mouth of hers too. All of them well-earned and well-deserved." He passes her the blade like he's offering her a sandwich or a cup of tea. She takes it from his hand. "We'll leave you ladies to it." He squeezes her arm, and she nods.

She turns to her pocket-sized friend. "You staying or leaving?"

Laila bites her lip. "I'll stay."

Razr looks proudly at her before placing a comforting hand on her shoulder, then us three men exit the room.

They have exactly half an hour. We have forty minutes before the cleaners arrive. In an hour, it will look like this shitshow never took place.

SARAH

"You there, Jaine?"

"I'm here, babe."

"Just thought you should bear witness."

"Thank you for thinking of me."

I take in her bandaged wrists on the screen. We've been spending a lot of time together as I've been helping her with things around her apartment. It's the least I can do since she saved my life. Again.

"I met him, Jaine."

"My Irish?"

"Yeah."

She smiles, but it's a sad sort of smile. It mirrors the one he gave me. Cheerful on the outside and hiding pain and misery underneath. Is mine and Cillian's future to follow suit? Empty smiles burying heartache? Tears prick my eyes. I finally meet the man of my dreams, only for him to be taken from me. Still. What can I do? Life sucks, and then you die, like the asshole in front of me will soon find out.

"Why?" I stand in front of him, but he just stares at me and smirks. Even facing death, he's an arrogant fucker.

"Laila, you want to cut him first?" I offer her the blade, but she shakes her head. She looks like she's going to pass out or throw up.

Instead, I give her my phone. "Hold it steady so Jaine can watch."

Then I do what's bred into us Delaneys. I walk behind the fucker, and I tilt back the head of the nameless smoking hot guy.

"This is for everyone you've ever trafficked. Rot in hell, you motherfucker."

Then I cut him from ear to ear.

CILLIAN

We re-enter the room half an hour later, and the Colombian's blood is spilled all over the floor, his throat cut ear to ear as is the way of a Delaney.

I'm proud of her. So fucking proud.

Red disconnects the call she was on—Jaine, most likely. Paddy walks over and stands beside her, and they admire her handiwork. She throws her head back and laughs heartily, and then she passes him his blade. They're already the best of buddies.

She'd have made a great Duster. I sigh with regret.

Razr has his arm wrapped around her pint-sized friend. At least she watched. For someone not from the life to willingly witness another be so brutally murdered is a tall order.

He leads her away from the carnage, and I seize the opportunity. I walk over to Red and Paddy. Her hands are covered in blood, despite using the towel Paddy's passed her. Then again, even when it's washed off, our hands are still invisibly covered.

"Red. We need to talk."

Paddy looks between us both, then makes himself scarce. He knows I love her. That I think she loves me too. That my situation is no better than his.

"What's there to say, Cillian?"

She stares at me, those hazel eyes of hers drinking me in. She's not angry. She looks defeated, but she also looks determined. Like she's already decided to move on with her life without me in it because she has no choice.

"You were fucking me at the same time as your family-approved fiancée. That much is blatantly obvious. I don't need to explain the birds and the bees to you, do I? To explain how she ended up pregnant? You know, your dick…."

"Enough, Red. I wasn't fucking her at the same time. There wasn't anyone else, and there hasn't been anyone since."

She laughs dryly. "Shit. Should I feel honored? That you and I were sort of exclusive in a Stockholm Syndrome kind of fucked up way and that you've since managed to abstain from sex for a few weeks?"

"Why are you being a bitch?"

"Because I don't need a fucking explanation about what's happened, that's why! Or about what it means," she hisses. "Whatever comes out of your mouth right now is not going to change anything."

"I could speak to my family. Maybe there's a way..." I don't even finish the sentence. I'm talking shite. She knows it.

I try to wrap my arms around her, but she pushes me away.

I don't want it to end right here, right now. Not like this. Surely to fuck there's a way for me to get out of this mess. For us to be together.

There has to be.

"Don't flatter yourself, hotshot. I'll survive. It's what we Delaneys do fucking best."

SARAH

I reach the cage, and I get in. Thankfully, there's no sign of Paul or Laila. He's probably comforting her somewhere after she had to witness my bloodbath from earlier.

Tears blind me. I wipe them away with the back of my hand and wipe my nose on my sleeve. Gross, I know.

I cry for my fatherless baby, and then I cry a bucketful of tears of self-pity for myself. I'm not proud of the latter, but after the past twenty-four hours, I need it.

"Jaine." I look at the woman on my phone screen—the one who's become like a sister to me in such a short time. I don't need to tell her why tears are tripping me or why I'm snotting and hiccupping.

I take a deep breath and try to compose myself so I can get the words out. She waits patiently until I can find my voice. She understands. She's the only one who truly fucking does.

"How do you cope?" The words are barely audible. She knows exactly what I'm asking, and she lets her own grief show, but only briefly.

"One day at a time, Sarah. You just have to cope one day at a goddamn time."

CHAPTER THIRTY-NINE

ROISIN

The O'Connell Home, Darling, New York

"Finally, Roisin, our families will be joined, just as we've always hoped. Your Cillian and my Cara. God has at last given his blessing to their union."

I doubt The Almighty had anything to do with the tampered-with condom that most likely resulted in this pregnancy, but if Helen wants to believe the Lord was party to it for biblical reasons, then who am I to contradict her?

She's on spirits. She's already well on her way to being wasted and it's only mid-day. I watch as she downs another gin and tonic.

I smile in response as I take in my childhood friend. I'm not saying I'm a prize by any means, but I've maintained my weight and tried to preserve my looks over the years. I was thankful for what God gave me, and I've taken care of myself as best I can. I take pride in my appearance. Every woman should, in my opinion. At my time of life, to look presentable involves a lot more effort, combined with a little third-party assistance, but my Fergal deserves me to be at my best at all times. I expect the same effort from him in return.

Helen? Well, she's let herself go over the years. She's bloated and rosacea-cheeked from the drink, and her short, brown hair, which she has styled in tight curls, does nothing to flatter her heavyset features. She's always been a curvy woman, but her ever-expanding backside now takes up almost two seats on my dark green Chesterfield couch. They're not small cushions, either.

Some might argue that my life's been easier than hers, but I'd beg to differ.

I appreciate when I was entered into an arranged marriage with Fergal O'Connell at the age of twenty-eight that I was the envy of all the Irish girls. Everyone wanted him—the handsome lad who was destined to become the future Da Duster.

I also appreciate that the O'Connells have always been extremely wealthy. I married into a family with more money than we could ever spend in a lifetime, so I've never known any financial hardship.

But as Ma Duster, I've had to roll my sleeves up on many occasions over the years. I've put to ground my fair share of men, but, in the main, it's the traitorous women that I've had to deal with. Any female who betrays our loyalty or our trust is handled by me. Regardless of sex, the O'Connells do not tolerate lies or deceit of any kind, either in our ranks or from our peers.

Both are punishable by death.

Helen's never had to do any dirty work. And being married to Jack, Fergal's school friend and right-hand man, she's certainly not poor by any means. He'll be rewarded handsomely for holding such a high-ranking position in the Duster hierarchy.

I only hope Cara takes better care of herself over the years. Our Cillian deserves the very best. I know he doesn't love the girl, but she's carrying an O'Connell in her belly now. That changes everything. The child deserves a father who's present in their life at all times. They need to be. Born a Duster heir, they will be targeted by our enemies—of which we have plenty—from the moment they take their first breath.

A blessing to our family? Yes. Our first grandchild. The first of many, hopefully. But also our biggest Achilles heel.

We can't have any O'Connell offspring not tied to the family by marriage. That would be unthinkable. They must immediately be brought into the fold. If any of my boys get a girl pregnant, they take the vows together whether they want it or whether the girl wants it. End of story. Their own wishes become irrelevant. They all know that.

Duster babies must be protected at all times and at all costs.

I glance around the sitting room. We seldom use it, but as we're having a small get-together to celebrate our families' upcoming union, I decided to have it aired out for today. I take in the antique walnut furniture covered in countless photos of my boys over the years. I'm a proud mother. My lads are my pride and joy, and I want the world to know it.

Tasteful pieces of art hang from the walls, and everything's finished in green and gold, down to the heavy tapestry curtains and other accents. The room screams luxury and wealth.

I pour myself a cup of tea from the white bone china teapot that's been placed on the glass-topped coffee table. I offer one to Helen, but she declines. Instead, she fidgets with the hem of her purple dress. She wants another alcoholic drink, but I'm not offering to have one mixed for her, even though we have kitchen staff hired for today. I don't want to encourage her mid-day drinking. Our Paddy was heading down that slippery slope until very recently. Thankfully, he's turned the corner. I don't need Helen's unhealthy obsession with the bottle encouraging him to embrace the demon drink again.

I'm sure she'll make off in a minute or two, though. Pretend she needs to visit the restroom and help herself to another from the bar in the family room. This place is like a home from home for her. She knows where everything is.

"Ah, here comes the happy couple," Helen gushes, raising her arm in a small, welcoming wave as Cara and Cillian enter the room. The movement causes the scent of her heavy lavender-based perfume to fill the air.

I take a sip of tea to try to wash down the floral notes that have gathered in my throat. It doesn't work. Maybe I'll buy her a new fragrance as a gift. Something a bit more subtle. I'm going to be spending a lot more time with her now. She'll make sure of that. She's well aware her family is marrying up.

I take in my future daughter-in-law. Cara's wearing a cream pantsuit and looking immaculate, as usual. She's beaming, flicking her long blonde hair around her shoulders and looking as pleased as Punch himself. And so she should. It's every Irish girl in Hell's Kitchen's dream to bag one of my sons.

She's carrying a bundle of wedding magazines under one arm, her other linked possessively through Cill's. My poor boy looks miserable. Eoin's mentioned that he's in love with this biker girl he met recently. The one he was meeting up with in the yet-to-be-opened hotel. Eoin's not given me or his da any further details about her. He says there's no point. Plus, her family isn't aware of their short-term hook-up. If they find out, it may not sit well with them, apparently.

I've not pushed. He's right. There is no point. Cillian's fate is sealed.

The reason for today's little soiree?

Observation.

When everyone's arrived, Fergal makes his congratulatory speech. It's then I feel it in my bones. Something's off. Something's amiss. I've had these bones for sixty-five years, and they've never let me down yet.

I'm a firm believer that the truth will out.

It always does.

This time will be no different, I'm sure.

PADRAIG

Jaine: *How's it all going, Dyl?*

Padraig: *Ma's forensically watching all the goings-on while sipping on a Bloody Mary. Cara's looking at wedding magazines. Cill looks like his life's about to end as his future wife points out things in said magazines. The future mother-in-law is drinking like a fish, and the men are all watching the Yankees game.*

Jaine: *Sounds like fun.*

Padraig: *It's not. The engagement is being announced a week Saturday.*

Jaine: *Shit. So soon?*

Padraig: *You know us Dusters, darlin'. We...*

Jaine: *Go big or go home.*

Padraig: *Exactly.*

Jaine: *Poor Cillian.*

Padraig: *He got Cara pregnant. Regardless of what he thinks of her, his child deserves a father. They'll be a Duster, after all.*

Jaine: *It's all a bit old-fashioned.*

Padraig: *If we had to follow the rules of The Almighty, we'd all have to abstain from sex until we were wed, so he should consider himself lucky he's been allowed to get his dick wet for so many years and in so many different women.*
Jaine: *I'll ignore that valuable insight into Cillian's varied sex life. I really don't need that visual. You forget he's in love with Sarah Delaney.*
Padraig: *Then he should have been more careful.*
Jaine: *So, you're in favor of all this?*
Padraig: *He's being given a precious gift. He's going to be a da. Unfortunately, not everyone is granted that privilege in life.*
Jaine: *Do you want kids, Dyl?*
Padraig: *More than anything.*
Jaine: *Really?*
Padraig: *Why does that surprise you?*
Jaine: *Not sure. You never struck me as the paternal type—all those grubby, sticky little fingers all over your laptops and screens.*
Padraig: *LOL. Never judge a book, Jaine.*
Jaine: *You're still young. You've got plenty of time.*
Padraig: *I'll never have kids.*
Jaine: *You say that like you're certain.*
Padraig: *I am certain.*
Jaine: *Why say never?*
Padraig: *Because I'd only want to have them with one woman.*
Jaine: *And it's the woman who doesn't love you back.*
Padraig: *Exactly.*
Jaine: *You're breaking my cold biker heart.*
Padraig: *Sorry. I'm feeling a bit melancholy today, darlin.*

Jaine: *Envious of Cillian?*
Padraig: *Something like that.*
Jaine: *You want me to have a word with your cliché blonde?*
Padraig: *Maybe. I've a feeling you're the only person she'd listen to.*
Jaine: *As if she'd listen to a random stranger.*
Padraig: *You'd be surprised.*
Jaine: *Anyway, I need to go. Sarah will be here shortly to take me to see Dr. Kelly.*
Padraig: *Let me know how you get on. Enjoy the rest of your day, Robin.*
Jaine: *You too, Batman.*

SARAH

Upper East Side, New York

We've just left Dr. Kelly's office. The stitches and bandages on Jaine's right wrist have been removed. Her left wrist has finally been stitched up and the dressing replaced. I feel rude, but I just can't stop staring. I also feel guilty. The scarring is atrocious. Dr. Frankenstein would have done a better job than that asshole, although I think he was scared shitless of Jaine, so he probably wasn't performing at his best. Her wrists will forever be a visual of how determined she was to save both our lives. All four of our lives, in fact. She doesn't seem bothered by the mess the bindings have left behind.

"The engagement's being announced a week Saturday." She just comes right out with it as she stares out the window.

Rip that band-aid right fucking off, why don't you?

A couple of taxi drivers cut us up, one waving in apology, the other flipping his comrade the bird. I lower the window and inhale the almost comforting smell of exhaust fumes and trash. I'd generally banter with the drivers by yelling abuse and waving my fist angrily, but I've been stunned into silence by that unwelcome piece of news.

I stare out the rear-view mirror of Cherry's mom's SUV. Jaine couldn't ride on the back of my hog, so we borrowed a cage. Apparently, it's been sitting at the clubhouse since before they traveled to Rising.

I'm not sure how much time passes. I know I need to acknowledge her statement.

"So soon." It's more an observation than a question.

"Yup."

I'm not sure what I expected. I knew it was never going to be a long, drawn-out process. Why delay the inevitable? Tears prick my eyes, but I blink them back.

I rub my hand over my stomach. Jaine notices the movement.

"You should tell him, Sarah,"

"What difference will it make?"

"He has a right to know."

"He has no rights."

"He's the father of that goddamn child you're carrying. Of course he has rights."

"What if I tell Cillian and his folks try to take the baby away from me?"

"You think Delaney would allow that to happen?"

"I wish I had never taken that test. Ignorance really is bliss."

"What made you think you were pregnant anyway?"

I shrug. "Missed my period. Eating for two. When I thought I might be I stopped at the pharmacy on the way to the function."

"You took the test at Leo's function?"

"Yes. In the ladies' restroom."

Jaine turns to stare at me.

"What?" I glance at her then quickly turn my attention back to the road.

"Nothing."

CHAPTER FORTY

JAINE

Jaine's Apartment, Upper East Side, New York

"JAINE, how are you? To what do I owe this unexpected pleasure?"

I don't reply, completely ignoring his fake niceties. The asshole doesn't give a fuck how I am.

He continues, ignoring my lack of response.

"I've just spoken with Dr. Kelly, and he's happy with how your wrists look. He's fine with you having the stitches removed when you return to California. Then, I'm sure he's already told you that."

I ignore his mundane conversation. My wrists look like shit. Dr. Kelly is a lying asshole. The truth is, he couldn't get me out of his goddamn clinic fast enough. He was visibly shaking the entire time I was in there.

I eventually answer, but only when I'm sure I've wound him up satisfactorily by delaying my reply as long as possible.

No one would dare keep Eoin O'Connell waiting. Well, except me.

"Eoin. I'm not calling for a social chat. I'm pretty sure you don't give a shit how I am or what my wrists look like."

I pause before I go on. Not because I'm trying to piss him off further, but because my conscience is now gnawing away at my brain. Am I doing the right thing? Given what I suspect, what other choice do I have?

"I did consider speaking to Dyl about this matter, but after what happened with the trafficking situation, I'm aware he doesn't hold enough clout in the Duster ranks to do anything about it and that he'll just direct me to you."

"Go on." He sounds smug. Asshole.

"How do you know for sure Cara's pregnant?"

"I believe she showed my ma a positive pregnancy test."

"It may seem a crude question, but did anyone see her piss on the stick?"

"Not that I'm aware of."

"So, you just believe her?"

"Her da is my da's right-hand man, Jaine. Our parents went to school together. Why would she lie? She knows what would happen if she betrayed our trust."

"She's in love with Cillian, yes?"

"Yes. She has been her whole life."

"She threatened Sarah at their hook-up spot. You've heard about that shitshow?"

"Yes… look, Jaine, where are you going with this?"

"Just hear me out. She knows she has competition for Cillian's affections. Real competition."

"Yes." He exhales loudly. It makes me want to drag it on even longer.

I pause. Rightly or wrongly, I'm going to have to spill Sarah's secret.

"Well?"

"This is in the strictest confidence, Eoin."

"Not again." He sighs.

"Although I'm not sure how quiet you'll be able to keep it."

"Stop talking in riddles, Jaine. Look, I'll be passing your apartment in the next five minutes. Expect me then."

He hangs up before I can decline. Great. Well, if he thinks I'm offering to make him a drink, he can kiss my ass.

I OPEN THE DOOR, AND WE GLARE AT EACH OTHER.

I'm in my usual tank top and cargo pants. For once, Eoin's not wearing a ten-thousand-dollar suit. Today, he's casually dressed, wearing dark blue jeans and a white t-shirt with a black leather bomber jacket thrown over the top. Even his hair looks less groomed than usual. On the outside, he appears borderline normal, not like the always-immaculate business-suited mobster I've seen in the past.

Aside from the shorter hair and the sprinkling of grey, I can't believe how much he looks like my Irish when he's dressed down like this.

It's then I realize I'm staring and have been for some time. We make eye contact, and his are laughing at me.

"You look different. You look like Padraig," I mutter.

He smirks. "I'll take that as a compliment given how much you admire my brother. I was just on my way to a lunch date."

"Then don't let me hold you up. I didn't ask you to stop by." I realize I'm sounding pissy and petulant, and I curse myself for being so reactive around this asshole.

"I've canceled. I can meet with her another time. Your news

sounded important."

I stare at him again. "You date?"

"Is that so hard to believe?" He crosses his arms and leans against the doorframe.

"I just thought you fucked your way through your overpaid staff."

"Careful, Jaine. Anyone would think you were jealous."

Smirking aquamarine eyes stare down at me. "You fucking wish."

The annoying smug smirk reaches his mouth like he doesn't quite believe me. What planet is he living on? Does he think I would ever be jealous of the poor women who are subjected to a dicking by him?

"Well, are you going to invite me in?"

I roll my eyes at him. I'm tempted to slam the door in his arrogant GQ model-like face, but I need his help. Again. He'll be loving how frequently I have to ask for it these days. Then again, who's actually doing who the favor this time?

I don't reply. I simply open the door wider, allowing adequate space for him to walk past before motioning my head to say that he can. Once inside, he scans my apartment.

It's expensive, and very tastefully decorated. It's minimalistic, all monochrome with black leather sofas, white walls, and silver and anthracite furnishings finished with crystal fittings and lights.

"Did you ever consider renting it out?"

"Nope. It's not like I need the money. But, then again, you already know that."

I couldn't resist the jibe that I'm aware he's been snooping through my bank statements with a fine-tooth comb. I won't expand on my reasoning for not renting. It's not like I can mention the safe room full of sniper gear located on the property.

We don't speak for several moments, both of us no doubt

reflecting on the last time he was here. The unexpected and unwelcome news he delivered then.

How many months has it been since I spoke to my Irish? I don't even know. What I do know is it feels like a fucking lifetime ago.

Without being offered, he sits on the black leather sofa, same as last time, stretching his arms out across the back.

Where the fuck do I start? What do I do if I'm wrong with this? My guts are telling me I'm not. They're seldom wrong. But still. Sarah's news is life-changing for so many people.

"So." He's staring at me. Waiting. I have no choice but to trust him.

"I don't think Cara's pregnant."

"Why would you say that?"

"I don't think the pregnancy test is hers. I think she gained access to someone else's discarded one."

He frowns at me. "Why would she do that? She may not be the sharpest tool in the box, but even she realizes her deceit would be unveiled in due course when there's no physical offspring produced."

"To keep hold of Cillian. As you've said, she's loved him her whole life. She was going to lose him. He loves Sarah. Sarah loves him. And as Delaney's sister, she's the perfect match. My guess is Cara was going to get him to marry her then fake a miscarriage."

He nods. "Go on."

I sigh. "Eoin, this isn't sitting right with me. I really am breaking a confidence here. A massive one."

"Do you have any choice? It's not likely if you've had to lower yourself yet again to contacting me."

At least the asshole knows I'm doing this as a last resort.

I shake my head. "No, I have no choice. If my suspicions are correct, I'm doing the right thing."

I pace the floor. Then I stop and look at him. "Sarah's pregnant.

It's Cillian's. She took a test the night of thc function. I think Cara found the discarded test. I saw her leaving the restroom only minutes after Sarah, looking smug as fuck. It didn't cross my mind at the time. It only dawned on me earlier today when Sarah mentioned where and when she'd tested."

There's a lengthy pause.

"Listen, Eoin, I can't be one hundred percent sure, and I'm having to break Sarah's trust to tell you this, but I can't just sit back and watch two people who love each other being kept apart."

I break eye contact and start pacing again. "I've been there, done that, and am currently living my life with the consequences. It's soul-destroying. Sarah's had enough bad luck in the past. She deserves a shot at happiness. As does Cillian. Plus, there's a child involved."

"What if you're wrong? What if Cara really is pregnant?"

I shrug. "Then we need to decide what we do with this information. Sarah's worried the Dusters will try to take the baby from her, but you and I both know Paul Delaney would never allow that to happen."

"Does Razr know?"

"He knows nothing about Cillian and Sarah or about the fact that she's pregnant."

"So, we've got that reaction to look forward to in the very near future."

He stares at me, and I can tell he's digesting this breaking news. Welcome or not? I can't tell.

"I'm not sure how my family will react to this knowledge. As you will appreciate, I can't keep this to myself. If there's a Duster baby to be born out of wedlock, my family has a right to know—a right to be involved in their life. Any O'Connell child will be born into a world filled with ready-made enemies. Their welfare and safety must be paramount. My ma and da will insist upon it. My concern is, I'm not sure the MC can offer the same level of protection we can."

"So, what are you saying? That the Dusters would take on the Iron Scorpions and fight over custody of the child? You'd seriously want to go head-to-head with Paul Delaney over this?"

"The child would be a Duster. We have considerably more enemies than the Scorpions."

"Only if anyone knew they were a Duster."

"We'd know. My ma would spend the rest of her life worrying."

"Cillian can only marry one of them, Eoin."

"I realize that."

"Then we'd best hope that my gut is right and Cara's lying."

We make our way to the door, and he stands and stares down at me. His attention drifts to my exposed wrist and the extensive scarring.

He lifts my hand and gently rubs his thumb over the puckered, discolored skin.

"I'll have a word with Dr. Kelly. I'm not happy with how this looks," he murmurs, frowning at the scarring.

I snatch my arm away. I don't want him touching me.

"It's fine, Eoin. He did his best, which is all anyone can ask. The man was quite clearly terrified the entire time."

I ignore his scrutiny at the unsightliness of my wrist. It's not important. My own situation is now front and center in my mind. The fact that the child in my belly might be a Duster. The fact that it would also be born out of wedlock. Would the O'Connells attempt to take them from me? Going by that conversation, I honestly think they might.

Have I done the right thing by Sarah? Only time will tell. I pray to God that Cara is lying and she's not pregnant.

If not, then I've potentially just kicked off outlaw war in Manhattan.

CHAPTER FORTY-ONE

SARAH

The Delaney Home, Brightling, New York

"I HOPE you're happy that your baby daddy's a mobster. And not just any mobster, but one of those extremely dangerous O'Connell brothers."

How many times must she lecture me? I'm seriously tempted to wring her minuscule neck. Like I need to be constantly reminded of how much of a disappointment I am in her eyes and how seriously lacking all my life decisions have been when I'm having to contemplate my future as a single mom.

I sigh. "I'm not bothered about the career choices of their daddy, Laila. I'm just sad that he won't be in my baby's life."

Even if I decided to tell Cillian, I'm sure his blonde bimbo fiancée would never allow him to play happy families with me—even part-time.

I'm sitting on the kitchen worktop, watching my pint-sized friend put away shopping. She's bought enough to feed a small village, and it's only ever me here unless she or Paul visit. It's all healthy stuff this time. No exceptions. I've already had the wagging finger lecture telling me what I can and can't put in my mouth. She's even bought me a smoothie maker to make nutritional shakes. I'm just praying Paul drops by later so we can order some take-out.

She graces me with a fleeting flicker of sympathy from around the fridge door, and then she smiles. It's clear where this discussion is headed now. Who the topic of conversation is turning to.

"Who needs a daddy? Paul will make a great uncle. He'll love that baby as if they were his own."

Jumping down from the counter, I start putting away the produce. "I know Paul will love the baby, but it's not his, is it? It's mine and Cillian's. And I remember the wonderful relationship I had with my own daddy, so I guess I'm just disappointed that my baby will never get the chance to experience that."

"Why did you have to fall in love with him of all people?"

"I ask myself that very same question every day, Laila, and I think those sorts of game-changing decisions are taken out of our hands. I think The Almighty likes to meddle in these matters, and He makes these decisions on our behalf."

She stops what she's doing and stares at me. It's clear she's having a eureka moment. "That's it. Sarah. Have you tried praying?"

"Praying for what?"

"I don't know. That by hook or by crook, things will work out in the end with Cillian?"

Am I surprised by that question? Nope. At least, not from my bible-bashing best friend. I roll my eyes inwardly as I take a bite from an apple. "No, I haven't tried praying."

"Then maybe you should. I mean, what have you got to lose?"

I shrug.

She's right. What do I have to fucking lose? But given the one percent badge that's inked on my soul, I decide to direct my prayers to Lucifer instead.

EOIN

The O'Connell Home, Darling, New York

"Eoin, this is a surprise visit."

"Sorry, Ma. I know it's Sunday, but it's urgent."

I called them on my way here to let them know I was coming. After kissing her on both cheeks, we walk through to the main family room. It's a comfortable space where my brothers and I spend our time when we're at home watching sports and playing poker. It's all neutral colors, with a large TV hanging from the wall and two large black-leather sectionals to lounge on. Like everywhere else in the house, the walls and surfaces are filled with a shrine of photos of us growing up. Ma wants it filled with images of grandchildren. We're all well aware of how desperate she is, as she's taken to reminding us almost daily that it's our duty to provide them. Our Cill's off the hook, for now at least. As soon as the first one's dropped, she'll no doubt be back on his case, wanting more.

Da appears a few minutes later. They're both dressed down in casual lounge pants, woolen sweaters, and sheepskin slippers. Ma would never let anyone apart from her immediate family see her this under-dressed. Like me, she believes appearances are everything when it comes to promoting the Duster brand.

They'll smarten up later, of course. Old Father O'Reilly wouldn't thank them for entering St. Peter's Church dressed casually, and he always gets his way. He holds the key to the pearly gates as far as my folks are concerned, so within reason, they bow to his bidding. It's a major event in the weekly calendar when the Duster masses take over the holy building to confess their plentiful sins.

The collection plate will be heavily laden with Benjamin Franklins for Father O'Reilly's troubles by the end of his tedious sermon. More than adequate compensation for any damage caused to his saintly ears by having to listen to the murderous activities we've been up to during the preceding week.

I'm only grateful Paddy and Cill operate a drop-in service for the atrocities they carry out, or Sunday confession would definitely roll into Monday, maybe even Tuesday. But, then again, they have no choice as they need as much time as possible to deal with their lengthy, much-deserved penance.

"Is it about the Bratva, son?" Da immediately starts peppering me with questions, curious why I've turned up at the crack of dawn on a Sunday morning.

"No, Da. They've gone quiet for now. They and their silent partner are probably still trying to locate the two Colombians we chucked in the Hudson."

"No news?"

"Nothing. Despite our Paddy being on the case, we still couldn't get him to talk. He was likely a high ranker."

He shakes his head in disappointment as he peers at me over the top of his reading glasses. "What is the world coming to? That these kiddie-fiddlers think they can walk in and kidnap two young women from under everyone's noses, and at Leoluca's shindig of all places. Jaine Jones was one of them, you say?"

"Aye, Da. She was. Thankfully, they're both fine. The other girl was one of the trafficked victims. She recognized one of the men on sight, so he needed to silence her. Jaine was either in the wrong place at the wrong time, or she deliberately got herself captured to make sure the other girl wasn't taken alone."

"That was big of her. Likes to make a habit of getting herself abducted, does she, this Jaine Jones?" Ma replies. The bitterness in her tone instantly gets my back up. She loathes bikers. She especially dislikes Jaine since our Paddy is besotted with her.

"Jaine would never walk away from a dance with the devil, Ma."

"You sound like you know her well. Our Paddy's former fancy woman."

"She was his girlfriend, not his fancy woman. And yes, I've spent a lot of time with her recently."

She raises an eyebrow at my tone. "Well, you've changed your tune about her. It wasn't that long ago you delivered her the news about Paddy's arranged marriage. You didn't seem to have too much of a conscience when you told her that."

"Things have changed."

"What do you mean?"

"I'm not here to talk about Jaine and me."

"Jaine and you? You say it like you're a couple." She looks at Da, egging him on to pry.

Da's frowning at me now. They're like a pair of matching bookends. I'm pretty sure one can tell what the other one's thinking at any given time. Ma tries to add something else, but Da holds up his hand to silence her.

He's got a bee in his bonnet now. Over Jaine, no doubt.

"One question, Eoin, before we move on to the reason behind this unexpected visit. Would you actually be considering this Jaine Jones for the role of Ma Duster?"

I pause before replying. Do I tell them the truth? Do I actually know the fucking answer?

"Yes, I am." I'm admitting it to myself as much as to them.

Ma goes to interrupt, but Da raises his hand once more. "You think this girl has what it takes to run this empire with you, lad?"

I nod. "Aye, Da. I think she does."

"Does she know of your intentions to court her? Potentially take the vows with her?"

"No, Da. She does not."

He nods again before turning it into a head shake. "I'm sorry, Eoin, but I can't allow this courtship to take place."

Anger billows through me. I don't like being told what to do. As the future Irish king, I should be able to choose my bride.

"Why not?”

"Because you'd break our Paddy's heart, son, that's why not. He's in love with the girl. Has been for years. As you know, we weren't made aware of her existence until after we'd agreed to the union between him and the Ruocco girl. The whole sorry situation had your youngest brother turning to the drink."

"I know." I sigh as I run my hand through my hair in frustration.

"So, no. We can't consider her for your union, I'm afraid. It would cause too much upset within the immediate family."

"But what if I can prove she's the right woman for the role, and what if I can also get our Paddy's blessing?"

Why the fuck am I pushing this? Why don't I just let this madness go? Because that's what this is. Sheer fucking insanity. Setting my sights on a woman who wouldn't piss on me if I were on fire.

Ma looks at Da, her mouth agape. She's probably as surprised by my insistence as I am.

"Then, of course, we would have to consider her."

"It's obvious you have feelings for this biker woman, Eoin, but how does she feel about you?" Ma's tone is argumentative. It's clear she doesn't like Da's reply.

"She hates my guts."

She smiles smugly, delighted with that response. "And she's just an old lady or whatever it is the bikers call them? So, what can she offer? What can she bring to the Duster party?"

"What's Sophia going to bring? By the looks of her, she's never broken a fingernail before now, let alone taken a life."

"Sophie will bring a new ally! The Sicilian mafia will become our friend, not our foe. They will be tied to us. So, tell me, what will this Jaine Jones bring that you would consider her for Ma Duster? The matriarch of our organization. Someone who would step into my very own shoes."

"As well as having the ability to kill a man with her bare hands, Jaine also runs one of the most prestigious and successful law firms in Manhattan."

"But we have a lawyer. Padraig deals with these matters on our behalf."

"Jaine's client base boasts outlaws, mobsters, bent politicians, and pigs, many of whom we'd only be too happy to do business with or have on our side. She's already introduced me to several key people, Leoluca being one of them."

We're glaring at each other now. It's not often Ma and I bicker, but it can turn very nasty very quickly when we do.

Da holds his hand up before either of us can speak further, nipping our heated exchange in the bud.

"You have feelings for her, son?"

"Aye, Da. I believe I do."

"Then I want to meet her. Can you arrange for that to take place?"

"Dyl's mentioned that she goes back to California next week." I'm speaking out loud more than anything. How can I convince her to meet my da? That girl will take great pleasure in telling me to fuck right off.

"California? Does she not live in New York? How can you court her if she lives three thousand miles away?"

"It's where her hometown is."

"Is she seeing anyone there? Living with anyone?"

"A biker. The prez of the Angels. But it's nothing serious, I don't think. They haven't taken the vows together, and they have no children."

Da nods.

"I need to meet her. I'll know the minute I look her in the eye if she's got what it takes to be Ma Duster."

"I'll make the necessary arrangement, Da."

"Well then. Enough about this, Jaine Jones, for now. What did you come here to tell us?" Ma interjects.

"I spoke with Jaine yesterday." She immediately rolls her eyes at the mention of her name again. "Ma, this is important. Extremely important. More so if it turns out to be true."

They look at each other.

"What is it then, son?"

I look at my da. "Jaine thinks that Cara's pulling the wool over our eyes about the pregnancy. That she's lying about it to trap our Cill, with the intention of announcing a miscarriage at a later date. Jaine thinks the pregnancy test Cara produced belonged to the girl he's been hooking up with. Sarah Delaney. She's the one who's pregnant with an O'Connell baby."

"And why would Jaine Jones come to you with such a revelation?"

"Jaine needs us to find out if Cara's lying. How else can she possibly do that? She realizes she had nowhere else to go with this. And for me to take her seriously, she had no choice but to tell me why. She knows the Dusters would never question Cara without good reason. Why would we? She's been known to our family her whole life. Jaine's convinced she's lying. She would never have come to me, betrayed Sarah's confidence, if she wasn't completely sure."

"So, this Sarah Delaney. Is she related to Paul Delaney, by any chance?" Da asks.

"She's his baby sister."

"So, Jaine Jones has broken a confidence, taken her life in her own hands, in fact, by betraying Razr's sister? That madman has slit people's throats for far less."

"She's aware of that. She wants what's best for Sarah, our Cillian, and their wee one. So, I'm guessing with that in mind, she's prepared to take that risk. Then again, she also knows Paul Delaney better than anyone."

There's silence while they digest what I've said. While they consider the ultimate of betrayals by the daughter of their closest friends and what her deceit will result in.

"Cara wouldn't lie, Eoin. She knows what this would mean." Ma mutters in disbelief, but I can tell by her face she already doubts Cara's loyalty. She looks between me and Da. We all know what this betrayal would signify for her best friend's daughter.

"Desperate times, desperate measures, Ma. She's invested a lot of time in our Cill. Who knows, maybe she saw the discarded test as an opportunity and seized it?"

"So, the girl our Cill's been fucking is Razr's younger sister? And he's got her pregnant?"

"Aye, Da."

"Does Razr know?"

"No. Our Cill would have no throat if he did."

Ma's eyes are cold, hard, and calculating as she switches into Ma Duster mode. "So, we need to find out for sure if Cara's lying to us."

"Aye, but then what if she's not?" I toss that in there.

"Then we have a problem, son," Da interjects. "See, if Sarah Delaney is carrying a Duster, then that child is at risk from the moment they're born. We'd need to bring them into the O'Connell fold, ideally by Sarah taking the vows with our Cill."

"But if Cara’s pregnant? He can’t wed both."

"Let’s cross that bridge if we come to it. Let's just hope for everyone’s sake that Jaine Jones's gut instincts are correct."

CHAPTER FORTY-TWO

JAINE

Jaine's Apartment, Upper East Side, New York

"What's the plan, Eoin?"

"My ma's going to find out one way or the other today."

"And how is she going to do that?"

"I don't think I need to concern myself with that level of detail, now, do I?"

"Off to the ob-gyn?"

"You sound like you know how this whole pregnancy malarkey works."

"Not at all." I lie through my teeth. My own big reveal will take place once I'm safely back within the confines of Rising, not before.

"It's not likely they'll go anywhere too public. I'm sure you know what this means for Cara if she's found to be lying. The moment my ma raises the question, she'll be fully aware of it too, and she may try to run."

"Yes, I realize exactly what it means, and deservedly so. Her lies could have had a major impact on a lot of other lives, including that of an unborn child."

"You're so sure she's lying?"

"I can't be one hundred percent, but my gut is telling me she is, and it's seldom wrong. I would never betray Sarah's confidence based on a whim. I'm doing this for her sake and for her baby's sake. I'm just hoping she'll thank me later as opposed to wanting to slit my goddamn throat."

"Razr still might."

"You leave him to me. I know how to handle him."

"I've noticed."

"Anyway, I'm not sure if Dylan's mentioned it, but I'm heading back to California imminently."

"Is there a reason you're telling me this?"

"None in particular. I just thought you should know. My business reins are handed over. Once this situation with Sarah and Cillian is put to bed, there's nothing keeping me in Manhattan."

"Nothing?"

"Well, Irish isn't keeping me here, is he? Thanks to you, I'm not allowed to speak to him or contact him in any way. I can easily maintain that ongoing deathly silence no matter where I am and with zero effort."

"It wasn't my decision. It was my family's decision." His response is almost a snarl. I can tell the frequency with which I blame him is starting to grate on his last nerve.

Fucking hurrah. Asshole.

"My da would like to meet you. Will you meet with him, Jaine?"

I frown at that unexpected question. Where the fuck did that come from? That's the last thing I want to do.

"Why?"

"He's heard a lot about you."

"That's even more of a reason for me to ask why."

"He's intrigued by you. Your name comes up a lot."

"It's nice to know I'm a popular topic of conversation at your Reservoir Dogs-style weekly meetings, Eoin, but the answer's no. I have no wish to meet him."

"Can I ask why? Are you scared to meet the head of our family?"

"Can you even hear yourself right now? Let's get one thing straight, I am scared of nothing and no one. Not even your da."

"Then why won't you meet him?"

"You've just given me the reason in your last breath. I quote, 'it was my family's decision.'"

"So, you'll hold that against us forever."

"Of course I will. Why the fuck shouldn't I?" I lash out.

"No one knew you were part of Paddy's life. Decisions were made without that knowledge."

"Listen to me." I'm aware I'm hissing, but I've had enough of his conversation now. "I don't want to hear your goddamn excuses. If you had wanted to find out about Irish's past relationships, you could easily have done so. I have to live with the consequences of you not doing so every day, as does Irish. Then again, you never have done your homework where I'm concerned, have you? The answer is no. The answer will always be no. Anyway, I'm leaving Manhattan, so even if I wanted to, time will not permit it."

"Yes, you've already mentioned you're leaving."

"Will you miss me, Eoin? Is that why you sound so grumpy?"

"Your mouth's too smart for your own good, Miss Jones," he snaps back.

"Ah, so we're back to the formal Miss Jones. Well, hopefully, when I'm back in Rising, we'll have no need to speak to each other again."

There's a pause.

"Will you ever come back to New York, Jaine?"

"Not until after the wedding."

"You're getting wed?"

I laugh at his shocked tone. "I'm talking about Padraig's wedding. A girl has to be asked before she can say yes, and Ace hasn't asked that question of me, and likely never will. As you know, bikers don't follow tradition."

"Would you marry him if he asked you?"

"Surely that's an answer I'd owe him first and foremost, don't you think?"

"Sorry. Yes. Of course."

"So, you'll keep me posted on tonight?"

"Yes. As soon as I hear anything, I'll let you know."

"Thank you. Sarah is picking me up at seven. If it's a false alarm and Cara's pregnant, which I highly doubt, then I can cancel her."

"Maybe you shouldn't cancel."

"What do you mean?"

"She's still carrying a Duster, so she'll still have to meet with the family."

"And she still has to break the news to Delaney beforehand. Unless you have a death wish, I wouldn't suggest any discussions be had without his participation. So, your parents obviously know about Sarah's condition. Do your brothers know?"

"Yes. All bar Cill as he'd likely drag her straight in front of Father O'Reilly and to hell with the consequences."

"A man who knows his own mind."

"A foolish man."

"A man in love, Eoin. Something your mobster heart is incapable of feeling."

"I wouldn't be too sure about that, Miss Jones. Anyway, about meeting with my da."

"I'm not meeting him."

"I'm helping you. You owe me a favor."

"Are you manipulating me again?"

"Call it what you wish."

"Where would you like me to meet him and when?"

"Thursday at noon at the Palace Hotel."

"Keep me posted on the Cara situation," I reply bluntly before putting the phone down.

PADRAIG

Padraig's Apartment, Hudson Yards, New York

Jaine: *You there, Uncle Dyl?*

Padraig: *Very funny. I can't believe our Cill has got two women with child.*

Jaine: *With child? What sort of old-worldly expression is that? I'm changing your title from uncle to grandpa!*

Padraig: *LOL. I'm an old-fashioned kind of fella, darlin'.*

Jaine: *Are you going to be there tonight?*

Padraig: *No, but everyone else will be if it turns out Cara's lied. It'll be a family event. You going?*

Jaine: *Yes and no. I'll be taking Sarah, but I won't be going inside.*

Padraig: *Because of Padraig?*

Jaine: *Yes.*

Padraig: *You know, I've been thinking. Why can't you just speak to him? Where's the harm in it?*

Jaine: *You already know the answer to that. Leave it now.*

Padraig: *Surely friendship is better than nothing?*

Jaine: *Jesus Christ. Have you banged your head today? Have you spent too long staring at screens and your brain's* *finally melted and run out of your ears? You know what I had to do. What I had to agree to.*

What the fuck does she mean? What she had to agree to?

Jaine: *You there, Batman, or have you spotted the Joker trying to scale one of your properties?*
Padraig: *I'm still here, darlin'.*
Jaine: *So, I won't see you tonight? I can't believe I've been in New York all this time and you've managed to avoid me at every turn, Dylan O'Connell. You're giving me a complex.*
Padraig: *Sorry.*
Jaine: *No worries. If you change your mind, Sarah's picking me up at seven, and then we'll be heading straight there.*

"Dyl."

"Paddy, I'm not liking your tone. What have you done?"

I can tell he's rolling his eyes while pushing the glasses that he probably doesn't even need further up his nose.

"I've not done anything."

"What is it, then?"

"Jaine mentioned she had to do something, agree to something."

"She told you that?"

"No. She reminded *you* of that."

"Paddy, where have you been sticking that nose of yours?"

"Nowhere. Anyway, I can't ask her about it because she thinks I already know."

"Good. Because you can't question her on any of this."

"Why can't I?"

"Because no good will come of it. Because you're engaged. And she's moved on, Paddy. She has a new life. She's pregnant with Ace's baby. I've no doubt she'll be announcing that news as soon as she's back in California. She leaves this week."

I can hear the worry in his tone. He probably regrets letting me message her. Still. It's too late for that now.

"I need to see her. Speak to her. Before she goes."

"You can't, Paddy. The family won't be happy if you do anything rash. Promise me you won't do anything stupid."

"Sorry, brother. I can't do that." I know exactly what I need to do. I just need to work out when.

CHAPTER FORTY-THREE

ROISIN

Private Dining Room, Palace Hotel, Manhattan

"I CAN'T BELIEVE I said yes to the dress!" Cara shrieks.

I pretend to laugh at the unfunny comment like it's the first time any bride-to-be has ever uttered those words. I let her have her moment, however short-lived it may turn out to be. For now, she thinks she's bagged herself the lad from her dreams, and they're going to get wed and have a baby.

Live the happily ever after. Then again, maybe not.

I take in the girl who should have been my daughter-in-law. She might still be. Who knows? She may or may not have broken a commandment. Thou shalt not lie. Her future is currently in God's hands.

She's positively glowing. I'm not going to spoil her joyful mood just in case she isn't the lying, deceitful little bitch that Jaine Jones is making her out to be.

My thoughts drift to the biker woman. I've been reading up on her. Both online and from all the intel Eoin's had Dylan produce. As much as it pains me to admit it, I have to agree that she appears a good match for him on the surface. She's wealthy, so she's clearly no gold-digger. She's also highly successful career-wise, with an unrivaled legal reputation for getting the job done. Eoin's right. She boasts a plethora of outlaw connections and politicians that could see us expand our organization considerably. Just from her images, she exudes strength and determination. Her eyes hide well the multitude of sins she's committed. Only people from the life would recognize those tell-tale signs.

She's hiding something else, though. See, her eyes also betray her. Jaine Jones shouldn't have committed a lot of atrocities in her life, but her gaze is telling me otherwise. From one murderous female to another, their green depths hold the final moments of way more souls than she's letting on. I'm convinced of it.

Ma Duster material? We'll know for sure when we meet with her here on Thursday. My Fergal is right. He'll know straight away; we both will. It's just a pity she's a biker.

"You looked like a princess. I can't believe I birthed someone as bonnie as you," Helen gushes, interrupting my thoughts.

She's already borderline pickled by the drink. I smile politely at my larger-than-life friend. Unfortunately, I have to agree with her comment. I realize it's unkind, but I can't believe it either, more so when her husband Jack is also no oil painting and is almost as wide as he is tall. Maybe Cara was switched at birth.

I sip on my Bloody Mary and let them chatter about weddings while they finish what could be Cara's last lunch.

"Where to next, Roisin?" Cara asks giddily.

I put my glass on the table and pat the corners of my mouth with my napkin. "I need to drop by Play. I've some items I need to pick up from John Paul. We can stop in there for a drink if you wish before moving on to the next boutique."

Cara nods excitedly. She probably thinks today is turning into an intimate and impromptu hen party by chance.

Play is one of the many gentlemen's clubs the Dusters own throughout New York. It sounds upmarket. That's because it is. In amongst the gambling that goes on within its decadent four walls, the all-male clientele also has access to strippers, prostitutes, drugs, and weapons. A one size fits all establishment for society's elite. Every patron has a seven-figure net worth minimum. It's essential given the price tag that comes with the exclusive membership. Every applicant's background is double-checked before they are permitted to join, and they also have to sign a non-disclosure agreement. Not that anyone would breathe a word of what goes on on the inside to anyone on the outside. No one wants to feel the O'Connell wrath if they dared breach our confidence.

"I'm so excited. I've always wanted to see inside Play." I'm glad Cara's enjoying what might be her last day out.

"Well, there's a first time for everything." Unfortunately, there's also a last.

Underneath Play is the subway. We own several disused areas of the New York system. They're sealed, completely soundproof, and easy to hose down.

"Ready to go?" I smile. It's a saccharine one, I know it is, but the Ma Duster red mist has already started to descend at the thought of being betrayed by one of our closest.

Play Gentlemen's Club, Manhattan, New York

"Thank you."

I glance at the waitress from the booth we're sitting in. Her *uniform*—a black tube dress—doesn't leave much to the imagination, but it's of exceptional quality which is only befitting of a Duster establishment. I smile at her, and she returns it. She's Asian and very petite and attractive. Then again, all the girls who work in our clubs are beautiful and offer their own unique look or set of skills. The clientele who frequent our venues want something they can't get at home, and they pay handsomely for the add-on services. There's no shame in it. It's a simple case of supply and demand. We all have to earn a crust in some shape or form—even these girls.

I glance around the club. Play is newly opened, and like all of the others of its type, the seating is easy to wipe quality black leather, studded in a Chesterfield design. Everything else is in muted tones of grey and contrasting white. Small tables and tub chairs line the walls. There are several booths like the one we've been shown to, most fitted with privacy screens. Our wealthy members, many of whom are actors, politicians, and other influential people, don't wish to be disturbed or witnessed in any compromising situations or positions. What goes on within these four walls stays within these four walls. The exorbitant price they pay buys that Duster guarantee.

I'm told the gambling den is in the next hall along, but we don't need to frequent that. We already know Cara's situation is all or nothing. Either black or blood red.

Helen downs her drink in one, which is her norm these days. I motion at the waitress to keep them coming. Depending on the outcome of today's events, it's probably best she numbs the pain in advance.

"So, Cara, I've got an ob-gyn who comes highly recommended." She knows I'm not asking her if she wants to use this doctor's professional services. I'm telling her. In the blink of an eye, her demeanor switches from happy and bubbly to defensive as she straightens her back and clasps her hands tightly in her lap.

After that noticeable shift, I'm not sure I need any further proof, but I have to give her the benefit of the doubt. She deserves that, at the very least.

"I'm happy to go with your suggestion, Roisin," she replies hesitantly, spinning a now-empty champagne flute nervously between her fidgeting fingers. She's been drinking all day. Is it another sign of her guilt? Anyone with half a brain knows you shouldn't drink alcohol when pregnant. Maybe Helen condones it. Maybe she did. She is a lush, after all. If it transpires Cara *is* pregnant, then I'll step in. She's not pickling my first grandchild. I watch as she places the glass on the table, observing when she then runs what I'm now guessing to be very damp hands down her fitted black jumpsuit.

I smile politely. "Good. We'll need a blood sample. As you know, John Paul is studying medicine, so he's more than capable." I nod towards the twenty-something newly-appointed ginger-haired manager of Play. "The doctor has also sent some tests she'd like you to complete. I'm not sure what they measure exactly, but she'd like them to be taken and returned today. We can pop into the staff restroom and get them out of the way before continuing. Liam can then drop everything off at her clinic." I nod at my bald-headed driver of thirty years or more. He's my age. Liam looks back at me impassively. He's been well-trained. He never gives anything away.

"What, right now? I mean, I've just had a glass of champagne and…."

"That won't affect the results," I interrupt her. "Shall we?" I motion my head towards the restroom.

"Come on, Cara. Maybe the doctor will be able to give you a due date once she has all the results." Helen motions excitedly with her hands for her daughter to make her way to the restroom.

Not that it will change her outcome, but I would have more respect for the girl—if she is lying—to just own it right about now. Instead, she stands and makes her way into the brightly lit restroom.

It's not as grand as the one for members, but it's still nicely finished in white tiles floor to ceiling and kept exceptionally clean. Our staff works hard on our behalf, and we reward them with excellent working conditions and above-average levels of pay. It's the very least we can do for every echelon of the Duster ranks.

When done, I hand everything to Liam. I've not lied. I do have the best ob-gyn in Manhattan waiting. She also has mouth swabs taken from my boy this morning. Not that Cillian knows why he needed to give them. Just routine, I told her to say if he asked. Within the hour, we'll know if Cara is pregnant, if she ever has been, and if she is, if our Cill is the father.

We sit in silence. The almost party-like atmosphere from earlier has now totally evaporated. I ask the waitress to bring a bottle of top-shelf gin to the table, along with some bottles of tonic. She'll be run off her feet later tonight, so there's no point in adding to the poor girl's workload. Helen can pour her own. Does she suspect anything? Who knows? Maybe she's using this lull in proceedings to reflect on her own life. On whatever has caused her to turn to drink.

Cara's staring into space. She looks pensive. I just need the message from the doctor to confirm what I pretty much now already know.

Why does she not just say? Admit what she's done before she's found out to be a bare-faced liar. Does she think with her parents being our oldest friends that she won't suffer the same fate as anyone who betrays the Dusters? She can't be that naïve, surely? The rules and consequences are universal. No exceptions.

I discreetly check my phone, having switched off all audible notifications.

Message received.

Negative. Not pregnant. Never has been.

I message the rest of the family with the unfortunate update. Eoin will deal with Cillian. He'll likely bring him without breaking the news beforehand. Fergal will bring Jack to say his farewells to his daughter before she goes to meet her maker.

I believe we're also to expect Sarah Delaney.

"Ladies, it's almost opening time at the club, so I think it's best we go somewhere a little more private."

Liam flanks us. If Cara attempts to make a run for it, she won't get very far. I've also asked John Paul to secure the place until given Duster approval to stand down just to be sure.

I walk towards the elevator, and Cara and Helen follow me.

Once inside, I press for the subway level. It's a sad day. A sad day indeed. For all of us, but more so for Cara.

Stupid girl.

JAINE

Jaine's Apartment, Upper East Side, New York

"Well, Eoin?"

"You were right. She's not pregnant. Never has been."

I exhale loudly. I know what this means for Cara. Do I feel guilty? A little. She's about to lose her life because she fell in love with the wrong man. Like Emilia did with Ace.

"In some ways, I wanted to be wrong, but in others, I'm relieved."

"You'd never have betrayed a Delaney confidence if you thought you were wrong."

"True. And my betrayal might still cost me my neck."

We both know that's still a potential reality. I haven't known

Sarah long, and I've seen her in action with a blade. She won't hesitate if she thinks I've stepped too far over the line. I've also witnessed the ferocity with which Razr kills. I've betrayed them both. If today's my day for meeting Beelzebub himself as a result, then so be it.

"What do you expect from this outcome for Sarah?" Eoin asks

"I want her to be able to end the bitch's life if that's her choice."

"If she can't? If my ma or Cill want the honors?"

"Then I want her to bear witness."

"Then what?"

"Then it's up to Cillian and Sarah what they do. They love each other, so I'm pretty sure it will all work itself out."

"You put a lot of faith in love."

"My soul may be condemned, but even our kind have to put our faith in something, Eoin."

"My ma and da are looking forward to meeting you."

"Good to know." I lie.

CHAPTER FORTY-FOUR

SARAH

Play Gentlemen's Club, Manhattan, New York.

IT'S JUST GONE seven p.m., and darkness has already fallen. A festoon of glittering stars hangs in the night sky, worshiping the full moon, and the familiar cacophony of yellow cabs honking and sirens wailing somehow warms the frigid air.

New York. New York. Home sweet fucking home.

Jaine steps down from the back of my hog and types in the code to the parking facility of Play Gentlemen's Club. I know just by looking at the exterior that it's a Duster establishment. It screams luxury and wealth while silently warning you that you enter at your own risk. That by simply crossing the threshold, you take your life into your own hands. It's not far from one of our own clubs, but the Scorpion venues are more lap-dancing establishments. Both offer men the ability to fuck a woman who isn't their wife or girlfriend while also offering the opportunity to buy drugs and weapons before or after. The only difference is, the MC is offering these services at a far more reasonable price. Then again, it won't be quite as discrete, the girls won't be quite as pretty, and the floor will be sawdust-covered to absorb any spilled bodily fluids.

The black matte metal gates swing slowly open, and I ride inside. Jaine makes sure they're firmly closed before following down the ramp behind me on foot. She motions for me to pull up as she yanks off her full helmet and swings her blonde hair free. She screams old lady. The biker's blood that runs through her veins shows on the outside and she doesn't give a damn who can see it. She's leather-clad from head to toe, same as me. Her jacket is patched to the Angels, whereas mine is patched to the Scorpions.

She strides over to me. We haven't spoken much. I don't know why I'm here, but my gut is telling me that she's betrayed me. She's broken the first outlaw rule. The golden one. And she knows I know.

He's here. Somewhere inside. Cillian O'Connell. And all because she's spilled her guts. To what extent has she betrayed me? That, I don't know. Will I slit her throat for her disloyalty? Will my brother? How this situation maps out will decide her fate. We both know it. She's fearlessly dicing with death.

I know she has my best interests at heart, so for now, I'll say and do nothing. I'll simply follow her lead.

"We're here." She speaks two words into her phone, then hangs up.

"You're staying. I'm going, Sarah." She holds out her hands for my hog keys, and I pass them across without hesitation.

She then confronts her disloyalty head-on.

"I'm not going to say what I've done, but if you or Paul decide afterward that my betrayal has seen me crossing too far over the line, then I want you to know that I'll accept I will have to live and die by my own decisions and actions. I'm fine with that. Death comes to us all. Some sooner than others."

I look at her. She's saved my life twice, and as a result, I'd put my neck on the line for her in a heartbeat. But betrayal, deceit, and disloyalty? That falls outside the scope of payback. That's a death sentence right there on its own, no matter how many credits you've earned.

I nod and hug her to me. She hugs me back and kisses me on the cheek. A modern-day Judas? I'll find out soon enough, I'm sure. I don't reply. I can't. Not until I know exactly what she's done.

The parking lot elevator announces its arrival, and we both turn towards it.

"Eoin."

"Jaine. You look…"

He's staring at her like he wants to eat her alive.

"Like a biker?" she replies as she slowly mounts my Night Train.

"Are you sure you're not coming in?" I interrupt his silent worship of Jaine, and both turn to stare at me.

She shakes her head. "Irish will be inside. Eoin will take you to where you need to go."

I nod. I understand her dilemma. Her shitty reality.

"Will you come back for me?"

"Of course. Call me or message me, and I'll pick you up."

She pulls on her helmet, then nods at both of us separately before revving up the hog and pulling out of the parking lot.

"Shall we?" Even as he asks me the question, Eoin continues to stare after her. He turns to look at me only after she's completely out of sight, motioning for me to follow him. We both step inside the elevator.

My eyes scan my environment.

The venue is a disused part of the New York subway system. Not the same area as before, so they must own several. This section feels way more dank and depressing, and the sound of dripping water is the only noise disturbing the utter silence. It's a concrete prison where no one can hear you scream. How many killings have these walls witnessed? How many death gurgles have they captured and now hold within their cold, grey confines?

The floor is wet, so it's recently been hosed down. Padraig O'Connell has undoubtedly taken his life frustrations out by spilling someone's guts today. Maybe more than one. Their tortured endings are all deserved, of course. Does this family have a never-ending sea of foes? Will my baby have to face the same deluge of enemies? Of course they will. This is the life of all O'Connells.

My hand drops to my belly as I take in the entire family, bar two. Cillian is missing. The other missing person must be Dylan as I recognise Paddy having met him before. The other two parties present are older. I drop my hand to my side quickly to not draw attention, but its temporary placement hasn't gone unnoticed. They all stare at me. Clearly, they all know. Does *he* know?

"What the fuck's going on?" I whisper.

The older lady steps forward, and I scan her as she walks toward me. She's tiny. Smaller than Laila even. She's immaculately dressed in beige slacks and a cream twinset. Her almost totally grey hair has stubborn hints of auburn glinting through it, and it's tied up in a chic bun atop her head.

I know I'm looking at Roisin O'Connell. The matriarch of The Hudson Dusters.

"There's no need to be frightened."

She looks at me, whispering her words of reassurance like I'm a cowed dog. Like I need them. I don't. I frown at her.

"I'm not frightened." My tone is firm.

My attention then swings to the older man in the room. Dressed in grey pants and a cream button-down, he looks like a typical grandaddy. My gaze lifts to meet his, and it's then I see what the bowels of hell itself will look like. I want to look away, but now I've made eye contact with the devil himself, I can't. I'm transfixed by the reigning Irish king. I take in his features. His hair is shockingly white, and his piercing blue eyes are the same shade as Paddy's. Eoin looks like him. This is exactly what the eldest brother will look like in thirty years. The only difference between them? The number of lives taken. The atrocities carried out by this man compare to none as the soul of each of his victims is still being held hostage within his penetrating gaze. If time permitted I'm sure I could count every single one of them.

I eventually turn away. I'm not sure if I'm allowed to break eye contact with Da Duster without it first being granted, but fuck it. If I'm being put to ground, then I'm doing so on my terms.

"Sarah." Paddy walks over to me, his cheeky chappy grin front and center. As always, his eyes smile on the surface, doing their best to hide the pain and desperation hidden underneath that's slowly eating him alive. "How have you been?"

I smile at him. It's impossible not to warm to him immediately. His hair is wet from the shower, so it's pretty obvious the hose job on the floor is recent. Who? How? Why? It's better not to ask questions.

"I've been fine, Paddy. It's good to see you again."

It's then I hear the footsteps. The footsteps I hear in my dreams. I'd recognize their sound anywhere. My senses all tune in at once when Cillian O'Connell steps into my eye-line. Even though we're twelve or so feet apart, the familiar scent of peppermint, cigarettes, and his woodsy cologne still envelopes me. A memory, or can I actually smell the heady combination?

I sob. Not a fear sob. It's a sob that escapes when a woman is unexpectedly confronted by the man she loves, the man her heart beats in time with—the man she can no longer have.

“Cillian.” Is it audible? It feels like I’m shouting out loud, but is it only in my head?

“Red.”

My eyes drift over him. The handsome red-haired Irishman who was mine for a fleeting moment. His eyes do the same with me. For the briefest interval from this circus of madness, it’s just him and me.

“Cillian, Sarah, you’ll be wondering why we’re all gathered here today.”

The trance is broken. Everyone turns to stare at Roisin O’Connell.

CHAPTER FORTY-FIVE

CILLIAN

Play Gentlemen's Club, Manhattan, New York.

THIS WHOLE SITUATION IS SURREAL. All my family, save for our Dylan, is gathered underneath Play. Something's going on. Something else that the one who does all the real work around here's not been party to.

And why the fuck is Red here? To tempt me? Rub my nose in it? Show me what I can't fucking have?

"Cara lied, son."

The oxygen rushes from my body. Is Ma saying what I think she is? I need to be sure.

"About?"

"She's not pregnant. She lied to you, Cill. To all of us."

I frown at her. Does she realize what she's saying? What this means for Cara? Why would the girl be so fucking stupid?

"Are you sure, Ma?"

"Yes. All confirmed by the doctor. She never has been. She's led us all up the garden path."

"But how? Why?" I run my hands through my hair. I mean, I've never loved Cara. Not like that. But I do care about her. We've known each other our whole lives. We played together as kids.

My thoughts drift to her folks. To her brothers, who are two of my high rankers. They know what we have to do. They know we have no choice. We can show no mercy, not even to the oldest of family friends.

"Why is an easy question to answer, son." Ma puts a comforting hand on my arm. "Cara loves you. Always has. She knew she had competition." She motions her head towards Red. "She saw an opportunity, and she took matters into her own hands."

"But the test…?"

"Was Sarah's."

There's complete silence. They're letting me digest this ground-breaking fucking news. My head starts to thud. I know it's my blood pounding through my veins and reverberating in my ears. My heart feels like it's going to explode in my chest. Have my prayers been answered by The Almighty after all?

I look at Red. My Red. Her eyes are filling up as she stares back at me, and her hands drop to her belly.

"You're…"

She nods. "Around six weeks."

I lick my lips before I speak, then realize I'm tongue-tied. I mean, how do I phrase what I need to know next? It's not a gentlemanly thing to ask. Even as mobsters, we were brought up to show respect to others, but especially to our women. I frown as I think about how best to say the words without sounding insulting or unkind.

"It's yours."

She knew what I was trying to ask. What I need to know. My

bold, brave Red's cheeks go as red as her name as she glances around my family. "There hasn't been anyone else," she admits, her embarrassment now evident for all to see.

I reach her in three strides, dropping to my knees in front of her. She's come on her hog as she's wearing her leather pants and her big biker boots. I want to tell her she can't ride it anymore. That I forbid it. It's too dangerous. I want to tell her that I won't risk her. But I know she'll just tell me to fuck off, then ride it all the more. I look up at her, my eyes searching hers. My gaze flicks between her belly and her face. Silent tears run down her cheeks as she watches me gently lay my hands against her stomach, my brain trying to register the fact that she's growing a baby inside her. My fucking baby.

It's a miracle. I am the luckiest bastard God ever put breath in.

I press my lips against her still flat skin, and then I stand.

She looks vulnerable with her tear-streaked face. I want my Red back. My reactive as fuck woman with the fierceness in her heart and the fire in her belly that mirrors my own.

My soulmate.

I cup my hand to her cheek, and she covers it with hers before pressing her face against it and closing her eyes.

I want to say so much more, but here and now is neither the time nor the place. Everything now belongs to me. Only me. Call me a possessive fucker, but I don't want to share any part of her. Not with anyone. Not ever.

She's fucking mine. All mine.

I press a gentle kiss on her forehead, and then I turn to face my family. My da's holding my ma close as they witness the miracle that has been granted for me this day. Eoin nods, giving Sarah and me his silent blessing. Paddy rubs his hand over his face as his own emotions threaten to burst from him. I feel a pang of guilt that he has to witness something he'll never have.

The woman he loves carrying his child.

My heart fucking breaks for him now that I can fully understand how he feels. The desolation. The emptiness. When you think they're lost to you forever.

"How… how?" Red stutters. She wants to know how we know. Truth be told, I'd like to know that too, so I can thank the fucker personally.

"Jaine came to see me two days ago. She saw Cara leaving the restroom at the function just after you did, and she put two and two together. She couldn't be one hundred percent sure, but she was prepared to take the risk. To gamble her own life for the greater good." Eoin tells us what we need to know.

Sarah nods. We all know what the end result could have been for Jaine Jones had her instincts been wrong. What the end result could still be depending on how Sarah and Razr deal with her blatant betrayal. I mean, we all know what Cara has in store for her.

"No one lays a finger on Jaine." Everyone turns to stare at our Paddy.

"That's not your decision, now, is it, Padraig? She's betrayed the bikers. It's their choice what they do with her now. We have no say in the matter." Ma glares at him.

"She's given you a grandchild today and our Cill the love of his life back. You should be showing your gratitude to her. NO ONE LAYS A FINGER ON JAINE." He motions at us all one by one, using a switchblade as a pointer.

"I'm fed up hearing about Jaine bloody Jones," Ma mutters. Her dislike for the biker chick is evident in the abruptness of her tone.

"If anyone attempts to lay a finger on Jaine, then they'll have to get through me first. She's saved my life twice recently, and the second time, that included the life of your unborn first grand-child," Red interrupts as she turns to smile at me. "Cillian and I will be asking her to be a godmother to this little one." She places a hand against her belly, and I cover it with my own in silent agreement.

Pride roars through me as I witness her fiery temper rise to the surface once more as she takes on my ma to defend her friend. To defend her family. My own kin will respect her for doing just that, even if they don't like her choices. Family means everything to us. It's what binds the O'Connells together.

"But we have a whole host of good people who are better suited to being godparents. Good Catholic people," Ma argues back.

"Jaine is good people. The best. I'd trust her with my life, and I'd trust my baby's life in her hands. There is no one I trust more, except for me, Cillian, and my brother."

"Plus, Jaine was raised Catholic," Paddy adds smugly.

I turn my attention back to Red. We both know what happens next. It's time. She nods at me.

"Bring her in," I say out loud, my eyes never leaving hers.

SARAH

"Daughter?"

I turn to stare at Roisin O'Connell. On the surface, she doesn't look like a mass murderer, but I know she is one. Of that, I have no doubt. Underneath the twinset and pearls exterior, there's a woman who would kill and die for her beliefs. For her family. As I would. Do I trust this tiny woman? No. Do I like her? No, I don't. But she's Cillian's mom. My baby's grandmother. I have no choice but to tolerate her. Maybe trust and like will come in due course, but I very much doubt it. I believe in going with your gut instincts, and from what I can gather, she wanted Cara to become family. To be Cillian's future. Always has.

This toleration will be shared both ways.

She looks at me, and I can see the distaste. Is it because I'm not a practicing Catholic? Because I'm not Irish? Because I'm a biker?

She motions her head towards a stainless-steel wheeled trolley, the top of which is covered in knives, blades, and various other instruments of torture. This is a test. She's making sure I'm worthy of becoming one of them. That I have what it takes to kill someone in cold fucking blood.

I also know that as soon as I pick up my weapon of choice, I'm accepting that I'm one of them. That my baby is one of them. Our silent agreement will be signed in blood.

Cara's blood. Spilled by my hand.

The lady herself walks into the room, escorted by Eoin, her blonde head held high. She's on her own. Maybe she said her goodbyes elsewhere. To her parents. To her siblings, if she has any. I pray she has, as she's not leaving this space alive.

Cara faces me from the same spot Cillian stood only moments before. Paddy and Eoin flank her, each holding an arm so she can't run. She jerks her limbs from their hold, her expression one of defiance. She's clearly insulted that they'd think so low of her that she'd try to run. She's from the life. Her family are high rankers. She wants to die with honor. It's her final wish. I have to respect her for that. I'd expect the same.

"I'm sorry for betraying you all. Especially you, Roisin." She nods at her. "And you, Cill." She looks at him, and I can see the love shining in her eyes.

Tears threaten, but I blink them back. Even though I hate the scheming bitch, I understand. I know what it's like to love this man, only to lose him.

But I didn't betray him. Not even when presented with the opportunity. I would never fucking betray him.

She turns her attention to me. She knows she's my problem to deal with now. That my new family expects it. The physical proof they need that I'm worthy of becoming one of them. Only then can I rightfully claim my place beside Cillian.

I ignore the trolley covered in deadly weapons. I walk across to Paddy, and I hold out my hand. He passes me the switchblade he threatened us all with earlier. It's clean. Then again, maybe it's new. Perhaps it's a Duster tradition that every soul sent to the bowels of hell at the very least deserves to be killed by a weapon with their own name invisibly engraved on it. I look down at the silver blade. Its weight feels good in my hand. Too good.

I turn back to look at Roisin over my shoulder. "Delaneys use a blade. Always." I raise my chin.

She nods at me. Do I detect a hint of pride in her green eyes? Eyes that are identical to Cillian's. Probably not. Methinks I'll have to do a lot to earn her respect. I'm being handed the O'Connell name because they have no option, not through choice.

I turn and face the woman who tried to take Cillian from me with her lies and deceit. She hates me. I can see it in her eyes. But she will say nothing as she knows she didn't play the outlaw game fairly. Every action has a consequence. Every consequence has a reality.

This is hers.

I nod at her, and she nods back. It will be a quick death. Painless almost, aside from the initial sting when the blade first connects with her throat.

I walk behind her, and I tilt her head back so it's almost resting on my shoulder. She doesn't fight. I stare into Cillian's eyes as I cut the woman from his past from ear to ear. I feel the warmth of her lifeblood as it sprays and runs down my hand and arm, then listen as it drips to the floor.

Her body tenses briefly, and then she slumps to the ground, her bodily fluids quickly pooling at my feet.

I can feel the pride radiate from Cillian. From the entire family.

I've defended their honor. Taken the life of someone who dared disrespect them. I am now one of them. I offer the switchblade back to Paddy, but he smiles and shakes his head to decline it before holding up the new one he's now playing with. The one that's waiting for the next Duster victim. I wipe both my hands and the blade down the front of my black tank top, then I fold the weapon down and stick it in my back pocket.

Roisin walks towards me and hugs me tightly against her.

"Welcome to the O'Connell family."

I accept her embrace, then step back and take in her cream twin-set, which is now also covered in Cara's blood.

I nod back in response, knowing I've just signed a deal with Lucifer himself for the remainder of my life.

"We need to go," Cillian interrupts.

"Go where?"

CHAPTER FORTY-SIX

CILLIAN

Play Gentlemen's Club, Manhattan, New York.

I MOTION my head towards the elevator to let Eoin know that we're leaving, and he nods. He knows what I need to do now.

The cleaners will come and deal with the aftermath of Cara's unfortunate demise. She'll be given the best of send-offs, and a credible reason will be found as to why she's gone to meet her maker at such a tender age. Thankfully, our engagement hadn't been formally announced, so only a handful of people knew about the intended nuptials. They won't say a word if they know what's good for them. And trust me, they do.

Rumors will circulate, but then, they always do.

I grab Sarah's hand and pull her towards the elevator, but she digs her heels in. She doesn't like being told what to do. My dick reacts immediately at her blatant show of defiance, but I won't act on my physical urges. Not until we're man and wife. What we share now is way more than just fucking.

This is a lifetime commitment. Mutual respect is a necessity.

"Go where?" She's glowering at me now, her chin raised, her hazel eyes flashing rebelliously. She's covered in the lifeblood of someone else, yet still, she's never looked more fucking beautiful.

"I need to go speak to your brother."

"Why?"

"So many fucking questions." I smile as I roll my eyes at her and cup her chin in my hand. "I need to ask him for your hand, Red, that's why." I place a soft kiss against her lips.

I pull on her gently, and this time, she inches forward slowly, then stops and shakes her head.

"Are you insane? He'll fucking kill you."

"That's what I reckon too, so I suggest you let Jaine know where we're headed so she can meet us there. We may need her to control that madman. When he sees us together, I'm not sure he'll even allow me to speak before he slits my throat."

JAINE

The Iron Scorpions' Clubhouse, Brightling, New York

I pull the Night Train up at the familiar compound entrance and take off my helmet, shaking my hair free. The clubhouse's grim exterior is shrouded by darkness. The only light afforded me is from the moon herself. It's silent, aside from the sound of music coming from inside. I inhale the smell of petrichor that lingers in the air after the recent shower. It reminds me of home.

Of Ace.

I miss him so goddamn much. Tears threaten, but I blink them back. I'm becoming more emotional each day. Pregnancy is a blessing, but the associated hormonal spikes are a curse. They're giving me a conscience and making me feel guilty. There's no place for either in my life. Not when you pull a trigger as often as I do. One split-second delay could see the tables turned, and then it's game over.

Would I have done what I did? Would I have betrayed the MC's confidence if there wasn't a baby involved? If I wasn't carrying myself? Definitely not. I rub my hand over my rounded tummy. It's time to shelve my extra-curricular activities until this little one is born.

My life means nothing. Theirs means everything.

I gaze at the building in front of me. I haven't been here since before I set off for Rising. So much has changed since then. I lose myself in my thoughts, recapitulating over the events of the previous months.

The temporary reprieve from reality doesn't last as the security lights come flooding on. I didn't tell Delaney I was paying a visit. I merely took the call from Sarah, and she asked me to meet her here. She didn't give anything away. Maybe my betrayal was too much. Maybe things didn't work out as I hoped.

The music switches off on the inside. I'm not expected, so the place will now be on high alert. For many, I'm sure I'll be a blast from the not-too-distant past. Welcome or not? That remains to be seen.

"Jaine."

"Jamie."

The young prospect salutes me, then winks as he keys in the code for the gates. I smirk at his brazen cheek, genuinely pleased he's managed to hold on to it and that it hasn't been sucked into the goddamn shit we trawl through living this fucked up existence.

"You fucking those cum sluts yet?"

"Patched in next month, and then I'm going to work my way through every single one of them."

"Jesus Christ. I'll bet those ladies can't wait for that."

"Happy to service you too, Jaine. I'm sure I can make it good for you." He smirks, rocking back and forth on his feet as he runs his hands up and down the seams of his cut.

I smile, shaking my head in disbelief at the words coming from the mouth of this eighteen-year-old man-child.

"As much as I'm sorely tempted, I'm not sure the prez of the Angels would appreciate me taking you up on that very kind offer, but thank you for thinking of me all the same."

He snickers as he closes the gates behind me before pulling on them to make sure they're firmly closed, causing them to creak loudly in protest.

I park up Sarah's hog. Maybe I was always meant to arrive here on it.

More so if I'm destined never to leave.

I TAKE IN DELANEY'S ALTER-EGO, THE MADMAN HOPEFULLY ONLY present due to my visit being unplanned. I watch as he struggles to flick that internal switch of his. When he does, he folds down the switchblade he's been holding in his hand and puts it in his back pocket.

My eyes scan over the prez of the Iron Scorpions. My former partner of four years. I frown as I walk up to him, my hands instinctively reaching up to touch his hair. He's shaved off the sides, and what's left on top falls into his tortured green eyes.

Its beautiful strawberry blonde length has also been hacked away, and a beard has now replaced the stubble that he always kept so immaculate on his handsome features.

"Delaney," I whisper. I don't have to ask why. He's struggling. His inner demon is clawing at his brain and tearing him apart. Delaney and Razr are fighting for control, and the latter is currently winning. It's when he reaches this stage that he starts to physically rip out his hair in chunks. It's been years since he did, but it's obvious that's what he's preparing for or has already started doing. He's heading for rock bottom if he hasn't already reached it.

As I did so often in the past, I wrap my arms around him to absorb his pain.

He returns my embrace, his arms wound so tightly around me that it physically hurts. But I don't complain. I never have. I let his familiar sandalwood cologne soothe me as I do my best to comfort him in return. I can almost feel his mental anguish passing from him before sinking and settling deep into my bones. I welcome it. I'm only glad I can offer him some respite, no matter how little or how temporary.

Do I feel guilty? Of course I do. I wish I could have loved him the way he needed and wanted me to. When we were together, I was able to stop him from drowning in his thoughts. He was almost normal. Now? Well, now I don't know what the hell the answer is. He may be able to hide his personality disorder from people in the short term, but the demon will win in the end unless he takes drastic action.

He needs someone to share his life with to ensure Delaney keeps control. He also needs professional help. A proper diagnosis.

I nod at Flame, and the quiet albino nods back in response before passing me a bottle of water from behind the bar. I'm guessing the other council members must be on a run, as the clubhouse is relatively empty. Maybe that's just as well. It won't be long before Cillian and Sarah arrive. I have no idea what will happen then, but blood will be spilled, I'm sure.

"Let's go through to your office, Delaney."

He kisses my forehead, then takes my hand like we're still a couple. I want to ask him not to do that, but I don't want to antagonize him. Not when he's already struggling. And not when I feel partially responsible. If I needed another reason why I need to escape New York, this is it. I can't encourage him, not that I have been. I can't have him think that there could ever be an *us* again. There won't be. Hopefully, out of sight and mind will allow him to realize that, move forward, and find someone else.

"I wasn't expecting you, Jaine."

I stare around the familiar space. Like his bedroom at the clubhouse, everything in his office is black leather or walnut wood and screams luxury. Unlike Ace, Delaney likes to display his wealth. He wants people to know how well he's done in life. Aside from the O'Connells and one or two others, there are very few people in Manhattan who are as wealthy as this man.

Money can't buy you happiness, though. He sits here, a perfect example of that fact.

"I'm meeting Sarah here."

I'm not sure how much to say. At the moment, I don't know precisely why I'm meeting her. Do I tell Delaney that I betrayed his sister, so in turn, I was disloyal to both him and the Scorpions? It may see him slit my throat before she even gets here. Maybe I should keep it intact for now. She should have first refusal, after all.

"She didn't mention anything."

"It was a last-minute decision."

We spend a few moments drinking each other in. I've spoken with him regularly. I saw him at Leoluca's function and during the shitshow that took place afterward, but it's not the same as being face to face, just me and him.

"So, how have you been? I like your hair. I didn't at first, but it's kind of growing on me."

He smiles as he rubs his hands up the shaved sides. Then, as quickly as it appeared, it vanishes. "I was pulling it out."

"I know the reason you did it, Delaney." I pause. "Do you think you need some professional help?"

"Maybe."

"You want me to go with you?"

"You'd do that? For me?"

"Of course I would. I'd do anything for you, Delaney. You know that."

"Apart from be with me."

"Apart from that, yes."

"I hear congratulations are in order."

I frown at him. "What do you mean?"

"When you and Sarah were taken, I called Ace. He told me you were pregnant. He told me I had to get you safe as you're carrying his baby."

I'm pissed off with Ace. Why the fuck did he say that? Especially to Delaney. As someone I spent four years of my life with, he deserved to hear that news from me. Has this added to his inner turmoil? I always told him I wasn't old lady or mom material, and yet here I am, doing both with another man.

"I would have done everything to find you, even without that knowledge."

"I know you would."

"Thank you for saving her life."

"Thank you for saving mine."

"I don't know what I would have done…."

"You don't need to know. You don't need to think about that. She's safe. Stop punishing yourself for shit you had no control over and for shit that didn't even happen, Delaney."

I make no apology for my terse response. He's his own worst enemy, and it needs to stop. He rubs his hand over his beard.

Both my phones vibrate.

Padraig: *You there?*

Sarah: *Can you meet me outside in ten minutes?*

I ignore Dylan for now. It's time to see what my immediate future holds, courtesy of Miss Sarah Delaney and her brother.

CHAPTER FORTY-SEVEN

SARAH

The Iron Scorpions' Clubhouse, Brightling, New York

TAM'S DRIVEN us to the clubhouse, and we've sat in silence the entire way.

Me and Cillian. Together. Forever. Forever may be short-lived if my big brother has anything to do with it.

We need Paul's blessing. I doubt Cillian would take the vows with me without it.

Cillian's hand squeezes mine as we pull up at the gates of the Scorpions' compound. I'm nervous. As much as Paul's my brother, he's also a fucking headcase. I have no idea how he'll react. I agree that it was best to involve Jaine. I'm not the one to try to control him. We lost seven years. We're just getting to know each other all over again.

For now, he's a paradox. Straightforward but complex. Level-headed but completely insane.

I watch as Jamie walks over to the gates, steps outside, and then closes them behind him. I put down my window as he won't recognize the cage.

"Sarah? You brought some visitors?" He nods his head suspiciously at Cillian.

"I need to speak to Paul. Can you let us through?"

"Sure thing. You know the rules, though, Sarah. Mind telling me who these two are first and foremost?"

"This is Cillian O'Connell and his right-hand man, Tam."

Jamie and Cillian stare at each other. Jaime quickly backs away. Maybe he saw the death and destruction in those green Irish eyes and the sheer blackness of Cillian's condemned soul.

"The Duster?"

"The Duster. I'm sure he's been here before, Jamie. The Dusters are our allies, after all."

He pauses for a moment before keying in the entry code and opening the gates. We drive through, he closes them securely behind us, and we park up beside my hog.

Then we wait for Jaine.

"JAINE."

I jump out of the SUV as soon as I see her approach, running across to wrap my arms around her.

"Thank you." Tears of gratitude spill down my cheeks, and a sob escapes me.

She wraps her arms around me to return my embrace. "I'm glad it all worked out, Sarah." She moves to hold me at arm's length. "I'm sorry for betraying you, but there was no other way. I knew the risks. I still do."

I know she's referring to my brother. Regardless of the positive outcome, at least from mine and Cillian's perspectives, Paul might still see fit to end her life for her blatant betrayal.

"He doesn't need to know, Jaine."

She shakes her head. "He does need to know, and I'll be the one to tell him. I'm not keeping things from him. I promised him no matter what that I'd always be honest with him. I fully intend to stand by my word."

"Jaine."

I watch as Cillian approaches her and hugs her. She keeps her hands at her sides. Out of all the brothers, he's the one she knows least. I want to change that. They both mean the world to me. I want them to be friends. Well, as much as you ever can be in this life.

He pulls back, sensing her reluctance to accept his tactile embrace. "The Dusters will be forever in your debt for what you've done."

She nods but says nothing.

I take Cill's hand in mine, and we look at each other.

"We want you to be godmother."

She immediately shakes her head. "I can't, Sarah. I'm sorry." She wipes at the tears that have started to fall with the back of her hand. I understand why. As a godparent in an Irish Catholic family, you would be expected to be active in the child's life. It's not just a case of sending gifts at Christmas and on birthdays. Being a godparent would tie her to the Dusters for life. To Irish. To Sophia. She'd have to face them at every single family event. It's too much to ask of her. Well, at least for now, it is.

I place my hand on her arm. "You don't have to decide right away, Jaine. We've got a while to go yet," I say softly.

She nods, but only to appease me, I'm sure. I know she'll fight me every step of the way, but I'll win. There's no one I want in my baby's corner more than Jaine.

"So, what do you need from me?" She looks between us both.

"I need to ask Razr for Sarah's hand," Cillian replies.

She exhales loudly. "Jesus, you couldn't have picked a worse time. Have you seen him recently, Sarah?"

I shake my head and frown. "Not for a few days. Is he bad?"

"The worst I've seen him in years." She sighs, running her hand through her hair. "I guess you want me to take my life into my own hands by being the intermediary?"

"There isn't anyone else who can calm him down if he takes the news badly, Jaine. Especially when he hears Sarah's already pregnant. He'll want to chop off my hands and my dick before slitting my throat."

She chuckles. "Yes, most likely. Come on, let's get this over with. You ask the question, then let me handle the rest."

JAINE

"What the fuck is going on?"

Delaney looks like a man possessed as he stares at each of us slowly. He's already got a blade in his hand, and he's flicking that weapon in perfect timing with the rapid beat of my heart. Hopefully, it'll still be beating in half an hour and, just as importantly, still doing so from inside my chest.

"Stay right where you are, Delaney, and just listen. Cillian? You have something to ask?"

I turn to look at Irish's brother. Cillian will be carrying a weapon for sure and could easily go toe to toe with Delaney, but he won't want to do that. If they're to be kin, this needs to be amicable. He needs to convince Delaney. If he can't, I need to.

"Razr… Paul, I'd like to take the vows with Sarah, and I've come here to ask you for her hand. Will you give your blessing to our union?"

The question is now out in the open.

Delaney runs his hands across the shaved sides of his head repeatedly in the absence of having any hair to yank on. Then, in an instant, he roars like the madman he is and flips his desk clean over. Everything crashes to the floor as he stands there, the vein pulsing angrily on his neck.

"Have you been fucking my sister?" He points his blade threateningly at Cillian. "HAVE YOU BEEN FUCKING MY SISTER?"

"Put the blade down, Razr," I warn him.

He ignores me, leaving me no choice but to step in front of him. It's either that or one or the other will end up dead today. The rage emitting from him is almost tangible. I know there will be little reasoning with him as he can't hear anything now apart from the demon screaming inside his head.

"PUT THE GODDAMN BLADE DOWN!"

He moves to strike at Cillian, and I reach for his arm, causing the blade to connect with my wrist. Blood immediately starts pissing everywhere.

"RAZR, PUT THE FUCKING WEAPON DOWN!"

He stops, staring at the blade, then at my open wound, which is now pooling blood on the floor. The trance is broken.

"Jaine…" He whispers in regret.

"Shut the fuck up and listen to me, Delaney. They love each other. Of course he's fucked her. Sarah's pregnant. You're going to be an uncle. Now, if you want to kick the shit out of each other, then be my guest, but no fucking weapons. Do you hear me?" He stares at me. "I said, do you hear me?"

Delaney nods slowly as he passes me the blade, then, with a roar, he launches himself at Cillian.

I grab Sarah and drag her out of the room.

"But…"

"Leave them to it. They won't kill each other, and that's all that matters. Now, as you're the closest thing we've got to a nurse, I need you to stitch me up. There's a kit behind the bar." I motion my head towards the communal area. "I'll wait in Paul's bedroom."

"BY BETRAYING MY SISTER, YOU ALSO BETRAYED BOTH THE Scorpions and me. You do know that Jaine." His voice is barely audible. He's disappointed in me. How much will decide whether I leave this room alive.

Sarah and I returned to find Delaney and Cillian sitting and sharing a whiskey over the uprighted desk. Both are beaten up and bloodied, but Cillian now has the blessing he needs.

"I'm aware of that, Delaney, but it was to ensure your sister and her unborn baby's happiness, and I'd do the same all over again."

This is my battle. Neither Cillian nor Sarah can influence Razr's decision. They both know that.

Delaney stands and walks towards me with his blade back in his hand. I won't beg for my life, and he knows it.

He folds the weapon and puts it in his back pocket before taking my hand in his and turning my arm over.

He inspects the two-inch cut on my wrist, which now complements the healing tissue caused by the bindings. The stitches are at least neat this time. Sarah will make a good nurse, even if she just uses those skills to tend to the countless wounds these MC men come back from runs with.

"I'm so sorry, Jaine." His face is etched with guilt as he lifts my wrist and places a gentle kiss against the bloody wound. "I'll forgive your disloyalty if you forgive me for hurting you."

I smile at his offer of a truce.

"Deal."

CHAPTER FORTY-EIGHT

SARAH

The Delaney Home, Brightling, New York

I KNEEL beside the inked Irish mobster who's contrasting against my white metal-framed childhood bed and surrounded by poster-covered pink walls and cuddly toys. He lies there with both hands behind his head and stares at me. I'm finding this situation surreal. We both are. I can't take my eyes off him either. I feel the need to pinch myself to make sure this is all really happening. That I won't wake up only to find he's been married off to Cara.

All my life, if I had any luck, it was bad. I've always been dealt the shittiest hand.

Now I've been well and truly fucking blessed.

Cillian O'Connell is beautiful. He's not classic, magazine-cover good-looking like Eoin or Padraig. He's more a mixed bag of features that culminate to create someone who looks breath-taking. He's all angled features and pale skin, and for a redhead, he has virtually no freckles. He also has the body of a god. Which I already knew, even if before I could only see it with my hands. He licks his bottom lip as he watches me take in every perfect inch of him. My clit throbs at the sight of his tongue piercing, my body remembering what he can do with that thing.

"You're really good-looking."

"I know."

"And vain."

"You knew that already."

He smirks at my blatant admiration. He'll be used to being ogled, I'm sure. Used to having to squeeze that massive head of his through open doorways.

"You asked Paul, but you didn't ask me."

"Didn't ask you what, Red?"

I love it when he calls me that. Not that I'll ever admit to it.

"To marry you. You've just assumed I'll say *I do* when prompted. Who's to say I will?"

"You will."

"Why will I? You're awfully cocksure of yourself, Irish boy."

"Because you love me, and you're carrying my offspring."

"Who says I love you?"

"I do."

"How do you know?"

"Are you saying you don't?" He raises one eyebrow, his mouth curving into an over-confident smirk as he calls my bluff.

"I do." I instantly feel my cheeks redden, and I bite my lip, unsure how to phrase what I need to know. He must see my brain whirring.

"Yes, I love you too, Red." He runs his finger slowly down my cheek.

"Then why haven't you kissed me?" I ask the question that's been bothering me since we left the subway. Even now we're alone, he's not trying anything on, and his kisses have been more pecks than anything toe-curling.

"I have kissed you."

"Not properly. Not like you mean it."

"I can't do that, Red."

"Why?" I frown

He drags me down beside him before tucking my head under his chin, and I inhale the woodsy smell of his cologne.

"Because if I kiss you properly, I'll want to fuck you."

"And what's wrong with that? It's not like this baby is the result of an immaculate conception." I run my hand over my flat tummy.

"That's not how it works, Red."

"What do you mean?"

"I've made a commitment to you that goes way beyond fucking. As a mark of my respect for you, there won't be any sex between us until we're man and wife."

I sit bolt upright and stare down at him. "Abstinence? You're kidding me, right?"

"No joke."

"Then we need to get married tonight."

"You want to fuck that bad we need to get married tonight?"

"Yes."

He laugh snorts. Well, I'm glad he finds this situation amusing.

"Do you not want the works? Most girls want to make a big deal out of their wedding day."

"Well, I'm not most girls. Plus, I need Jaine to be there, and she'll be heading back to California any day now."

"She'll come back for the event, surely?"

"She won't. Trust me."

I won't divulge any details, although I'm not sure how long I can keep what I know to myself about what Eoin did. I don't want to have any secrets between us. Then again, maybe he already knows. I can't really mention my suspicions about the baby's father either.

Moving to straddle him, I deliberately rub myself against his dick, causing him to growl and grip my hips hard to get me to stop.

"Fuck, Red. Have a heart, sweetheart."

I repeat the movement despite his protests, and he instinctively grinds against me.

"Nope." I lean forward and cover his mouth with mine, my tongue pushing past his lips to taste him. He's mine. No other woman will taste his peppermint and cigarette flavor ever again.

If any try, I'll fucking kill them. If he lets any try, I'll fucking kill him.

His hands grip my ass, his fingertips digging into my flesh as he starts to thrust his hard-on slowly and deliberately against me, angling the head of his cock so it teases my swollen clit. He can't even control it. It's clear he's hanging on to this self-imposed abstinence of his by a thread.

Deepening the kiss, he fists my hair in one hand as his tongue sweeps the inside of my mouth, then he flips me over.

I anchor my legs around his hips, and he rubs the entire length of his erection against me. "I need to fuck you, Red," he whispers against my mouth, cursing when I drop my hand to rub his dick through his jeans.

"Better sort out that wedding, then."

"You're going to be a cock tease to get your way?"

"I'll do whatever it takes to get my way. You'd better bear that in mind for the rest of your days."

"We'll be wed tonight, and once we are, I am going to fuck you into next week."

He bites my neck before soothing it by sucking on it. "Witnesses?"

"The two people without whom we'd never have met."

"Jaine and Eoin?"

"Jaine and Eoin."

PADRAIG

Padraig's Apartment, Hudson Yards, New York

Jaine: *Sorry it took so long to message back, Dyl. Cillian and Sarah asked me to go with them to the Scorpions' clubhouse.*

Padraig: *Why?*

Jaine: *Cill wanted to ask Delaney for Sarah's hand. They wanted me there to deal with Razr's pretty much guaranteed adverse reaction.*

Padraig: *I'd say how romantic, but my guess is it was probably a blood bath.*

Jaine: *No blood spilled. Well, apart from mine.*

Padraig: *What do you mean?*

Jaine: *Razr skewered my wrist with his blade.*

Padraig: *I'm going to gut the fucker.*

Jaine: *Talk about an over-reaction. And since when did I nominate you as my personal protector? For the record, I'm a big girl. I can handle my own shit. Thank you.*

Padraig: *Did our Cill not try to stop him?*

Jaine: *It was all too quick. Delaney didn't mean to cut me. He apologized afterward. Anyway, spilling guts is Irish's party trick, and how can you gut anyone when you never leave the house? I mean, I've been in New York for weeks and you've avoided me at every goddamn turn.*

Jaine: *Sorry, two ticks.*

Padraig: *Jaine?*

Padraig: *Jaine!*

Jaine: *Alright, keep your goddamn hair on. It was my other phone.*
Padraig: *Who was it, darlin'?*
Jaine: *It was Sarah. I've been told I need to make my way to St. Peter's Church. I'm not supposed to tell anyone as they don't want your ma and da to know. She and Cill are taking the vows tonight. They want me and Eoin to be witnesses. Why the fuck does it have to be that asshole?*
Padraig: *You really do hate him, don't you?*
Jaine: *Can you blame me?*

CHAPTER FORTY-NINE

JAINE

St. Peter's Church, Upper East Side, New York

I CAN FEEL *HIM*. All around me, I can fucking feel him. Having parked the hog on the small street in front, I now stare up at the church. Irish's church. It's impressive, I have to say. A place where, had it been part of God's masterplan, I'd have taken the vows with him. Ancient grey stone walls and a spire that reaches into the night as though to touch the very heavens themselves form the imposing building. Bats flit playfully around my head as I stare up into the star-laden night sky. I close my eyes and inhale the earthy scent of fresh soil, then lower my gaze and take in the small graveyard that makes itself known by placing an array of uneven headstones in my line of vision. The start of a small plethora, I'm sure. And these days, with space at a premium, only for the extremely wealthy.

Will Irish be buried here one day? Sophia? Their children?

I can't do this. My heart physically aches. With a shaky breath, I turn and stride back towards the hog. I need to leave. I need to get the fuck away from here. I'll message my apologies to Sarah. I'll tell her that the strong biker female I make myself out to be was too yellow-bellied to enter this holy place. His place. Facing this most sacred space was just too much to ask of me in the end.

I'm weak. I can't deal with it. The pain is still too raw and intense. Then again, it always fucking will be.

When was he last here? A day ago? Two days? Today even?

I curse myself, stop, then turn back towards the building. Get a grip, Jaine.

I place my hand on my rounded tummy and gasp as I feel my baby move. For the first time ever, I feel the fluttering inside me as I walk towards the most aged of imposing doors.

They'll all already be inside, I'm sure. Waiting for cowardly little old me.

Life. Moves. On. Jaine.

It has to. I have to. As much as I don't want to leave him behind, I have no goddamn choice. Eoin didn't leave me with one.

I touch the black circular metal handle. How many times has Irish touched it? I turn it and push the door forward. It creaks loudly in protest, its weight pressing against me as though to keep me out before finally relenting and letting me in. It's clear The Almighty doesn't want me inside his place of worship. I don't belong here.

The bright lights inside contrast the darkness I leave behind. I breathe in the smell of this holy place. I'm expecting it to be dank and musty. A sob escapes me. It's too much. Because now I can smell him. Old Spice. I swear to fucking God that's what I can smell. Or is it just my imagination? His whole life, his whole being, every single part of him will be ingrained on the inner walls of this church. From boy to man, this place has been a staple throughout his life.

It's like he's here. Watching. Listening. Ever-present.

Does he miss me? The question crosses my mind fleetingly, and I quickly push it away. Of course he doesn't. I remind myself how it all ended. What I had to do. But then, Irish hasn't made any effort to contact me. He could have if he'd really wanted to. Did he give up so easily because he didn't care after all? Was it a simple case of out of sight, out of mind? Does he love Sophia now? Is he in love with her?

Would I have responded if he had? We'll never know.

Then again, I asked him not to contact me. I told him I didn't love him. That I never fucking had. Try telling that shit to my heart as the painful grip of his loss surrounds and tightens around it like a vice.

My guard down, I turn around.

"Jaine." Sarah's tone is sympathetic.

I don't want her fucking pity. I don't want anyone's pity. She frowns at me, taking in the pain that, for the briefest of seconds, I know is etched all over my face. Pain that should never be displayed in the life unless you want others to know that you're weak.

Still. Maybe now she realizes she should never have asked me to come here. I wasn't ready to face the loss of him head-on. Not yet. Maybe not ever.

My smile is shaky. Both of us know I can't confront the Dusters like this. An emotional goddamn wreck. Not Cillian. Definitely not Eoin. I won't give that fucker the satisfaction of seeing me on my knees.

I take a second to compose myself.

Deep breaths. In for four. Out for four.

"I'm sorry, Jaine. I never thought of how hard coming here would be for you."

I exhale slowly. "I'm a big girl, Sarah. I've suffered through far worse." But I haven't.

"Jaine."

I turn to look at Eoin O'Connell. Rage billows through me. He doesn't realize how lucky he is right now. If I had a gun in my hand, I'd shoot the fucker right between the eyes for the part he played in the demise of my soul. God may strike me down for doing so in His place of worship, but it would still be worth it.

"Eoin." My voice is monotone as I take in his expensive suit. Money. Position. Power. It's all that matters to this unfeeling man with a heart of stone.

I suddenly feel under-dressed wearing my clothes from earlier. The biker chick. The scum of outlaw society. Then again, Sarah is wearing the same. She's just changed her tank top for one that's bridal white.

"Let's go, Jaine."

I break eye contact with Eoin as Sarah snakes her arm through mine and leads me into the depths of the church. My eyes glance over the tall, vaulted ceilings, the ancient wooden pews, and the abundance of stained-glass windows that no doubt look breathtaking with the daylight streaming through them. It's a beautiful place. Serene. I can feel its history wash over me.

"I'll just fetch Cill," Sarah whispers in my ear.

I take in Father O'Reilly. A man I've heard mentioned a million times before now. So many times I feel like I already know him. He's short and rotund, with rosy cheeks and a mop of bright white hair. If he had a beard, he'd resemble Father Christmas. He smiles at me welcomingly.

"Jaine Jones?"

I nod.

"Have you been baptized, Jaine?"

"Both baptized and confirmed, Father." It's true. Had all that shit done well before I started killing people as a hobby and for obscene amounts of wealth. Not that anyone present is aware of that fact.

I turn to look at Eoin, who's now standing to my left. He looks proud for some reason. Why? I don't want the asshole to look at me proudly. Or like he wants to fuck me. I don't want him to look at me in any way at all.

The door behind the altar opens, and Cillian and Sarah step out. My heart warms at the sight of them. At the love that's almost tangible flowing between them. I did good. I know I did. I couldn't have them going through life without each other. Not when I know what that truly feels like.

I watch as they take their place in front of Father O'Reilly. Cillian takes Sarah's hands in his and stares down at her with a mixture of love and lust. The same way his baby brother used to look at me.

"You need a song." The words tumble from my mouth. Everyone turns to stare at me when I speak, the girl trying desperately to hide the fact that she's falling apart. "Have you got a song? Something that makes you think of each other? A song that even from the first note, you'd recognize it anywhere?"

I can feel my cheeks redden. Is it hormones? The romance of the moment? This sacred place? Probably a mixture of all three. But I have a song. Two songs, actually. And they mean the world to me. Just like the people I share them with mean the world.

One for Ace. One for Irish.

Sarah looks at Cillian, and he shrugs. They haven't. And why would they? Their relationship has been far from run of the mill.

"We don't. Will you choose one for us? One that you think is fitting?"

I nod and take out my phone. I know just the song. It's perfect for them.

"I'll set it to play on loop."

How Long Will I Love You by Ellie Goulding fills the silence.

Tears prick my eyes as my thoughts drift to Irish. There's only one response to that question.

Forever.

SARAH

As soon as I hear the song, I struggle to hold back the tears. It's perfect. I look at Cillian. He's perfect too. I can feel his love for me flowing from his large hands to my small ones, which he clutches tightly in his like he never wants to let them go. I feel truly blessed. I've gone from having pretty much nothing to having absolutely everything in such a short time. This man. My handsome Irishman with that beautiful lilt of his, and his baby growing in my belly.

I listen as he says his vows to me in this sacred of all places that, even as a mobster, he holds so close to his heart. This is his one place of calm in a world of murder and destruction. His one place where nothing bad can happen. Or at least where nothing bad *should* happen. His green eyes sparkle, and I know he's holding back tears. Just as I am. From now on, where he goes, I go.

He's my life. My home.

CILLIAN

I look down at my Red as I say my vows to her. Vows I will only ever say once in my life. Tall and slender, she looks like a gust of wind would blow her over, but I know my fiery woman packs a punch with her mouth as well as her fists. I fucking love her. Every day the Lord lets me live, I will tell her and show her just how much. For once, I have something, have someone who's solely mine. I don't have to share her. Not with my brothers. Not with my family. Not with the Dusters. She is mine, and I am hers. I will love, honor, and protect her always and forever. Side by fucking side. Bring the future on.

EOIN

My phone vibrates, and I frown in annoyance.

Dylan: *Paddy's missing. I think he might be there. I'm almost there. Will use the side entrance.*

I stare at the message and curse silently. Padraig shouldn't be here. How the hell does he know where we are? This could be disastrous for all parties. If Jaine sees him, there's no telling how she'll react. How he'll react.

"I now pronounce you husband and wife. You may kiss your bride, Cillian."

I watch as my brother kisses his new wife like he wants to eat her alive. They'll want to get off. Consummating their marriage will be the only thing on their mind, but if Paddy's here, that will need to wait.

Jaine walks over to congratulate Sarah, and I use the opportunity to approach Cill.

"Paddy's here," I whisper as I give him a congratulatory hug.

"What do you mean?"

"He's missing. Dyl thinks he may be here."

We both look at Jaine. We know what this means.

"Shite."

"Exactly. They cannot under any circumstances see each other."

CHAPTER FIFTY

SARAH

St. Peter's Church, Upper East Side, New York

"PADDY'S HERE." It's a whisper against my ear, likely done so as not to draw attention to this grand reveal.

"What do you mean?"

"Exactly what I just said. Paddy's here."

"Why?"

"Why do you think, Red?"

"So, what do we do?"

"We stop them from seeing each other by hopefully finding my brother and talking some fucking sense into him."

We both stare at Jaine, who's currently having a conversation with Father O'Reilly. She's painted a polite smile on her face. Pretending on the surface that she's listening intently, but it's clear she's paying no attention whatsoever, and she's miserable underneath.

Am I doing the right thing or the wrong thing? When you tempt fate, does it work in your favor or not? Knowing my luck, probably not. Still, there's only one way to find out.

I walk across to her my gaze drifting over her arms. With the number of scars she's acquired since returning to Manhattan, she'll probably never want to come back. I don't like the thought of her never returning. We're family now—biker sisters.

"Jaine, have you got a song?" I interrupt their conversation. Father O'Reilly frowns at me, probably pissed off with my blatant rudeness at interrupting his well-rehearsed spiel as he touts for charitable donations. He then smiles politely. He'll have remembered who he married me off to less than five minutes before. He'll also have remembered which side his bread's buttered on. I'm an O'Connell now, and with that brings instant respect from the likes of him, whether earned or not.

Jaine frowns at me. She's probably thinking I've finally lost the plot on account of all the madness that's surrounded me since I've returned to New York.

"For?"

"You and Ace."

She nods slowly, looking at me suspiciously, trying to gauge what game I'm playing. She knows I've got something up my sleeve. There's no pulling the wool over her eyes.

"Yes, of course we have. We've had the same one since we were teenagers."

"What about you and Irish?"

"Why do you ask?"

"Do you have one?"

"Yes."

"Will you play it for me? Now?"

I can feel two murderous glares boring into the back of my skull, courtesy of Cillian and Eoin. They know I'm playing with fire. Well, fuck them. Who's to say Jaine can't be with her Irish as well as Ace? If they really want to be together, I'm sure something could be figured out.

"I don't want to play it, Sarah," she whisper hisses at me.

"Please? For me? I'd like to hear it, Jaine. Think of it as my wedding gift."

I know she's falling apart at the seams right now, but maybe in this holy place, God will listen to her plight and change their fates. Let them be together.

She looks at her phone. She's aware we're all watching her. All waiting. All listening.

Her cheeks redden as the song she and Irish share starts to play, echoing all around and filling the church. I recognize it immediately.

Kiss Me by Ed Sheeran.

I'm conscious that the two Irishmen behind me have now stormed off because I've just opened up the biggest can of fucking worms the Dusters have ever seen. I'm sure I'll be told off for my interference in something they consider to be none of my business. I'll be punished for my sins. Right now? I don't care. They can't kill me. Anything else will be a minor detail.

"I'm going to have a look around, Sarah."

Jaine walks away, her fingers slowly trailing over every available surface. She's touching things that Paddy might have so she can feel a connection with him, no matter how ridiculously small it is. Tears prick my eyes as I watch her suffer in silence.

DYLAN

"Paddy, you're going to get me in so much trouble."

He went suspiciously quiet earlier, which is not at all like him. Paddy is never quiet. When I went to his apartment to investigate, he wasn't there. As I suspected, I found him here inside the safe room at the church. I've managed to join him without being seen. If Jaine spots me, she'll know straight away something's going down.

She misses nothing and suspects everyone and everything at all times. It's the lawyer in her; it's also the sniper.

The safe room is a bullet-proof space that my family had built a few years back. Given our line of work, my da reckoned that we weren't safe, even within the confines of this holy building. Heathens don't care about Christ and religion. And as he places most of our foes under that irreligious heading, he wanted to create somewhere to accommodate up to half a dozen people. Better to be safe than sorry in his mind. It's not for us Duster men. We'd be expected to be on the front line at all times. One space is for old Father O'Reilly as he holds the entry ticket to those pearly gates. The others are for our ma and our wives. Not that any of us are married yet. Well, apart from our Cill.

The room is plain white and only offers up two black leather sectionals, both of which can be used for either seating or sleeping. There's also a basic toilet and wash facilities. A store cupboard is the only other item, and it contains just enough supplies to sustain the six inhabitants for around a week or so. We had hoped this facility would never be used. Today, our Paddy's decided otherwise.

On the main wall facing into the church is a large window. It's mirrored so no one can see in from the outside. From the inside out, it's like looking through clear glass. The room is also sound-proofed. Folks on the outside can't hear us, but we can listen to them just fine.

This room is just past the confessional booth and then down a long corridor, so Paddy can't see anything that's going on. Then again, I'm not sure that matters. I think he just wants to feel close to Jaine. At least, I hope that's all he wants. God forbid he attempts to confront her over what happened. God help us all then, especially our Eoin. That truth could destroy our family.

"Just tell them I saw the message on your phone, Dyl."

I frown at him. I'm just glad I've been monitoring his communications with Jaine since the last episode. I can't say I'm happy at being drawn into a lie as big as this one, but I've only myself to blame. I allowed their exchange to start, same as I allowed it to continue. I actively encouraged it. My intentions were good. I just wanted to save my brother from his demons before the family completely lost him to the drink.

"Why, Paddy?"

I take in my brother. His black hippy hair, as Da calls it, now falls below his shoulders.

"I need to ask her a question."

"What question?"

The sound of Ed Sheeran fills the church. I don't know what's going on, but I've got a feeling that it's not going to end well unless The Almighty himself intervenes.

Eoin and Cillian stride around the corner. Eoin looks furious. Cillian looks like he's been in a brawl. I suspect his cuts and bruises are a 'welcome to the Delaney family,' courtesy of Razr.

They enter the room and close the door quietly behind them. Paddy's unstable, so Eoin will have to handle this situation with kid gloves. Then again, he is the reigning outlaw chess master, so he's used to defusing tense situations. If and when he can be bothered, that is. No one plays the game as well as Eoin O'Connell because no one cares about winning as much as he does. Despite what he lets others think, Eoin has zero conscience. He doesn't care who he tramples on to get what he wants.

Even his own brother.

"What the fuck are you doing here, Paddy?" Eoin asks, keeping his voice as calm as possible and doing his best to hide his inner rage.

Paddy doesn't reply.

"It's our song. Ed Sheeran. It's mine and Jaine's song." He's talking to himself more than anything while no doubt reminiscing over exactly when they made that song their own.

"You've not answered my question, Paddy." Eoin is losing his cool. He has a vested interest these days. I know what it is. Who it's in. I wonder if our Cillian suspects.

Paddy continues to ignore him and instead rests his forehead against the window while humming along.

"I need to ask Jaine a question."

Eoin looks at Cill and me. He's expecting one of us to know what that question is. Like it's our Duster duty to find out such things in advance and then advise him accordingly. I have my suspicions, but it's not for me to say. It's not my place. I shrug my shoulders to indicate I don't know, and Cill shakes his head to signal the same.

"What do you need to ask her, Paddy?" Eoin's frustration is now evident. The kid gloves are off. He's showing zero understanding or empathy towards our youngest brother's situation or feelings.

It's then that we all see Jaine. She's about to walk past the corridor. I say a silent prayer that she keeps right on going, but she doesn't. She stops, then turns and looks straight at us. I'm only glad she can't see through the glass.

"Jesus Christ! She's right there? Can you fucking see her? Can you?"

It's like Paddy can't believe she's actually in front of him. He looks at us, wild-eyed, while waving his pointer finger at her in disbelief. Holding his breath, it eventually releases as a sob. I'm only grateful Jaine can't hear it. I know the gut-wrenching sound would break her heart. She frowns and slowly approaches the room as if sensing he's here.

"Lock the door, Dyl," Eoin orders.

I do as I'm told, like I always do. Maybe one day I'll stand up to him. Then again, likely not. He's the future Da Duster, after all—he who must always be obeyed.

"Someone told me once that the eyes are the windows to the soul. I need to ask her face to face if she loves me. I need to be sure. I can't move on otherwise." Paddy's voice is barely audible.

We all watch as the love of my baby brother's life approaches the window. As she approaches the love of her own life. Not realizing she's being watched, her face hides none of her mixed emotions. She's an open book. On display for all the world to read.

Sad. Broken. Tortured.

"What difference will it make, Paddy?"

"Because if she told me she loved me, I'd marry her right here right now and fuck the consequences, Eoin."

He brushes his hand across his face as he wipes away the tears that have started to fall. I watch his shoulders shake as he weeps—my poor brother.

I know.

I fucking know that he loves her and that she loves him. So does Eoin. Our Cill's always thought it was one-sided, that Paddy's love for Jaine was unrequited. Does he now suspect what's gone on? What Jaine was made to do? He must be a blind man if he can't see it. He looks at me and frowns.

He knows.

Paddy lifts his forehead off the glass just as Jaine stops in front of it. It's like she knows he's here.

He places his fingertips against the cold surface just as she does the same. If the glass wasn't there, their hands would be touching.

A single tear to signify her own heartache and loss slides down Jaine's cheek, and she quickly wipes it away.

Jesus Christ, what have we done? Soul mates, that's what they are. Or at least that's what they were until us O'Connells waded in and stopped them from fulfilling their destiny.

"Jaine, darlin'," he whispers to her.

"Do you have any idea how much I fucking love her?" His raised voice is wracked with pain and emotion as he starts yanking on his hair. "Do you? I need to ask her. Please, Eoin. I just need to fucking know."

He'd get on his hands and knees and beg if he thought it would help. I know he would. But it won't. Eoin doesn't care. Paddy looks between him and Jaine. He knows he has seconds before she turns and walks away. Before she leaves his life for good.

Eoin places his hand on his shoulder. "Paddy, you need to stop punishing yourself. You can't change anything. You're betrothed to another. If you dishonor the agreement, the Sicilian mafia will seek revenge. They may decide to focus their attention on Jaine. Would you want anything to happen to her?"

There's a pause—a deathly silence. Paddy shakes his head defeatedly before his face falls into his hands. In that split second, Jaine turns, and the inked I above her ear becomes visible. The tattoo Eoin told me about. I pray to The Almighty for Paddy to lift his head in time to see it. Then he'd have his answer. Then he'd know.

He doesn't, though. It's like even God himself is helping Eoin break our Paddy's heart. Then again, he's probably got him in his back pocket like he has everyone else.

Eventually, Paddy jerks his head up, the realization hitting him that it's now or never, even though it's clear that, deep down, he's already accepted his fate.

"Please don't go, Jaine. I'm begging you, darlin'. I love you so fucking much. Please don't leave me again," he cries quietly to himself, the palms of his hands pressed flat against the glass as he watches her walk away.

When she turns the corner out of sight, my baby brother sinks to his knees in defeat. The silence is deafening.

He's lost. Eoin's won.

I stand there and take in the scene. I've just had to witness my eldest brother tell Paddy exactly what he told Jaine all those months ago. He's used their love for each other to keep them apart. The first time it was for all the right reasons. This time, I'm not so sure. I pray to God that he's not doing it purely for his own selfish gain.

Sadly, I suspect I already know the answer.

CHAPTER FIFTY-ONE

CILLIAN

Cillian's Apartment, Hudson Yards, New York

"PUT ME DOWN, CILLIAN."

She's trying to sound firm, but the giggle in her voice gives her away.

"I'm carrying you bridal-style over the threshold, Red. It's tradition. Did you not dream when you were a young girl of being carried over the threshold by your husband?"

Her body relaxes, and she rests her head against my chest. She loves it. The fact that I'm her husband. And I fucking love that this little strawberry-blonde firecracker is my wife.

"But we're way past the threshold now." Still, she tries to complain, but her efforts are unconvincing. She knows exactly where I'm taking her.

"I'm carrying you to the bedroom now, Red."

"And what are you going to do with me once you get me in there?"

"I'm going to fuck my wife into next week."

"Oh, you think?"

"No, I know."

I can feel the shiver run through her, and my body reacts. This love-lust thing we have going on magnifies every thought and every touch. My dick is rock hard, and the only way it's going to be satisfied is when it sinks into her.

I stop when I reach the bed, lowering her feet to the floor, then I stand and look down at her. She's so beautiful. I'm a lucky fecker.

"Lights on or off, Red?"

She bites her lip, and I watch as her cheeks redden. I know what she's going to say. She doesn't want to miss a thing, even though it embarrasses her to admit it.

"On."

I smirk at her, then, reaching for the hem of her top, I pull it over her head, throwing it to the floor, then I unclip her bra and repeat the throwing.

I cup those magnificent tits of hers in my hands before rubbing my thumbs across the tips. They tighten instantly, and she groans her appreciation. She gazes at me, watching my reactions just because she finally can.

Yanking my Henley over my head, she trails her hands across my chest, her fingertips outlining each of my tattoos in turn.

My throbbing dick is telling me to throw her on the bed and just give her a right good pounding, but my brain is telling me not to rush. To savor our first time together as man and wife.

Dropping to my knees, I unbutton her pants, dragging them down her legs. She's pantie-less. She groans as I run my fingers through her folds, her slickness immediately coating them.

"This soaking wet pussy is mine, Red. No other man will ever touch it. No other man will ever set fucking eyes on it." I'm aware I sound like a possessive neanderthal, but not a fuck do I give. It is mine. "Who's pussy is it, Red?" I ask as I thrust two fingers inside her, her walls instinctively clenching around me.

"Yours," she answers throatily as she parts her legs to give me better access.

I fuck her hard and fast with my fingers, and when her legs begin to shake, I tease her clit with my tongue piercing before sucking on it hard. Gripping my hair, she cries out her pleasure, her wetness drenching my hand as she comes. Lifting her leg over my shoulder, I thrust my tongue deep inside her to savor every last fucking drop.

"I need to fuck you right now, Red."

I stand and kiss her, letting her cum coat both our faces before pushing her backward onto the bed. I discard my jeans. No condom needed. No rubber will ever come between us again. Skin to skin always. I want to feel that hot, wet pussy of hers as it tightens around my shaft every single time she comes on my dick.

I sink into her warm, welcoming heat, and she clenches around me, causing me to hiss and pause.

"You're pussy's fucking perfect, Red. So perfect, I'll be lucky to last thirty seconds."

"Don't you dare pump and dump on me!"

I snicker as she anchors her legs around my hips. I pull out and drive straight back in. "Well, it's been a while, sweetheart."

"You didn't fuck Cara?"

"She wishes," I grunt. "There's been no one since you, Red."

Her mouth finds mine, and she kisses me hard, her tongue sweeping against mine, and her hands fisting my hair. I can taste the love on her tongue. Her appreciation that there's been no one since her. That there will be no one ever for me but her.

I start to fuck her hard, fast, and deep. I know when she's close as she starts with that incoherent mumbling shite she does when the blood leaves her brain and travels to her clit.

"Look at me, Red." Using one hand, I pin her down by the throat so she has no choice but to do just that. I want to see into her fucking soul when she comes around my cock.

I fuck her harder, faster, deeper, the slapping sound when our flesh connects filling the silence, along with our appreciative mutual groans of pleasure.

"Cillian." She digs her fingers into my shoulders, and I watch her mouth part and her pupils dilate as she finds her release, her warm wetness coating my dick. Her walls contract around me, encouraging me to empty my balls to complete our furious coupling.

Roaring in appreciation I pump in and out of her, making sure there's no part inside that's not coated with my seed. I want to fill her with my cum every fucking day. Ten times a day. I want her to walk around wearing my scent, so every other man knows she's mine.

I lie on top of her, my deflated dick still nestled in her pussy.

Both of us know there'll be no sleep tonight. This insane need we share for each other is too intense to be sated with just one fuck. We'll talk and get to know each other, then we'll fuck again, and we'll repeat that process all night long.

I push her hair gently behind her ear as I stare down at her. I'm the luckiest bastard alive. I say a silent prayer of thanks to The Almighty for letting me have her.

"I love you, Cillian O'Connell."

I smile when a blush sweeps over her cheeks as she utters the words. So bold. So shy. She's a heady combination of everything.

I'm looking forward to spending the rest of my life trying to figure her out. Even then, I'm not sure I ever will.

"I love you too, Sarah O'Connell." I drop my mouth to hers, and I kiss her, my tongue stroking deep.

The time for talking is over. At least for now.

CHAPTER FIFTY-TWO

JAINE

Jaine's Apartment, Upper East Side, New York

Jaine: *Is everything okay? You're worrying me now, Dyl.*

I STARE AT MY PHONE, hoping to see that he's typing a response. It's been almost twenty-four hours. Nearly a full day. Irish and I never went a day without speaking or messaging. Well, at least not until after big brother Eoin paid me *that* visit. I realize it's not the same, but Dyl's lack of response still fills me with an almost overwhelming feeling of loss and sadness. It's like deja-fucking-vu. I've sent countless messages. Nothing.

Padraig: *Do you ever wish you could go back in time and make changes? You know, to your life?*

I exhale loudly as tears of relief prick my eyes. I don't mention his noticeable absence. I'm just glad he's back. I'm guessing what's been on his mind isn't something he wishes to discuss or he would have mentioned it right off the bat. His last couple of days can't have been anywhere near as bad as mine, that's for goddamn sure.

Jaine: *Are we sharing a melancholy moment and doing reflective shit, Dyl?*
Padraig: *I guess. I'm in that sort of mood, darlin'.*
Jaine: *Yes, I wish I could go back and make changes. You?*
Padraig: *Just one.*
Jaine: *The cliché blonde Disney Princess?*
Padraig: *That's the one.*
Jaine: *Did you confront her face to face like I told you to?*
Padraig: *I tried. She was right in front of me, but I didn't. I couldn't. I can't.*
Jaine: *There's no such word as can't.*
Padraig: *There is when you're a Duster.*
Jaine: *Your family disapproves of her?*
Padraig: *It's not that.*
Jaine: *Please tell me your life's not been signed away in an arranged marriage? Fight for what you goddamn want, Dyl. For who you want.*
Padraig: *It's too late for that now. The moment's passed. I can't get it back. I can't get her back.*
Jaine: *So, you're going to live your life with regret?*
Padraig: *Probably. Should I give up? Forget about her? Move on with my life?*
Jaine: *You want advice from me even though I'm a crap actor in my own personal shitshow most of the time?*
Padraig: *Yes.*
Jaine: *Then my advice is this. Never lose hope. If things are meant to be, then they will be. When will it happen? When*

you least expect it to and just when you think all hope is gone.

Padraig: *You could make that into a sign and sell it. You'd make your fortune.*

Jaine: *Last I checked my account, I already have a fortune.*

Padraig: *True.*

Jaine: *I'll be heading back to Rising soon. I'm sorry we didn't get a chance to meet up.*

Padraig: *Me too. Maybe we're just meant to be messaging buddies.*

Jaine: *Thank you, Dyl.*

Padraig: *For?*

Jaine: *For being there. For making things that bit easier.*

Padraig: *For being your replacement confidant, you mean?*

Jaine: *Something like that.*

Padraig: *Thank you, Jaine.*

Jaine: *For?*

Padraig: *For being there. For making things that bit easier for me too.*

Jaine: *But I'm not replacing anyone.*

Padraig: *No, you're not and no one will ever replace you for me, darlin'.*

Jaine: *No more, Dyl. You've made me cry.*

Padraig: *Sorry.*

Padraig: *Friends forever. Forever friends. Pinkie promise?*

Jaine: *Pinkie promise.*

Padraig: *Love you, Robin.*

Jaine: *Love you too, Batman.*

EOIN

Private Dining Room, Palace Hotel, Manhattan

I take in the ostentatious room with its gold, cream, and crystal décor. It's extravagant. But then, money is no object when you're a Duster.

My parents have dressed for the occasion. My da and I are wearing suits. My ma is dressed in a cream pantsuit accessorized with freshwater pearl jewelry.

Outlaw royalty. We definitely look the part.

Knowing Jaine, she'll turn up looking like Tank Girl. Does it bother me? In some ways, yes. In other ways, no. She dresses exceptionally well when she has to. She knows precisely how luxurious this establishment is, so I know if she arrives dressed down, she's doing so to purposely wind me up. I'll take that. If she's putting thought and effort into fucking with my head, then she's thinking about me.

I sip on a glass of whiskey. I seldom drink, so that's something Jaine and I already have in common.

My parents are staring at me. I must admit to feeling something alien. Something akin to nerves. I've no doubt they'll approve of her as the future Ma Duster.

My courtship of her will have to be undertaken covertly until she starts to trust me. Until she starts to develop feelings for me. Then I'll take her to my bed and make her mine.

As mine she will be. There's no doubt in my mind that will be the eventual outcome for her and me.

"Are you sure about this biker, Eoin?" Ma has to get one last dig in. She can't seem to help herself.

"Sarah's a biker too," I reply as I swirl the amber liquid around the crystal glass.

"She's carrying a Duster in her belly. Jaine Jones isn't."

"She's late," Da interjects, frowning at his watch to emphasize his point. He hates tardiness. No doubt Ma will take great pleasure in blaming Jaine for raising his blood pressure as a result.

I take out my phone to message her.

Eoin: *Where are you?*
Jaine: *California.*

There's no delay in her response. I put my phone back in my pocket, clenching my teeth and trying to control my inner rage. Throwing my whiskey back in one, I motion for the waiter to bring me another. I now have to explain to my parents that the woman I hand-picked to head our organization at my side has intentionally stood me up and, in turn, has intentionally stood them up.

Jaine Jones will be made to pay for making me look a fool this day.

JAINE

Four Weeks Later
The River, Rising, California

We dismount from Ace's hog, and he takes off his cut for me to sit on as he always does. I smile up at my sinfully handsome broody biker boyfriend.

I lie back on his leather, stare into the cloudless blue sky, and inhale the sweet floral scent of the wild flowers that cover this area. I sigh contentedly as the warmth of the Californian sun sinks deep into my bones. I never thought I'd miss my hometown as much as I did. Missing Ace was always a given, even though we spoke every day.

He lies on his back beside me. How often have we laid here like this through the years in the exact spot he first showed me how to skim stones? I've lost count.

We turn our heads to face each other. My heart flips as I take in his features. My heart will always flip when I take him in—my first love. Like a fine wine, the beautiful Jason Steele improves with age.

"I love you, Ace." The words just tumble from my mouth. He smiles, and my eyes drop to his wolfish canines.

"I love you too, PJ."

Ace moves to lean on his elbow so he can look down at me, his hand reaching out to lovingly caress my belly. I haven't got a big bump by any means, but it's noticeable now at almost thirty weeks. I can't quite believe that in a few months, I'm going to be a mom.

"I've been thinking, PJ."

"Yeah? What you been thinking about, Ace?"

"I've been thinking that maybe we should make things official between us."

"Meaning?" I frown at him. Is he saying what I think he is?

"Meaning, I know you're my old lady, but I'd really like to make you my wife."

"Is that a proposal?"

He closes his eyes and lifts his face to the sun. "I guess that's what it is."

I sit up and stare at him. I don't know what to say. My beautiful boy is asking me to marry him?

He stands up and walks towards the river, and I can't stop my eyes from trailing down his lean, muscular body before resting on that ass of his that's perfectly displayed in snug-fitting pale blue jeans. He runs his hands through his black wavy hair which is even longer these days.

He's thinking about what he's going to say next. I can read him like a book. He turns around and walks purposely towards me before dropping to one knee.

Tears prick my eyes. "Ace?"

Taking my hand in his, he presses his lips to my palm.

"Jaine Jones. Will you marry me?"

A sob escapes me. There's no hesitation. No need to even think about my response. If asked a million times, my reply would always be the same.

"Yes, I'll marry you, Jason Steele."

His mouth covers mine, his hand pinning both of mine above my head as his tongue strokes deep. The time for talking is over.

SARAH

The Hudson Dusters' HQ, Manhattan, New York

Do I just come straight out with it? I mean, Jaine talks to Dylan a lot. Does he already know? Maybe I should have asked her about who knows what. That would have been the sensible thing to do. Way to go, Sarah O'Connell. Then again, common sense escapes me even more these days now I have full-on baby brain.

I approach the door to the meeting room, where they have their weekly get-togethers. I can already hear my father-in-law barking out his orders.

Candice, Eoin's PA, sits at the desk just outside to ensure no one crosses the threshold. Not that anyone would. It would be a death sentence for anyone who dared enter or eavesdrop. Her dark eyes scan over me. She fucking hates my guts. I'm glad. Fuck her. Does she know what happened to Cara? Suspect? My guess is it's the latter. She won't know the details as she'd be dead if she did.

My eyes scan over her in silent response. She's tall and slim with creamy skin and long dark hair. She's beautiful. Unfortunately, she's also the sort that lets her boss fuck her over his desk whenever the mood takes him. My ears have been subjected to the sex noises that come from Eoin's office on more than one occasion. Fortunately, the door was firmly closed each time. I'm not sure I could have coped with that visual.

Does Candice realize the mobster she's got her sights firmly set on is in love with someone else? That Eoin's just dicking her so he has somewhere to empty his balls. That he's just biding his time and waiting for Jaine to return.

Well, that's his current intention. That may change when he hears the news I have to spill. News I'm permitted to tell with Jaine's blessing, of course. Lessons have been learned since the last time a pregnancy announcement was made to the Dusters.

Candice scowls at me as I reach the door. I want to tell her to back off. That I'm an O'Connell now. I can't, though. No one knows Cillian and I are married, apart from our immediate family. We're to pretend like it didn't happen and have a full ceremony with all the works so all of New York's finest can attend.

On the one hand, his folks were disappointed about what we'd done. On the other, I think they were just pleased to have me locked in. There's no escape for me now. Roisin will have her wish. Her first grandchild will be here in around thirty weeks.

I knock on the door.

"Come in." It's Fergal's voice, his Irish accent much more pronounced than that of his sons.

I push the door open, and my eyes immediately scan the room. I take in the leather-topped black circular table, the marble floor, and the walls filled with some of the ugliest artwork I have ever seen. It stinks of vanilla furniture polish. I hate vanilla. It turns out Cillian does too.

"Yes. What is it, Sarah?" Eoin leans back in his chair. He looks annoyed. Probably fucked off that I've interrupted him listening to the sound of his own voice. I've worked out that he's a chauvinist in the main. A bit like my brother. He's likely wondering why a silly woman is interrupting important men's business.

My eyes go around the table as I take them in one by one.

They're all suited and booted in ten-thousand-dollar suits and looking quite the business professionals.

They're all watching and waiting. I smile at Cillian, and he smirks back. He knows what I'm going to say. I've already given him the heads up.

No secrets. Not ever.

"I've just been speaking to Jaine. She didn't want there to be any Chinese whispers circulating about her, so she wanted me to let you all know personally. She's pregnant. She's having Ace's baby. It also turns out that he's asked her to marry him, and she's accepted. I just thought you should all know before the rumor mills start."

I'm met with deathly silence.

The only sound is the Newton's Cradle in the corner.

I daren't make eye contact with Eoin or with Paddy. Having dropped the bombshell, I simply turn and leave the room, closing the door quietly behind me.

On the one hand, I rejoice that I've just pissed off the eldest O'Connell. Serves the arrogant fucker right. He lost.

On the other, I'm saddened that I've just broken the heart of the youngest—her Irish. I know in his mind he'll think she's now lost to him forever. Everyone knows taking the vows in this game is a lifetime commitment—a life sentence.

Who knows what the future holds for them?

Me?

Well, my guts are telling me their journey is far from over, and they've never let me down yet.

EPILOGUE

SARAH

Twelve Months Later
Jaine's House, Rising, California

WE PULL up the hired SUV in front of the ranch-style property with its white walls and dark red-tiled roof. This is for sure the most important stop on our short tour of the west coast.

Jaine's childhood home is larger than I expected it to be, and it's set in its own fifty acres of complete nothingness. Each inch of land is covered by the white poppies that grow wild in these parts, their sweet floral notes filling the air.

The house is picture-postcard pretty, with a white-painted porch that holds a rocking chair and a little two-seater swing. I can't help but frown as I look around. It just doesn't feel right. I can't envision Jaine living here. She's a city girl. She belongs in Manhattan. The pace of living in Rising must bore her to tears. Then again, it's the perfect place to raise children, so I guess you have to figure out your priorities.

There's also Ace. Her husband. As prez of the Angels, his role will be hands-on. It's not like he can commute from Manhattan doing what he does. My eyes drift to the two classic hogs parked side by side outside. They really are the perfect biker couple.

"You ready, Red?"

I turn to look at my own husband. A man who gets more handsome with each passing day. His auburn hair glints in the warm Californian sunshine. We're fucking like rabbits these days, trying for baby number two. Roisin's not happy that she's getting older and she's still only got one grandbaby.

I nod at him and watch as he steps out of the vehicle before opening the other door. My heart fills with such an indescribable feeling of love as I watch Cillian gently lift our sleeping daughter, Caoimhe, from her car seat. He places a tender kiss on the top of her head, which is covered in strawberry blonde curls.

At almost five months old, she's still so tiny, and Cillian is so very protective of her. He carefully passes the sleeping bundle to me, then gathers the small mountain of supplies that we need to take with us everywhere we go these days.

I'm sure Jaine will understand. Her son, Fin, is around ten months old, and she's currently expecting baby number two in three or so.

We walk towards the house, and the door opens before we even reach it. Finally, I get to meet the boy who stole Jaine Jones's heart when she was just seven years old. A man she loved so much, she left everything she knew behind for a whole decade.

Everything about Jason Steele is sinfully handsome. Jaine was right with her description of him. I don't think I've ever seen such a breath-taking brute, and man, does he wear that black mane of his well. I swear if he had his own biker calendar, it would sell out within minutes.

"You must be Ace."

I hold out my hand, and he takes it in his. "It's good to meet you at last, Sarah." Even his voice is dark and sinful.

The bluest eyes stare down at me, taking me in and silently assessing me.

He smiles at me, then turns his attention to Cillian.

"Cill, it's good to see you." I watch as they man hug, slapping each other on the back. They've worked together for a long time and know each other well.

"Sarah."

I turn to look at Jaine, and tears prick my eyes. Her blonde hair is now almost waist length, and her skin glows with health. She may not belong in California, in my opinion, but it clearly does wonders for her complexion.

"Jaine."

It's a whisper more than anything. I can't believe it's been around twelve months since all that shit went down. Since she saved my life twice.

"Cill and I will head on over to the clubhouse, PJ. Leave you two girls to catch up."

I watch as Ace wraps his arms around her, his eyes filled with love for the mother of his children. She stares up at him, her own mirroring the same. She loves him. How can she be in love with two men? I just can't get my head around it. I was sure when I saw her and Ace that it would be lacking, that she must surely love Paddy more. I mean, I can't imagine loving anyone apart from Cillian.

Ace kisses her, and it's a proper kiss. He loves her, and he doesn't care who's witnessing it as he shows her just how much.

"Ace." She snickers as she removes his hands from her ass, her cheeks reddening.

He smirks down at her before rubbing his hand over her belly, where baby number two is currently cooking.

"I'll see you soon, Red." In contrast, Cillian presses his lips to my forehead. He doesn't do sharing of anything. Even letting people witness our kissing. He's so fucking possessive. I love that about him.

He and Ace make their way to the SUV.

"Come on in, Sarah."

"Bring the little one through here."

I follow Jaine into the prettiest little girl's room I think I've ever seen. Its walls are pink, and there's a princess-style four-poster bed. Every accessory is either sparkly, feathery, or glittery.

"Your childhood bedroom?"

"You got it. We never had the heart to take it apart—too many memories. Ace and I figured if we had a little girl, it would be perfect for her. If not this time, then maybe next," she says with a smile, rubbing her hand across her rounded tummy.

She points towards the little white wicker Moses basket in the corner. "It's Fin's. It's a new mattress and everything. You can put Caoimhe in there."

I place my sleeping baby in the crib, and then I turn to hug Jaine. When I step back, my eyes immediately drift to her wrists. An inked bracelet tattoo covers each scar. On one wrist, it's a circle of poppies. On the other, it's a circle of four-leaf clovers.

Figures. One for Ace. One for her Irish.

"I've missed you."

"I speak to you most days, Sarah."

"Yeah, but it's not the same."

"Nope, it's not."

"So, how have you been?"

She shrugs. "I'm itching to get back to work." She folds her arms and walks across to look out the window. I follow her. The view is breathtaking. It's uninterrupted for miles around.

"You know, I thought that the moment I saw this place, you must be going stir crazy. You're a city girl for sure."

She continues to absorb the view. "Truth is, I need both to be truly happy."

I nod to myself. "Just like you need both Ace and Irish?"

She turns to look at me, and I can see the flash of pain at the mention of Paddy. It will always be there, just bubbling away under the surface.

"Exactly that."

"Ace loves you."

She smiles at me. "Yes, he does, and I love him."

"I didn't think I'd see what I did. Is that bad of me to say? I didn't think you'd love each other as much as you do."

"Why? Because I also love Irish?" She chuckles. "It figures you'd think my love for one or the other would be lacking. I don't claim to understand this shit either."

"Would you ever have considered a polyamory relationship with them both?"

"I would have signed up for that in a goddamn heartbeat, Sarah, but I didn't think it would be something either of them would have considered. It turns out I was wrong. Ace has already said he would have no problem with it. He just wants me to be happy."

"I doubt Paddy would have a problem with it either. He misses you."

She laughs dryly. "I'm not so sure about that. Anyway you're forgetting the part where he's engaged to the Sicilian don's baby sister." She shakes her head. "Nope. Mine and Irish's ship has sailed. Life moves on. It has to. For both our sakes."

"I'm sure the Dusters could come to some sort of amicable agreement with the Sicilians."

She exhales slowly while running her hand down her face. I can tell that, just like old times, I'm now grating on her last nerve. "It's never going to happen, so put that idea right out of your head."

"But…"

"But nothing," she hisses. "We've both moved on, Sarah, and even if we hadn't the Ruoccos can't be trusted. Why do you think two of their family members are already dead? I could never live with myself if anything happened to Irish. If he's seen to be publicly disrespecting them in any way, he won't last twenty-four hours."

"Surely they wouldn't mess with the O'Connells?"

She forces a laugh. It's clear she thinks I know jack shit about these things, and maybe I don't.

"Of course they wouldn't, Sarah. Irish would simply have a price put on his head. They'd hire someone else to carry out the hit and do the dirty work on their behalf. It's how these things work. It would never be traceable to the Sicilians, even though we'd all know who was behind it."

"What, like a sniper? Would they hire The Exterminator?"

She shakes her head.

"No, not him. He wouldn't get involved. He's got morals. He only kills scum, and Irish isn't scum."

"Dylan says he's gone AWOL at the moment, so the Dusters are having to use an alternative. Fergal doesn't like change, so he's constantly complaining and asking when the surreptitious sniper is returning."

"He'll be back soon enough, I'm sure."

She rubs her belly, causing my eyes to drift there. I can tell she wants to change the subject, so I oblige.

"You're bigger than last time."

"Yup. And the pressure on my bladder is even more extreme this time around as a result. In fact, I'll just go deal with that issue right now."

We walk back into the living area, and Jaine goes to the restroom. I look around. It's modern inside the house, and it's all in white with various shades of grey. Some of the furniture is old. Really old. Like the stuff I have in Brightling. Sentimental shit that you never want to get rid of as it holds a lifetime of ingrained memories, making each piece priceless. Photos line the surfaces. Images of Jaine and Ace growing up together through the years. There's a noticeable gap before they resume, no doubt signifying when she left home.

It's then I reach the little boy's room. Fin. The bedroom is in typical shades of blue, and it's motorcycle-themed in the main, but in a cartoon, childlike way.

I walk across to look down at the sleeping infant. I don't think I've ever seen such a perfect-looking child. Long dark eyelashes rest on the chubbiest of pale cheeks, and his hair is a mop of midnight black. As if he can sense someone is watching over him, he rubs his eyes before opening them. They sparkle blue on his baby face, and it's a gaze I instantly recognize. His lips pout as he makes little sucking noises, and then he stretches, lifting his two chubby arms. My fingers reach down to trace the horseshoe birthmark on his inner wrist, which is now clearly visible. Cillian has the same one. All the O'Connell men do.

I can feel her behind me, watching me take him in.

"I didn't want to message about this or say anything over the phone." She reaches down to lift the sleepy little boy from his crib. The little boy who is the double of Paddy. "You know, just in case anything is monitored."

I stare at her. Moments pass as I digest all of this.

"Are you ever going to tell him? He deserves to know. Shit, Jaine, I had my suspicions before you left New York, but I just figured the baby turned out to be Ace's in the end."

She frowns at me. "Of course I'm going to tell him, but only once he's wed. If I tell him before, there's no knowing how he'll react."

"But he's missing out on so much," I hiss, hating the reality that I'll be made to keep this secret.

"It's better he misses out on the first year or so than miss out on the rest of his goddamn life by doing something stupid." She's biting back her anger, trying to keep her voice calm for the sake of Fin.

"So, you're coming back to Manhattan, right? If you promise me you are, then I won't say a word. I'll keep this a secret from Cillian for now."

"I'll be back once this little one is born. Ace and I have already agreed that I'll alternate between Rising and Manhattan. We both know Padraig has a right to be part of Finian's life. Cherry's struggling to cope with running the business anyway, so I have no choice. Plus, Ace doesn't want me to give my career up."

"Finian? I thought it was Finlay?"

"Finian. After his Irish great-granddaddy."

I run my hands through my hair. What a fucking mess.

"Shit, Jaine. You have a Duster heir. A male Duster heir. Their first grandchild, and they don't even fucking know."

"I realize that."

"So, you'll be back in Manhattan when?"

I understand her reasoning, but she can't keep this a secret beyond Paddy's wedding. I won't allow it.

"Give me six months, Sarah. It's all I ask. Irish will be wed by then."

"Six months. No longer. Agreed?"

"Agreed."

JAINE

"How did things go with Sarah?" Ace wraps his arms around me, pulling me tight against his chest. We've only just waved her and Cillian off.

"She knows." I sigh.

"You were always planning on telling her, PJ. You were never going to be able to hide it or keep it secret long-term. Fin's his daddy's double."

"I know, but now it's out in the open, I guess I feel kind of exposed. It's like we were able to live in our own bubble, and now…."

"Now we can't. Now we welcome this little one into the world, and we do what needs doing. You introduce Fin to his family, and you resume your career. We've talked about this already. I won't have you giving up everything you've worked so hard to build. Not for me."

"Six months."

"Six months?"

"I've agreed with Sarah that I'll let the O'Connells know about Fin within six months. If I don't, I'm guessing she will."

I TAKE IN MY FATHER-IN-LAW AS HE STANDS ON THE PORCH. HE HAS his back to me and his face is raised to the clear midnight sky. Is he counting stars? Wishing on one? Saying a prayer? Maybe he's having a silent conversation with those he knew that have passed over, each one now polishing their own star. They'll be plentiful, that's for sure. Then again, most of them, except for one or two like my pop, will have ridden the fiery helter-skelter straight into the bowels of hell.

I take in Ace's daddy. A man I love like he's my own father. A man I've known since I was seven years old. His hair is getting whiter by the day. Much to do with his age. Much to do with still living this life. He turns to face me, taking me in before stepping forward and hugging me close.

I embrace his warmth and inhale his familiar smell. Everything about Duke is welcoming. Comforting.

Well, usually it is. Something's wrong. I can feel it.

"Duke?" I look into the face of my pop's best friend. What has he come here to tell me on a day that seems to be all about revealing secrets?

I usher him inside and close the door just as Ace appears.

"Jainie, there's something I need to tell you. I can't put it off any longer." He looks at Ace, and I turn to do the same. His face looks grim. I then realize that my husband knows about this. That he's kept something from me. For how long, I wonder?

"He wants to meet you formally. For you to know who he is, and he's threatening to tell you himself."

"What the hell are you talking about, Duke? Who wants to meet me?"

"Jainie, I don't know how to say this."

"Don't waste time thinking about how. Just tell me already."

"Your real pop, Jainie. Jeremiah wasn't your biological daddy."

Author's Note

I hope you enjoyed Cillian's Story

Although his book is standalone within the
Dirty Dusters Series
and can be enjoyed in its own right; Cillian's story is also the
second in a whole
CROSSOVER UNIVERSE
between the Angels, Scorpions, and Dusters.

As mentioned at the outset, Cillian is also BOOK 2 in an initial series of novels containing an ONGOING STORYLINE that concludes in BOOK 6 of the crossover universe, DIRTY PADRAIG.

The Crossover Universe Reading Order

ACE

Angels of Hellfire MC Series: One

DIRTY CILLIAN

The Hudson Dusters Irish Mob Series: One

RAZR

Iron Scorpions MC Series: One

DIRTY DYLAN

The Hudson Dusters Irish Mob Series: Two

DIRTY EOIN

The Hudson Dusters Irish Mob Series: Three

DIRTY PADRAIG

The Hudson Dusters Irish Mob Series: Four

FOR THE BEST OVERALL READING EXPERIENCE, THE BOOKS SHOULD BE READ IN CROSSOVER UNIVERSE ORDER.

Acknowledgments

To Wynne.
Thank you for your words of wisdom and encouragement.

To Sue.
Thank you for always being there, friend.

About the Author

Harley Diamond is a writer of romance novels with plot twists that will leave you begging for more. In every dirty story, an angsty bad boy and a badass queen lead the cast.

When Harley's not reading, she's writing. When not doing either, she's plotting to unleash her next novel on you from her non-working farm in West Yorkshire, England, surrounded by her faithful but very needy companions. Her seven rescue dogs.

Facebook Group: Harley's Hangout
Facebook Group: Harley's Spoilers

www.harleydiamond.com

Printed by Amazon Italia Logistica S.r.l.
Torrazza Piemonte (TO), Italy

41353879R00230